BLOCKBUSTER PRAISE FOR

"LUST, GREED, VIOLENCE, THE FRENZY OF THE AD BIZ . . . TONS OF SUREFIRE THRILLER ELEMENTS."
—*Kirkus Reviews*

"A WILD RIDE. . . . Marty English is an engaging protagonist who effectively combines slickness, intelligence, and fallibility."
—*Publishers Weekly*

"SUSPENSEFUL. . . .Leaves you wondering what will happen next."
—*Providence Journal*

AND FOR SAM AND CHUCK GIANCANA'S *NEW YORK TIMES* BESTSELLER *DOUBLE CROSS*

"AMAZING AND SHOCKING DISCLOSURES."
—*New York Daily News*

"CHILLING. . . .BRIMS WITH UNNERVING ALLEGATIONS."
—*Boston Herald*

"AS SHOCKING AS THE LIFE OF THE BOOK'S SUBJECT, CRIME BOSS SAM GIANCANA."
—*Associated Press*

Gia 520454

SAM AND BETTINA GIANCANA

30 SECONDS

WARNER BOOKS

A Time Warner Company

This is a work of fiction. Certain real locations, products, and public figures are mentioned, but all other characters and the events and dialogue described in the book are totally imaginary.

WARNER BOOKS EDITION

Copyright © 1998 by Sam and Bettina Giancana
All rights reserved.

Cover design by Tony Greco

Warner Books, Inc.
1271 Avenue of the Americas
New York, NY 10020

Visit our Web site at
www.warnerbooks.com

 A Time Warner Company

Printed in the United States of America

Originally published in hardcover by Warner Books.
First Paperback Printing: June, 1999

10 9 8 7 6 5 4 3 2 1

To the doctor with the red bow tie,
Clarence F. Sullivan, Jr.

Acknowledgments

We wish to thank our family, friends, and colleagues for their unbridled enthusiasm during the writing of this book.

We are particularly indebted to:

Laurence Kirshbaum and Maureen Egen at Warner Books, whose vision made this book possible.

Caryn Karmatz Rudy, our editor, whose terrific insights and suggestions brought this book to life.

Frank Weimann, our agent, whose encouragement and support have been unflagging over the past months.

Mark Hazeltine, John Oda, and Christopher Wilhelm, whose "insider" advertising industry expertise proved invaluable.

30
SECONDS

Prologue

From fifteen hundred feet, the forest looked tranquil, an idyllic expanse of nature unmarred by human hands. Suddenly, "Light My Fire" blasted out over a loudspeaker into the peaceful jungle night as the chopper's searchlights began swinging back and forth along the dense rainforest clinging to the water's edge.

The men in the chopper were dressed to kill, decked out in full camouflage: faces painted black, heads wrapped in bandannas, bandoliers of ammo draped around their necks—the works. Not because they had to be, but because they got off on it. Four were Americans, veterans of countless similar attacks. The remaining ten were mestizos who came cheap and were thrilled at the chance to hone their already flawless killing techniques. Tonight, some self-appointed defenders of the American way would get some blood on their hands. They came prepared, sporting Uzis, sawed-off shotguns, flamethrowers, handguns, and machetes.

"The baby's sleeping," the pilot announced. "We're going in."

The chopper banked and the men were suddenly restless; the ride had put them in the mood for some action. By the time they set down, they'd be aching for it. That's when they did their best work.

*   *   *

In the pitch-black night, the men eased across the jungle floor. At the outskirts of the tiny hamlet, they split up: six to the left, six to the right, and two in the center. They moved quickly now, running in a low crouch over the moist, spongy earth of the forest floor, taking up firing positions within the sleeping Maya village.

They waited, the silence excruciating. Then, at the leader's signal, there was a roaring *whoosh* and the flamethrowers ignited like firecrackers in the night, spitting long trails of fire into the thatched huts. Caught off guard, their terrified victims rushed out. The older among them hobbled into the village center—their clothes and hair afire—and fell into the dust, rolling and begging and sobbing.

The younger villagers tried to run to the safety of the river, children and infants flaming, shrieking in agony, in their arms. But they didn't make it; the defenseless Indians were torn to pieces by full automatic firepower from all directions.

It took only a few seconds—perhaps thirty—and then the village was still and the screams were silenced.

The flamethrowers finished the job, torching the huts, burning them to the ground, licking the bloodied corpses until they no longer bore any resemblance to human beings.

Dawn was breaking when the men boarded the chopper and lifted off. It rose through the mist of the rainforest slowly, like a huge black bird of prey that had feasted to the point of being sated. But only for a little while. Soon it would rise to satisfy its ferocious appetite again.

Chapter 1

Marty English was on his first cup of Starbucks when he got the call. He'd been feeling pretty damned good for such a dreary winter morning—he'd even taken a few minutes to lean back in his Eames leather chair and survey his plush corner office, to revel in the fact that if things kept going his way, he'd be named president of Wynn Bergman Advertising within the year.

At the thought, Marty smiled to himself, catching his reflection in the long expanse of window with its breathtaking view of Chicago's Michigan Avenue. He saw a handsome man with intensely serious eyes staring back at him, his dark hair sprinkled with gray, dressed in a charcoal pinstriped Armani suit, cut close to emphasize a lithe, muscular compactness. The carefully cultivated image conveyed confidence, a man secure with his position in life. And hell, why shouldn't he be? He was getting ready to make it to the top.

Of course, most people would've thought Marty English was already there. As executive VP of domestic operations for one of the world's largest ad agencies, he was paid over five hundred thousand dollars a year. Plus a twenty percent bonus. A merit incentive amounting to fifteen percent of his annual salary thrown into a retirement fund every year. And stock options, based on performance, worth six figures.

If he played it right, Marty could be a millionaire several times over. But this was about more than big bucks—advertising held the promise of immortality: that someday, your work would be as much a part of the American culture as the Marlboro Man. Money and immortality. Shit, what more could a guy ask for?

The harsh electronic jangle of his desk phone jerked Marty out of his reverie. "Hello . . . Marty English," he answered cheerfully.

"Morning, Marty."

"Hey, Gary, how's it going?"

"Uh . . . well . . ."

Marty's smile froze on his face; there was a strange edge in the man's voice.

"Look, Marty, I wanted to be the first to tell you . . . uh . . . I've got some bad news."

On guard now, Marty stiffened and sat straight in his chair. Gary was his best contact at NHP, Marty's biggest account, worth six hundred million a year in billings. Bad news for NHP meant bad news for Marty. "Go ahead, Gary, I'm listening."

"Jeez, I'm sorry to have to drop this on you first thing in the morning, Marty, but . . ." he cleared his throat. "But NHP's being bought out by Hexall."

"I see," Marty said evenly, his heart pounding. "So what's the bottom line?" His voice didn't betray his anxiety.

There was a deep sigh. "The bottom line is Hexall wants their agency to take over NHP's advertising. It looks like Bergman's out, Marty. You're gonna lose the account."

Stunned, Marty slumped back in his chair. So that was it? Just like that it was all over? He could forget about the presidency? And what about all those people working on NHP's account: Were they supposed to just forget about having a job? It was inconceivable. There had to be something he could do.

"But it's not a done deal, Gary . . . *right*?" he asked pointedly. "We're going to get a shot at presenting to Hexall for the business? As NHP's marketing director, surely you can see to that. Hell, out of courtesy Bergman should get that much. . . . After all, we've handled NHP for ten years."

"I wouldn't count on it, Marty. Hexall and their agency are tight, real tight. With NHP being bought out, I'm feeling my way on this thing, too. My job's on the line here. I have to watch my step. It's probably best to face facts—"

"Facts?"

"Yeah. You're out and there's not a goddamned thing either one of us can do about it."

There was a silence on the line.

"Marty, you okay?"

Marty frowned at the phone. Was he *okay*? What kind of fucking question was that? A son-of-a-bitch marketing director just told him he was losing a six-hundred-million-dollar piece of business, that his fucking dreams were going down the drain. And he was supposed to be okay?

"Sure I'm okay," Marty replied smoothly, like multimillion-dollar accounts grew on trees. "Hey, business is business, right?" He managed a chuckle that sounded sincere.

"That's right. Business is business." There was another sigh. "Look, I gotta go. Things might get a little hairy around here soon. But you know I'll keep you posted."

"Thanks," Marty said woodenly. "Take care, Gary."

"You too."

Marty hung up the phone and looked around his office, thinking about what a difference one damned phone call could make. His Starbucks was cold and gray in the paper cup. He could hear the tick, tick, ticking of the clock on his desk. It brought him back to earth.

Timing was everything, Marty reminded himself as he grabbed his briefcase and headed out the door. Hadn't he always believed that? So NHP was probably down the tube, but he still had an ace up his sleeve. An ace named Isaac Arrow.

In less than an hour he and his team would be pitching Arrow for its three-hundred-million-dollar pharmaceutical account. It might not be the whole enchilada, true. But it was halfway there. All he had to do was bring out the smoke and mirrors.

As the lights came up in the conference room, signaling the end of the presentation, Marty glanced down at his watch. From start to finish, the presentation had taken forty-five minutes—and cost more to produce than some people made in a lifetime. It sounded crazy, even decadent, but in light of the bad news about NHP, it made perfect sense to Marty. Right now, he'd do just about anything to snag Isaac Arrow, an account that not only had a fat ad budget, but whose campaign promised to have worldwide exposure thanks to an unusual alliance with the Belizean rainforest foundation, Planetlife, and its eco-resort, Escoba.

Marty smiled at the nine Arrow executives seated before him. Usually, after a presentation, you got some indication of the way a client was leaning. But this bunch was damned near inscrutable. Hell, they even looked alike—weird, nerdy guys, all of them, with backgrounds in things most people had never heard of, like nanotechnology, ethnobotany, and virtual reality—with the exception of Arrow's president, Frank Torello, who, if Marty didn't know better, was really Elvis gone corporate. And then of course there was the vice president of marketing, Carson Page, a dangerously good-looking woman who looked as though she liked to play more than office politics.

Carson Page, with her leggy, curvaceous physique, flawless skin, and exquisite bone structure, took your thoughts away from any business at hand, but her probing gaze quickly alerted you to the brains and guile behind the beauty. Carson had all the right moves, all the right words, too. Marty imagined they probably had a lot in common.

As he pondered the enigma that was Carson Page, Marty

felt the weight of a stare pierce his consciousness and turned to see Lee Wilde observing him coolly.

A steamroller of a woman, sixty-year-old Lee had probably been beautiful once—before all those long nights as a media director spent studying Nielsen ratings and dreaming up ways to beat down the TV reps. Still, Lee had her appeal; she had a hell of a brain. And there was a strong elegance about her, too. The way she pulled her steel-gray hair up into a smart French twist, showing off all those refined bones. The cut of her custom-tailored suits. And those high Italian heels. If sex was power, Lee Wilde had it. Even at sixty.

At the agency everybody called her the Queen. And to her face at that. But Lee Wilde didn't give a shit; she was a vice president now and near retirement. An agency stockholder. Probably worth several million. With no husband and no kids, she was financially set for life. But then of course Lee had no life except the one at Wynn Bergman—which was probably why she and Marty got along so well. You didn't make it up the ladder by having backyard barbecues with the spouse and kids. Sex life? Family life? Social life? The agency *was* your life.

Lee had become a close friend over the years, to both Marty and his girlfriend, Reiki, so when Marty realized Lee was watching him watch Carson, he started guiltily and returned to the business at hand. Looking over at the Arrow crew, he asked, "Are there any questions?"

"Just one, Marty," Frank Torello said from his place at the head of the conference table. He stood up and buttoned the coat of his off-the-rack suit over his middle-age spread and walked to the front of the room.

Marty tried to look unconcerned. Only one question? Marty smiled again, but his mind was racing. All those great graphics and clever headlines his creative team had put together would never snap, crackle, or pop across a TV screen if this guy Torello wasn't crazy as hell about them, but right now that was only the half of it. What about that small detail called NHP? What about an agency shortfall of six hundred million bucks? Marty's heart began to pound. Shit, he *had* to land this account.

Torello's narrow lips broke over his teeth, exposing a gleaming white grin as he extended his hand. "When can Wynn Bergman start?"

Marty tried not to look shocked: Clients almost never awarded an account on the spot; he'd assumed Arrow would make him sweat a few days, not a few seconds. His words betrayed his astonishment. "Are you serious, Frank?"

"I sure am."

Marty struggled to control the broad smile creeping over his face; hell, maybe the presidency wasn't a pipe dream after all. With Arrow in his hip pocket, it looked like he'd have that ace he needed. "We can start right now, Frank," he replied, giving Torello a firm handshake.

"Great!" Torello exclaimed. He motioned to the rest of the Wynn Bergman people. "Well, let's cut to the chase, shall we? When is the Super Bowl? Three, four weeks away?"

"It's three weeks away," Marty answered, puzzled. He looked at Lee and she shrugged. There'd been no mention of the Super Bowl.

"I know we've never discussed it," Torello conceded, "but we want to see our new rainforest botanical line in the Super Bowl."

"That's right," Carson said, coming to the front of the room. She patted Marty on the back like she'd known him half her life, adding, "Those great concepts of yours deserve a special showcase."

"I'm glad you liked them," Marty said cautiously, feeling his way. "But producing an ad like the one you just saw in three weeks is unrealistic. And besides, it's probably too late to get a spot in the Super Bowl at any price."

Lee nodded politely. "Marty's right. We placed our clients' buys for the Super Bowl months ago. And just to set the record straight, today's Tuesday, the sixth, which means the

game's only nineteen days away, not three weeks." Marty
tried not to smile; Lee Wilde was a precisionist; no detail, not
even a small one, escaped her attention.

Looking annoyed, Frank Torello cleared his throat and nervously unbuttoned and buttoned his suit coat and, suddenly,
Marty felt a mounting sense of panic. Was he going to blow it
all now? And over a goddamned placement in the Super
Bowl? But shit, it would be almost impossible to make a
deadline like that.

"Don't misunderstand us, Frank," he explained evenly.
"We don't have a problem with the *strategy* of placing a spot
in the Super Bowl; it's the time frame we're uncomfortable
with. We didn't plan on producing a major TV spot on such
short notice."

"You're our agency, aren't you?" one of the scientific types
still seated at the conference table called out. "We want in the
Super Bowl. So put us there. That's what we hired you for."

"An ad in the Super Bowl will put us on the map," Torello
insisted, his dark eyes flashing. "That's what we want . . . a
big splash."

Both men, roughly equal in height, locked eyes momentarily, Torello's challenging and Marty's meeting that challenge.
Then, Marty broke his gaze to glance over at his agency team.
They looked pretty grim. If he agreed to produce an ad and
get it in the Super Bowl, his team would revolt. If he didn't,
well, they'd probably lose the fucking account. And he knew
better than anybody how much the agency needed this account. Damned if he was going to let it slip through his grasp
now.

"A big splash is fine, Frank. . . . We all want that," he said
soothingly. "But we also want to make sure Isaac Arrow puts
its best foot forward. And that takes time. We've spent over a
thousand man-hours researching your market, your demo-
graphics, your product line and competition. We've done a lot
of work. But there's still a lot more to do. There are the focus
groups to copy-test the campaign. And then there's talent and

music and a thousand other details that can make or break an ad. And let's not forget the filming at Planetlife in Belize and postproduction here in Chicago." Marty paused. "I'd hate to see us blow a great campaign now . . . just to get one spot in the Super Bowl. Wouldn't you?"

Torello shook his head and grinned. "Oh, now I get the picture—you're worried. Well, don't be. We know you can pull this off."

Marty didn't think Torello got the picture at all. "I appreciate your vote of confidence, Frank. But if we produced an ad that didn't work, you'd look bad to your board of directors and we'd lose your account. That's what I'm trying to avoid. When your campaign hits the air, I want us both to look good."

Zak Restin, the team's creative director, nodded furiously, his thick black dreadlocks bouncing up and down. "One bad ad will ruin the entire campaign, Mr. Torello."

Torello adjusted his wide blue necktie and, glaring at Carson Page, snapped testily, "I thought you said Wynn Bergman could pull this off."

"I did, Frank." She smiled, her voice level and confident, with a steely resolve echoing in it. "And I'm still sure they can." She looked back at Marty and the six agency people standing alongside him and cooed, "We know what we're asking may seem unreasonable. Really, we hate to put you through this. But our board of directors wants the Super Bowl. They've got it in their heads that's the best place for our kickoff. They don't care how much the production costs. They don't care what the airtime costs. All they care about is seeing Isaac Arrow in the Super Bowl. They want the ad there . . . just like the other big boys . . . IBM and Bud and Coke." Carson paused, her features turning to stone. "So there it is. Either you produce the spot and get us in the Super Bowl or we'll have to take our three-hundred-million-dollar account elsewhere."

The conference room went quiet except for the sound of

one of the Arrow scientists clicking his plastic ballpoint. Lee shot a look at Marty and Zak. The look said she too had been caught off guard and was pissed as hell. But it also said they had no choice, they had to give it a shot.

Lee might not know about the possibility of losing the NHP account yet, but she knew enough to know things were getting lean everywhere, even at a major agency like Bergman. She'd given the company her life and she wanted to retire someday with her head up, not pushed out because some Generation X turk from another ad agency would promise to get a spot in the fucking Super Bowl. Go for it, her blue eyes commanded. Go for it.

Of course Marty would. He smiled at Frank Torello and Carson Page and said, "You've got it. Super Bowl here we come."

"That's what we like to hear," Torello boomed, smiling like he'd just conquered K2.

Carson leaned over and whispered in Marty's ear, "You made the right decision."

He nodded, trying not to sigh. So that was that. There went that crazy idea he'd had about taking a few days off. But hell, he'd lost count of his canceled vacations. The most important thing right now was figuring out how they'd pull off this Super Bowl thing. Just how they'd do it, he didn't know at the moment, but dammit, this account was too big. And way too important.

He and Lee and Zak would go back to Bergman's headquarters, open a bottle of champagne, and curse up a blue streak. Then they'd all put their heads together and come up with something. They'd done it before. That's what those eighty-hour workweeks were all about.

"So now that that's settled," Torello announced smugly, "let's plan on meeting here tomorrow to review your production timetable."

"How's two o'clock?" Marty asked, flipping through his Filofax pocket diary.

Carson nodded. "Two's fine," Torello agreed.

With that, there was the rustle of papers and the sound of chairs on chrome rollers being pushed back in place, and the nerds at the conference table shuffled up to the front of the room. They had all the personality of wet Kleenex, the whole lot of them, with those limp handshakes and stammered Thank yous. Naturally, they dribbled out one by one. Not with a bang but with a snivel.

"Given our deadline, Frank," Carson suggested, "what do you say Marty lets his people get back to work while I give him a tour of our herbal research facility?"

"Good idea." Torello smiled at Marty. "You'll be impressed."

Chapter 2

So how'd the presentation go, Frank?" Del Waters called out from behind Torello's desk. He waved Torello into the office, his tropical-tanned face breaking into an unusually sunny smile, a smile Torello had only recently come to know and fear.

Frank Torello paused in the doorway and smiled back obligingly. From the looks of things in his office—*his* office, Torello reminded himself resentfully—Arrow's chairman had made himself right at home. Hell, the guy even had his feet propped up on Torello's priceless mahogany desk, probably admiring those expensive Italian slip-ons he always wore. And as usual, he was puffing on one of those goddamned Cuban Cohibas; Waters knew Torello couldn't stomach the smell of a cigar, and yet he still went right on smoking them every chance he got. Torello had started to wonder if it was one of those psychological warfare tactics Waters liked to use to "put the enemy off balance." Trouble was, Torello thought now as he pulled a chair up to the desk, keeping a wary eye on his boss, *he* wasn't supposed to be the enemy.

"Everything went just like we planned, Del," Torello said, shaking his head at Waters's offer of a cigar.

"So they jumped through hoops?"

"Yeah, went the whole nine yards. It must've cost Wynn Bergman a goddamn fortune." Torello sounded both regretful and astonished at the same time. He shook his head and rubbed his fleshy palms together in his lap. "Talk about a fucking waste."

Waters let out a low, disdainful laugh. "Your roots are showing, Frank," he jabbed, knowing Torello's soft spots well by now.

Torello averted his aviator-framed eyes and nodded accommodatingly. "Maybe so . . ." he offered, trying to be diplomatic, swallowing his desire to snap back at the man. So he hadn't grown up with a silver spoon in his mouth like Del Waters, Torello thought. So he found this whole agency review process absolutely shameful. So what? In his estimation it was decadent having those ad agencies waste all that money on presentations.

And that's what it was, after all: wasted. Truth was, Waters had decided weeks ago that Marty English was their man. All the expense and hoopla hadn't been necessary. All those thousands of dollars had been nothing more than Del Waters's idea of a good smoke screen, a camouflage for what he really had in mind. And what he had in mind, Torello had to admit, was a thing of beauty. Indeed this time Del Waters had outdone himself, devising a scheme that would put them in the driver's seat for a change.

Torello's eyes returned to the chairman. Waters was rolling the cigar around between his fingers. He didn't seem very concerned about much of anything today, a troubling change of personality for the intense, hard-driving man who hunted through stacks of Arrow audits and reports like he was tracking the Cong back in 'Nam. In fact, Waters treated corporate problems just as he had the enemy. The thought crossed Torello's mind that Del Waters had lots of enemies.

"It had to be done, Frank," Waters commented, giving him a sharp look, the familiar authoritarian demeanor returning. "You know as well as I do we couldn't just pick up the goddamned phone and give English the account. The agency had to make a presentation. That's the way it's done." Waters drew on his cigar, making its tip glow red. A swirling raft of smoke escaped from his lips. "If we hadn't asked for a presentation, English would've been tipped off. He's not an idiot."

"No," Torello agreed stiffly, sensing Waters's patronizing tone. He sat up straighter in his seat. "No, of course he's not. From what I understand, Marty English is about as sharp as they come. Carson says he went from account executive to director of client services in less than ten years. He's next in line for agency president, you know . . . and shit, he's only forty-five."

Waters took his feet off the desk and stood up with the crisp snap of a military man. "Did you know that Marty English was also with Charlie Company in Vietnam?" he demanded harshly, as if Frank Torello had no earthly idea about the life and death of war and what it did to a man.

"I believe I heard that somewhere," Torello admitted uncomfortably.

"Well, for your information, Frank," Waters said disdainfully, "war and advertising are a lot alike. They're both about *survival.* Marketplace . . . jungle . . . it's all the same. It's life and death on Madison Avenue just like it is in a rice paddy. And as cutthroat as any Central American coup you'll ever want to find. To get that far, that fast, in *that* business . . . a man has to be more than intelligent. Or ambitious. He has to be ruthless." Del Waters's Nordic blue eyes held Torello's for one long, cold moment, and then the smile Torello knew well—the smile of a man who reveled in hand-to-hand combat with the enemy, who lived only for the battle—that smile, returned, and Waters said, "And you know what, Frank? I like that in a man. I like that a lot."

Chapter 3

I see you've met our founder," Carson called out as she entered Isaac Arrow's steel-and-glass lobby. Marty had been staring up at a huge oil portrait; he smiled now as Carson joined him in art appreciation.

"'Man's salvation rests with God's creation,'" Marty intoned, reading Isaac Aronstein's most famous quote from the engraved brass plaque hanging squarely beneath the painting. "Looks like Mr. Aronstein was right all along."

"Yeah, he was," she replied earnestly as she guided him across a connecting bridge and into the next building. "Of course the industry forgot that for a while ... went wild for synthetics. But now it looks like we've gone full circle. From herbals, liniments, and patent medicines to synthetics—and now back to this new product line of rainforest herbals. Here at Arrow we believe the natural world is where the future of pharmaceuticals lies. In the rainforests mostly. Because of that, we're determined to save them. At least what we can." She paused, her eyes running over him in a strangely familiar way. "But you already know all that."

He nodded. Yeah, he knew all that. That and a lot more. Most of it was a matter of public record, stuff his staff dug up while researching the account. "I'd say with that kind of forward-thinking strategy, Arrow's empire is really going to grow," he complimented.

Carson smiled. "Empire . . . I like that word. Arrow is quite an empire, isn't it?"

He nodded. "It sure is. And to think it all started with an eleven-year-old German Jewish immigrant boy with a dream of making a fortune in America. He came to Chicago in what? Eighteen eighty-nine? And he changed his last name to Arrow and founded Isaac Arrow Patent Medicines in nineteen ten. Not bad for a kid of twenty-one."

Carson smiled proudly. "And just twenty years later, he was a millionaire; held on to his fortune right through the Depression, too, and then took the company public in 'thirty-nine."

"McCarthyism after World War Two almost got the best of him, though, didn't it?" Marty added. "I understand he was convinced some commies were plotting to take over his company."

"Yes, that's right," Carson acknowledged. "That's when he decided to take the company private again. He got Arrow Pharmaceuticals off Wall Street and back on track with a special board of directors. After that, things really took off. In just ten years, Arrow's board took a company that's only real claim to fame was an aspirin called Endall and turned it into a high-tech superstar."

"I read somewhere that the original formula for Endall came from the local Indians," Marty commented as they turned down a corridor.

"Bull . . . all of it." Carson laughed. "But what the hell, it makes for good press with the ecology freaks." She gave him a wink and he felt the uncomfortable yet somehow enticing familiarity come back again, and he suddenly realized he was tired of hearing her drone on about Isaac Arrow.

He wanted to know more about her. Who was this beautiful woman leading him around this megalopolis of a company? How the hell had she gotten so far up the ladder in this

old boys' club? He hated to think it—he tried not to be sex-
ist—but dammit, Carson Page had to be banging somebody at
the top. Still, he couldn't believe it was Frank Torello. Not in
this lifetime, anyway.

"So," he said offhandedly, "you from Chicago originally?"
He'd posed a nonthreatening question, hoping she'd open up.

She smiled and shook her head. "No. I'm from a little
country town in southern Missouri."

"You go back often?"

"For the holidays, you know, to see my folks."

"Well, they must be proud. You're quite a success." He offered a teasing grin and added, "For a country girl."

She smiled as she led him into a gleaming brass elevator. The
door closed and she pushed the Down button. "Well, you're no
slouch yourself. I mean, you're in *Ad Age* all the time."

"Drawn and quartered," he acknowledged dryly.

She threw him a playful glance and laughed softly, her
hand brushing his forearm. "You're pretty modest for a guy
who graduated four-point-o from Duke with a double major
in psychology and business and then went on to Wharton."

She was flattering him, he knew that, but it felt good anyway. He gave her an appreciative nod. "I see you've done
your homework, Ms. Page."

"I have my spies," she declared with a teasing smile, then
her voice turned serious. "Besides, that's what they pay me
for. . . . The big shots wanted the best ad agency. And that's
what they got."

Even if she was buttering him up a bit, Marty knew she
spoke the truth; Wynn Bergman Advertising was the most respected agency in the country, generating three billion dollars
in annual billings. Bergman's thirty-three offices spanned the
globe from London to Tokyo and boasted the only full-scale
satellite communications system outside network TV, with capabilities extending to the company Gulfstream jet and yacht.
Rumor had it, though tongue-in-cheek, that the agency rest
rooms were next in line for linkups.

"So what else have those spies of yours uncovered?" Marty asked as the elevator door opened and they stepped off.

"Hmm . . . well, let's see," she began, her green eyes meeting his. "Marty English drives a 'sixty-three Jaguar E-type roadster, plays the harmonica, and likes to kick back in blues bars. He prefers Dewar's to Chivas. He has a computerized telescope. Likes a good Robusto No. 1 cigar after dinner at a fine restaurant. He's traveled all over the world: Nepal, African expeditions. . . ." She stopped, breathless now, and frowned. "Did I leave anything out?"

"Only that I sleep on Egyptian cotton sheets." He laughed uneasily; he preferred his private life be kept private, but obviously that was going to be wishful thinking with Carson Page. His discomfort with her was growing. "So," he said, motioning down the golden travertine marble hallway, "where does this yellow brick road lead?"

"To Isaac Arrow's pride and joy," she replied matter-of-factly, leading him to a steel door. She ran an ID card through a scanner at the door and added, "It's all very hush-hush. Only VIPs are allowed beyond this point. But you're a VIP now. We'll get you a temporary security card so you can come and go while you're working on the ad campaign."

A light above the scanner turned green and the door glided open, revealing an underground lobby that branched out into seven passageways leading off in all directions like the tentacles of an octopus.

"There's a lot more to Isaac Arrow than aspirin," Carson explained as they started down one of the corridors. "Every one of these corridors leads to a different division of Arrow's research. Each division has its own library, cafeteria, administrative offices, and labs."

She stopped at a windowless door. Unlike the others they'd passed, this one had no identifying features, no department title or office number. "A word of warning before we go in," she said. "Eric Bachmann, *Doctor* Bachmann to you, is the head of

the lab you're going to see. He takes his work very seriously. He
thinks he's going to save the entire human race someday."

"Thanks for the warning. I'll treat him like the god he is."

"Good." She put her hand on the door. "Now, prepare to be
amazed."

Eric Bachmann's laboratory was designed in the finest scientific tradition. It reminded Marty of his old college chemistry
class. There was white everywhere: white tile, white walls,
white coats. The rest was halogen and fluorescent lights and
chrome and glass. The usual array of centrifuges and micro-
scopes. A dozen or so earnest-looking chemists scurrying
about. Some things never change, Marty guessed. And, despite
Carson's dramatic pronouncement, he wasn't amazed. But for
three hundred million he could damn well pretend to be.

At the sight of Marty and Carson, a slight man dressed in a
lab coat looked up from a microscope and peered over
horned-rimmed glasses.

"Dr. Bachmann, I'd like for you to meet Marty English,"
Carson volunteered. "Marty's the man who's going to tell the
world about all the great things you're doing here at Isaac
Arrow. You mind giving him the nickel tour?"

Bachmann's eyes lit up and he looked at Marty. "You're
really interested?"

"Absolutely."

Bachmann pushed his glasses up on his nose and beamed.
"Right this way," he said, leading them through a maze of tub-
ing and beakers and into another room. "I hope I'm not too
rusty. We don't get much company down here, you know." He
stopped in the doorway.

"This is it, Marty," Carson announced with an almost reli-
gious awe. "You're looking at our crown jewel."

Unlike the stark white lab Marty had just seen, this one was
all gray and stainless and looked more like mission control at
NASA than a college chemistry class. Now he really was impressed.

There were dozens of monitors suspended ceiling to floor, their screens throwing an eery green light onto two enclosed glass chambers. One of the chambers had a tangle of cables hanging down from a large contraption that looked like some kind of robotic extraterrestrial. The other chamber was completely empty.

"Is this some kind of VR setup?" Marty asked as Bachmann strolled across the room and sat down in front of a computer monitor.

Surprised, Bachmann looked up from the workstation. "Why, yes . . . that's right. Virtual reality. Man's greatest attempt to create his own universe with computer-imaging technology. So you're familiar with VR?"

"Not enough to be dangerous," Marty confessed as he walked over to Bachmann's side. "I'm fascinated by the concept, though. I've done some research—just to satisfy my own curiosity." He looked down at the monitor as a triangular logo came up on screen. "You've got quite a setup here, sir," he complimented, turning his gaze to the rest of the room.

"It's the finest VR lab in the entire world," Carson boasted. "Our chairman, Del Waters, is determined to see us with the most advanced computer technology. Right, Dr. Bachmann?"

"Nobody can touch Isaac Arrow's VR lab," he agreed, patting the computer monitor affectionately. "Or for that matter, Trinity here."

"Trinity is the backbone of the entire company," Carson explained. "It's the world's fastest computer. It takes up about two thousand square feet down here. It's got eight hundred gigabytes of memory and a capacity of two trillion operations a second." She smiled. "That's more than the supercomputer at Sandia National Laboratories. And more than the Pentagon."

"More than anybody," Bachmann declared proudly.

"So you see," Carson said, "without Trinity, we'd be lost."

Bachmann nodded. "Trinity handles everything . . . from this lab's VR research with herbal medicinals to the company's banking and inventory. Every piece of information that comes in or goes out of Isaac Arrow is handled by this computer. I guess you could say Trinity's our key to the universe." He smiled with satisfaction. "In fact, thanks to Trinity, we're so far ahead of my old colleagues back in North Carolina—that's the home of VR, you know—that it's not funny."

"Wow! I'm impressed," Marty offered politely.

"Speaking of impressive, I don't know if you're aware of it or not, Marty," Carson added, "but there's one problem everybody in VR's been wrestling with."

"The time lag?" Marty offered, looking up from the monitor. He had their attention now.

"You really do know something about VR, don't you?" Bachmann exclaimed in admiration. "That's right. The biggest problem in VR's been the time lag between real motion and the computer's feedback of motion. Before we tackled that problem, you'd move and you wouldn't see or feel the movement in virtual space for, say, a sixtieth of a second. That doesn't sound like much, but believe me, it threw the whole experience off."

"It was a computer processing problem," Carson said. "And with the help of Trinity, Dr. Bachmann solved it right here, at Isaac Arrow. Of course, no one knows it yet." She smiled at Marty and added, "That's where you and your agency come in."

"It sounds like you're making incredible strides here," Marty said appreciatively.

"Well, unfortunately, experiencing events in real time is just part of the equation," Bachmann admitted. "If we agree that perception is reality, then we have to take VR a step farther in order to make the experience seem completely *real*. As you know, just seeing something doesn't make it real, no matter how real it looks. There are all the other senses to consider. And most important, in my estimation, is the emotional aspect of the experience."

"Under Mr. Waters's direction," Carson added, "Dr. Bachmann's created a software program for our computer system that does just that." She motioned toward the empty chamber. "It provides an emotional experience with virtual feelings."

"Virtual feelings?" Marty inquired. "I'm intrigued."

Carson nodded. "With the help of VR technology, our scientists are exploring human emotions, especially the emotional states of the schizophrenic. Things most of us have never experienced before. And best of all, without all the gadgets. You know, stuff like goggles and hardware."

"How's that possible?"

"The software program doesn't stay outside your head with miniature TV screens and Disney World effects. Dr. Bachmann's program goes *inside*."

Seeing Marty's puzzled expression, Bachmann explained, "The software I've designed utilizes sound waves and vibrational frequencies to target specific neurotransmitters in the brain. These neurotransmitters induce a totally new set of emotions in a subject."

"*New* emotions?"

Bachmann crossed his arms across his chest and nodded with pride. "That's right."

"Isn't that amazing?" Carson exclaimed. She was practically bubbling over. "The regular emotions are part of the software, too—there's pain and joy and grief. It's an incredible breakthrough, integrating virtual feelings into the VR experience, let alone not having to be hooked up to some cable."

Marty's polite interest had turned into genuine fascination.

"It's like Sensurround," Carson continued, "only a whole lot better. Like real life."

"Real life in hell," Bachmann interjected soberly. "The program's still highly experimental."

"So how does all this fit in with herbal pharmaceuticals?"

"VR and pharmaceuticals are a natural fit," Bachmann answered. "The applications of VR in medicine and research are limitless. VR will accelerate the time it takes to find cures for all sorts of diseases. We're actually manipulating molecules in virtual space. Making 'good' proteins ride piggy-back on 'bad' viruses and render them harmless. We'll have the cure for most forms of cancer this decade, thanks to VR. Instead of spending years creating new drug compounds in a test tube, with VR we can create them right before our eyes, in a matter of hours. We can shift atoms to make new molecules . . . right now, we're taking rainforest herbals and transforming them into totally new drugs."

Carson looked at the doctor conspiratorially. "How about giving Marty a demonstration?"

"I'd be happy to."

Marty started toward the empty chamber, but Bachmann grabbed his arm and steered him away. "No, not that chamber. That's the one we use for our new software program. We're testing a simulation of a psychotic experience in there. We're hoping to find a cure for schizophrenia someday."

"I think I'll pass," Marty said wryly.

"Good idea," Carson laughed as they walked into the other glass chamber and Bachmann directed him onto a platform positioned in the middle of the room.

"So we won't be going top of the line here, with your new wireless software program?" Marty remarked, nodding at the hundreds of cables snaking up into a gleaming knot of hardware overhead.

"No," Bachmann admitted. "But I think you'll find this experience satisfying all the same. May I have your right hand?"

Marty extended his hand and Bachmann pulled a stretchy black glove connected to the cables over it. Over his eyes, the doctor placed a pair of dark goggles that held tiny TV screens.

"Hey, who turned off the lights?" Marty joked. He could hear Bachmann's footsteps as the doctor walked out of the chamber and over to the Trinity workstation.

"May I, Dr. Bachmann?" Carson asked eagerly, sitting down in front of the monitor, fingers poised over the keyboard.

"Be my guest," Bachmann replied with a chuckle. "Pretty soon you and Mr. Waters will be better at this than I am."

"All right, Marty, here we go," Bachmann called out over the intercom. "You're in good hands; Carson's at the helm."

There was a sudden emerald flash in front of Marty's eyes and then a series of Ping-Pong-type balls magically appeared, suspended in midair.

"Wow! What are these balls?"

"What do they look like?" Carson asked, her voice sounding tinny through the microphone.

"Like Play-Doh. You know, the stuff kids play with. Hey, now there's some red and blue and yellow balls, too . . . sort of lumpy round globs floating all around."

Bachmann leaned over the intercom. "Those are molecules," he explained. "But that's not really important. Just think of this as a game, Marty . . . a game for chemists."

Marty grinned from beneath the goggles. "Did Carson tell you I'm not exactly a chemist?"

"You don't have to be to get the idea," she said. "Just use your gloved hand and make the globs of Play-Doh fit together, like putting flap A into slot B."

Marty fished his hand around in the virtual space and gave the red glob a shove toward the blue one. It pushed back hard, and he laughed aloud. "Wow . . . it's fighting me—they're like magnets."

"That's the resistance of the molecules you feel," Bachmann said. "When you locate the point where the molecules connect, you won't feel that anymore. You'll have a stable molecule. We call it docking."

Marty tried again. "Yeah, you're right," he exclaimed, "it worked!"

"Congratulations," Dr. Bachmann boomed over the intercom. "You've just created a whole new chemical compound."

Carson smiled. "Welcome to the brave new world of Isaac Arrow."

Chapter 4

Marty English knew all about brave new worlds. Born in 1951, he was a baby boomer and the product of one of the bravest, after all: that Pandora's box of human history known as television. Before TV, men fought in wars. After TV, they watched them. Splitting the atom might have defeated a nation, but television captured the world.

It had also captured Marty English.

Like the rest of his generation, Marty grew up feasting his eyes on Howdy-Doody and Captain Kangaroo. He ate sugar-coated cereal because a smiling tiger said it was great, and he worshiped John Wayne. But unlike the rest of his generation, Marty didn't want to grow up to be Dr. Kildare or the Man from U.N.C.L.E. No, he wanted to be the power behind it all. And that power, he reasoned, was in those thirty-second commercials. In advertising.

"Sight, sound, motion, and emotion"—that's how they described it in the television industry. But whatever you called it, in those thirty seconds of nothing—that half minute of thin air, hype, and razzle-dazzle, you could create a star. Or an entire universe.

Ever since Marty had figured out that somewhere in those thirty seconds was nirvana—hidden like the Tootsie in the Pop—he'd wanted to make it in the advertising world.

But it hadn't been easy. He'd gotten sidetracked in the sixties, grown his hair long and gotten his head bashed in at the Democratic convention in '68. The following year, he was drafted into the army and ended up with a group of guys who called themselves Charlie Company.

When he finally got back to the States, Marty was a decorated veteran and the world was a different place. It was the seventies and the innocence that had pervaded American advertising was gone; selling a product took a better line than "Trust me." People didn't trust their president anymore, let alone the man who wore the Texaco star.

Things were global; Coke was teaching the world to sing. Mr. Peanut had been replaced by social realism. And Marty's passion for advertising was again sparked. He entered Duke University, got his degree in marketing and psychology, and headed for Wharton. A flurry of jobs in various ad agencies followed, each one taking him another rung up the corporate ladder, another step closer to his goal of making it to the top. In the late eighties, he joined Wynn Bergman Advertising, and the rest, as they say, was history.

When Marty finally made it back to his office, it was after five. Even so, Wynn Bergman was still an eighteen-story beehive of activity; the only clue that there'd been a celebration over landing the Isaac Arrow account was an empty Dom Pérignon bottle teetering on the edge of his sleek steel desk. At the sight of it, he swore under his breath and tossed the bottle into the trash. It landed with a hollow clatter.

It wasn't missing the party that pissed him off—he was used to that. No, it was getting behind in his work; he had a thousand things to do and each one was more important than the next.

Over the next few hours, Marty made over twenty calls, pacing back and forth, up and down the long expanse of window overlooking Michigan Avenue, barking out orders, asking the tough financial questions nobody wanted to hear,

stroking egos where he had to. With six group account directors to oversee and thirty U.S. accounts to look after, he had
to be able to hard-line it one minute and smooth-talk it the
next. But Marty had no problem turning it off and on. He was
a chameleon par excellence.

The streetlights were gleaming against the darkness outside
his window when Marty finally dropped into his chair and
loosened his tie. He glanced at the antique Rolex on his wrist
and then dialed Zak Restin. It might be after seven, but Zak
would still be in his office; you didn't work on a time clock at
Wynn Bergman.

"Let's get moving, Zak," he ordered. "This Arrow deadline's already breathing down our necks. Round up your people and get the hell up here."

Marty paused, listening. "Yeah, yeah . . . Lee's on her
way."

He paused again, tapping his Mont Blanc on the desk, riding out the creative director's storm of rage and frustration.
"No, Zak," he said, rolling his eyes. "We can't talk Arrow out
of a spot in the Super Bowl. Get your ass up here. Now." He
hung up the phone and sighed. Management. It was truly
overrated.

It was quite a three-ring circus Marty had brought together.
There was Account Service. Creative. Media. Broadcast Production. Legal. Account Planning. Twelve people in all.

"Congratulations," he declared, leaning back in his chair.
"You folks did a hell of a job." They nodded and muttered
their thanks and then he smiled grimly and added, "But
you've still got a hell of a job to do."

The smiles faded and they nodded in unhappy agreement.
Lee Wilde was the first to speak out.

"Hell of a job to do?" She laughed acidly. "Forget about it.
Frank Torello and his little sugar pop, Carson Page, are fucking nuts. I checked on getting them in the Super Bowl. Not a
chance. And by the way, while we're on the subject of the il-

lustrious Ms. Page, she's gonna be trouble—it's written all over her."

"Don't give me that, Lee," Marty shot back. He was tired, on a short fuse. Ignoring her personal commentary on Carson Page, he pressed on. "I expect to have Arrow in the Super Bowl. No excuses."

She shrugged, caught between fury and resignation. "Well, if we *can* get it, it's gonna cost them an arm and a leg."

"I know."

"Thirty seconds might go as high as a million and a half bucks." Lee glanced down at her notes. "Hell, maybe two, and, no bullshit, I still don't know if I can lock it down."

Zak shook his head. "I think we should just tell Arrow we can't get the airtime in the Super Bowl and be done with it." He screwed up his youthful face. "Jesus, Marty, you know what pulling this off is gonna be like?"

Marty laughed. He'd started working at Wynn Bergman before Zak Restin had finished junior high. "Excuse me?" he asked, leaning forward in his chair and feigning offense. "Do *I* know what it's going to be like?"

"Restin, you're a real piece of work." Lee chuckled. "Did anybody ever tell you you're full of shit?"

The room erupted in laughter.

Zak Restin was full of it, all right. And even worse, he liked to bitch. But there was no denying he was talented. A street kid from Detroit, Zak's artistic roots were in the graffiti of buses and subways—"the poor man's billboards," Zak called them. When he'd gotten a scholarship to California Institute of the Arts, the only African American in his high school to receive such an opportunity, a career in commercial art and advertising had evolved naturally.

At twenty-seven, Zak was Bergman's youngest creative director, a diamond in the rough with the promise of true brilliance. If he hadn't been so talented, Marty would've tired of his whining and had the director of creative services bounce him out on his ass a long time ago. But in this business, talent mattered more than temperament; as long as Zak was manageable, the creative product would keep flowing. The kid could deliver, and that was what mattered most.

Marty held up his hand and the office fell quiet. "Hey, folks," he growled, "the bottom line is we're going to produce a commercial that should take four months in a little over two weeks. We're here to figure out how we're going to do that. Not piss and moan."

He gave Zak a look that told the kid to get with the program. Then he looked back at the other eleven faces. "Speaking for myself, I'm not in the mood to tell old man Bergman we lost a three-hundred-million-dollar account because we couldn't get a lousy thirty-second spot in the can and on the air."

They nodded back at him solemnly; neither were they.

"Okay. So now that that's settled, let's talk timetable. The clock's already ticking. I have to present a schedule to the client tomorrow afternoon. . . ." Marty's voice trailed off as he looked at the monitor on his desk. "Here's how it shakes out," he began. "Today's the sixth of January. D-Day is the twenty-fifth, Super Bowl Sunday. Before we can even start production, the spot's got to be approved by the client *and* by Network Broadcast Practices and Standards in New York. Once that happens, we can get going."

"By the way," Lee offered, "the spot can be in the network's hands as late as Saturday, the twenty-fourth . . . as long as we give them advance notice that it's gonna be down to the wire. Of course they'll want us to give them a backup spot, just in case."

The agency's production manager, a redhead named Bill Kidman, rubbed at his freshly sprouting goatee thoughtfully. "Maybe we can use one of their old Endall spots?" he suggested in a deep southern drawl that betrayed his Georgia heritage.

"Yeah, that's a good idea," Zak declared sarcastically. "Because it's gonna be a goddamned miracle if we get this new spot produced in time. In case anybody here hasn't noticed, even with a network grace period of the twenty-fourth, we've still only got eighteen fucking days to get this done."

"I'm glad to see you managed to pass arithmetic," Marty commented sarcastically. "But we're not going to cut it that close. I expect this spot to be approved and ready to air by Wednesday the twenty-first. That means we've only got fifteen days, Zak. Not eighteen."

"Looks like you're already behind, Restin," Lee taunted.

Marty frowned at her and continued. "The rest of this week is for creative development and final budgets. We'll get client approval this coming Monday, the twelfth."

He turned to the team's attorney, Marcia Levine, and added, "On Monday we'll need Legal to overnight the storyboards to New York for network approval. We have to have approval by Tuesday morning."

"That shouldn't be a problem," Marcia replied. "It'll be preliminary, though. We'll have to get final approval after the spot's finished, of course."

"I can live with that. Just make sure we get a preliminary nod from Network first thing Tuesday because Zak, Kidman, and I will have to leave for Belize that afternoon if we're going to get the spot produced on time. Right, Kidman?"

"Right." Kidman nodded.

"So then," Marty went on, "from Wednesday through Sunday the eighteenth, we'll be in Belize. On the nineteenth, the following Monday, we'll be back in the office and Creative will start editing."

Marty turned to Bill Kidman and added, "You'll have to supply Legal with your rough edits on Tuesday, the twentieth, so Marcia can review it with Network on Wednesday while I'm getting the client's approval. If Network's got a problem, I want to know right then, before we go to the final cut on Thursday."

"So do I," Kidman agreed.

Zak looked at Marcia and added, "Don't worry . . . you'll have those edits."

"Sounds like you guys have it covered," Marty commented. "Maybe I'll take that vacation after all."

Lee wagged a well-manicured scarlet fingernail at him. "Don't even think about it."

"Well, maybe not." He chuckled. "So that's our timetable," he said with finality. "Now I suggest you all get moving— we've got an ad to produce."

It was almost nine o'clock by the time everyone left Marty's office. Some, like Kidman, had left quickly to get to work, while others, like Lee and Zak, lingered a while, good-naturedly bitching and moaning. Before leaving for the evening, Marty checked his E-mail. Only one message made him stop to think:

GOOD JOB MARTY. YOU LANDED ANOTHER BIG ONE. ARROW
WILL MAKE OUR YEAR. CONGRATULATIONS, WYNN.
P. S. WHEN DO WE START BILLING?

Marty sighed. He hated to burst Wynn's bubble, but he had to tell him about the possibility of losing NHP before someone else did. He figured early the next morning would be the best time: Wynn had an early morning open-office policy; he kept the hours between seven and nine open for senior execs, claiming this fostered good company relations. Marty hated to start a morning off with news like this, but it was better to bite the bullet and just get it over with. Resigned, he typed back:

THANKS WYNN. I'LL COME BY AND FILL YOU IN FIRST THING
IN THE MORNING. MARTY

He sighed for the second time in two minutes, then hit a few keys on his keyboard to bring a profit-and-loss statement up on the screen. Whatever illusions he might have about creative contributions, he knew the real story in advertising was billing. What you thought about the client or the ad campaign didn't matter. What mattered was dollars.

This time, with Arrow, he'd hit the mother lode. If he handled the account right, Wynn Bergman Advertising could walk away with thirty-six million. With a five percent bonus, he himself could expect a check for two, maybe three hundred grand. He smiled to himself and leaned back in his chair. "Damn!" he said under his breath.

But it didn't take long for the glow of the computer screen to pull him back to earth. If they didn't make deadline and screwed up this Super Bowl spot, nobody would ever see a dime of all that money.

And what about NHP? As exciting as it would be to tell Wynn about Arrow, the truth was the agency would still be down three hundred million without them. Shaking his head, Marty reached around the computer and shut it off. Tomorrow would be here soon enough. It was time to go home.

Chapter 5

Image is everything. That's the advertising motto, both in the office and out.

For Marty, that meant living on Walton Street—just a block from the John Hancock Center and Water Tower Center—on the top floors of the Astor, a ten-story brownstone that looked out onto Lake Shore Drive and Oak Street Beach. That was about as far as Marty would go with the charade: having the right address, letting a valet park his car, greeting a doorman that looked like he could pass muster at Buckingham Palace. Once he stepped inside his three-thousand-square-foot condo, that was it. No more games. No more bullshit. It was recharge time.

Before Marty could get his key in the door, it flew open, revealing a tall, tanned woman with warm brown eyes and a waterfall of long straight hair that shone like autumn wheat. An ivory cashmere sweater and a pair of faded Levi's hugged her long, athletic figure. From the oval entryway, she flashed a broad smile and held up a bottle of Cristal champagne.

"Congratulations!" she cried, throwing her arms around him, enveloping him in the heady scent of Chanel No. 5.

He was surprised at the reception, but reminded himself that he shouldn't be. After all, he'd lived with Reiki Devane for seven years and she was still as unpredictable as the Chicago weather.

"Lee Wilde called," she explained, closing the door behind him. "She said you got the Arrow account. I thought we'd celebrate."

He nodded and followed her into the living room, a grand, decadent space with twelve-foot ceilings and French doors leading out to a balcony overlooking the water. Ever the romantic, Reiki had placed candles around the room for the occasion; the tiny flames bathed the walls in amber light.

"You look great," he said, his eyes moving over her appreciatively. Even at her most casual, Reiki had her own unique style, a cross between ethnic and classic—sort of Ralph Lauren goes Katmandu—that, somehow, worked exquisitely for her. Tonight her long, soft sweater was lashed at her narrow hips with a knotted leather belt she'd picked up at a backstreet bazaar in Marrakech.

She beamed at him now, her full, pouty lips forming a childlike smile, and he had to remind himself that her innocent facade masked a globe-trotting freelance photojournalist with more guts and grit than most men Marty knew.

"Lee also told me about Arrow's marketing VP," she said softly, a vulnerable undertone to the words. "What's her name? Carson Page?"

He frowned to himself and took off his hat and coat and tossed them down on a wingback chair. "Yeah. Carson Page."

Reiki nodded thoughtfully, twisting one long strand of hair around her French-manicured finger. "So what's she like?"

"Carson?" He shrugged. "I don't really know, not yet anyway . . . we just met. You know, when she asked us to present for the account. She seems nice enough. A real corporate type. Pretty buttoned down."

"So, then, she's a . . . *professional*." Reiki said the word "professional" cautiously, as if questioning its legitimacy in the case of Carson Page—as if she suspected there might be something more to Arrow's vice president than oxford cloth and corporate power.

He set his jaw defensively and retorted, "Yeah, I'd say that." Why the hell was Reiki asking all these questions? It wasn't like her to do that—at least not until recently, when the subject of marriage and commitment had started to come up. But whatever the reason for her sudden insecurity tonight, Marty didn't like the direction things were taking. He'd end this game right now.

"Okay," he demanded, "what's the problem here?" She averted her wide, almond eyes and he smiled, pulling her to him. "Come on now, let me tell you what you really want to know." He cupped her face in his hands, looked directly into her eyes, and spoke: "Carson Page's got nothing on you."

He saw her tanned cheeks flush with pleasure; for all her exterior toughness, Reiki was an absolute softy. But he wasn't kidding. Carson Page was no different from most of the women he saw marching up and down Michigan Avenue every day. Most of them could have been run off on a copy machine. But not Reiki Devane. She was a different story entirely. In all his life, Marty had never been with a woman like Reiki. A one-of-a-kind, the consummate iron fist in the velvet glove. Her tough exterior masked a sultry feminine passion. Marty loved her contradictions; they made her the sexiest woman alive.

He could feel the heat of her body against him as she stared up into his eyes. "I take it," he said, "that Lee was bashing Carson Page?"

Looking embarrassed, she nodded.

Marty sighed. Sometimes he wondered why he'd ever introduced the two women in the first place. Reiki and Lee had hit it off right from the start, becoming fast friends who "did lunch" at Neiman's, shopped at Bendel's, and shared confidences. Girlfriend things, that's what Reiki called them. But Marty suspected the two of far more devious activities—like plotting against the men of the world. Or, at the very least, him.

"So," he asked, "what else did Ms. Wilde have to say?"

"Well . . ." Reiki smiled impishly. "She mentioned something about how you should be richly rewarded for all the hard work you've put in these past few weeks."

He gave her a skeptical grin. "Lee said *that*?"

"Uh . . . no. Well, not *exactly* that." She paused, searching his eyes knowingly, and added with a mischievous whisper, "But you wouldn't mind . . . would you?"

"Not a bit," he chuckled as she led him across the hardwood floor to the sofa.

She tossed off her brown suede loafers, sat him down, and started loosening his tie. "You must be tired."

"Yeah," he agreed, leaning back. "I am." He threw a teasing grin her way and added, "I suppose it's all that male bonding and protecting the tribe I do all day. It drains a guy something awful."

She laughed softly and knelt down beside him and buried her face in the open collar of his shirt. He closed his eyes and she began nibbling up his neck to his earlobe. "Kiss me," she whispered. He pressed his mouth to hers, tasting the moistness there, breathing in her scent.

"Hmm . . . that's nice," she said dreamily. She ran one long finger over his lower lip. "Did I ever tell you how much I love to kiss you?"

"All the time." He smiled. He started to kiss her again, but before he could, she jumped up and spun away, golden hair flying, laughing like some fairy sprite. He smiled again; sometimes living with Reiki was like living in the Keebler hollow tree—uncommonly good.

"You hungry?" she called out from the doorway of the kitchen.

A guilty expression crossed his face. "Uh . . . not too."

She gave him a suspicious look.

"Sorry," he apologized. "I couldn't help myself. I grabbed a hot dog on the way home."

She shook her head the way she always did when she didn't approve. Health food was Reiki's thing, those godawful algae and barley drinks. It certainly seemed to work for her. She had flawless skin and a figure that was so toned and lean that she could easily allow herself a hot dog or two. But Reiki never yielded to temptation, remaining a perfectly proportioned, yet statuesque, one hundred eighteen pounds.

"Good," she said, surprising him; he'd expected a lecture on nitrites or food coloring or some other hot-dog ill. "I thought we'd just have some fruit and *reggiano* and a loaf of bread from that Italian bakery on Taylor Street." She paused and held up the bottle of champagne. "Oh, and this."

"Sounds great," he said. "I'll make the fire."

Marty changed into a pair of old jeans and a shirt and put on some music while Reiki laid out the food. By the time they sat down on the floor in front of the fireplace, the champagne was well chilled.

"So, here's to shady deals and good slogans," he said, hoisting the bottle.

She nodded absently. "Hmm." She frowned. "Something's missing. . . ." She looked around the room and then snapped her fingers. "Damn it, that's it. I forgot the flutes." She got up and started toward the kitchen, but he caught her hand and pulled her back down to the floor.

"Hey, remember the old college days?" he said. "When you drank cold duck right out of the bottle?"

Her large brown eyes went wide and she shook her head, feigning horror. "We didn't do that at the Sorbonne. . . . *Civilized* people use glasses."

He tried not to laugh. Truth was, Reiki's parents had spent a fortune trying to "civilize" her and it had been a miserable failure. Though it was still a wonder she wasn't a snob. Her mother was an opera singer, a real Italian diva. Her father was an American diplomat in Germany. Between the two of them, they'd seen to it that Reiki had the best of everything. But it was all to no avail; she hadn't been the little princess of her parents' dreams. She'd been too independent and willful, a truly rebellious kid. So they sent her to Paris for her education, hoping she'd come back a deb. Instead, she came back a libertine. Marty imagined they'd been pretty disappointed.

"Forget civilized," he said, tipping up the bottle. He took a long drink and then handed it to her.

She grinned and put her full lips around the mouth of the bottle and lifted it. The champagne trickled down her chin and she wiped it away with the back of her hand. "Now I know why we didn't do that in Paris." She sniffed. "It's *so* gauche."

He laughed. Reiki might have the high cheekbones and perfect, aquiline nose of some European aristocrat, but this was no hothouse flower sitting here next to him in front of the fire. This was a woman who could swim with the sharks and play poker with them, too. But he'd go along. "Gauche? You poor thing." He clucked. "You need to loosen up."

"*I* need to loosen up?" she cried, sitting upright. "Shit, if it weren't for me, you'd be sleeping in a tie. I'm the one who drank shots of tequila with Baptiste the bandit down in Peru, remember?"

He narrowed his eyes, as if the very name Baptiste sent him into a mental frenzy of jealousy. "Yeah, I remember, all right. And I keep meaning to ask you if drinking with him was part of the assignment."

"Yep." She giggled. "All in a day's work. Want to see the shots I got of Baptiste in his fatigues?"

"I already saw them, in *Time*." He paused. "Speaking of assignments, you heard anything about Rwanda?"

She shook her head. "No." She sighed, pulling her knees up to her chin. "I'm still waiting. God, I hate waiting. But as much as I hate waiting . . . I hate talking about it even more. Let's talk about you. Tell me about this new piece of business you got. You've hardly said two words about it. Lee sure had a lot to say. . . ."

Marty shot her a look.

"Lee said Arrow's going to be a ball buster."

"Leave it to Lee to put things so eloquently," he remarked, taking another drink from the bottle. "Arrow may be a ball buster, but they've got three hundred million to spend." He paused, his thoughts flitting to the prospect of losing NHP. He wouldn't say anything to Reiki about his concerns; somehow talking about his problems at work had always seemed unmanly to him, more like pissing and moaning than what Reiki called "opening up" and "sharing."

"Three hundred million, huh?" she said, her expression teasing. "Not bad for a day's work."

"Believe me, right now we can use every dollar we can get."

"Well, you're talking about more than a few dollars. That's a hell of a budget for a company like Arrow, isn't it? I've never really noticed their ads. Why the sudden push?"

"It *is* a big budget. But they're going to need it. They've decided to revamp their entire image and branch out into rainforest herbals."

"Really? Rainforest herbals?"

He had her full attention now; saving the rainforests was one of Reiki's favorite topics. "Yeah, but it's not all fruits and nuts. They're putting a spin on it, using virtual reality to make new drugs from herbs. I saw their VR lab today. God, you wouldn't believe it. It's amazing. They've got one software program that actually simulates emotions."

"Really?" She didn't look like she was buying it.

"Yeah. *Really*. But it's still experimental, so I didn't get to try it."

"That's good." She giggled. "I think the sixties were enough of a trip for you."

A brief smile passed over his face and then he sighed, turning serious. "You know, sometimes I think things were better back then. Back when what you were inside counted for something and it was *in* to be real. Feelings were something you got in touch with, not something made up by a machine. Sounds funny coming from an ad man, doesn't it?"

"Not to me."

"It wouldn't to you. You're weird to begin with."

She laughed.

"I guess seeing that VR lab today made me wonder where it's all headed."

Nodding, she picked up an apple with her long, elegantly shaped fingers and took a bite. "So where is it headed?" she asked between crunches. "Arrow's technology, I mean."

"To the limit, I'm sure. Nobody can touch the shit they've got. And with this new line of rainforest products we're introducing—"

"But herbals aren't high-tech," she objected, handing him the apple.

"No, you're right. They're not. But they will be when Arrow's through with them." He looked down at the apple in his hand. "I got the impression today that they honestly think they'll be improving on nature. Or, at the very least, revolutionizing medicine. From what I can tell, Mother Nature's herbs are just a means to an end for Isaac Arrow."

"Where are the herbs coming from?"

"Belize. That's where we're going to film the Super Bowl spot, at a place called Escoba."

"Escoba! The eco-resort?" she exclaimed. "Jesus, you're kidding!" She jumped up and scurried over to the coffee table, grabbing up a *National Geographic*. "There's something you've got to see. Ever heard of a foundation called Planetlife?"

"Yeah, Escoba's on a Planetlife preserve. Arrow's got some cooperative thing going with them. They're using the rainforest for their research into herbals."

Reiki sat down cross-legged next to him and opened the magazine. "Look," she said, fanning the pages. "There's a whole spread on the Planetlife preserve in Belize. And see this"—she tapped the page—"here's Escoba. God, isn't it beautiful? There're some great shots in here. They even have NASA photos."

She stopped turning the pages and started studying the photos. "I'll tell you one thing," she said, looking up at him with a puzzled expression, "Planetlife must have some unbelievable pull. You can't just ask NASA to send a satellite over and take pictures like these."

"Why not?" he asked, taking the magazine. "I thought NASA was doing some work with private companies."

"Yeah, they are. But they're not taking photos like the ones in here. The technology for these shots is supposed to be reserved for government intelligence."

"Well, they must have some government connection, then."

"Or some friends in high places."

He shook his head in exasperation. "With all the research we did for the Arrow presentation, how the hell did we miss this article?"

"You didn't," she soothed, "it came in the mail today." She looked over his shoulder and smiled. "Escoba's some place, huh? They even serve gourmet food. Of course it isn't the lily pad. . . ." She sighed wistfully and gave him a quick hug around the neck.

He nodded. "No, it's definitely not that."

"Lily pad" was what Reiki called Bermuda, comparing the two of them to frogs sunning themselves in the middle of a pond. For a while they had managed to go there every year, retreating to a little cottage on the western end of the island, basking in sybaritic luxury. It had been three years since Marty had felt that soft sand between his toes. Despite its supposed splendor, he didn't think Escoba would be much consolation.

"Escoba does look wonderful, though," Reiki prompted. "I mean, for a place in the wilderness. It's really meant to be a whole other kind of experience."

"Oh, it sounds like that all right." He chuckled, scanning the fold-out of wildlife photos. "Grass huts, Maya ruins. Two hundred–plus species of birds. Jaguar. Snakes . . ." His face went tight at the word; he'd hated snakes ever since his tour of duty in Vietnam. "What's this about snakes?" he said, flipping hurriedly through the pages.

"Oh, there're snakes down there, all right."

"Why don't we change the subject?"

"Sure," she agreed, not wanting to dig up the past. "Okay, then, when do you leave?"

"Next Tuesday."

"I see." She gave him a sidelong glance. "You know, a good photographer might come in handy."

"And we know you're a good photographer." He grinned, putting down the magazine. "But are you a magician?"

She shook her head. "Do you need one?"

"Yeah. And in the worst way, too. That Super Bowl deadline's got us under the gun. Lee was right—it's going to be a bitch." He shook his head. "I guess I'm a little spooked about it all."

"Hey, relax, you've done it before," she said, lying back on the rug. She pursed her lips together. Marty loved to watch her when she was trying to make sense of something. "Hmm . . . maybe it's the way you got the account that's making you feeling jinxed. Lee said it was pretty strange. I mean, the way you got it right away, like that."

"Yeah, it *was* strange. You just don't give a presentation and get the account on the spot. I was as surprised as anybody when they did that—" Marty stopped, taking in the way the firelight played across Reiki's face, the way it caught the deep brown of her eyes and turned them to fire. "What the hell," he said, moving closer to her. "What have I got to complain about? I just landed a three-hundred-million dollar account. Why question good fortune?"

"That's right," she agreed. "Why tempt fate by asking the hard questions?"

"Exactly," he murmured, leaning over her. "I'll take the easy ones instead."

Eyes twinkling, she slipped her arms around his neck. "And what questions are those?"

"Did you miss me these past weeks?"

"You've been here every night."

"You know what I mean."

"Well, now that you mention it, you have been a bit negligent in your manly duties."

"Then I guess I'll just have to redeem myself," he said. He kissed her hard and she sighed under his mouth with open pleasure. "Is that better?" he asked.

"Much."

Chapter 6

With its lush rolling woodlands, gracious terraced lawns, and walled estates laden with English ivy, Lake Forest, Illinois, was about as far away from Taylor Street and Chicago's old Italian neighborhood as a man could get.

Tony Inglesia took great pleasure in reminding himself of the sharply contrasting worlds in which he'd lived. It gave him a deep sense of self, a certain unshakable confidence, to know he'd made it, to know he'd clawed his way out of poverty to make his home in one of America's foremost bastions of wealth and respectability.

He'd carried that knowledge with him for seventy years, and he knew it had served him well; he called it a gift, that knowing. Knowing he could do it all over again if he had to. Knowing what he was made of. And, indeed, Tony Inglesia took pride in what he was made of—he was hot-blooded, with just the right combination of nerve, guts, and brains.

Muscle and a handgun hadn't been enough to pull the only child of Sicilian immigrants out of Chicago's back alleys and juke joints. He'd needed to use his head to do that. And he had. In spades. It was the American way, after all, getting ahead by using your brains. He'd used those brains so he wouldn't grow up to be like his father, an uneducated man who barely spoke English, who spent his life pushing a broken-down vegetable cart through Chicago's poor Italian neighborhood.

Though he'd spent his boyhood days rolling Irish boys for quarters, Tony Inglesia hadn't been a greasy-haired little *goomba* for long. In forty years, he'd risen through the ranks of Chicago's Mob to the number-one spot. Nobody called it "godfather" nowadays, but that was what he was: Tony Inglesia ran the whole shebang. From Chicago to LA.

He'd faced a lot of competition on the way up, of course, other greaseballs with less brains and more brawn than he had. But Inglesia had outwitted them all. And then he'd turned his attention to the one thing he believed would save the Italian Mafia in America: bringing Chicago's organized crime syndicate into the twentieth century.

He'd done that by learning how to play the corporate game, by shedding the Old Country gangster crap of his immigrant parents' generation and passing as one of the crowd; these days, Tony Inglesia went to the Chicago Athletic Club and steamed with the best of them.

It hadn't been that hard for him to pass inspection; had he been legit, he could have made it into the *Forbes* Four Hundred. The men he encountered knew who and what he was, but they let it pass—as much out of fear as for the thrill of rubbing elbows with a mobster who didn't act like one. A mobster who looked like one of them. Polished. Sophisticated. A mobster who looked the part of a mogul.

Instead of sharkskin, Tony Inglesia wore two-thousand-dollar suits and custom-made leather shoes that cost more than most people made in a week. But he wasn't flashy or ostentatious; no gold chains and gaudy rings for him. He even smelled like a WASP: of Dunhill and tweed, not garlic and cheap cigars.

Although he was self-educated, he could have gone to Princeton or Harvard or Yale for all anyone knew. He was well informed, educated in history and the arts. And in the social graces, too. *That* had been especially important, and Inglesia prided himself in having learned the correct behavior for every social occasion.

And so it was that he'd replaced the gangster swagger with the all-American businessman's stride and a good firm handshake, a handshake that said that, even in the twentieth century, there really was honor among thieves.

Inglesia was settled in his library chair, staring into the orange and blue flames shooting up in a fieldstone fireplace, when his guests arrived.

At the sight of them, standing in the arch of the doorway alongside his very proper-looking butler, Inglesia's deep-set eyes glinted out from his aristocratic face, revealing a sly nature beneath the facade. "Hello, Frank, Carson." He smiled. "Del . . . good to see you!" He unbuttoned his Harris tweed coat and waved them over. "Come in, have a seat . . . How's Escoba doing? How's Arch?"

"They're doing great," Waters answered, his deep voice filled with unabashed pride as he folded his long frame into one of the leather chairs. "Arch sends his apologies. He just couldn't make it, Tony. His plane doesn't get in from Belize 'til late tonight."

"I see," Inglesia said, and added, tongue-in-cheek, "so Arch Templeton's just too busy to pay his respects to an old friend now, is he?"

Del Waters took the ribbing about his partner in stride. He broke into an easy grin and replied, "You know Arch is never too busy for you, Tony . . . but he sure as hell has had his hands full at Escoba."

"Arch has done a fabulous job," Carson gushed.

"Fabulous." Torello nodded, admiring the way Waters handled the mobster. Anyone else might have betrayed himself by acting too smug, too self-satisfied. But not Del Waters. The culmination of Waters's plan for Inglesia would be more gratifying than any adolescent one-upmanship he'd have now.

Waters would save his gloating for later. When he had the Mob boss where he wanted him.

"So I take it business is good?" Inglesia asked.

"Couldn't be better," Waters asserted. "Last month we even had some officials from the Audubon Society stay at the place. Christ, they ate it up." He held up a copy of *National Geographic.* "You see this yet?"

Shaking his head, Inglesia took the magazine and started thumbing through the pages.

"Looks like we made the big time, Tony," Torello crowed.

"Arch has even got NASA working for us," Waters added. "NASA took those satellite photos in there." He smiled the calculating Nordic smile at Inglesia. "They're supposed to be for an ecological study, but they're pretty damned good at finding those Guatemalan rebels."

"I bet they are." Inglesia chuckled warily.

"*National Geographic* gave Escoba and Planetlife some of the best coverage I've ever seen," Carson added. "That's a twenty-page article in there . . . full-color, too."

Torello nodded exuberantly. "On top of all this publicity, Tony, *The New York Times* just named Escoba the five-star eco-resort of the year. My God, you couldn't ask for a better endorsement than that."

Inglesia smiled and looked over at Waters. "I have to hand it to you, Del, you guys at the CIA came up with a hell of a cover for this operation. But, cover or not, it's nice to see Escoba's profitable on its own, without our other side businesses. It must be a hell of a place, to get that kind of press. Someday I'll have to get down there and see it for myself." He grinned disarmingly. "That is, if you promise to keep the scorpions out of my hut."

"You come down to Escoba, Tony," Waters offered, "and we'll make sure of it."

Inglesia pulled a small gold case from his pocket and took out a cigarette. "So, Frank," he said, lighting up as he turned to Torello, "where do you want to begin?"

"With your son?" Torello tried not to smile; the trap was being laid.

"I take it he got the Isaac Arrow account?"

"What are friends for?" Waters smiled cagily. "Just a little token of our appreciation. But I gotta tell you, Frank says the kid's got his work cut out for him."

At Inglesia's puzzled expression, Carson added, "That's because of the Super Bowl, Tony. You see, Marty's only got two weeks to get Isaac Arrow's spot produced and in the game."

"Why all the pressure?" Inglesia demanded, his paternal instincts suddenly aroused. "What's so special about a goddamned football game that your ad campaign can't wait a few days?"

"There's just nothing like the Super Bowl, Tony," Torello answered earnestly. "With thirty seconds in that one football game Arrow's message will reach millions of people. Satellites will send it to TVs all over the world. Oh, I admit it costs a fortune, but even at that, it's very cost effective."

Inglesia nodded politely. "I see," he said in a tone that told Waters that he didn't.

"Arrow's herbal product line may serve as a cover for our operation," Waters added stiffly. "But don't forget that, unlike you, Carson, Frank, and I have to answer to Arrow's board of directors. They expect their new herbal product line to be a big success, and our job is to make that happen. The fact is, introducing it in the Super Bowl will do more for sales than all the other ads we'll run the rest of the year. If there's a little pressure on your kid to get the job done . . . well, I think you'll agree he's being well compensated for his trouble."

Inglesia couldn't argue with that. "If I know Marty," he said with an ingratiating smile, "he won't let three hundred million dollars go down the drain because of a deadline. Hell, he's at his best under pressure." He took a long drag on his cigarette and then exhaled, enshrouding his gray mane of hair in smoke. "Marty doesn't suspect my involvement, of course—"

"Of course not!" Torello exclaimed.

"He's not at all suspicious," Carson declared, an arrogant note in her voice. "I took him all over the company today and he never asked a single question about anything unusual." She smiled smugly. "But then I didn't expect him to. He's a man, isn't he? And we all know about you men and your egos. Marty won't ever question why we gave him the account on the spot—he'll be too busy patting himself on the back."

"He's a man, all right," Inglesia retorted testily. He'd often questioned why Waters had included a woman in this whole affair. She was ruthless, perhaps, but nevertheless she was a woman. As far as Inglesia was concerned, that made for trouble. "But I can assure you, Carson," he went on, "my son doesn't have a vain bone in his body."

"I don't know about vanity," Carson declared, crossing her lovely legs. "But he does have a typically male talent for dissembling. When I asked him about his family, he told me you were dead, Tony."

"He always did know how to keep a secret." Inglesia sighed.

"So, Carson," Torello jumped in. He was well aware of Inglesia's bias against women and he was eager to change the subject. "How did Marty like the tour?"

"He had a good time. He's bright, curious, and he asks the right questions."

"Exactly. So don't underestimate him," Inglesia said, eyes flashing. "Marty's even brighter than he looks. He's hardheaded, too. Once he gets his teeth into something, he doesn't let go. His involvement with Arrow is legitimate right now and I expect it to stay that way. He gets a piece of the action, but it has to be on the up-and-up."

"That won't be a problem, Tony," Torello said reassuringly. "Carson will make sure everything's under control at Arrow."

He glanced at Waters and nodded. "But there are a few other things we'd like to discuss tonight." Torello held his breath. This was it. Waters would make his move and, soon, if things went as he'd planned, Tony Inglesia would be taking orders from him.

Waters cleared his throat. He was pleased with himself; just a hint of encouragement—and his promise of a big ad budget for Inglesia's son—and the mobster had taken the bait and involved his only child in their enterprise, an only child Inglesia clearly loved and would do anything to protect. Indeed, blackmailing the Mob boss was going to be even easier than he'd imagined. Waters tried to hide his excitement, but Inglesia saw it in his eyes, in the sudden dilating flash of his pupils, and the Mob boss was instantly wary.

"Tony," Waters began, "we've been receiving cocaine from your Colombian associates at our Escoba airstrip in Belize for what—fifteen years now?"

Inglesia nodded and put out his cigarette. "Something like that," he agreed.

"All those years we've being using the escoba tree as a cover for our smuggling operation into the U.S. . . . and, I must say, it's worked like a charm." Waters paused and smiled. "Of course we have to give credit to Arch Templeton for the idea to use the tree's bark and thorns to hide the cocaine in, in the first place. *That* was a stroke of genius. Maybe even pivotal to the success of our plan."

Inglesia nodded and crossed his arms over his chest. He was waiting, wondering where this was headed.

"Thanks to the escoba tree's status as a medicinal herb," Waters continued, "and my contacts in the government, it's been pretty easy bringing our shipments in. We've shipped thousands of tons of cocaine into Miami, duty free, without any search by Customs. From Florida, you've moved the coke through your import front, Curandero, and out onto the streets. It's been a hell of a success."

"Yeah, we've done well for ourselves," Inglesia agreed cautiously. He didn't need a history lesson. "So what's the point, Del?"

"The point is, now we can do better. It appears the escoba tree is much more important than we ever realized. The Maya Indians call it the give-and-take tree." He grinned. "But I think we're going to have to call it a—"

"A money tree!" Carson finished breathlessly as she put her briefcase on her lap and unlocked it.

Frank Torello nodded eagerly, rubbing his fat palms together. "We've had a breakthrough at the lab, Tony," he said. "Bachmann says we're sitting on a gold mine. He played around with the escoba bark in the VR lab and came up with some stuff that's better than cocaine. And cheap?" Torello rolled his eyes. "Bachmann's turned a useless bunch of land-fill into a drug worth billions of dollars."

"Which means we don't have to buy any more cocaine," Waters added matter-of-factly. "We don't have to be middle-men anymore. We can run the whole damned show. From harvesting to distribution. And forget about growing—the escoba tree is everywhere. Our supply will be unlimited, at least as long as the rainforest holds out and Arch Templeton continues to grease those Belizean palms."

"But you would be cutting down more trees," Inglesia broke in. "Wouldn't that be suspicious in an eco-resort, especially now, with all this publicity?"

Del Waters shook his head, emphatically disagreeing. "Isaac Arrow intends to use the escoba tree as the cornerstone for its new herbal product line. Like tea-tree oil or mineral salt from the Dead Sea. It will make an excellent cover for all the material we'll be shipping up from Belize."

"We'll process it up here," Torello added, "at Arrow. Some of it will be legit, for the company's herbal line, of course, but most of it will go out on the streets . . . after a little doctoring."

Carson leaned forward. "The advertising campaign your

son is working on at Bergman will be part of our cover, furthering Isaac Arrow's conservation image. You know, we'll hit all the hot buttons, use all the buzzwords. On top of that, we're saying that a portion of all the proceeds of Arrow's products will be earmarked for the Planetlife Foundation." She folded her hands on top of the briefcase and smiled. "We're going to look like heroes to the entire world."

"And all the while"—Torello chuckled delightedly—"we'll be making millions on the street with this new drug."

"That's not exactly a low-profile plan," Inglesia remarked skeptically as he rose from his chair and walked over to the fireplace.

Frank Torello glanced over at Del Waters and saw him stiffen. To pull this off, they needed a distribution network. They had counted on Curandero, Inglesia's thriving herb and spice import front, to serve as the hub for their smuggling activities. The mobster's street connections were invaluable. Without them they'd have to start from scratch. But Torello knew Del Waters wouldn't allow that to happen; Marty English would be his trump card in this game.

"That's the beauty of it, Tony," Waters said smoothly, slyly. "The very fact that we will be so high profile will raise few suspicions. Who would ever think that Isaac Arrow, the world's most respected pharmaceutical giant, and Planetlife, a rainforest foundation full of bleeding-heart liberals, would be tied up with rogue CIA agents and the Chicago Mob?" Waters's blue-gray eyes went to steel and he smiled into Inglesia's eyes. There was something confrontational about the smile; he was challenging the Mob boss now.

Frank Torello was chuckling, rolling his eyes. "That's so far out that the public would never buy it, Tony," he said, chortling. "Even if they saw it in black and white."

"Or in color." Carson laughed.

Inglesia stared back at Waters for a moment and then looked away, stoking the fire. He shook his head thoughtfully. "I'm not convinced the American public is as stupid as you'd all like to believe." He put down the poker and turned back to face them. "But in any case, there's the issue of the trees themselves. They won't last forever. A few pieces of bark are one thing, but you'll be cutting down acres of trees. That's got to cause problems. First, with supply. And second, with guests at the resort."

"You know as well as I do," Waters retorted evenly, an impatient edge mounting in his voice, "that Planetlife controls over three hundred thousand acres and our guests at Escoba see what? Maybe twenty. We fly them in from Belize City. Drive them around in our jeeps. Show them a few Maya ruins, some birds. Arch arranges it so that our Indian guides are with them constantly. The guests see what we want them to see, Tony." He smiled coldly. "And *only* what we want them to see."

"That may be," Inglesia allowed, his tone saying he wasn't backing down. "But there's not an endless supply of escoba trees. Okay, so the guests don't get wind of what you're up to, but there's still the problem with supply."

"No," Carson corrected, "our supply is sustainable. The natives won't be cutting down that many trees to begin with— that's what's so remarkable about the escoba tree. One acre will yield over a half-ton of useful material, stuff we used to throw away. That half-ton will be shipped through Customs as a medicinal herb. Once it arrives at Arrow, it'll be turned into a drug that will be ten times stronger than the cocaine we've been getting out of Colombia."

Frank Torello nodded eagerly. "That means one acre of trees has the equivalent yield of five tons of cocaine, Tony. And a street value of four hundred million." He beamed. "That's *one* acre. And Del and Arch have three hundred thousand. Hell, even if we never replanted, that's endless enough for me."

Carson opened her briefcase and took out a small vial of brown powder. She studied it reverently for a moment and then handed it to Inglesia. "This is it, Tony. Our old escoba scrap with a little VR magic, courtesy of Dr. Eric Bachmann. On the street, they'll call it Brown Sugar."

Inglesia studied the vial, turning it over in his hand.

"We used to supply about half of the U.S. coke trade," Waters added. "But with Brown Sugar, cocaine will be a thing of the past. If we play it right, we can have the entire market. That's a thirty-billion-dollar-a-year business, Tony. With distribution through Curandero, it would go out on the streets just like the coke always did. Basically, it would be business as usual." He gave Inglesia a wink. "With a little give and take."

Inglesia walked back to his chair and sat down on the edge of his seat. "And what about our Colombian partners?" he demanded.

Waters shrugged indifferently. "What about them?"

"So you're saying we'll turn our backs on them and run this shit ourselves?"

"You're worried about some Colombians?" Waters asked incredulously.

"I've worked with the Colombian cartels from the beginning, Del, remember? You and Arch Templeton came to *me* and wanted in. I put it all together, got the Colombians to go along. Now you're asking me to cut them out?" Inglesia shook his head and turned to stare into the fire's shooting blue-red flames. Even if he wanted to do what Del Waters was suggesting, he knew he'd be a fool to try it—the Colombians wouldn't take this lying down. He'd be a marked man. Hell, he didn't need a bull's-eye tattooed on his forehead; he wanted to live to enjoy that nice Palm Beach retirement he'd been planning. He looked back at Waters. "That's not the way I do business, Del."

"Not the way you do business?" Waters sneered with the arrogant smile of an aristocrat. "Jesus Christ, wake up. Business is conducted differently today. This isn't the fifties. Maudlin sentiments like loyalty, I'm afraid, have gone out of fashion." He paused, his smile widening to a smirk. "Or perhaps you just don't like the fact that this new technology is going to change your Old-Country way of doing things?"

Waters saw Inglesia bristle and he knew he'd struck a nerve. But that's what he enjoyed most about doing business with more challenging men like Inglesia: He liked finding that soft spot, digging at it, cutting it out. "Let's get down to business here, Tony," he said, his tone now gentle and disarming. "We've been working with the CIA since Vietnam; let's not throw all that away now."

"*You've* been working with the CIA since Vietnam," Inglesia corrected, voice rising. "I've been working with them since Castro."

"Okay," Waters conceded. "You're right. My mistake. Since *Castro*. And all that time, we've all done well, probably you most of all. We had our boys in the DEA eliminate your competitors south of the border. I personally put the pressure on law enforcement and arranged for them to crack down on those black gangs that were in your way. Hell, we've even kept the FBI off your back—"

Inglesia cut him off. "And *I've* taken care of those little problems of yours around the world." His dark eyes glinted, turning to gleaming obsidian. His words came out like rapid-fire bullets, piercing, accusing. "Who set up that heroin plant in Laos back in the sixties so you guys could get the money you needed for that coup in Indonesia? Who ran guns for you to the Contras? Who helped you build this sham of a resort in Belize so you could keep an eye on Guatemala and run dope at the same time? And who made sure for the past thirty years that the CIA had all the fucking money it needed for its dirty work?"

Frank Torello and Carson Page looked at one another and then at Del Waters.

"You did, Tony," Waters replied with a warm smile that masked his hatred for the man. He wouldn't play his trump card yet. He wanted Marty English so deep in this operation that Inglesia wouldn't have any choice but to go along. He could wait a few days. "You're invaluable, Tony. That's why we want our relationship with you to continue. We've both benefited all these years. And we both know it."

"And we still can," Torello added quickly.

Carson nodded. "Absolutely."

Inglesia shook his head. "No. I'm afraid not. Not this time. I'm not cutting the Colombians out. You can find another mule for this one." He paused and smiled sarcastically. "Go get the Chinese Tongs, the Triads, or the Jamaicans. I'm sure you'll find them trustworthy."

Del Waters would like to have beaten the old man to death at that moment; he was sick of Inglesia's arrogance, sick of coddling his ego. "I guess the rumors are true, then?" he remarked offhandedly. "The ones that say you're losing your nerve." As Inglesia's face filled with rage, Waters smiled in satisfaction. He was getting to the soft spot. He decided to cut farther, deeper, go all the way to the heart, and he nodded, raising one eyebrow. "Yes. That's what they're saying in New York. They're saying Tony Inglesia's on the way out."

Inglesia glared back at him. "Is that what they're saying?" He let out a low chuckle. "I think you've been visiting too many prisons these days, if that's what you heard. Half of the goddamned New York families are behind bars. I've never even gotten so much as a parking ticket in my entire life. That's why you came to Chicago in the first place. You wanted more than some two-bit thug who'd end up in jail, shooting his mouth off and landing everybody else in there with him. You wanted somebody with brains." He stood up. "I'm sticking with cocaine, Del. That is, unless you guys plan to shut me down."

Waters shook his head. "Why would we do that? That little enterprise is all yours. Of course," he added slyly, "you won't have our protection at the border anymore."

"Of course," Inglesia repeated coolly.

"Perhaps you should take some time," Waters suggested. "We can wait for your decision. But once this Brown Sugar hits the streets, it'll be too late. Cocaine will be history. It'll be *obsolete*, Tony. I strongly suggest you give this more thought."

Inglesia stood up. "There's no need for that. You've got my decision. I'm out. I'm not like those politicians you deal with. I don't waffle."

Waters assessed the Mob boss carefully and then said, "We'll need your disc."

"You'll have it tomorrow . . . after I get my share of the profits from our last shipment." Inglesia paused. "What about my son?"

"We promised Wynn Bergman would handle Isaac Arrow," Waters replied. Dropping Bergman was the last thing he wanted to do. "That won't change. Besides, from what I hear, Marty's one of the best in the business. Frank and Carson won't let our differences affect what's best for Isaac Arrow."

"Of course not," Carson declared.

Torello nodded in agreement. All three of them knew that Marty English was now a piece on the chessboard.

"As far as the money you've got coming," Waters added, "I'm meeting with Arch Templeton at Planetlife at eight tomorrow morning. The transfer won't be any problem. What do you say we settle this at eight-thirty?"

"That's no good, Del," Torello said quickly. "Bachmann's lab is tied up until nine. We can't get on Trinity until nine-thirty."

"Nine-thirty's fine with me." Waters looked at Inglesia, waiting.

"Yeah, that's fine," Inglesia replied. "We make the transfer at nine-thirty and you'll have my disc by ten." He ushered them to the door and they stood there, faces strained, in uneasy silence.

"I think you're making a big mistake, Tony," Waters said as Inglesia opened the door. "We'll find another distributor and when we do, things will take off. We'll make billions."

Inglesia set his jaw. He had nothing more to say. And so he

simply said good night to his three guests. And closed the door.

They sat quietly as the sleek black limousine motored down the drive and out into the suburban Lake Forest street.

"Once we get the disc," Waters said coldly, smiling at Carson and Torello, "I'll make sure Inglesia cooperates." He'd always hated Tony Inglesia for the power, the control, the man wielded over his world. Just as soon as he had Inglesia's disc in his hand, he'd make that final cut. Right to the heart.

Chapter 7

Shit, Tony, why didn't you just cut our motherfucking balls off?" Mike D'Angelo yelled.

As Inglesia's right-hand man, D'Angelo had been more than a little unhappy at having been excluded from the boss's meeting with Del Waters, but this? Hearing that Tony Inglesia, Mob boss extraordinaire, had just turned down an opportunity to make millions—no, billions—of dollars? Well, it was more than the tough little D'Angelo could stand. Shit, he'd been waiting most of his life for Inglesia to pass the baton and now, goddammit, it looked like he'd be lucky if he was waiting tables when Tony was done.

"What the fuck are we supposed to do now?" D'Angelo ranted on, pacing back and forth in Inglesia's firelit library. "Stand around with our dicks in our hands? Sure, Del and his boys'll leave us the fuck alone. Why the hell should they give a goddamn? They're gonna have a drug that's ten times stronger than coke. Coke's gonna be shit, Tony. And so will we."

Inglesia listened calmly until D'Angelo had finished, then he handed D'Angelo the vial of Brown Sugar and said, "Cut out the Colombians and sell this, Mike, and we won't be shit—we'll be dead. They won't stand for it. And that's the way it should be: a double-crosser gets what he's got coming.

The way I see it, friends take care of friends. Enemies get taken care of."

"Hey, I'm not afraid of the fucking Colombians," D'Angelo countered, drawing up his small frame like a prizefighter. "This isn't about just one lousy fucking drug; it's about our whole goddamned future. Can't you see that? If I've got to choose between a handful of greasy fucking Colombians and the CIA, I'll take Uncle Sam any day." He paused, his tone now pleading. "Goddammit, Tony—we need them."

"No. They need us," Inglesia declared flatly. "Del Waters will be kissing our ass in a month."

"You're wrong this time, Tony!" D'Angelo shouted, his anger rushing back to pound through the veins in his temples. "Del and his boys are just as organized as we are. . . ." His voice trailed off and he let out a hollow laugh. "Shit, what the hell am I saying? They're *more* organized. They've got power, Tony. And that's what we need. Without them we're fucked, that's what we are. We're gonna lose our hold on the streets. Waters'll see to it. And what's gonna be left? Some half-assed business with your friends, the Colombians, that's what."

"That's enough, Mike," Inglesia snapped sharply. "I expect more from you than this, this hysteria. I expect you to think before you open your mouth. To act like a man. It takes a man to run this organization, a man who has what it takes to get the job done. A man who knows the difference between friends and acquaintances."

"I have what it takes and you know it."

"No, Mike," Inglesia retorted coolly. "I don't think you do. At this rate I'd say you won't make it to the finish line."

D'Angelo's swarthy face blanched at the threat.

"Now go on and get the fuck out of here," Inglesia growled, waving him away.

The vial of Brown Sugar was still in Mike D'Angelo's trembling hand when he stalked out of the room.

*   *   *

It was after ten o'clock when D'Angelo finally walked back into the library. "Guess I lost my head, Tony," he began cautiously.

Inglesia nodded. "Losing your temper like that, Mike—it's not smart." He put his arm around D'Angelo and hugged him heartily. "Now, you listen to me. We don't need Waters and his friends. They need us. But I'm starting to think we don't want to be in business with them anyway. This drug they've got may sound good, but it'll do them in. I can feel it in my gut. And that's what I listen to, Mike, not what a bunch of greedy idiots have to say. Greed gets more guys killed than anything I know of."

D'Angelo nodded slowly, fingering the vial of Brown Sugar that was still in his trouser pocket, turning it over again and again in his sweaty palm.

"I want you to go down to Miami," Inglesia continued. "Pick up our old shipping contacts. Let's get this under control right away." He sighed and added, "And forget what I said a while ago. Dammit, Mike, you're like a son to me . . . you know that. When you get back, let's talk about turning over a few more of the operations to you."

D'Angelo forced a rubbery smile. He'd heard it all before. All that talk was nothing more than a broken record, that's what it was.

"How about a drink . . . to put this behind us?" Inglesia suggested.

Nodding, D'Angelo started toward the bar. "What do you want?" he asked offhandedly.

"Scotch," Inglesia replied over his shoulder as he sat down in the leather chair facing the fireplace. He lit a cigarette and sat back, admiring the roaring fire.

As D'Angelo poured their drinks, he paused to study the amber liquid glistening in the glasses, turning his plan over in his head. Brown Sugar was ten times more powerful than cocaine—that's what Tony had said. It was simple. All he had to do was pour the contents of the vial into the scotch in front of him. That would be that. With Tony out of the way, he could go to Del Waters and get things back on track.

Now or never, prompted a voice inside D'Angelo's head. Now. Or never. He heard the voice over and over again. Would he ever be free of Tony Inglesia? Would he always play second fiddle? Loyalty was one thing, but stupidity? Was he stupid enough to think Tony Inglesia would ever step aside?

"Hey, Mike," Inglesia barked impatiently, "where's that drink?"

Inglesia's command pierced D'Angelo's thoughts like a knife in the gut. *Now or never,* the voice repeated. *Now.* He slipped the vial from his pocket and hurriedly emptied its contents into one of the glasses.

"Just like you like it," he said, handing Inglesia the drink. "Not too much ice."

Inglesia lifted his glass. "*Salud.*"

"*Salud.*"

"Here's to the future, Mike. Here's to a kid that's like a son to me. Someday you'll be in charge."

D'Angelo held up his glass. "*Someday,*" he repeated with a tight smile as he settled down in the chair across from Inglesia; he wanted a clear view.

D'Angelo looked on as the man in front of him sipped at his drink. He watched until it was all gone. Every last drop. He felt euphoric. "Want another?" he offered, trying to conceal the sudden lilt in his voice.

Inglesia shook his head.

It took longer than D'Angelo had thought it would: exactly three minutes. But then it happened. Inglesia's face turned a terrible bluish purple, the color of an eggplant. Then his lips tightened into a grimace and he grabbed his chest and doubled over.

"Call emergency, Mike," he gasped. "I'm having a heart attack." He struggled to breathe, to speak over the pain. "Nine-one-one. Hurry. Call nine-one-one."

But Mike D'Angelo didn't move from his chair; instead, he sat there, watching. Waiting for that pot of gold he'd been promised.

"Mike!" Inglesia cried. He was shuddering, panting now. "Help me . . . for God's sake . . ." The Mob boss tried to stand, but his legs wobbled and gave out from under him and he crashed into the coffee table, turning it over as he fell to the floor.

Helpless, Inglesia stared up at D'Angelo with the eyes of a cow at the butcher's knife. He saw the man looking down at him. Saw that he was unmoved by his agony. And it was then that Inglesia realized he'd been betrayed by the only man he'd ever trusted, aside from his own son. "Mike," he pleaded. "Mike. Don't do this."

But Mike D'Angelo didn't move. He only smiled as the powerful man writhed in pain. And when it was over, he smiled again and lifted his glass over the corpse at his feet. "*Salud*," he said. He'd made it to the finish line.

Chapter 8

"How did it happen?" Reiki asked gently as they drove down Sheridan Road toward Lake Forest. Only minutes before, the shocking phone call had wrenched them both from a sound sleep. "Did D'Angelo say how?"

Marty shook his head. "He didn't know for sure, but he said they think it was a heart attack. Hell, I knew my father was getting old. . . . I guess I just never really got it straight that he was going to die someday." He glanced at her and gave out a bitter laugh. "Isn't that fucking crazy? I mean, we're all going to die. Right? And him, a Mob boss at that? Jesus, he's had his life on the line for as long as I can remember and I still never thought he could die."

Marty paused, looking out the window, trying to recall the last time his father even had a cold. "Christ, the old guy was as tough as they come," he said at last. "Inside and out. I guess if I'd thought about it, I would've figured he'd be hit, not die of a heart attack like everybody else. Men like Tony Inglesia usually don't just up and die. They're put away."

"Really, now," she objected. "Hits and all that? This isn't the nineteen-twenties, you know."

"No, but just because the Mob isn't in the headlines every day doesn't mean they've folded their tents. Believe me, they're not out of business. I'm sure my father was at the front of the line these last few years, with riverboat gambling and offshore casinos. . . . Hell, business had to be booming. And let's not forget about heroin and cocaine."

Reiki lowered her eyes. She'd done her share of pot smoking and sitting around a bong under a black light—she'd expanded her mind, so to speak—but cocaine and heroin? That was going too far. To her way of thinking, those drugs had nothing to do with the spirit and everything to do with the flesh.

"Hey, I don't approve either," he declared defensively. "You know that. But that was his business. That's what he was, that's what he did." Marty sighed and looked away. "Hell, he was my old man. I guess I cared about him anyway."

"I know you did." Shivering, she pulled her coat tight around her shoulders and bit her lip. "Hey, he was your father. You didn't make him what he was. We can't control our parents any more than they can control us. I guess nobody can take the credit or the blame when it comes to their family." She smiled ruefully and shrugged. "They're who they are. And we're who we are. And that's that."

"Yeah. That's that," he said, sounding morose.

She reached out to stroke his arm. "How long's it been since you were out to see him?"

"Hmm . . . when you were in Cairo, I think. What's that? A month or two ago?"

She shook her head. "Three months."

"What the hell." He shrugged, flashing a cynical grin. "Time flies when you're having fun."

"You work too hard," she said softly, taking his hand in hers.

He nodded and turned his attention to the road. It was hard to find something to say.

But then it always had been like that when it came to talking about his family. Maybe it was because he was afraid that if he started talking, he'd never stop. Or maybe it was because he wouldn't know where to begin. He knew where it ended, though. It had ended on the day Kennedy was assassinated. But not for the same reason as everybody else. Not because Marty had lost his president. But because he'd lost his mother.

As the car sped down the highway toward Lake Forest, Marty's thoughts reached back to that time. He'd been in the library, hiding in the secret closet his father had built behind the mirrored bar. They wouldn't find him there, he'd told himself, out of earshot of those screams and shouts and angry words his parents had used with one another so often back in those days. But he couldn't escape for long. They'd come into the library, his mother's gentle voice strangely shrill, his father's harsh and matter-of-fact. Marty had peered out from behind the closet's one-way mirror, his hands clasped tightly over his ears, watching, waiting until they took their argument into another part of the house and he could escape to his own room.

Later than night, his father called him downstairs. "Say good-bye to your mother, Marty," he commanded.

His mother was sobbing when she held him; the arms of her wool coat felt rough. He often wished he'd felt the warmth of her skin against his, one last time. She said she loved him, that someday he would understand. And then she was gone.

But he didn't understand—after all, he was only a twelve-year-old kid. He only knew enough to blame his father for what happened. To hate him for it, in fact. He just didn't know enough to forgive him. Or to forgive himself.

Years later, his father had finally explained what happened. Marty's mother hadn't wanted to leave, he'd said, she just couldn't handle being a mobster's wife anymore. But a Mob wife didn't just run out on her husband and child—and she didn't have a messy public divorce, either. Instead, Marty's parents agreed to a quickie Mexican divorce.

Tony Inglesia received custody of his son on one condition: that Marty never be involved in his father's activities, that he be cut free of all potential power and danger that came with being Inglesia's only son and heir.

It wasn't much of a concession for Inglesia. He had no desire to see his son become a part of the Chicago Mob. Instead, Marty would finish his education in boarding schools far from Chicago and begin a new life under a new name.

It had taken some doing, of course. Inglesia had been forced to line more than one VIP's pockets before a judge finally granted his son a new name and social security number. All records of Marty's past were sealed by order of the court. Short of some government agency snooping around, his secret was safe.

"Sometimes I think it hurt my father pretty bad to have my name changed," Marty said, abruptly coming back to the present. "We never talked about it, but I think he thought I ended up being ashamed of him."

"You've never been ashamed of him . . . or who you are," Reiki soothed.

"No, you're right about that. God, it's always killed me to have to pretend my father was dead. But I have to admit it was easier than answering a bunch of damned questions about a man who made headlines as Chicago's godfather every other day. Shit, Lee Wilde doesn't even know about him."

"And we know Lee knows everything," she gently teased.

"*Almost* everything," he corrected. "We may be pretty good friends, but to tell you the truth, I think things would be different between us if Lee knew who my father was."

"Come on, Marty. Give people more credit. You told *me* and it didn't hurt our relationship."

"You were in love with me—that's different. But, hell, my mother was in love with my father, too, and look what happened to them. Hey, I may call Lee a friend, but she's really just another co-worker with something to lose. The ad game's all about image. Having a mobster's name doesn't exactly open doors. And at places like Isaac Arrow? Come on, you know what would happen as well as I do."

"Don't you think your father knew that? Didn't he use another name when he traveled? You said he hated the limelight."

"Yeah, he didn't want to attract any attention. He's the one who took the Chicago Mob out of the news and found legitimate businesses to invest in. That's where he saw the future."

"And that's what he wanted for his son," she insisted. "He wanted you to have a future, a college education. He wanted you to have what he couldn't have. He wanted you to be *legitimate*, Marty. He had to know that you could never pull that off . . . not with the Inglesia name."

"Maybe he did. What's in a name anyway?" Marty shrugged bitterly as he turned into a drive and pulled up to a gate. "A rose by any other name . . . hell, it's all just one big goddamned game." He turned to look at her now. "It's just that sometimes that game turns on you. Sometimes you change your name trying to escape one thing and what the fuck happens? You end up losing *you*. . . ." His voice trailed off as a light shown across the windshield.

"What the hell are cops doing here?" Marty grumbled as he rolled down the window. "Yes, sir?" he said coolly to the burly officer shining a flashlight in his eyes.

"This area's restricted, sir," the cop barked. "You'll have to turn around."

"I'm Marty English," Marty retorted, not bothering to conceal his irritation.

"Marty English? Detective Sinclair's been waiting for you. You go ahead. I'll radio up to the house and let him know you're on your way. You may want to hurry."

"Yes sir," Marty said agreeably. But he didn't hurry. He took his time. He knew that after he walked in that door, nothing would ever be the same again.

Like a lot of cops, Ford Sinclair didn't like to play games. In fact, the detective's attitude about that kind of crap was so well known among his fellow officers at the Lake County Police Department that they'd finally gone and dubbed him "Just the Facts, Ma'am, Ford," which was fine and dandy with Sinclair. After all, running Homicide wasn't supposed to be a social event. No, you had to cut to the quick, see through all that bullshit—that's how you solved a murder. At least that's how Sinclair did.

Besides, with the shit he saw every day, the facts were more than enough to screw your head up; a fella didn't need some fool rambling on about the ugly and the obvious. Grabbing a moment of silence in what promised to be a long night, Sinclair pulled a half-eaten Almond Joy candy bar out of his coat pocket and surveyed the chaotic scene at the Inglesia estate.

Marked and unmarked cars crisscrossed the drive, their blue and red and yellow flashing lights casting a spook-house glow over the surrounding lawn and woodland.

Yeah, it was spooky, all right. Sinclair took a bite of the candy bar and frowned. The spookiest part was who the hell all these bastards were running around here like they owned the place.

By the time Sinclair had gotten there—and he surely was one of the first to be called to the scene—Tony Inglesia's house was lit up like one of those birthday cakes he'd always wanted as a poor little ghetto kid—and never got. And the front door? Well, it looked like the entrance to some high-security prison instead of a rich guy's house, even a rich mobster's, with those four gorillas in flak jackets standing there, eyeing everybody who went in or out.

So what the hell *were* all these guys doing here? That was what Sinclair wanted to know. And that was what he'd asked, too, when he finally found somebody who thought he was in charge, some goddamned FBI guy with an attitude who acted like he had a stiff one up his ass. No way they'd be working together.

But really, why should they? Why shouldn't Sinclair kick the guy's ass right off the crime scene, if that was what it was. Just because the guy who died happened to be a Mob boss, the feds thought they could just come right in and make themselves at home.

The guy had died in Lake County, hadn't he? And Sinclair was from Lake County Police Department's Homicide Division. Right? That meant this was *his* investigation, not some snot-nosed little bastard's from the FBI.

But obviously, what Sinclair had to say about it all didn't mean squat to the God knows how many storm troopers and their dogs swarming over the place, a feature Sinclair's trained eye found peculiar. They were looking for something—that much was clear to him. But what that something was was a goddamned mystery. There wasn't a murder weapon; during his examination of Inglesia's body, Sinclair had found no sign of blunt injury or gunshot or stabbing. No, they were looking for something else. Though they wouldn't tell him what. Or even admit they were actually looking.

Angrily, Ford Sinclair crumpled the empty candy bar wrapper in one hand; with a dead body on his hands, playing hide-and-seek with the feds was the last thing he needed.

"Wow! What's all this about?" Reiki exclaimed, wide-eyed, as they pulled up in front of the two-story Tudor. She motioned toward the half-dozen or so men roaming the yard with police dogs. "Are you sure they said it was a heart attack?"

"Yeah, I'm sure," Marty replied somberly as he stepped out of the car and surveyed the scene. "But it looks like a hell of a lot of attention for a heart attack."

A tall black man in a rumpled topcoat walked up beside them. "Yes, it does, doesn't it?" he observed, sticking out his hand; he had an Almond Joy candy bar wrapper in the other. "Name's Ford Sinclair. I'm the detective on this case. You must be Marty." He lowered his voice and added, "Mr. Inglesia's son."

Despite the bitter cold, Marty found Sinclair's handshake warm and genuine. "Yeah, that's right. I'm Marty English. This is Reiki Devane."

"Pleased to meet you, Ms. Devane," Sinclair said, giving her a gentlemanly nod. His brown eyes came to rest on her camera and he shook his head. "I'm afraid photography is restricted here, ma'am," he said apologetically, almost angrily.

"This happens to be my father's home," Marty objected.

"Hey, I know where you're coming from," Sinclair replied with a shake of his head. "But I didn't make the rules." He motioned across the lawn at a tall man in a trench coat standing by the door. "Some highfalutin government guy name of Shelby did."

The words rang in Marty's ears: highfalutin government guy? Why would some bigwig be interested in his father's death?

Sinclair smiled uncomfortably at Reiki. "Sorry about the camera."

"No problem," she said, slipping it into her handbag and giving Marty a sideways glance.

"Why don't we go inside, where it's warm," Sinclair suggested, shoving the candy bar wrapper into his pocket. "We can talk in there."

Inside, the place was a madhouse. Forget about talking; shouting barely cut through the racket.

"This isn't exactly conducive to good conversation," Marty grumbled. He looked around at the plainclothesmen marching from room to room, barking out orders into walkie-talkies. There were a few cops standing around the kitchen drinking coffee out of white foam cups, laughing, telling jokes like they were standing at a dime-store counter.

"I thought my father died of a heart attack. Why the hell are all these guys here?" Marty demanded. "This sure looks like a crime scene to me." He glared back at the detective, waiting for some answer that made at least some sense.

Sinclair frowned and lowered his voice. "Hey, there's no reason to shout. Just keep your pants on. I'll be happy to explain everything, at least what we know at this point." The detective hesitated, looking unhappy about what he had to say next. "After you make a positive ID on your father." He glanced over at Reiki. "You might want to wait here, ma'am."

Reiki nodded politely, and they left her on the sofa in the living room. When they got to the library door, Sinclair lifted a piece of yellow tape and waved Marty inside. Then he walked over to an orange blanket lying on the floor and lifted it up. "Is this your father?" he asked frankly.

Marty sucked in his breath. Yeah, it was his father all right. And he was dead, as empty as an autumn leaf. He hadn't expected this. But then what had he expected?

Whatever it was, it wasn't seeing his old man cold and gray and fast getting stiff, with all the life gone out of him and only a waxy shell left behind. No, he hadn't expected this. He hadn't expected the sadness, either. Or the goddamned terrible finality of it all.

Ford Sinclair saw the look on his face. "I'm sorry." He sighed, dropping the blanket.

Marty looked up. Sorry? He didn't believe this Sinclair guy gave a damn.

"You think I'm being polite, don't you?" Sinclair remarked as he led Marty out of the library and into the sunroom. They sat there, in the shadows amid the white wicker and ferns.

Sinclair pulled out a pen and notepad. "It just so happens I had a lot of respect for your old man. He helped my daddy out when I was a kid, got him a job on the railroad . . . said he wasn't cut out for the numbers game." He smiled. "Hell, we wouldn't have had a pot to piss in if it hadn't been for Tony Inglesia. After I grew up and went away to IU, I kept my eyes on him." He paused. "I guess you could say I admired him. Most cops wouldn't come out and say that, I know. But I always felt like I understood him, somehow. Maybe I just saw something other guys didn't. Your old man had brains and guts, Marty. But most of all he had honor."

A wave of sadness washed over Marty. "Yeah, he did, didn't he?"

Sinclair scrawled something on his notepad. "So how long since you last talked to him?" he asked.

"Not in a while."

"How long is 'a while'?"

"A couple of months."

"I see. Okay, so did your father have any enemies?"

"Enemies? What kind of question is that?"

"An important one," Sinclair replied. "Well . . . did he?"

"I thought you said you knew a lot about my father. If you did, you'd know he had more enemies than Saddam Hussein."

Sinclair sighed. "Hey, I just want to get to the truth here."

"The truth?" Marty frowned. "I thought he had a heart attack."

"The coroner said it *appears* to have been a heart attack," Sinclair corrected. "But after a few years in this line of work, well . . . let's just say I'm not too hot on appearances. Things aren't always what they seem." He paused and looked Marty in the eye. "To be perfectly honest, if I didn't know better, I'd say this was a homicide."

"A homicide?"

"Yeah, a homicide. Did you see the look on your father's face back there? I've been on the streets twenty years and I've seen my share of dead men. You learn to notice the little details. That wasn't the look of a man in pain. That was the look of a man who'd just been betrayed."

"Betrayed how?"

"Hell, there's a million ways to kill a fellow."

Marty nodded; after what he'd seen in Vietnam, he couldn't deny that. "Well, when will we know for sure?"

"Tomorrow," Sinclair replied, stifling a yawn. He glanced down at his Timex and then shook his head. "I guess I mean *today*. It's already after midnight. We'll have the preliminary autopsy report back by late this afternoon." He held up one of Marty's business cards. "This your number at the office?"

Looking surprised, Marty nodded.

"It was in your father's wallet," Sinclair explained.

"So you'll call me?"

"Oh yeah, I'll call you." Sinclair smiled wanly and gave him a thumbs-up. "You can count on it."

Chapter 9

At the news of Tony Inglesia's death, Del Waters had gone into shock. But now, as the limousine sped down the dark Chicago streets toward the Sears Tower, he felt something else. Fear. He wasn't used to that. And at the realization, the fear turned to rage.

The threat of losing the Mob's distribution network was one thing—a threat, nothing more. Waters had intended to use Inglesia's son to make the Mob boss see things his way. But now, with Inglesia dead?

Not that Waters held any sentimental affection for the man; he would have enjoyed offing Inglesia himself. No, it wasn't that. He wouldn't have had any problem whatsoever with Inglesia dying except for one small detail: Inglesia hadn't turned over his disc.

And all Waters could think of now was how little time he had to find it. The Super Bowl was only what—eighteen days away? Not much time . . . just long enough to run out of excuses. The Iranian arms dealers he was working with weren't interested in excuses. Cold hard cash was all they cared about. Cold hard cash he didn't have now—now that Tony Inglesia was dead and had taken the disc to the grave with him. At least that's the way it looked: His men had searched the mobster's estate all night and hadn't turned up a goddamned thing.

Waters's thoughts fixed on his dangerous position, just as they had a long time ago, back in 'Nam, when he'd laid in stinking rice paddies for hours, his eyes just grazing the top of the water, while twenty or so armed gooks searched for him and Templeton. After a while his finger had gone numb on the trigger of his M-16 but still he'd waited, waited like a cobra waiting for a rat.

Waters gazed out the tinted window at the Chicago River and smiled ruefully; right now he almost longed for those days. Outthinking the enemy—that was what it was all about. And he'd always been masterful at that. But now? Now he had only one hope. He had to find Tony Inglesia's disc. And he had to find it soon.

On a clear day, a guy could stand on top of the Sears Tower and see seven states. But even so, it had always amazed Mike D'Angelo that tourists came from all over the world just to stand fourteen hundred feet above the pavement. Yet come they did, tens of thousands of them each year. They looked out the enormous span of windows, chattering excitedly in a hundred different languages from Japanese to Portuguese, all the time ogling the three-hundred-and-sixty-degree view of Chicago and beyond.

D'Angelo had gotten to the Sears Tower early and, to kill some time, he milled around in the crowd, trying to find just the right view. He was glad Waters chose this as the setting for their historic meeting. There was a wonderful symbolism in it, he thought, as he paused and stared out onto the cityscape. With Tony's death he was, no question about it, on top of the world. It was all under his control now, as far as the eye could see.

"Entertaining delusions of grandeur, Mike?" a voice from behind him asked coldly.

Surprised, D'Angelo turned to see Del Waters, his usually tanned face as gray and chalky as the Chicago winter sky.

There were two men dressed in black topcoats, agents no doubt, loitering nearby.

Waters surveyed D'Angelo coldly for a moment, as if he were a cheap cut of meat, then he looked out the window, pretending to take in the scenery. He'd always despised Tony Inglesia, but he had only contempt for the Mob boss's right-hand man; Mike D'Angelo was too rough for his refined taste, too wrong side of the tracks, too uneducated.

"I guess you heard Tony's dead?" D'Angelo asked under his breath.

Waters's face grew more somber, but he kept looking straight ahead. "That's why I wanted to see you."

D'Angelo nodded smugly. He'd been right: Waters was going to bring him in on the Escoba deal. "They're saying it was a heart attack." He tried to sound properly solemn, but he couldn't help but smile.

"You're a goddamned fool," Waters hissed through his teeth. "You did him, didn't you? If this weren't a public place, I'd kill you myself."

Struggling to maintain his composure, D'Angelo took a step back. He wanted to grab Del Waters by the shoulders, to shake some sense into him. To make him understand that he'd put things right by getting rid of Tony Inglesia. But he couldn't do that. Not here. Not with hundreds of people standing around.

"I'm surprised, Del," he said, trying to act casual about the man's vicious threat, as if Waters had said nothing more deadly than "What time is it?" "I thought you'd be pleased. With Tony out of the way and me in charge, we can move on this Escoba thing. You'll have your distribution. That's what you wanted, isn't it?" He paused. "After you guys left, Tony told me everything."

"So I take it you got the disc?"

Confused, D'Angelo shook his head. "Disc?"

"That's right. *Disc.*"

"I don't know what you're talking about, Del. I don't have any disc."

"Then obviously Tony *didn't* tell you everything. I see now your employer was a man of his word, after all. He didn't tell you shit about this operation. Thanks to you and your rash behavior, four hundred fifty million dollars are now tied up in a Swiss bank account." Waters smiled bitterly at the shocked expression on D'Angelo's face. "That's right. Four hundred fifty million. And with Tony dead, and his disc gone, we can't get at one goddamned dime of it."

"What the hell's this disc got to do with getting some money out of a bank account?"

"You really are in the dark, aren't you?" Waters shook his head at the man's stupidity. "The disc has the access code a computer requires to enter the account. We each have one. Me . . . Torello at Isaac Arrow . . . and Tony."

Mike D'Angelo's world was crumbling down around him. "Shit, Del, Tony never said a thing about a fucking disc. I swear." He shook his head. "Four hundred fifty million? What the fuck are we gonna do?"

"Find Tony's disc, that's what."

D'Angelo's face suddenly turned hopeful. "Hey, I'm no computer whiz, but why can't you just get inside Tony's computer at Curandero and get his code?"

"Because it's not that simple. It's not *in* the computer, it's on the disc. It's a sort of password. No disc, no code. No code, no access. We had a retired military cryptographer put together a three-way code and he's the only one who knew the whole thing. Each of us has a third of it. We have to enter our discs at our own locations, within an hour of one another, otherwise no money can be transferred."

"Tony never said . . . he never told me."

"Well, forget feeling left out. We have to find that disc. I have to make a hundred-fifty-million-dollar payment on an arms shipment in two weeks."

"What about that military code guy? Can't he just give you another disc?"

"He could," Waters acknowledged grimly. "If he were still alive. But after the code was delivered I had him eliminated"— he glanced at D'Angelo defiantly—"to avoid any possibility of a double cross in the future."

D'Angelo's mouth fell open and he turned to gape at Del Waters. He'd thought he had ice water in his veins. Shit, he'd known some cold sons of bitches in his life. But this guy? He took the cake. It really was true what Tony had said all those years: The CIA made the Mob look like choirboys. "So then where do we go from here, Del?" he asked nervously. "Sounds like there's only dead ends. Where would I look for this, uh, disc? At Tony's house?"

"No. I had agents out there last night. They combed every square inch of the place. I even had the FBI on it."

"Where else, then? Over at Curandero?"

"Tony was too smart to leave something like that at a fucking warehouse on Goose Island."

"What about his kid, Marty? Tony kept him out of the business, but hell, it's a long shot. He might know something."

Waters smiled icily. "He might."

"I guess Marty's our only lead, then." D'Angelo noted. "It's a shame we have to go after him—he's really not a bad guy."

"Are you the same man who just murdered English's father?" Waters snorted in disbelief. "I suggest you get your priorities in order. We're talking about four hundred fifty million dollars here, and a third of it's yours. I don't care if Tony's son is ground up for dog food. And neither should you. If English has the disc, we have to get it. And once we do, he's out of the picture. No loose ends. No prisoners. That's the only way I do business. Understand?"

D'Angelo nodded uncomfortably. "So what's next?"

"I've already got some men tagging him. They're going to

question him this morning at his office. Isaac Arrow will work him from their side."

——"Sounds like you've got it covered without me."

"Without you?" Waters glared at D'Angelo. "What are you trying to say, Mike? That you don't have the stomach to play hardball with Tony's kid? That you want to bail out? You just killed a man, remember? You're in this up to your eyeballs. I suggest you pull your weight if you want a piece of the action in Belize. Or are you telling me that I should make other arrangements?"

D'Angelo paled. "I'll pull my weight. Don't worry, you'll have your fucking disc. Chicago's never let you down."

"*Tony Inglesia* never let me down." Waters grabbed D'Angelo by the shoulder and looked him in the eye. "Don't you let me down either, Mike," he whispered. "I'm counting on you, you hear me? I hate to be disappointed. Or didn't Tony tell you that, either?" He smiled a thin cruel smile and loosened his grip on D'Angelo's shoulder. "You know where to find me."

Heart pounding, D'Angelo watched as Del Waters strolled nonchalantly toward the elevators. He turned back to the frigid winter scene outside the window, his eyes scanning the length of the icy Chicago River. He'd really fucked up this time, D'Angelo thought furiously. If he didn't come through on this deal with Waters, he'd end up floating in that river. Del Waters would just as soon kill him as not. Yeah, no question about it, things were getting ready to heat up. But when they did, Marty English was the one who was going to be on thin ice. Not him.

Chapter 10

Reiki was standing in the bedroom doorway, holding up a large manila envelope. "This just came for you," she whispered. "Hurry, hang up."

Marty nodded and turned back to the phone. Though only a little over an hour had passed since they'd talked in Lake Forest, he'd called Ford Sinclair in the hope the detective might have something more on the case. "Nothing else, Sinclair?" he declared impatiently. "Well, you'll call me tomorrow then . . . because I want to know right away what the story is." He nodded and then a faint smile flitted across his face. "Yeah, okay, Sinclair. I'll keep my pants on. You just let me know the minute you hear something from the coroner. And listen, just so you know . . . all your help . . . well, it's been appreciated."

When he hung up the phone, Reiki was sitting on the bed, looking at him expectantly. "A messenger gave this to the doorman, just now," she said breathlessly.

"Are you sure?" He glanced at the bedside clock. "It's after two in the morning."

"That's what our doorman said. It just came."

Marty took the package from her hand.

"So what is it?" she asked impatiently as he pulled out a sheaf of papers. "A map to buried treasure?"

"No, it's not the map." He smiled sadly and held up a black-and-white photo of a boy and a dog. "It's the treasure. Just old stuff, really. Some pictures of me and my dog, Spot, and my father . . ." His voice trailed off as he leafed through a stack of photos. "And Mom."

Reiki smiled at him sympathetically. "So here's Spot— where's Dick and Jane?" she asked, picking up one photo after another. She stopped all of a sudden and her face lit up. "Oh my God, is this you? What an adorable *naked* baby!"

"Nice ass, huh?" he said, still rifling through the papers. "Why, I'll be goddamned! *B. B. King Live at Cook County Jail.*" He held up a CD and smiled the broad smile of a boy with his first bike. "I liked the Doors. My father liked Glenn Miller. But B. B. King was *our* favorite." He tapped the back of the CD. "Too bad I've already got a copy. But hell, I guess I can always use another one. . . ." For an instant, his eyes took on the faraway look of a traveler exploring his past. Then, just as suddenly, he was back, smiling wistfully into her eyes. "God, I love the blues."

"I know."

"Guess the whole world knows, huh?"

"Well, everybody at Bergman, at least. Lee says you play B. B. King in your office constantly." She affected a look of reproach. "I think you've driven the poor thing half crazy with 'The Thrill Is Gone.'"

" 'The Thrill Is Gone' . . ." Marty's voice cracked momentarily and his eyes welled up. "That was my father's favorite." He paused and looked away. "You know, Reiki, we had some good times . . . me and my father. It wasn't all guns and gangsters. Or fights over politics. There was something more between us. . . ."

Marty suddenly recalled the day he'd come home from Vietnam, a hero with a crew cut and a silver star on his chest. That was the day they put Marty's stormy adolescence behind them, the day his father declared him a man and they started to rebuild their relationship. They turned to music, and blues in particular, as the one thing they both loved.

"What was it Pablo Casals said?" Marty asked abruptly. "That music might save the world?"

"Something like that." She nodded.

"Well, it sure as hell saved us. That's what we had between us." He held up the CD. "Sure doesn't seem like much."

"Most people don't have *anything* in common with their parents," she said softly. "What do you say I put it on?"

Nodding, he handed it to her and she went over to an antique Indonesian chest and opened the door, revealing a TV, stereo, and collection of CDs. She fiddled around for a few minutes before announcing, hands on hips, "The stereo's not working."

"Not working?" He glanced up from the papers and photos spread all over the bed. "Shit, we just bought that stereo."

"Yeah," she shot back. "*Just* four years ago."

"Has it been that long?"

"We've been together *seven* years."

He flashed her an "I know what you're up to" look. Lately, Reiki had managed to remind him of the length of their live-in relationship at every chance. "Well, even so," he said, letting her remark pass, "it can't be broken already. Shit, we hardly ever use it."

"Why don't you try?" She held out the CD and teased, "We all know men are so much better with high-tech stuff."

Laughing, he took the shimmering disc, put it in the player, and hit Play. Nothing. He scowled and hit Play again. Again nothing. "You're right," he conceded. "It's dead as a fucking doorknob."

"Maybe you should do what other men do when their brains fail them. . . . You know, hit the stereo real hard, call on those testosterone-filled muscles." She grinned. "Or you could use a more intellectual approach. Try your copy of the CD—maybe this one's defective."

"No, it wasn't sealed. My father must've played it before.

Let's try your idea, the one that requires brains." He thumbed through the CDs on the shelf, and finding his copy of the disc, he dropped it into the player and with as much pomp and circumstance as he could muster at that hour, hit Play.

Instantly, the room was thrown into a maelstrom of blues riffs as B. B. King broke into "The Thrill Is Gone."

"Jesus Christ!" Reiki yelled, clasping her hands over her ears. "Turn it down!"

"Sorry about that," he apologized, turning off the stereo. He frowned down at the B. B. King CD in his hand and collapsed in a heap in the chair, trying to figure out why the hell his father would want him to have a defective music disc. His thoughts flowed through a confusion of images, until only a shimmering silver disc remained, bobbing up into his consciousness like a dead man at sea. Silver disc. The image stayed there, right before his eyes, refusing to go away. And then suddenly, he knew—

Silver disc.

Marty jumped up, grabbed Reiki by the arm, and started dragging her out the bedroom door and down the hall.

"Where are we going? . . . Marty . . . what in the—"

"I've got something to show you."

"Well, it had better be good."

"Trust me. It will be."

As they entered the study, Reiki caught on and rushed to turn on their PC. The computer monitor flashed on a brilliant blue as Marty sat down. "Here we go," he announced, giving the mouse two clicks.

As the file menu materialized on-screen, Reiki patted him on the back. "All right, Einstein, let's see if that theory of yours holds water."

"Yeah, let's see . . ." Two more clicks of the mouse and the menu was replaced by a dialogue box. *Click, click* and they were in the drive field.

Marty put the B. B. King disc in the CD-ROM drive. Two more clicks and there was a whirring sound as a directory came up on the screen.

"You're right," she cried, "it's not a music disc at all."

"Yeah, but so what? There're no files in the directory."

"Maybe there's a file saved in another format?"

He brightened. "Yeah. I'll check the list of file types." *Click. Click.* On the left-hand side of the screen, the words appeared:

ING.TIF.

"Look at that," Reiki said excitedly. "TIF. Tag Image File Format."

Bewildered, he frowned. "An image file. That's weird."

"You think the 'I-N-G' might stand for Inglesia?" she ventured.

"It makes sense." He clicked the mouse and then let out a heavy sigh of frustration. "Shit, what the hell's wrong with me? It's not going to open. We need an image program like Photoshop to get in." He pointed to the screen as a dialogue box came up with the message:

CANNOT FIND APPLICATION IN WHICH FILE WAS CREATED

He gave the mouse a click and then another and took the disc out.

"Zak has Photoshop, doesn't he?"

"Yeah." He spun around in the chair to face her. "Creative has a fortune tied up in software."

"You think this disc has something to do with your father's death?"

"Maybe," he said thoughtfully, taking the disc from her hand. "But the only way I'll ever know for sure is to find out what's in that file. And I will," he said, setting his jaw, "tomorrow."

Chapter 11

The Wynn Bergman building was a missile of a structure, a marble-and-steel Erector-set rocket, a Freudian irony that agency detractors snickeringly referred to as "The Big One."

But there was more to Wynn Bergman Advertising than an awe-inspiring facade: Once you passed through the etched glass doors, you knew you were on hallowed ground. The lobby was an architectural wonder, an atrium soaring like an ancient cathedral to an enormous skylight, giving real meaning to the company's slogan: "The sky's the limit."

The atrium's cascading fountain and botanical wonderland gave way to eighteen floors of escalators and elevators connecting the agency's fifteen hundred domestic employees in a labyrinth of modular workstations. Two floors were dedicated to Finance and Human Resources. Three to Production, four for Media, and three floors each for Client Service and Creative. It was all topped off by the company's two executive floors. There, in the rarefied air of upper management, a guy could get high on power. But today, as he took the elevator to the top, Marty didn't find the air at all intoxicating; today he found it stale.

It was just after seven when Marty walked into Wynn Bergman's office. He wanted to be the first to speak with the agency's seventy-five-year-old founding father.

"Congratulations, Marty," Wynn whispered, waving him in through a haze of smoke, his sinewy hand cupped over the receiver of the telephone. As usual, the old man was on the phone. And as usual, he was chain-smoking, puffing away like the FDA was about to make cigarettes a controlled substance.

Wynn nodded at a leather chair across from his desk and Marty nodded back and sat down, amusing himself while Wynn finished his call by surveying the immense office he hoped would someday be his—minus the interior design, of course.

Wynn Bergman's idea of contemporary high style was a mortifyingly expensive version of Jetsons home decorating: white pedestal chairs and tables and low sleek leather perched atop a gleaming slate floor. The walls were papered in grass-cloth and hung with Lichtenstein comic book–style originals, print campaigns, Addys, and Clio awards, symbols of the agency's creative excellence over the years. It was all pretty stunning—in a Teen Angel sort of way. Marty was more an Eames man himself.

Wynn finished his conversation and turned to smile at Marty. "Good work, Marty!" he exclaimed. "This is a huge account for us!"

"One of the biggest, Wynn." Marty smiled.

The older man eyed Marty keenly, and Marty felt his smile fade.

"You didn't drop by just to crow about Isaac Arrow," Wynn observed.

"No," Marty admitted.

"So you still trying to decide how your desk is going to look in here? Or . . ." Slipping his bifocals down on his nose, Wynn gazed back at Marty quizzically. He was waiting.

Marty had been dreading this moment. Jesus, he hated to be the bearer of bad news, and after just landing Arrow on top of it. But Marty was executive vice president of domestic operations and this was a business, not *Fantasy Island*. The buck stopped with him. "I'm afraid all's not well in Shangri-la, Wynn," he said simply.

"Hell." Wynn shrugged. "Is it ever?"

Marty smiled, but it was a solemn smile. A smile that said they had bigger problems than getting a client into the Super Bowl. And, as if he could sense what was coming, Wynn's heavy frame went on alert and he snuffed out his cigarette and lit another.

"The board of directors at National Home Products has just approved a hostile buyout by Hexall Industries," Marty began.

"And?" Wynn leaned forward, flicking his cigarette in the ashtray.

"Well, I'm hearing through the grapevine that Hexall wants NHP to move their account to Hexall's New York agency."

"To Todd, Gattwick, and Lorenz?"

Marty nodded, surprised that Wynn hadn't flinched; though on second thought, Marty realized his boss's reaction was really in keeping with Wynn's carefully constructed image. Bergman might be advancing in years, his trim physique replaced by what those in the social security set referred to as "well-rounded dignity" thanks to decades of T-bones at Gene and Georgetti's, but he was still every inch the hard-edged industry mogul. Wynn knew as well as anybody that the ad game wasn't a game at all; it was just one hell of a hard job.

"Hexall manufactures appliances and electronics, right?" Wynn asked calmly. "So Todd knows appliance advertising . . . but what do they know about marketing health-care products and cosmetics?"

"Not a damned thing . . . which, of course, explains the client's fascination." A bitter chuckle escaped Marty's lips.

"I see." Wynn leaned back in his chair and stared thoughtfully into space, lighting his umpteenth cigarette. "NHP's our second largest account," he remarked at last through a billowing cloud of smoke.

"Six hundred million in billings."

Wynn crushed out the cigarette and sat up. "Fifty percent of it is in media and we're generating a twenty percent margin, right?"

"Right. One hundred twenty million a year for the agency."

"That buys a lot of Christmas turkeys," Wynn murmured, fiddling with his half-empty pack of cigarettes, crackling the cellophane in his hand. "So let's talk the flip side, Marty. What's your projection for new business this year?"

"About two hundred million."

"A four-hundred-million-dollar loss?" Wynn looked cool enough when he said the words *four hundred million dollar loss*—hell, Wynn had seen a lot of ups and downs in all those years on the playing field. But even so, Marty figured the guy had to be sweating.

"I didn't include Isaac Arrow in that figure, Wynn," Marty replied. "With Arrow, we'll add another three hundred million."

"So if we lock Arrow in on some healthy fees and a good media schedule, we'll generate five hundred million, *total*, in new business? Is that what you're saying?"

"That's what I'm saying." The Isaac Arrow account was suddenly taking on staggering importance.

Wynn let out a heavy sigh and, as if he'd read Marty's thoughts, said, "Sounds like we've got a lot riding on Arrow. Without it, we stand to lose nearly four hundred million in billing. If that happens . . ." He shook his graying head, his face going hound-dog sober. "Well, if that happens, we'll come as close to life and death as you can in this business."

"That *won't* happen, Wynn."

Bergman smiled soberly and stood up. "So I take it you've got a few tricks up your sleeve?"

"Don't I always?" Marty grinned.

"Yeah . . . what the hell am I thinking. You're the sorcerer's apprentice, right?"

"Right," he said, nodding confidently. But the truth was, he didn't have the faintest idea how he was going to get out of this one. The waters were rising fast and he didn't know the magic word. And this time, neither did Wynn.

After leaving Wynn's office, Marty decided to tackle the mystery of the CD-ROM disc. What exactly was on the disc and what that information could possibly have to do with his father were two questions that had burned in his thoughts ever since he and Reiki had uncovered its first secret: that it wasn't a music disc at all, but had only been made to *look* like one.

He hurried down to Creative to find Zak Restin; when the elevator door opened, the quiet of the building was pierced by the whine of an electric guitar. Marty followed the sound to Zak's headquarters, where alternative rock blared out of a stereo, and found Zak, looking more Sergeant Pepper than General Patton, bouncing back and forth among the dozen or so artists seated at their computer workstations.

The Creative Department was all loud music, funky hairstyles, and arty types. Still, if it hadn't been for those "small" details it could have passed for a clerical office. Ten years before, when Marty had started at Bergman, Creative had been crowded with mechanical boards, drafting tables, and rolling carts loaded down with sticky cans of spray mount, colored markers, tissue, and X-Acto knives. What had been an art department had given way to a hackers' paradise: Rows of computer workstations lined the walls and there was not a hand-drawn sketch to be found.

At the sight of Marty standing in the middle of the room, Zak waved. "Hey guy, what's happening?"

Marty glanced around the room. "Can we go in your office and talk in private?"

"Sure thing." Zak's eyes darted to the papers under Marty's arm. "Guess it's pretty crazy out here, huh?"

"As usual."

"So, this sounds serious." Zak offered cautiously as he led Marty into his office.

"Not really."

"Why is it I don't believe you?"

"Beats me." Marty grinned, surveying Zak's cluttered office, looking for a place to sit down, as Zak closed the door.

The office was a mess, as usual. Next to a chessboard, its pieces awaiting the next move, a cardboard box lay open, exposing the moldy crusts of a half-eaten veggie pizza. Magazines were stacked around the floor alongside pyramids of empty pop cans. Art supplies rounded out the eclectic "junque" style.

There were signs of work in Zak's office, of course: The tacked-up mechanical specs and charts of computer command instructions. Trays of computer discs and racks of job folders bursting with laser printouts of ad designs. The sleek, high-tech workstation stacked high with everything from *Ad Age* and *Communication Arts* to *MacWorld* and *Wired*.

"Sorry about the mess," Zak called over one shoulder as he hoisted a duffel bag bulging with dirty laundry off a chair and onto the floor. "Have a seat."

Marty sat down and Zak sank into a battered swivel chair.

"Okay." Zak grinned between loud slurps at a bottle of wheat grass. "Just tell me one thing before we start. Is this gonna be painful? Am I gonna have to bend over and grab my ankles?"

Marty laughed and shook his head. "I promise you won't feel a thing."

"Shit, that's what they all say," Zak cracked. "Okay then, so what is it? Something wrong with the Arrow account? Or am I fired?"

"You know there's not a chance of that. Hell, after Arrow's spot hits the air, Zak Restin's headed for greatness. And probably a promotion and bonus on top of it."

"So what's all that stuff?" Zak asked, pointing to the envelope and papers in Marty's lap.

Marty pulled the disc out of the envelope and held it out. "Actually, I just need to get a look at this in Photoshop."

"B. B. King?" Zak groaned. "Jesus, Marty, that's not gonna work. You can't read a music disc in Photoshop."

Marty smiled patiently. "Just put it in, Zak."

"Hey, no problem, you call the shots." He took the disc out of its case and spun around to face his PC. "So just what the hell do you expect to see?" he asked, slipping the disc in the drive.

"That's why I'm here, Zak," Marty replied innocently; he thought his father's old Mob adage about "the less a guy knew, the better" fit this situation to a T. "I don't have the slightest idea."

"Well, my guess is you're not gonna see anything," Zak declared, putting his pointer on the launcher icon and giving the mouse two clicks. They were suddenly in Photoshop. "I'll be damned . . . there *is* something on here."

Marty caught his breath. He knew his father well enough to be pretty sure that Tony Inglesia wouldn't have sent his son any secret information pertaining to his line of work—he'd been totally committed to Marty's living a straight life—but Marty found his heart beating wildly nonetheless.

There were more clicks and commands and then ING.TIF appeared on screen. "It's an image file," Zak said in amazement, giving the mouse two clicks. A dialogue box opened. Two more clicks and the dialogue box was replaced by an empty window.

Marty watched, his anxiety steadily rising, as an image gradually took shape. From top to bottom, pixels lined up like rows of marching soldiers. Bit by bit, the computer built the graphic until, at last, a final picture emerged: an image of a twisted, gargoyle-like creature.

"Looks like that alien dude from *Predator*, huh?" Zak kidded. "You taken up hieroglyphics?"

"No, not lately." Thoughts racing, Marty leaned over Zak's shoulder for a closer inspection. He wasn't sure what he had expected—row after row of cryptic numbers, a list of Mob guys, maybe his father's financial records—but not *this*. He shook his head in exasperation. "It's a glyph, all right. But from where? It's not Egyptian."

"No. It's definitely not Egyptian." Zak screwed up his face. "Too weird for that."

Marty nodded absently, wondering what the hell hieroglyphics had to do with his father. As he scanned the image more closely, he noticed that two groups of numbers were positioned alongside the glyph, one to the left, one to the right. "What do these numbers mean, Zak?"

"Hmm . . . I-N-T followed by nine digits." Zak shrugged, tapping the right side of the screen. "You got me. I've never seen anything like this in Photoshop before. But this series over here . . ." He pointed to the other set of numbers. "This is the resolution setting and format size . . . and number of bits in the image. You know, all the data the computer needs to reproduce the image exactly. To the computer it's an identification code, sort of like a fingerprint."

"Do me a favor and print it out."

"Sure thing." Zak gave the mouse a click and a green light blinked on the printer. There was the sound of a sheet of paper *whooshing* over rollers and then two beeps. "Here you go," he said, handing Marty the printout and mysterious disc with a courtly flourish. "By the way, how come this . . . this thing . . . whatever it is, is on a music disc?"

"It's a long story," he said, slipping the disc back into the envelope.

Zak's dark face darkened further. "This isn't something Arrow's popped on us at the last minute, is it? Some goofy fucking logo they just pulled out of the air and want us to use in their ad? We've got a deadline, you know. The Super Bowl's just eighteen days away."

"No last-minute surprises." Marty lifted his hand in mock solemnity. "Scouts' honor." He smiled reassuringly at the creative director. "No, whatever this is, it's got nothing to do with Isaac Arrow." He stared down at the strange image on the printout. "Nothing at all."

Chapter 12

It was nine-fifteen when Marty got back to his office and started wading through E-mail. A message from Carson Page flashed on the screen:

> MARTY
> NO MEETING AT ISAAC ARROW TODAY. I'LL BE COMING OVER
> TO BERGMAN INSTEAD. SEE YOU AT ELEVEN. CARSON

He looked around the office; it was a wreck. "Shit," he said under his breath.

"Marty?"

He looked up. "Yeah?"

Lee Wilde was standing in the doorway with two men he'd never seen before. "Excuse me, Marty." She smiled, all saccharine. "But I was on my way over here with those figures I promised"—she held up a piece of paper—"when I bumped into these gentlemen at the reception desk. They said they were looking for you and, being the good Samaritan that I am, I offered to show them to your office."

Marty walked around his desk and, shooting Lee a knowing smile, took the paper. Lee Wilde hadn't been a good Samaritan in her entire life; she was probably dying to know what two guys who looked like they just stepped out of an episode of *Dragnet* wanted with a top executive in an ad agency. But then he couldn't blame her for that—so was he.

One of the men glanced uncomfortably at Lee and then at the open door. "Would it be possible to speak with you in private, Mr. English?"

"Sure," Marty replied genially. "No problem." Turning to Lee, he motioned to the paper in his hand. "What do you say I get back to you on this later?" She nodded hesitantly as he closed the door.

"So, it looks like you know my name," Marty remarked to the two men staring back at him. "But I don't believe I know yours."

They smiled—stiff, poker-up-the-ass smiles. G-men. Federal agents. That's what his father would have guessed. That was Marty's guess, too. These two guys had all the makings of the Friday and Gannon of the detective world: drab guys in drab suits, cookie-cutter, square Johns with an attitude.

"We're federal agents, Mr. English," they answered, flashing their IDs.

Bingo. Marty smiled to himself.

"I'm Roger Kemper and this is my partner, Max Harper," the one with the wooden face said as he shoved his hand into Marty's.

Marty's father had taught him that you could read as much in a man's hands as you could in his eyes. Roger Kemper's handshake was firm, but it was also robotic; the skin was rough and calloused. Marty looked into the man's eyes, hoping to find something more demonstrative there. But, no—the eyes weren't giving up anything either.

"Sit down," he offered, pushing aside a sudden uneasiness and taking a seat behind his desk.

They nodded and sat down, keeping their coats on.

"How can I help you?"

Kemper folded his hands in his lap. "I think you know."

"No." Marty shook his head. "I don't think I do."

There was an awkward silence. The agents looked back at him impassively, waiting.

"Maybe this is too sensitive," Kemper said at last. "Would you be more comfortable talking someplace else? We could come by the Astor tonight if that would be more convenient."

Marty tried not to look shocked. The Astor? So they already knew where he lived, the bastards. He wasn't about to let the feds intrude on his personal life. No way.

He gave them a studiously polite smile. "That won't be necessary. We can talk right here."

"Good," Kemper said, retrieving a pen and notepad from his Burberry trench coat. "We appreciate your cooperation. So, Mr. English, when was the last time you saw your father?"

"A few months ago." He answered the question before he had time to think, before he could take it back. Before he realized that it wasn't really true. Actually, he'd seen his father just last night—stiff and blue under a coroner's blanket. "Oh, and last night of course," he said quickly.

Agent Kemper looked suddenly hopeful, like some puppeteer up above had pulled a few strings and put a smile on that wooden face of his.

"I mean, last night when I went out to Lake Forest and identified his body."

"Oh." Kemper's face fell. "I see. Well, when you last spoke, did your father mention anything about his business dealings . . . anything about his activities outside the country?"

"We never talked about his business. He kept me out of that part of his life."

"Of course he did," Harper acknowledged, nodding at his partner. "But over the years, in passing, surely he mentioned the names of some of his associates."

Marty frowned. "Like I said, he kept me out of his world . . . completely. And I kept him out of mine." He felt a pang of regret; he suddenly wished he had something to lie about, that he and his father had actually been that close. But truth was,

Marty didn't have the slightest idea what went on in his father's day-to-day existence.

"Kept him out of your life by changing your name, you mean?" Kemper asked.

"Yeah." Marty nodded. "Gangsters don't play too well in my line of work."

"I'm sure they don't," Kemper agreed sympathetically, like he understood just what Marty was going through.

"Have you been contacted by anyone since your father's death last night?" Harper asked.

"Or," Kemper added, "received any messages or correspondence?"

Marty shook his head. "Should I have?"

"Well, it's a distinct possibility," Harper replied.

Kemper nodded. "We have reason to believe you may be contacted, Marty." He paused. "You don't mind me calling you Marty, do you?"

Marty did mind, but he had more important things to do than give these guys a lesson in manners. "You think I'll be contacted?" he asked skeptically. "By whom?"

"I'm sorry," Harper jumped in. "We can't divulge that information, not at this time. You understand . . . not during an investigation."

"Well, if you can't tell me that, then at least tell me where you got the idea to begin with."

Kemper smiled stiffly. "From our informants, of course."

"Informants?"

"Have you been contacted or not?" Kemper demanded impatiently, tapping his pen on the pad of paper.

"Who the hell would be contacting me? And why would you guys care?"

"I can't answer that," Kemper said.

Marty rolled his eyes.

"It's confidential."

"Confidential?" He looked from Kemper to Harper incredulously. "What agency did you guys say you're from?"

"The FBI."

Marty stood up. He hadn't liked this little game from the start and he liked it even less now. "FBI?" he repeated. "Well, I already talked to some of your buddies last night. And I talked to the police, too. I didn't know anything then and I don't know anything now. I don't even know what it is I *should* know. Or what you think I should know." He paused, his voice trembling with controlled anger. "As far as I'm concerned, *I'm* the one who should be asking the questions."

The two agents stood up and Kemper surveyed Marty coolly, as if to say he'd dealt with plenty of other victims and grieving family members who weren't in the mood to be questioned either. He shook his head. "All that's left by a man like Tony Inglesia are questions," he said. "That's why we're here."

"Then you're wasting your time," Marty snapped. "You guys come walking in here like you're asking directions to Comiskey Park. Tony Inglesia may have been a gangster to you, but he was *my* father. I already told you I don't know anything more than he was found dead last night at his house. Hell, I haven't even heard from the coroner how he died."

Stuffing his notepad into his trench coat, Kemper gave his partner a nod. "Suicide," he said as he opened the door. "Your father killed himself."

Chapter 13

Suicide? That's what they said?" Even over the phone, Ford Sinclair's gravel voice couldn't hide his astonishment. "Are you sure they said *suicide*?"

Marty had been leaning back in his chair, doodling on a yellow-lined legal pad, but he sat up now and held the receiver away from his ear and looked at it in exasperation. Was the guy deaf or dense or what? He put the phone back to his ear. "Yeah, that's what they said. Suicide."

"What time were they there?"

"Uh . . . around nine-thirty. Why?" Absently, Marty doodled *Why?* on the paper.

"Why?" Sinclair exclaimed. "Shit, Marty, I've been standing over the poor son of a bitch doing the autopsy for the past two hours, *waiting* for the report on your father. I've got it right here, in my hand." He paused. "It *just* came out."

"Then how the hell did those agents know the cause of death before the coroner?" he demanded.

"Damned if I know," Sinclair growled.

"What else does the report say?"

"It says your father died of a massive drug overdose. Cause of death is listed as a heart attack. But they're ruling it a suicide."

"My father didn't kill himself. He'd never do that."

There was a silence on the line.

"What agency did those guys say they were with?"

"FBI."

"What were their names?"

Marty studied the paper on his desk, deciphering his scrawl. "Kemper and Harper. *Roger* Kemper and *Max* Harper."

"Those names don't ring a bell—not that I know every agent in the state of Illinois. You sure they said FBI?"

"Yeah, I'm sure. Jesus, Sinclair, they showed me their IDs."

Ford Sinclair let out a throaty laugh. "Aw, shit . . . IDs don't mean diddly nowadays, Marty. Didn't that daddy of yours teach you anything?"

"Yeah, he taught me some things."

"Well, did he teach you that nothing is ever what it seems?"

"No." Marty smiled. "I learned that in advertising." He heard the detective chuckle. It was hard not to like Sinclair, even if he was a cop. Marty had been brought up to think of cops as the enemy, but his gut told him Ford Sinclair was different, that the guy was a straight shooter.

"Listen, Marty," Sinclair said. "I don't think your old man did himself in, either. It just doesn't jibe. On a hunch, I went down to the lab and had a little talk with one of the chemists."

"And?"

"Well, I gotta tell you . . . what he said scared the shit out of me."

"What did he say?" Marty asked, sensing the detective's hesitation. "Well, go on."

"It's big, Marty. Too big to be yapping about on the phone. Can we meet someplace? Tonight maybe?"

"The sooner the better."

"How about the Domino over on West Broadway? You know it?"

"The Domino? Yeah, I know it. Best blues in the city. How about ten?"

"Ten's good for me."

"Okay," Marty said. "See you then."

He hung up the phone and turned around in his chair to face the window, turning over in his mind what Ford Sinclair had said. Yeah, there was more to all this than a simple suicide. He had to believe that. Kemper and Harper had to think so; they sure as hell wouldn't give a damn about a mobster's suicide. Unless—

"Big date tonight?" a voice said, interrupting his thoughts.

Marty swiveled around to see Carson Page, her coat in her arms, standing at his desk.

Caught off guard, he managed a smile. "Carson . . . hello." He tried not to let his irritation show. He wanted to ask her how the hell she got past the reception desk but reined himself in enough to state mildly, "I wasn't expecting you so early."

She affected a wounded expression. "You weren't expecting me so early?" she said, her lips forming a pout. "Is that any way to greet one of your most important clients?"

Carson's theatrics made him laugh. "Sorry. I'm being rude, aren't I? Sit down, make yourself comfortable." He walked around and took her coat. "How about a cup of coffee?" he offered as he hung her coat in the office closet.

She shook her head. "I've been sitting in meetings all morning," she answered, walking over to the window. "I've had enough caffeine to jump-start a car. You know how it is. If you don't mind," she said, her eyes still directed out the window, "I think I'd rather just stand here and enjoy this fantastic view."

"It is a nice view, isn't it?" he agreed, walking over beside her. He could smell her perfume now, a warm, musky scent that was surprisingly unprofessional.

She looked at him and smiled. "You know, I should be jealous."

"I beg your pardon?"

"Well, you're asking other clients out on the town, now

aren't you?" She motioned toward the phone. "You haven't even asked me out to celebrate . . . and I helped you get a three-hundred-million-dollar account."

His easy grin masked his surprise; she'd heard him talking with Sinclair. "Hey, once we get past the Super Bowl, dinner's on me," he promised. "Your choice. Fair enough?"

"Fair enough." She nodded, moving closer.

"Let's have a seat," he suggested, guiding her over to a grouping of chairs.

She paused at his desk and leaned over his computer, running her fingers across the keyboard. "It's a whole new world, isn't it?" she remarked. "You know, with computers and all. They've changed everything . . . well, just about. We still have all that stuff to file, don't we? All those discs. Even with a computer I have a storage problem. God, it's a mess. . . ."

She shook her head and picked up a disc lying on Marty's desk. "I bet I've got a thousand of these damned things lying around . . . but *you*? You must have millions. Where in the world do you keep them all?"

"Let's just say they're out of sight, locked away in our vault in Finance," he said, gently extracting the disc from her hand. "Given Arrow's emphasis on security, I'm sure you're happy to hear that." He grinned. "After all, you wouldn't want your newly selected ad agency to be involved in any industrial espionage, now would you?"

"No," she agreed with an easy smile. "Arrow's board will be happy to know their secrets are safe with Wynn Bergman." She sat down and crossed her long legs. "You have a computer at home?"

"Yeah, a PC," he replied, taking a nearby chair.

"How about a CD-ROM? I've got one for my computer and I really love it."

"I got one a while back. It's great, but I wish there was more software on the market."

"Oh, from what I read in that huge stack of computer magazines I subscribe to, there will be soon enough." She gave a careless shrug and added, "But I have to admit what's out there in software hasn't grabbed me yet—when I'm home, I'm on the Internet most of the time. God, some nights I can't pull myself off."

"I know what you mean." He nodded. "Sometimes I think computers are almost as addictive as heroin. After a while, you're like one of those lab rats pushing a lever for a fix."

She gave him a strange look and laughed. "I think I'm going to enjoy working with you. . . . Who knows, we might even stop being all business someday."

Ignoring her comment, he stood up and walked over to his desk. He liked Carson's spunk and the fact that she was bright, but he was going to have to be careful about preserving a professional relationship with her. He prided himself on his ability to handle any client situation, and he could see he was really going to have to stay on his toes with this one. "Speaking of business," he said, picking up a spiral-bound document and handing it to her, "here's the timetable for the production of the Super Bowl ad. It's a tight time frame. Real tight."

"But it can be done?"

"Yeah. We can do it."

She scanned the document. "Looks good. I see you're down here for the trip to Belize. You'll love it, Marty. Escoba's an oasis." She looked down at her watch and frowned. "Damn! I didn't know it was so late. I'd better get going." She stood up. "Oh, there's one more thing, Marty. We've decided to use Frank Torello as Isaac Arrow's spokesperson in the ad. So be sure and have that in your creative review when you come over to Planetlife on Monday."

At the stunned look on Marty's face, she added, "Hey, I know this is out of left field, but the board members got it in their heads that Arrow needs the same kind of presence that Wendy's has with Dave Thomas . . . you know, a more *personal* corporate image." She shrugged. "Anyway, it's settled—it's a board directive."

"A board directive?" Marty tried not to wince. Zak Restin was going to have a coronary over this one; he'd been looking at celebrities for the job of spokesperson, somebody with a tie to the rainforest.

Marty couldn't believe Isaac Arrow was foolish enough to spend over two million dollars to put Frank Torello's face in the Super Bowl. He cringed at the thought of Torello's Elvis-like hairstyle, his bulging midriff and double chin. Why was it that everybody wanted to be the next Lee Iacocca?

"That's right," Carson replied, flashing a cover-girl smile. "A board directive." She paused and then cooed, "Before I leave, tell me something: Is the Domino a dive? Or is it a place I'd like?"

She'd heard more than he'd realized. He was going to kill the receptionist who let her slip by. "It's a dive," he said over his shoulder as he took her coat out of the closet. "The Domino's a place where sweaty guys hang out and play the blues. A real low-life joint." He turned on the charm. "Not your kind of place at all."

"And what's my kind of place?"

"Well," he said as he helped her slip into her coat, "I'd say the Ambria's more your style."

Looking pleased, she nodded and started walking across the room. "You're right. The Ambria *is* my kind of place. Low lights. Champagne." She stopped at the door and turned around to face him. "The only question I have, Marty, is, Is it yours?"

Chapter 14

Later that afternoon, when Marty broke the news to his team that he would be out the following day "on personal business," they didn't take it very well. But they took Carson's news that Frank Torello would have to appear in the Super Bowl spot with even less enthusiasm.

"I'd like to wring that little bitch's neck," Lee snarled.

Zak Restin and Bill Kidman nodded.

"Well, before it's over," Marty remarked bitterly, "half the agency will probably want to."

"It's a fucking kick in the balls," Zak groaned. "That's what it is. Shit, I almost had the talent nailed down. It was going to be fucking perfect." He surveyed Marty intently. "You know, don't you, that this is gonna ruin the ad?"

"Yeah, and ruin us, too," Kidman added grimly, his fingers twisting at his red goatee. "After the Super Bowl, we're gonna be the laughingstock of the advertising industry."

"Oh, I wouldn't lose too much sleep over the Super Bowl, kids," Lee broke in. At the expression on Marty's face, she shrugged, then said, "Not much luck, golden boy. There's a fifty-fifty chance we might be able to get a spot in the pregame or the postgame. But that's about it." She paused and shot him a knowing look. "Guess we're going to have to come up with a good excuse for Wynn on this one, huh?"

Tired of fighting every step of the way, Marty drew himself up and declared, "So, you're telling me there's *nothing* inside the goddamn game?"

"Yep, that's what I'm saying. Nada. Zippo."

"Well, that's it, then," Kidman exclaimed. "We're screwed."

Marty set his jaw and leaned over the desk. "I want Arrow's ad to run *inside* the Super Bowl, Lee. You understand? I don't care how you get them in there.

"If you can't swing a network buy, then I suggest you get busy—go with local spot buys." He waited for the idea to connect, for the bomb to drop.

It didn't take long.

Lee's penciled eyebrows flew up in disbelief, then outrage. "Spot buys?" she shrieked, jumping up from her chair. "Are you fucking crazy? You want my people to spend their time negotiating with two hundred local TV stations? We don't have time for that crap. Besides, it won't give Isaac Arrow the national prominence they need."

"Yeah, she's right, Marty," Zak agreed. "There's something to be said for position. I mean, Arrow should be shoulder-to-shoulder with a Coke or a Bud . . . not with some mom-and-pop joint."

Kidman moaned. "Oh, I can just see it now, our spot running between Dave's Auto Repair and Mary's Pet Groomers."

"Does anybody have a better solution?" Marty demanded.

Zak and Kidman shrugged and Lee gave him a blank look. Marty knew damned well they didn't. "Well if you don't," he snapped, "quit bitching."

Lee let out a dramatic sigh and wilted into her chair. "Okay. You win. I'll get it done. Isaac Arrow will be *in* the Super Bowl. One way or another. But I can tell you right now, we're not gonna call two hundred TV stations to do it. I'll just have to get a buyout. There must be some sponsor out there who's willing to sell a spot back to the network for a profit."

"Let's just forget the whole goddamned thing," Zak blurted out. "The campaign's fucked now, anyway."

"Oh, too bad," Lee jabbed. "Zak Restin's dreams of a Clio award shattered by the client again."

Marty glared at her disapprovingly and then turned to Zak. "Sorry about that," he said. He understood; he really did. If there was one thing he hated, it was the client who knew it all. Things went fine when everybody did their own jobs. But when the client started calling the shots . . .

"Forget sorry," Zak shot back. "Tell them we won't do it, Marty. Let's have some fucking credibility here, some goddamned self-respect. What ever happened to the idea of creative excellence?"

"Creative excellence?" Lee chortled. "You reading Ogilvy again?"

Marty smiled patiently. "In this case, Zak, creative excellence went out the door when we found out we've got three hundred million dollars riding on one ad."

"This time I'm with Zak here," Kidman grumbled. "Shit fire, we don't even know if this guy Torello can put two sentences together in front of a camera. Can he read a cue card? A prompter?" He held up his hands. "Don't even fucking answer that—I already know he's no Lee Iacocca or Dave Thomas. And he sure as hell isn't an actor. The way I figure it, this guy Torello's probably about as photogenic as a broken toenail."

"Yeah, and about as credible as a gangster," Zak added. "Hell, that's what the guy looks like with those fucking aviators and that Elvis hair of his."

"Elvis hair?" Kidman moaned. "Nobody told me he had Elvis hair—"

"Hey, speaking of gangsters," Zak interrupted, ignoring Kidman's tirade, "did you hear the news? That Mob guy Tony Inglesia cashed in his chips last night."

"No fooling?" Kidman exclaimed.

At his father's name, Marty felt the sadness seep back in.

He might have rejected his father's world, his ways, hell, even his name, but he was his father's son, after all. But whatever grief he felt, he'd have to hide it. If his father had wanted Marty to distance himself while the Mafia boss was still alive, he certainly wouldn't want Marty to come clean after he was no longer around.

And so, not skipping a beat, Marty looked at Zak impassively, as if the death of a gangster named Tony Inglesia wasn't any more important to him than knowing what new hairstyle the nation's First Lady was sporting that week. "Yeah, that's what I heard," he remarked offhandedly, shuffling through the papers on his desk. "They said it was suicide."

Chapter 15

It was well past nine when Marty pulled up behind a rusted-out Chevy and parked his car. He was three blocks away from the Domino Lounge; it wasn't so much that he was worried somebody might see him, he just liked to walk the streets at night. At least he did when he had the blues.

He hadn't told Reiki where he was going. And she hadn't asked, though he could tell she'd wanted to; he saw the insecurity in her eyes, the questioning. But he wasn't in the mood for talks of commitment and relationships and houses in the country; instead he'd thrown on some jeans and a sweater and headed for the door, telling her he needed time to think.

He got out of the car and stood on the curb for a minute or two, shivering in the cold gusts that curled around the corners and alleys, blasting unsuspecting pedestrians.

Out here, on the streets at night, Marty could ignore the frigid climate; the cold wind was like a long-lost friend, coming out to greet him. Tonight, it carried the welcome scent of hickory-smoked ribs and Greek lamb turning on a spit in restaurants somewhere down the street, of burned coffee and stale booze. Other nights, the air smelled of boiled hot dogs and alley-cat urine and fried onion rings. It was never the same. But whatever it happened to be, Marty relished it. The air of the streets was reassuringly familiar.

He locked the car and stuffed his hands into the pockets of his worn leather jacket and set off down West Broadway toward the Domino Lounge. As he walked, the street got darker. The buildings lower, more run down; the cars bigger and more beat up.

He passed one joint after another. All-night diners with their usual customers slung around chrome-stripped Formica counters, heads down, slurping at watery soup with big stainless spoons. Strip clubs with worn-out peroxide blondes in G-strings wriggling their cellulite on a stage. Package stores with neon signs flashing blue and green and orange, hawking malt liquors.

Some of the places had nothing more than a hand-painted sign on the door that read *Tiger's Den* or *Jimmy Mack's* or *Ruby's*. Those joints came and went with the flick of a paintbrush.

All along the street, hookers hovered in doorways, hoping to stay out of the wind. For warmth, they clustered in brooding groups of twos and threes. The braver ones, with furs, stood alone on street corners. This time of year, a hooker's short skirt exposed her to more than a potential customer's lustful gaze. This time of year, she froze her ass off.

It was misery being a hooker—that was just one realization Marty had come to in his many years of walking these streets. Working girls didn't smile too much. They saved their best smiles for passersby. At least that's what a forty-something hooker named Suzy Q had told him.

Tonight, the big-haired brunette waved Marty over to her street corner. They shot the shit for a while, shivering in the wind, Marty listening while Suzy Q poured out her latest hard-luck story.

As unlikely as it seemed, Marty was a friend to Suzy Q. Marty's father, determined that his son not grow up a snob who thought the world consisted only of prep schools and country clubs, had instilled in him the belief that you were never too big or too rich to disdain the friendship of a good, honest soul, and that's what Suzy Q was to Marty, despite her profession.

Friendship with someone like Marty was a rare commodity for a hooker; the lonely woman would've given him anything. Street people didn't forget a kindness, even if it was only a few minutes bending your ear. They were loyal for life, which was just one of the things Marty had learned over the years roaming these streets.

Thanks to Mike D'Angelo, who'd shown him around the westside—broken Marty in, so to speak, while he was still just an underaged kid—Marty had gotten to know a fair number of street people. And they knew him. He knew the old wino Sloppy Joe, who always stood outside the neighborhood diners with the stray dogs and cats, hoping for a few scraps of leftovers. He knew the blues singer-turned-bag-lady whose hands shook so badly from the DTs she could hardly hold the change he always gave her. And he knew the crazy Hispanic pimp named Hector who claimed to have once had the biggest stable of whores on the westside and now wore heels and false eyelashes and turned tricks himself. No woman could give a better blow job for a five-spot—that's what crazy Hector said.

D'Angelo and his father needn't have worried about educating Marty about the other side of the tracks. Marty loved this part of town. He found it liberating, for here he was finally free. Free of his mask. Free to be Martino Inglesia, a mobster's son, a streetwise kid who wasn't afraid of dark alleys and pimps and pushers and whores.

That's who he was, after all. And that's who he'd become, despite his father's best intentions to make him into a sanitized version called Marty English—he was still Tony Inglesia's son, a guy who understood the grit of life and could slip into the underbelly of society just as easily as he could slip into an Armani suit.

Sometimes, Marty wondered what they all would think: his clients, his staff, his friends in the ad business, those faces that stared back at him from the annual Wynn Bergman meetings. They'd think he was crazy, that's what they'd think. They wouldn't get it, he was sure of that. Just like they wouldn't understand that he'd actually cared about—hell, loved—an underworld gangster.

Of course, even those who knew the "real Marty," the Martino Inglesia side, could have disputed those claims of affection. And with some justification: Marty hadn't really seen much of his father since his life had taken its infamous U-turn in the summer of 1968. That year had been a watershed for Marty as well as for the nation. He'd let his hair grow past his shoulders and spent the days locked up in his room, listening to his stereo, a Hermann Hesse novel in hand. His father declared him a disgrace, a dirty hippie. Marty called himself an activist, a head—an intellectual.

Marty smoked his first joint that summer, ate his first mushroom, looked in the mirror and, for the first time in his life, saw God. When he was straight, he envisioned himself as a romantic revolutionary. When he wasn't, a spiritual warrior. It was a heady time. And then the Democratic convention came to town.

Marty was in Grant Park the night things went up for grabs and the rioting broke out, just another long-haired kid on the edge of seventeen who wore his heart on his tie-dyed sleeve and carried a chip on his shoulder. He said he'd come to protest the war in Vietnam, but more than anything he wanted to feel the comfort of other restless youth.

It was all a frightening blur of humanity moving around him. Boys with rocks and bricks. Men in blue with billy clubs and bullets. But for the first time since his mother had held him in her arms and said good-bye, Marty felt like he belonged to something larger than himself. He wasn't that kid with a pain in his heart. No, that night he didn't feel much of anything. Nothing except anger.

There'd been a lot of people like that in Grant Park that night. Most of them, like Marty, were arrested and hauled off to jail. But unlike Marty, their father wasn't a Mob boss with friends in high places; less than an hour after his arrest, Marty was released against his wishes and driven home by a "love it or leave it" cop who felt compelled to lecture him on the merits of America, Mom, and apple pie.

At home, Marty's father had felt compelled to lecture him on respect. They'd fought that night, tossing bitter words back and forth with no more forethought than they'd used playing catch in the backyard years before. "Are you going to run me off just like you did Mom?" Marty had finally shouted, wanting to hurt the man, to make him feel the pain he'd felt.

That was all Marty remembered of their argument. Most of what they'd said had been muffled by time. But he could still recall those words, could still feel the stinging slap of his father's hand across his face, the tears burning in his eyes as his father had opened the door and ordered, "Get out. And don't come back until you're a man."

Marty had left that night. And he hadn't come back until four years later, when he was a man and a Vietnam veteran. They never spoke of the incident again. Marty knew it was behind them when his father gave him a key to the house and told him the door was always open. After that, Marty had figured he could just walk through that door in Lake Forest and have a few drinks with the old man, bullshit over a Grand Avenue hot dog.

In spite of his father's unorthodox line of work, he hadn't really considered the possibility that someday it would all come to an end, that he might never be able to ask him the things he really wanted to know. Like what made Tony Inglesia tick. Like why his mother had left.

But Marty had other questions, too. Questions his father wouldn't have been able to answer. The kind of questions he'd asked back in Vietnam, when he crouched in his foxhole, smoking pot and drinking rotgut, wondering about the state of the country—as well as of the universe—instead of thinking about body counts.

The kind of questions he and the rest of the baby boomers had asked when they went through that notoriously rocky identity crisis of theirs. Yeah, maybe that was it, he thought. Maybe he was going through one of those. Maybe his father's death had made him think about his own mortality again; hell, he hadn't done that since Vietnam.

But Marty knew better than that; this wasn't an identity crisis—it wasn't anything so complicated as that. This was about grief, pure and simple. And the only question he had right now was what really happened to his father. He couldn't just walk out the door this time. He had to know.

As Marty walked down the steep iron stairs leading to the Domino Lounge, strains of a blues trio drifted up to greet him. The Domino wasn't much more than a dark, smoky, hole-in-the-ground joint, but at the bottom of the stairs, the beat took over and a person forgot all that. You were pulled into the room by the smell of hard times and reefer.

Marty took a deep breath and smiled and gave his coat to a sweet-faced girl with dimples on her cheeks and a dainty little gold ring through her nose. She pointed across the room to a table in the shadows. "Guy over there says he's waitin' for you, Marty." It was Ford Sinclair.

"Thanks, Celie," he said, putting a few bucks in her hand.

He headed off through the crowd and she yelled after him, above the grinding music, "You gonna play tonight?"

"Nope, didn't bring my harmonica," he called out over his shoulder as he elbowed past the little round tables that always jiggled when you rested your elbow on the top.

The place was packed. A good night to people-watch, he thought. There were a few out-of-work black musicians gathered around, tapping their feet to the rhythm of the bass. The occasional burnout crying in his beer. And, of course, the "Harvard Classics." That's what Marty called the white guys who ventured down to that part of the city, guys who always took a cab, naturally, and always looked over their shoulders and checked their pockets for their wallets when they ordered a Tom Collins. Those guys stuck out like a sore thumb in a place like the Domino.

But then, Marty thought as his eyes came to rest on Ford Sinclair, some guys just naturally stuck out like a sore thumb. Ford Sinclair was black and he didn't look over his shoulder or check for his wallet every two seconds, but still, he didn't fit in. He looked like a cop.

The detective was sitting at Marty's favorite table, right in front of the stage, watching Pork Chop, a moon-faced guitarist with skin the color of hot coals, pick at an electric guitar and belt out the blues. Sinclair was thumping his hand on the table in time with the beat. Marty couldn't help but smile; the poor guy didn't have a sense of rhythm worth shit.

"Hello, Sinclair," Marty spoke above the music. He pulled up a chair.

Sinclair looked up. "Hey, you made it! I was beginning to wonder."

"I walked a few blocks," Marty explained, taking out a cigar.

Sinclair's eyes widened. "Walked? Down here? Are you nuts? Jesus Christ, boy, didn't anybody ever tell you that walking around by yourself in this part of town is asking for trouble?"

Marty smiled. "Only the people who don't live here." He held up the cigar. "I've got another. You want one?"

"Hell no," Sinclair replied, shaking his head. "I quit ten years ago. And I'm not about to start again now. Quitting nearly killed me and my wife both." He grinned. "And Crissie didn't even smoke."

Marty laughed and lit the cigar and waved a waitress over.

"What'll it be, Marty?" she asked.

"A draft, Lacy." He looked at Sinclair. "Drinks are on me. What'll you have?"

"Just a cup of coffee, thanks." Sinclair smiled up at the

waitress, who shrugged and ambled away. When she returned with their order, the band was taking a break.

The detective's face went suddenly solemn. "I guess listening to music isn't why we're here tonight, now is it?"

"No, it's not," Marty agreed, putting down his cigar in the ashtray. "Not if what you said about that chemist is on the money."

"Oh, it's on the money all right. Pardon my French, but the guy fucking blew me away."

"Yeah?" Marty leaned in slightly. "Go on, what did he say?"

"He said it was a drug overdose that killed your father, all right. But he said it wasn't just any drug. This one's like cocaine, but a hell of a lot stronger. Something he'd never seen before, Marty, not some crap that came out of a back alley lab, either. He said this shit was made by somebody who knew what the hell he was doing. Somebody *real* sophisticated."

"So what?" Marty snapped impatiently. "So the drug they found in my father's bloodstream makes cocaine look like a fucking Tylenol. So it was made by somebody with a GED. So what? I still don't think he killed himself."

Sinclair frowned, his large almond eyes squeezing down to slits. "Well, maybe he didn't," he said slowly, a conspiratorial note in his words. "Maybe he was poisoned. That's what I think, Marty. And first thing tomorrow, while you're at the funeral, I'm gonna try to prove it."

"And just how do you plan on doing that?"

"Well, first off, I'm going to have another talk with that chemist. Then I'm going to find out if there were some other fingerprints besides your father's on that glass. I'll do a little snooping on my own after that. . . ." He shrugged and added, "Hell, shake enough trees and some leaves are bound to fall."

"Go ahead, knock yourself out. But it still doesn't make any sense to me. Why poison? I don't get it—it's not like the Mob. Why not just shoot him and be done with it?"

"I don't know," Sinclair admitted. "But I do know this isn't Al Capone's gang we're dealing with here. You know that as well as I do. Your old man had plenty of enemies. Like you said last night, there was a long list of guys who would've liked to pop him. Maybe one of them decided to move into the modern age of chemistry."

Marty picked up his cigar and thoughtfully rolled it back and forth in his fingers. If Sinclair was right, he'd probably come face to face with his father's killer at the funeral.

"By the way," Sinclair said, breaking in on his thoughts, "I checked out those two visitors of yours."

"And?"

"I was right. They're not FBI."

"Well, they aren't fucking Martians, Sinclair. The bastards were in my office, intruding on *my* goddamned life. I want to know who the hell they are and whose watch they're on." He paused, glaring at the detective. "You got that?"

Sinclair raised his hand in surrender. "Okay, okay . . . keep your pants on. Soon as I know something, you'll know something." He leaned in closer, lowering his voice. "But I gotta tell you, I got a feeling about those guys, Marty—"

"Yeah, well I got a feeling too," Marty interrupted, gulping his beer. "I got a feeling some bastard killed my father and he's going to get away with it."

"Not if I can help it."

"No . . . not if *I* can help it," Marty retorted, his dark eyes going cold beneath his heavy Sicilian lids. "I'll find out who did this, one way or another. And when I do . . . the bastard's gonna fucking pay."

Sinclair recoiled; there was another man sitting at the table with him now—a mobster's son. "Hey, just a minute," he protested. "That's for the authorities to do."

The alarmed look on the detective's face jolted Marty back to reality. He couldn't let a cop inside his head. There wasn't room for a man like Ford Sinclair in his life. Not now anyway. Revenge was a solitary sport. That was one thing he'd embraced from his father's world. He wouldn't forget that lesson now.

Marty nodded in reluctant agreement and watched Sinclair relax a bit. He slapped the detective on the shoulder, like they were long lost buddies. "Yeah, you're right . . . that's for the authorities to handle. But, goddammit, Sinclair, you can't blame a guy for wishing he could take the law into his own hands once in a while, can you?"

"Oh, the streets are full of guys that think like that. That think they're Rambo."

"Well, I'm no Rambo, so I guess we should play this by the book, huh? What were you saying about those two jokers? You got a feeling about them?"

"Yeah. A feeling." Sinclair frowned and took a quick sip of coffee. "My guess is somebody thinks you know something, something about your father's business, probably. Why else would those two guys pay you a visit? It's pretty plain something funny's going on here. So do yourself a favor. Until we know for sure, watch your ass. Okay?"

Marty grinned. "I thought you were doing that."

"I'm a Lake County cop, remember? I'm out of my jurisdiction down here."

"But you're here now . . . in Chicago," Marty objected.

"Yeah, but technically this little talk we're having is part of Lake County's investigation into the Inglesia case. When it comes to providing protection to a resident of Chicago . . ."

"Meaning me?"

Sinclair nodded. "Well, that's up to the Chicago police."

"So what you're saying is, I'm on my own?" At Sinclair's sigh of admission, Marty smiled cynically. That's the way it always was, wasn't it? When the chips were down, you were on your own.

Chapter 16

People had been celebrating life and mourning death for as long as they'd been roaming the planet.

But there was no time when the attempt to make sense of it all seemed more futile than when someone close to you died. A priest could talk all he wanted about leading you beside those still waters and restoring your soul. But the shadow of death? That would always be with you. No Escape key on the keyboard for that one.

Life wasn't like advertising; you couldn't just try a different slogan if things went bad. And all the money in the world couldn't buy you out of mortality. Nor could it buy you peace of mind, any more than it could buy you the stairway to heaven.

But then again, with a really good Italian funeral, you could give it your best shot.

The funeral for Mob boss Tony Inglesia had been orchestrated by Inglesia's lifelong attorney and was typical of Chicago's finest Mob funerals: A guy might not be able to take it with him, but he'd give it a hell of a try.

At a cost of twenty-five thousand dollars, Tony Inglesia had been laid out at Montclair Chapel, that darling of the Mob funeral set, with its garish red carpets and velvet curtains and greaseball guards with pinky rings standing in rooms filled with tacky wreaths and garlands and potted plants. The place looked like a whorehouse and smelled like the perfume counter at Marshall Field's. But no matter; to its mafiosi patrons, Montclair was all class.

As ostentatious as the trappings of Marty's father's funeral were, the service itself was simple and to the point. Rumor had it that for another ten thousand dollars, a man like Inglesia could receive High Mass, given by the cardinal himself. Maybe, Marty thought, you could buy the stairway to heaven after all.

In any case, his father's attorney hadn't coughed up the dough to pay off the church or whomever you paid off, and because of that there wasn't much to say on behalf of Tony Inglesia that day. Father Sullivan did the best he could under the circumstances; he offered a few prayers for the dead and that was that.

From where he and Reiki stood on the shadowy balcony, Marty counted over two hundred men filing past his father's open bronze casket. Sicilian mobsters had a long history of treachery and deceit, and, knowing that, Marty took their grief-stricken expressions with a grain of salt. His father's murderer was among these men—he had to be.

When the chapel cleared of its mourners, Marty and Reiki hurried down to the chapel's service entrance and a waiting limousine. The car's windows were heavily tinted, for Marty was determined to avoid the media circus gathered outside the chapel. He didn't need a front-page scandal; clients like Arrow didn't take to being connected to a mobster's son. He'd keep his identity, as well as his attendance at his father's funeral, under wraps.

Once they were inside the limousine, away from the news cameras and reporters, Marty relaxed his guard slightly and nodded at the mourners walking past the limousine. "All these people may look like they're going somewhere, Reiki, but the truth is, they're all standing still. Hell, their world hasn't changed for a thousand years. At a funeral for a man like my father, the women have always prayed and the men have always plotted. That's how it is in the Mob. The men are always looking for an angle, looking to make a score. If it weren't so politically incorrect I'd swear it was in their genes."

Reiki laughed softly and he flashed her a serious, bitter smile. "They killed him," he said in a resolute whisper. "One of those guys we just saw in there did it. My father didn't commit suicide. No way. A man who kills himself has regrets. I might have loved the guy, but my father had to have been one cold motherfucker. I doubt he ever had a single regret in his entire life."

She looked at him in shock.

"Hey, he was a Mob boss, not the good fairy."

Reiki nodded slowly, knowing he was right. "So he was murdered by one of the men who attended this funeral. But who?"

"I don't know. But there's always somebody waiting in the wings who understands that 'blood washes blood' just as well as the boss does."

Mike D'Angelo leaned over and tapped on the limousine window.

"Interesting timing," Marty said under his breath.

"Who's that?" Reiki whispered, smoothing her chignon.

"Mike D'Angelo," Marty replied, rolling down the window. She nodded; though they'd never met, Reiki had heard all about Marty's "big brother, Mike."

D'Angelo leaned in the window. "Marty, we need to talk," he said in a hush. "It's important." He pointed to the limousine behind them and added, "Your girl can ride in my car."

Marty looked over at Reiki. He wouldn't involve her in whatever it was Mike D'Angelo had up his sleeve. He'd always lived by his father's axiom: What you don't know won't hurt you. That had special meaning in the Mob, and it seemed appropriate now. "That okay with you, Reiki?" Marty was asking, but his eyes said she should go.

"Of course," she replied, giving him a quick kiss on the cheek. She slipped on her dark glasses and pulled a challis scarf over her head; then, looking like Mata Hari, she opened the door and got out. "See you later," she whispered, hurriedly closing the car door behind her.

D'Angelo climbed in and Marty gave the driver a nod.

As the procession to Mount Carmel Cemetery began, Marty wondered, for what seemed the millionth time that day, if this man could be Caesar's Brutus; none of the other men he'd scrutinized seemed to be plausible suspects, yet none, not even Mike D'Angelo, could be above suspicion if Marty was to find the killer.

But shit, he reminded himself, he'd known Mike D'Angelo for most of his life. The guy really was like a big brother. He'd picked Marty up at school, brought him Christmas presents—hell, he'd even given him a baseball signed by Mickey Mantle. On cold winter nights he'd come over to the house and fry up a few skillets of those sausages and peppers Marty loved so much. He'd taught Marty how to drive a stick, too. Took him down to the westside, showed him the real world. Sent him a bottle of Dewar's when he'd landed the job at Wynn Bergman.

Could it be possible that D'Angelo would turn his back on all that history? Marty studied the man's bearing, his hands, the set of his jaw, hoping to find the answer there.

D'Angelo felt his eyes. "Why are you looking at me like that, Marty? Like I'm a stranger."

"Sorry," Marty apologized. "It's just that this . . . well, it came as a shock, him dying like this."

"The suicide, you mean?"

So D'Angelo was buying it, that it was a suicide? Marty was surprised by that—and then suspicious—but he wouldn't let his words or actions betray him. "Yeah, the suicide," he replied. He wanted to sound sad, distressed, but not too off-

Broadway. No overacting. "I guess my father was pretty depressed, huh? I just didn't realize . . ."

"You couldn't have known, Marty. Tony kept those things to himself. But I was with him all the time. . . . I saw it. He'd been down for a long time, ever since your mother left. And jeez, you have no idea how hard it was on him when she remarried that guy out in Arizona. . . ."

Marty nodded. It had been hard on him, too. Try as he might, he'd never gotten over the feeling that his mother had walked out not only on his father, but on him as well. Visitations out west with her had been strained. They became more infrequent as the years passed. Then, after Vietnam, he lost touch. Maybe he couldn't handle the way the old pain always resurfaced every time he looked into her eyes. Or maybe—

"How many years has it been since she left?" D'Angelo asked, interrupting his thoughts. "Thirty?"

"Thirty-three."

"Well, you know, in all those years, your father never gave up on thinking she might come back. Time didn't heal the wounds Tony felt. It just made them worse. Of course, he didn't want you to know. You know how he was . . . always looking out for you."

D'Angelo glanced nervously out the windows, as if he were afraid someone might hear what he was going to say next. "I hate to have to come at you like this, on a day like today, Marty," he said in a hush. "But there's no getting around it. You see, ever since Tony died . . ." He looked Marty directly in the eye and started again. "Well, ever since then, the heat's been on—you understand what I'm saying?"

"Yeah, I understand. As a matter of fact, some FBI guys came to see me at work. The bastards were just full of questions."

"The FBI?" D'Angelo exclaimed. "They came to your office?" He sounded surprised, but the look on his face said something else.

"Hey, it was nothing, Mike." Marty wouldn't let D'Angelo

in on his suspicions about his two visitors. "Although I have to admit, I wish they hadn't come to my office, if you know what I mean."

"Tony would've loved that, having the fucking FBI nosing around his boy's office. Jeez . . . and after all the trouble he went to to keep you out of his world." D'Angelo shook his head. "So what did they want to know?"

"Oh, they asked the usual crap. Things like when my father and I last talked."

"Anything else? Did they ask about his property? His business? Dope, maybe?"

"Mostly they wanted to know who he dealt with . . . but you'd expect that, wouldn't you? I mean, my father *was* in the Mob. They're going to ask questions about who his friends were. No big deal."

"Don't fucking kid yourself, Marty. The feds are interested in more than who's on Tony Inglesia's dance card. They're on a fucking fishing expedition. They're just using Tony's death to get to the rest of us. No matter what a cop says, I wouldn't trust one of those devious motherfuckers for a New York minute."

Marty laughed out loud as the image of Ford Sinclair sitting at the table in the Domino, tapping his hand to the beat, suddenly came to mind. Sinclair was about as devious as Ranger Rick.

"No fooling, Mike. Has an Inglesia ever trusted a cop? Maybe I should remind you . . . I'm an adult now, not that twelve-year-old you used to baby-sit."

"Goddammit, Marty, listen to me, will you? I'm telling you all this 'cause I don't want you to get your ass in a sling."

"Okay, go on." Marty crossed his arms.

"Did Tony ever give you anything that might be incriminating . . . that might tie you or anybody else to the business?"

The image of the disc with its strange hieroglyphic flashed through Marty's mind. But he quickly dismissed the idea;

hell, what would Mike D'Angelo want with something like that? Marty shook his head. "You know as well as I do, Mike, my father never gave me anything that had to do with his business."

"Well, how about computer records or printouts ... shit like that?" Marty thought he detected a sly note in D'Angelo's voice and he instantly went on guard. "Your father had a computer in the office at Curandero, you know," D'Angelo said. "Did he ever give you any computer stuff? A computer disc, maybe?"

At the mention of a disc, Marty caught his breath. Maybe it was D'Angelo who was the one on a fishing expedition. "No, Mike," he replied, maintaining his cool exterior. "Like I said, he never gave me anything—not even a fucking Post-it note."

"Never?"

Marty's heart began to pound. *"Never."*

D'Angelo's face turned dark, almost desperate. "God-dammit, *think*, Marty," he hissed. "Think hard. Did Tony ever give you anything at all? Shit, it could be something simple ... a business card, a fucking key. Like I said, maybe it was a computer disc. Who knows what the feds are looking for. Whatever it is, I'll tell you one thing, if they find it on you, you'll be the one on the hot seat. Hell, they might even try to nail you with some trumped-up charge."

Marty smiled back at D'Angelo calmly, but inside he was reeling. He could only come to one conclusion: Mike D'Angelo knew about the disc, and whatever that glyph meant, the way D'Angelo was acting, it had to be important. "So, Mike, you expect me to believe that all this bullshit you're handing me is to save *my* ass?" He shot D'Angelo an arrogant smile. The guy had a temper, maybe if he got him riled he'd open up. "My father would be disappointed in you."

"Hey, that's hitting below the belt," D'Angelo said, his eyes flashing angrily. "Tony was your father ... okay, I know that. But he was like a father to me, too. It's because of that that I'm talking to you right now. Goddammit, Marty, I don't want to see you hurt. Will you just do me a favor here . . . and look around? Maybe you'll come across something." D'Angelo searched Marty's impassive face and then he sighed in exasperation. "Dammit, I wish I could tell you more, but you'll just have to trust me."

Marty gazed back into D'Angelo's eyes. On the surface they were pleading, sincere. But underneath? Behind the eyes? Nothing. Some acting job; anybody else might've given Mike D'Angelo an Oscar. But not Marty; he knew all about the bullshit that Mob guys—even a guy who claimed to be your "big brother"—threw around like confetti on New Year's. Marty's opinion of D'Angelo was sinking as fast as a guy in a pair of concrete overshoes.

"Okay," D'Angelo began in a tone that said he sensed Marty's distrust. "I admit this isn't just for *your* protection."

"Somehow I didn't think so." He smirked, giving D'Angelo a sideways glance. "So whose protection is it for, then?"

D'Angelo flushed red. "All right. You want the truth?"

"It would be a refreshing change."

"Look, the truth is, some of Tony's shit's missing. If the cops find it, well, the whole fucking Mob could go down. I can't let that happen."

"What kind of shit?" Marty demanded. He'd give D'Angelo one last chance to redeem himself, to tell him about the disc.

"Like I said, I can't go into it. I love you, Marty, like a brother . . . so the less you know the better. It's just that you're the only one who could have what the cops are looking for." D'Angelo gazed into Marty's eyes with a terrible sincerity and, suddenly, Marty realized that whatever bond they'd had between them was gone. Mike D'Angelo couldn't be trusted.

Marty's stomach turned. Could this man be his father's killer? He smiled back at D'Angelo like he believed every word. "I've already told you I don't have anything, Mike, but if you want to check it out for yourself, here . . ." He pulled a key ring from his topcoat. "Here's the key to my father's house. And the key to my place, too."

"Jesus, Marty. . . . I don't want your fucking keys."

"Then what *do* you want?" Marty exclaimed; he was losing his patience.

"I want you to work with me on this, goddammit. That's what I want. I want you to promise you'll call me if you come across something. Anything." D'Angelo paused as if struggling to calm himself. "And I want you to promise that if the cops come snooping around again, you won't try playing cops and robbers on your own. You do that and this whole fucking thing'll blow up in your face. I won't be able to help you then. You won't be Marty English, ad man. You'll be Martino Inglesia, gangland criminal."

Gangland criminal? Marty couldn't conceal a smile; Mike D'Angelo was really grasping at straws with a threat like that.

"Hey, is that what you fucking want?" D'Angelo demanded angrily. "You want to be ruined by a lousy piece of paper or some fucking computer shit?"

"What I want is the truth, Mike. I want to know what it is you're really looking for." He smiled at the expression on the man's face. "That's what *I* want. The truth."

As the limousine slowed at the cemetery, D'Angelo set his jaw and gazed out the window. A mist of cold rain had started to spatter across the windshield. "You know something, Marty?" he said as the car came to a stop beneath a stand of trees. "This cemetery is just full of wise-ass motherfuckers who thought they knew it all. Guys who wouldn't play ball . . . who said they wanted the truth." He opened the car door to get out. "And if I were you, Marty, I'd remember that."

Chapter 17

It was before five o'clock when the alarm went off on Friday morning. Marty grumbled into his pillow and hit the snooze button. Ten minutes later, the alarm went off again. He lost track of how many times he hit Snooze after that. He wasn't out of the shower until after seven.

"It's not like me," he complained later to Reiki as she adjusted his tie in front of the hall mirror. He wouldn't tell her about his conversation with D'Angelo or the fact that he'd been awake half the night thinking about it.

"I suppose you're referring to the fact that you're a man who's always in the office by six," she said. "A man of steel. Always ready."

"I'm confused." He smiled wanly. "Are you talking about work?"

"Maybe," she said with a playful smile. "Maybe not." She handed him a glass of orange juice. "Here, drink this."

Marty drained the glass in one gulp and asked, "So what've you got going today, my dear?"

"Still waiting, I guess." She shrugged. "You know, for that assignment in Rwanda. God, this is Friday. I don't think I can take another week like this one. And now, with you leaving for Belize . . ."

He gave her a reassuring kiss. "You'll get the call. You

always do. You just hate the part in between, that's all. Remember"—he grinned—"nobody does it better than Reiki Devane. *Nobody.*"

She shook her head and laughed. "Comparing me to a muffler shop again? You always say the most romantic things."

"That's because I'm inspired by great beauty," he said, opening the door.

"Just don't forget that when you're down in Belize," she said softly, her brown eyes suddenly solemn.

It was a strange thing for Reiki to say, Marty thought, and he started to ask her why she'd said it. Was it Carson Page again? Reiki probably assumed Carson would be going to Belize too, that she and Marty would be working together down there.

But Reiki would never ask. She was too smart for that. She didn't show her hand—not when it came to her heart. At least she hadn't since they'd been on the subject of marriage. Since then, she'd withdrawn a bit, held back. Even so, she couldn't disguise the feelings he saw in her eyes. What was it? Vulnerability?

But why should a woman like Reiki Devane be anything but confident? After all, she had everything going for her. She was so much in demand that she could afford to take on only those assignments that genuinely interested her. She was at the top of her game professionally. Still, Reiki Devane was a woman. And for a man, even a man like Marty English, that one little fact put everything up for grabs. He could read her eyes, but her heart . . .

She smiled again. "You'd better be going now or it'll be off with your head."

"Yeah, you're right," he replied awkwardly. Dammit, he knew he should stop, should do the sensitive, feeling thing: He should tell her he loved her, that she was the only woman in his life and always would be. After all, that's what women needed, wasn't it? Even a woman as independent and self-reliant as Reiki.

But Marty didn't stop. No, there was too much work waiting to be done at the office. All those meetings to attend. With the funeral, he'd been off a day, too, so he'd have to play catch-up. And of course he couldn't forget about Arrow. Or the importance of that disc. And shit, he was running late on top of it. He felt a sudden rush of adrenaline course through his body. It was a familiar, seductive feeling.

And so, before he knew what had happened—before he even realized he'd made a choice—Marty found himself standing in the empty hallway outside his condo, staring back at a closed door.

Marty had hardly hit Michigan Avenue when he noticed the car.

It was hanging back just far enough. Three cars back, to be precise. Not so far that you'd just shrug your shoulders and forget it, but far enough to make you wonder if you'd finally flipped out completely, thinking you were being followed.

Maybe D'Angelo hadn't bought his story. Maybe the mobster had put some guys on Marty's tail, just to check things out, to see if the disc turned up.

Marty looked in the rearview mirror again; he'd always had a good imagination, and it wasn't letting him down now. The car was a Buick, next to no chrome. A gray four-door sedan. A company car—that's how he'd describe it to Ford Sinclair. Of course he wouldn't mention to the detective his talk with D'Angelo and the very real possibility that the Mob was tailing him. Without that small detail to consider, he imagined Sinclair would have a good laugh at the notion of Marty being shadowed, and in broad daylight, through the streets of Chicago, at that. But then again, it did sound pretty crazy. Hell, he didn't have any experience with city-street tag. The only tag he played these days was on the telephone.

Yeah, he chided himself, he was probably way off base here. Maybe even paranoid; D'Angelo's threats had gotten to him. But when he glanced in the mirror again, the car was still there. "Try this, asshole," he hissed, taking a sharp turn, tires squealing, off Michigan Avenue and onto Ontario. Marty smiled. The car was gone.

But then there it was again, three cars back, just like before. He felt a pit in his stomach. "Son of a bitch!" he growled, slamming his hands on the steering wheel. Well, at least he knew. He really was being followed.

When he got to Rush street, he turned left and looked over his shoulder. It was no good; the car was still there, turning up like a bad fucking dream. One block later, at Ohio, Marty made another left. The car stayed with him. At the next light, he turned right onto Michigan. The Wynn Bergman building was just four blocks away.

The gray sedan shadowed him through the morning rush-hour traffic and across the Chicago River—until he turned into the agency's underground parking garage. He watched in the rearview mirror as the sedan edged past the entrance and disappeared down the street.

As he got out of his car, Marty made a mental note to call Ford Sinclair first thing.

"Did I mention that you've looked green around the gills these past few days?" Lee Wilde asked. She was standing in the doorway of Marty's office, waiting for him. He wasn't in the mood for any bullshit right now; he wanted to call Sinclair.

"Yeah, that's what you said." He tried to move past her, but she blocked his way.

"Well, I take that back. You're not green, you're white as a sheet. What the hell's wrong? You look like you just saw a ghost." She raised her eyebrows. "But just wait 'til you see that office of yours ... that'll put some color in those cheeks."

"What about my office?" He frowned and looked over her shoulder. Except for the glow of his computer screen, it was dark. The pit in his stomach returned; he never left his computer on. Somebody had been snooping around.

"What the fuck . . ." Stunned, he looked around the room. Papers—contracts, briefs, research, ad copy—were scattered across the floor like they were nothing more than useless ticker tape. Behind his desk, the credenza, emptied of its contents, gaped back at him. Bookcases were knocked over, ransacked and left lying in a pool of books freed of their spines. Cabinet doors hung perilously by their hinges next to chairs sprawling leg-up in the air, their sleek ebony leather upholstery slit open to reveal stuffing that billowed out in soft white tufts, looking like Orville Redenbacher's best. Somebody was looking for something and Marty had a pretty good idea *who* that somebody was—and what they were looking for as well.

"Old Roy the janitor mad at you again?" Lee asked.

He spun around. "I sure hope not," he replied, concealing his anger as he turned on the light.

"Well, it wasn't the staff," Lee cracked. "They may be pissed off about you taking a personal day with a schedule like this one with Arrow breathing down our necks, but they're not this pissed off."

Marty straightened a Jasper Johns print hanging cockeyed on the wall. "What I want to know is how the hell somebody got past Security."

Lee laughed and rolled her eyes. "Any cat burglar with soft shoes could make it past that guard of ours. The guy sleeps half the time."

Marty let out an exasperated sigh and started wading to his desk through a sea of papers. Lee was right about that. A job like this had probably been a snap for the Mob's pros.

"Listen, Marty," Lee said, her teasing expression suddenly replaced by maternal concern. "We've known each other a long time. You know you can talk to me. What's going on here? Is something wrong? I mean, first those weirdos in trench coats come around here and now . . . *this*." She made a sweeping gesture around the office.

Poker-faced, he looked in her eyes. "There's nothing wrong, Lee. Nothing at all." He forced a chuckle and added, "At least nothing that Housekeeping can't fix."

Sensing she'd intruded too far, Lee gave out a sigh. "Well, okay then. Whatever you say. I'll be in my office if you need me."

"Thanks. I appreciate that."

Frowning to herself, Lee sidestepped Zak Restin on her way out the door.

"Jesus!" Zak exclaimed, walking in to survey the damage. "What the hell happened here? Looks like our meeting's off, huh?"

"Not a chance," Marty barked from behind his desk. "I may have some cleaning to do, but I still want to know how Arrow's creative is coming along. Let's get together over lunch at twelve in the executive conference room."

Zak nodded dutifully. "I'll pass the word on to everybody else," he promised as he trailed out the door.

"Thanks," Marty said gratefully as he settled into his chair. He picked up the phone and dialed Ford Sinclair.

"Marty, the ad man . . . hey, what's going on?" Sinclair boomed as if he'd known him for a hundred years. "Things go all right yesterday?" he asked, his voice taking a sympathetic turn. "You know, at the funeral?"

"Forget yesterday," Marty retorted. "Let's talk about today. Right now things aren't going so good."

"How's that?"

"Somebody followed me to work this morning . . ."

"Followed you?" Sinclair chuckled.

"Hey, I'm not kidding around here. I was followed to work and I'd put money on it that it was the same bastards who broke in my office last night and trashed it."

"Somebody broke into your office?" The detective took a deep breath. "You're not kidding, are you?"

"I'm not a kidder, Sinclair."

"You're over on Michigan, right? Across from the Wrigley Building? I'll call the Chicago police and ask them to send a cop right over. You know, so they can dust for prints. Maybe they'll find something."

"No. No cops. I've had my fill of guys in trench coats hanging around here, thank you. People start asking questions, you know." He'd keep his mouth shut about D'Angelo and the Mob. It was bad enough as it was; he didn't need the rumor circulating that the Mob was responsible for trashing his office. How the hell would he explain something like that?

"Well," Sinclair said morosely, "I'm sure this little housekeeping problem of yours will be a hit around the company watercooler."

"I'm sure it will. So no cops, okay? Promise me that."

Sinclair sighed. "You're making a mistake, Marty. I'm a cop and I'm probably the best friend you've got right now. And, as your friend, I've gotta tell you, not getting the police in there to look around is against my better judgment."

"Forget judgment."

"Forget judgment? Are you crazy? Whoever came in there and tore up your office forgot judgment a long time ago. . . . All they care about is what they think you have. They're looking for something, Marty. And unless my gut's letting me down, I'd say you know what that something is. Hell, you probably have some idea who it was, too."

A smile of admiration for the detective crossed Marty's face. Marty had an idea, all right. But he wouldn't tell Sinclair that. And he sure as hell wouldn't tell him that he knew what they were looking for and that he had it, right now, in his briefcase. Besides, what if this Sinclair guy wasn't the straight arrow he'd assumed? What if Sinclair was after the disc too?

"Well?" Sinclair demanded. "Are you going to tell me what they're looking for or not? Talk to me, goddammit."

"Hey, I told you everything I know, all right?"

"Yeah, sure," Sinclair snapped sarcastically. "Whatever you say."

"Good. So now that we've got that settled, did you find any fingerprints on that glass?"

"Hell no, just your father's . . . which didn't make my day. I just knew I'd find some other prints. But I've got nothing, Marty. Not a goddamned shred of evidence that says somebody killed your old man."

"What about those characters who came calling the other day?"

"I was right. They're phonies. Probably Mob."

"No way," Marty scoffed. "The guys that came up here were too smooth. Too Anglo for that action."

"They were pretty good actors. . . . They fooled you."

"Yeah," Marty admitted, his eyes darting around the office now as he calculated how long it would take to clean up the mess.

"I'll do some more checking," Sinclair promised. "In the meantime, maybe we could put together an artist's rendering. You got a good look at them, right? We could run a sketch through our files. Who knows, we might turn something up." He paused. "You got a computer in that fancy office of yours, don't you?"

"I think I still do," Marty replied, turning to the screen and hitting a few keys. A menu came up. "Yeah, I do."

"Great. We'll handle this over the phone, by computer. I'll have an artist give you a call, set it all up."

"Sounds good to me. So we'll talk later?"

"Yeah, I'll give you a call." Sinclair paused. "Before we hang up—now don't go bustin' my balls here—but can't you think of *something* those characters might've been looking for?"

"I don't have the slightest idea." Marty shrugged and smiled into the phone. "A good ad?"

* * *

As Marty surveyed the disaster area that was now his office, a timid knock sounded on the door. Looking up, he saw Judy Heron, the Arrow account supervisor, peering in.

"Sorry to bother you, Marty," the petite brunette apologized, looking around at the paper-strewn floor, "but I had to catch you before the meeting. We've got a problem." She unloaded an armful of reports on his desk with a thud. "A big one."

"A problem? What kind of problem?"

"Well . . ." she began, leafing through one of the stacks of paper, "I think the facts pretty much speak for themselves." She handed him a document. "The focus group hated Frank Torello. They thought he should've been the one swinging from a vine, not some howler monkey."

If it hadn't been such bad news, Marty would have laughed out loud. Instead, he scanned the report for a moment and then looked up.

"It's pretty obvious, Marty. Don't you think? We can't use Frank Torello as Arrow's spokesperson. He's got the wrong look. It just won't work."

Marty nodded, taken with the image of Frank Torello decked out in a loincloth, swinging through trees. "So then," he said finally, dropping his little fantasy, "we have a problem with Torello. Using him on-screen wasn't our idea to begin with. I don't think anybody here is going to be surprised by this report."

Judy nodded nervously, twiddling her pen in her hand, looking like she wished she could be anyplace else in the world but there, in her boss's office.

"I take it there's more?"

"Yeah." She sighed. "There's more. Research says there's a problem with name recognition and product identification, too. The focus group couldn't get it straight who the advertiser was, couldn't hold an image of the product in their minds. The Isaac Arrow name and product got lost in all those fast edits of birds and shamans. Looks to me like Zak was trying to squeeze a minute-long message into a thirty-second slot . . . which, as the focus group points out, just doesn't work."

"And what about credibility?"

She shuffled through more papers. "That's an issue, too. With all those Maya shamans and healers in the spot, the focus group got hung up on witch-doctor crap. Zak may have been trying to honor the people of the rainforest and their healing arts, but all the focus group saw was hocus-pocus, mumbo-jumbo, not the beginning of some magical journey on the road to the production of wonder drugs."

"Doesn't sound good."

"No . . . no, it doesn't."

"So what are your conclusions?"

"Well, I think most people, at least the people we're targeting, just aren't ready to put their health care in the hands of some 'weird-looking Indian running around in the woods.' By the way, those are Research's words, not mine. The focus group evidently saw all this shaman business as quackery."

Marty leaned back in his chair and looked up at the ceiling. He heard what she was saying. Hell, the research didn't lie. But that didn't mean he had to be happy about it. Truth was, he was as crazy about the campaign as Zak Restin was. For one, even the client loved it—and shouldn't the client know its own target's likes and dislikes?

"You know the client loved the concept," he commented, returning his attention to the research document.

"Yes, I know. And that does present some problems, but Research doesn't think this ad is past the point of no return. I think Zak could put a spin on a few things and still keep the stuff everybody loves. Really, the main problem he has to address is our target's attitude. You know the one: 'Herbs are for California fruits and nuts.' "

"Yeah, yeah, yeah. Herbs belong in a shampoo bottle, or maybe a tea or health-food store—not in a *real* drug that really works."

"And that's what our commercial has to get through to the consumer, Marty." She was suddenly passionate. "We have to make them see that Isaac Arrow's new over-the-counter drugs are going to change their lives forever. That they'll change the way people eat, sleep, think . . . love." Judy hesitated, her ruddy cheeks flushing slightly at the realization that she'd forgotten herself.

There was a brief, awkward moment and then she cleared her throat and plunged on. "In my opinion, Marty, if we communicate that, we'll make the old melatonin craze look like a one-trick pony. Zak's biggest challenge isn't going to be what to do with Frank Torello—it's making sure the high-tech angle comes through in a spot filmed entirely in a rainforest."

"Hmm . . . that'll be a challenge, all right," Marty agreed thoughtfully.

Judy studied him intently, enjoying the opportunity to watch Marty English's legendary agency mind in action.

"I've got it!" he exclaimed, leaping up from his chair. "Since it can't all be filmed in the rainforest, we'll shoot some additional footage in Arrow's VR lab for this first ad and make sure the viewer really gets a look at the packaged product in the high-tech environment. And we'll resolve the Torello problem by using him as the announcer instead of putting him on-screen."

"Perfect!" Her wide face broke into an admiring smile. "I think that would work. Zak wouldn't have to trash the whole concept, either, just rework it."

"Which means we'd make deadline."

"I just hope Zak understands we can't wait to get into the nuts and bolts of the product line until later in the campaign. By then it'll be too late." She stood up, looking at him apprehensively. "I'm sure Zak's going to be pleased to hear this."

"I'm sure," he agreed bitterly.

"Oh yeah, one last comment," she said, heading for the door. "One I think Zak will appreciate. The focus groups said the ad was . . . too MTV."

Marty shook his head as he picked up the phone to call Housekeeping. Someone else was going to have to clean up the mess in his office; he had other messes to deal with.

"Too what?" Zak yelled, his dark face suddenly mottled. He looked up at Marty from across the conference table.

"Too MTV," Marty repeated calmly.

"Too MTV?"

"Hey, that's the word from Research. The consumer needs to see the product and they need a name they can hold on to. We have to enhance the line's credibility and show the benefit to the consumer." Marty paused. "It's all getting lost, Zak . . . in all the rainforest beauty shots and primitive music and Indians." At the expression on Zak's face, he added, "I'm just telling you what the focus group said."

"Well, except for the fact that they hated Torello, they're all fucking idiots." Zak shook his head in disgust. "So, what's the bottom line?"

"For starters, we're going to have to use Frank Torello somewhere. My guess is that voice-over talent is as good a place as any. At least his face will be off-screen."

Zak nodded sullenly. "And?"

"And, since the consumer needs to see the high-tech side of this product, you'll have to integrate some footage from Arrow's VR lab into the spot."

"Fuck them," Zak bellowed. He stood up, slamming his chair under the table.

"Sorry I'm late," Bill Kidman broke in, slipping into his chair. "I was waiting for Lee. She wanted me to tell you she can't make it. She's busy hammering out a deal for Arrow's Super Bowl spot." He looked over at Zak. "I'm afraid to ask. Is there a problem?"

"Problem?" Zak sneered. "What the fuck isn't a problem?" Trembling with anger, Zak glared at Marty. "This Arrow spot isn't supposed to be a motherfucking infomercial selling hair in a goddamned spray can. And we're not selling widgets

here, either. This is about sizzle, about *image*. This spot's supposed to evoke a primal emotion in the viewer, a spiritual connection."

Marty tried not to smile; it was obvious as hell Zak had
committed the cardinal sin: He'd fallen in love with his own
creation.

"This has to be more than sizzle, Zak," Marty said flatly.
"This spot has to *sell*. This isn't *Happy Days*, this is the
nineties. Price and item grab the consumer."

"I thought we wanted something more than just another
Endall aspirin spot," Zak snapped back. "Shit, if we want
price and item, we can just shoot Torello standing in front of
a few pill bottles in a fucking drugstore."

Kidman frowned. "I take it Judy Heron had bad news from
Research?"

Zak nodded. "They hate Torello."

"You're kidding!" Kidman exclaimed. "That's what this is
all about? That's not bad news." He looked at Marty. "You
mean we can get rid of Torello and his Elvis hair?"

"Oh no, we're stuck with Torello," Zak said sarcastically.
"He pays the bills, remember?"

"That's not exactly a revelation, Zak," Kidman taunted.

"Well, the rest is," Zak snarled. "Get this. According to
research, the focus group thinks the spot's too . . . are you
ready? Too MTV."

Kidman burst out laughing and turned to Marty. "How old
were the people in these focus groups anyway?"

"The focus group mirrored our target audience," Marty
said. "Adults twenty-five-plus. I wouldn't say that's limiting.
That's half the country."

"Well, what's the logic in going along with the research
anyway?" Zak argued. "The client liked the concept—"

"Hey," Marty cut him off. "Whether we like the results of
the copy-test or not, you know we've got to live with them.
We're here to do the best job we can for the client—in spite
of the client if we have to."

"But if we change the spot," Zak insisted, "we'll lose the inherent drama. We're introducing a brand-new product in the goddamned *Super Bowl* . . . the biggest TV event in the whole fucking world. The ad we produce has to compete with fifty-five other spots for the viewer's attention—it has to cut through the clutter. To do that, we *have* to have drama, Marty. And drama is rainforests, not fucking pill bottles."

"Don't let your desire to film the Second Coming overshadow the fact that we're selling something here," Marty shot back. "Drama's all well and good, but we can't let our core selling message get lost in theatrics. MTV or otherwise."

Pouting, Zak crumbled into his chair, refusing to look at them. "Yeah. So that's it, huh?"

Marty nodded.

"So what do you want me to do?"

"I want you to rise to the challenge. And I want you to do it without making major changes in the concept. Get the research report from Judy and look it over. If the focus group thinks all the stuff about the rainforest is hocus-pocus, figure out a way to overcome that perception. Back off on the beauty and spotlight the benefit. Make sure our consumer has a good reason to buy our product. Keep the benefit of the product top of mind. I know where you were going with this campaign, Zak. And believe it or not, I liked it. But that doesn't change the fact that we've got a few too many edits and not enough product."

"Marty's right, Zak," Kidman asserted. "This isn't just about potions from the past. It's about how Isaac Arrow has taken those things and used modern science to make them better." Kidman paused. "Hey, I admit I'm no creative director, Zak, but as far as I can tell, that's where we need to be with Arrow's herbal product line. Take the audience on a journey, fine, but don't forget to show them how Arrow's VR technology is going to take them into a whole new age."

Marty smiled to himself; sometimes he forgot how truly talented and bright these guys were. "That's where Arrow's credibility comes in, Zak," he added. "It's basically rainforest appeal combined with technology."

"Oh, that old shit," Zak scoffed. "High-tech, high-touch . . . Jesus, did I just step back in time or what?"

"No," Marty flared, "you just stepped back into reality."

Kidman moaned, "So now I have to revise my estimate, right? Thank God for the weekend."

"Yeah, thank God," Zak said, his voice barely audible.

The kid wasn't used to this kind of bullshit, not yet anyway. Oh, he'd toughen up eventually, get a few calluses. Or else end up leaving advertising to try his hand at something else. But it wouldn't take a guy like Zak Restin long to find out that there wasn't anything else. Everybody in business was a whore. When he got that straight, well, then Zak wouldn't be just a good creative director, he'd be a great one.

Zak didn't look up. "Do me a favor. Okay? Leave me alone for a while."

Marty nodded at Kidman. "Sure," he replied gruffly as they headed for the door. "But I expect you to deliver. Monday I meet with the client. And if they're not happy, we're in trouble."

The weekend flew by. Marty spent Saturday and Sunday in his office, doing paperwork and catching up on the trades. He dropped in on his team occasionally, as much as anything to let the troops know he was there, putting in the same hours they were, missing out on all those great activities he'd long since forgotten.

In Production, Bill Kidman hunkered down over his desk, poring over vendor invoices and old jobs while making urgent phone calls to suppliers, trying to get a fix on costs for the Isaac Arrow ad campaign. He stayed that way for most of the weekend, dressed the entire time in the same pair of rumpled khakis, held up by his regulation suspenders, and a hand-knit cardigan two sizes too big. Except for a quick hello and the gift of a Moon Pie, Kidman's favorite down-home treat, Marty left him alone.

On Sunday morning, the tension in the office was high; Kidman brought in two boxes of Krispy Kreme doughnuts and then disappeared into Creative with Zak to put together the final storyboards, talent selections, and music production.

It was after eight that Sunday night when Zak and Kidman finally marched into Marty's office and announced wearily, "We made it."

Chapter 18

With the office deserted late Sunday evening, Marty settled down in front of his computer to study the computerized sketches Ford Sinclair had modemed over to his office earlier that day. The artist had captured the two agents perfectly, all the way down to Harper's cold little snake eyes and Kemper's wooden smile.

Marty was scrutinizing the images on his computer screen when the phone in his office rang.

There was a silence on the line and then: "Looks like we've got a little misunderstanding, Marty."

Recognizing Mike D'Angelo's voice, Marty's heart skipped a beat. Still, his reply didn't betray his wariness. "Misunderstanding?" he said evenly.

"Yeah. Between you . . . and me."

Marty didn't reply; he'd let the mobster do the talking. He wouldn't say that he knew he was being tailed by D'Angelo's men or that he was sure they were the ones who'd trashed his office.

"I thought we agreed you wouldn't play cops and robbers?"

Marty felt a knot in his stomach as his eyes darted over to the expanse of window—hell, he was sitting in a fucking fishbowl. "Cops and robbers, Mike? What are you—"

"Cut the fucking bullshit, Marty, okay? You're good with pictures, so I hear, so let me draw you one."

You're good with pictures? Was D'Angelo playing word games? Or did he know about the artist's renderings? Marty looked at the image of the agents on his screen and flipped off the monitor. "Draw me a picture?" Marty repeated sarcastically. Mike D'Angelo was like a junkyard dog: if he thought Marty was intimidated, he'd go for the throat. "I didn't know you were artistically inclined, Mike." The sarcasm was still there, more pointed now. "I'm learning something new about you every day."

"Now's not the time to be a fucking wiseass. I happen to know you haven't been straight with me from the beginning. That's not smart, Marty. There's other guys in this besides me. They don't know you like I do; they don't give a fuck. They seem to think you have the shit we're looking for. So be smart, okay? Leave the cops out of this."

"I don't know what you're talking about."

"You're a liar, Marty." The words came out evenly, as if they'd been bitten off, one syllable at a time. And suddenly, Marty knew that Mike D'Angelo, family friend and surrogate uncle, could as easily put a gun to Marty's head and blow his brains out as tie his shoes. "I know you met with a cop at the Domino the other night," D'Angelo continued. "Don't try to bullshit me. I *know* you're a motherfucking liar."

Marty's hand went tight around the phone but he managed to keep his voice easy, almost indifferent. "So I sat at a table with a cop who likes the blues? You got a problem with that?"

"A cop's a cop."

"Well, that may be, but that's all there was to my 'meeting' at the Domino. A few drinks and some blues with a guy whose jurisdiction isn't even in Chicago."

"You expect me to believe that?"

"Yeah, I do." Marty paused. "Let's not beat around the bush here, Mike. Why the hell are you watching me?"

D'Angelo laughed into the phone. "The game's over, Marty.

I know you're a liar. And you know what happens to liars? A liar spends his life looking over his shoulder. But sooner or later, his day comes. He puts that car key in the ignition and . . . *boom*."

There was a click and then a dial tone. Mike D'Angelo was gone.

Stunned, Marty glared at the receiver in his hand. If his suspicions were right, it was the enemy too, a mechanical agent for D'Angelo and his thugs right there in his office. "Fuck you, Mike," he said aloud, slamming it down. He looked around the room. "Did you hear me, Mike?" he yelled. "I said fuck you. And while you're at it, fuck your friends, too."

The agency's parking garage was empty—and unusually quiet, even for eleven o'clock on a Sunday night.

Somewhere in the distance, Marty heard a steel door close and then the echo of footsteps on concrete. They were decisive, purposeful footsteps, footsteps that were coming his way through the fog and shadows. He stopped and listened, looking over his shoulder, into the fog.

Nothing. Nothing but empty space.

A damp winter fog had settled into the cavernous concrete tomb, draining the area of color and light and replacing it with a thick, flat-gray shadow. The walls and floor dripped with beads of condensation and what few cars there were had been glazed by the fog, their windshields coated with a tenacious mist.

They were watching, just like D'Angelo said. He knew it. Shit, Marty thought bitterly, D'Angelo had him spooked, and he suddenly realized the depth of his fear.

He searched the fog for his car and, at the sight of the Jaguar, felt for his keys in his coat pocket and hurried over. Yeah, D'Angelo had him psyched out, all right. The bastard.

He pulled his keys out of his pocket and fiddled with them at the car door. They clanged metallically in his hand, sounding louder than usual. Over the clanging came the sound of footsteps. They were coming his way again, closer this time. He opened the door and got in and slid behind the wheel, peering into the rearview mirror as he closed the door. The garage was empty. There was nobody there; he'd probably heard his own footsteps, echoing through the garage. Yeah, it was all in his head. That's what the Mob did: They made you paranoid, made you sick with worry, so sick you couldn't sleep at night.

As Marty raised the key to the ignition, D'Angelo's threat came back and he hesitated, his hand holding the key in freeze frame, in midair. No, goddammit, he wouldn't live like those guys D'Angelo was talking about. He wouldn't spend his entire life looking over his shoulder. A guy did that and the Mob had him; hell, he was as good as dead.

Not him. The only way to win this game was not to play. Marty set his jaw and stabbed the key into the ignition, turning it in the mechanism in one swift motion.

Hearing the reassuring purr of the Jaguar's engine, he smiled. "Fuck you, Mike," he mumbled under his breath as he put his hand on the gear shift.

At the abrupt jangle of his cell phone lying on the console between the seats, Marty jumped, jerking his hand off the stick.

He sat there, looking at the phone, listening to it ring again and again. No. He wouldn't let it happen. The phone was ringing more insistently now. *No. Not him.*

He reached over, punched the power button off and threw the gear shift into reverse, slamming the accelerator to the floor. Then, with a squeal of tires, he sped out of the garage.

There wasn't much traffic that time of night. The streets were foggy, a combination of car exhaust and the thick soup that always rolled in from Lake Michigan on nights like this. But it felt right, somehow, and Marty sighed a sigh of relief and flipped on the radio as he passed over the Chicago River. An old Doors tune was playing: "Riders on the Storm." Not exactly a lullaby. He cranked it up and stepped on the gas and Jim Morrison's words spun out, enveloping him in their velvet spell.

Marty was coming up on the Chicago Water Tower when he suddenly felt eyes on his back. He looked in the rearview mirror. Shit. Yeah, there it was. Big as fucking life: a car, hidden in the fog, gliding like a death ship. Slipping up behind him. Getting closer with each moment. Was it the same car he'd seen before? He slowed, trying to make it out, but the glare of traffic lights blinded him, obscuring his vision.

At Chicago Avenue, he took a deep breath and, tires screeching, whipped around the corner. He looked in the rearview mirror. The car was still there.

He drove two blocks, keeping his eyes glued to the mirror, and turned right on Rush Street, weaving in and out of traffic. He was forced to slow down; the yuppies were still out, flocking like lemmings to the bars. They were mostly white-collar types looking to wrap up the weekend with a microbrew, or desperate meathounds, still hoping to get laid. Taxi drivers and condom makers did a swift business on Rush and Division.

Marty turned onto Delaware and headed east, leaving the crowds behind. He crossed over Michigan Avenue, passing the John Hancock Building and Water Tower Place. Still he couldn't outmaneuver the car following him. He took another left, went a block, and turned on East Walton.

At the realization that the Astor was just ahead, he smiled to himself. The Astor wasn't exactly a dark alley, and the Mob didn't like the glare of bright lights. Maybe he was home free, he thought as he shot into the circular drive and, brakes squealing, came to a stop. He turned off his headlights and waited.

Ominously, the car pulled into the drive and parked behind him. Shit. Maybe he'd been thinking of vampires, Marty thought ruefully, not mobsters, when he'd considered the

Astor's bright lights some sort of protection. Obviously, it didn't matter to the guy behind him if this was Times Square.

So this was it. The showdown. D'Angelo hadn't wasted any time, had he? In the old days the Mob took their time, made their victims sweat.

But this wasn't the old days, Marty reminded himself as he took a deep breath and opened the car door. He heard the other car door open, heard feet hit the pavement, and his heart began to pound.

At the friendly wave of Flannigan the doorman, Marty saw his only chance: He'd make a scene, that's what he'd do—maybe that would make the son of a bitch think twice before pulling the trigger. The Mob might not care about the glare of lights anymore, but they definitely had a thing about witnesses.

"All right . . ." Marty yelled, getting out and slamming the door behind him. "What the fuck do you want?"

"A good ad?" a voice answered from within the heavy fog.

"Sinclair?" Marty went limp with relief. He wanted to laugh. "Ford . . . Ford, is that you?"

"Who'd you think it was?" Sinclair cracked, stepping out of the mist. "The good fairy?"

"Shit, I didn't know. I saw you back there. I thought you were one of the guys who's been tailing me."

"Oh, I was tailing you all right. Hell, I've been trying to call you on your goddamned cell phone for half an hour." He smiled grimly. "I've got some news."

"On the sketches?"

Sinclair glanced uneasily at the headlights of a lone car coming toward them. "Let's sit in my car for a minute. Okay?" He opened the passenger door. "I think I'm being followed too."

"*Too*? So, you believe me now?" Marty asked, climbing in and closing the door.

"Yeah, I do now . . . after seeing this." Sinclair tapped at a file lying in the seat between them. "Kemper and Harper?

They're anything but FBI." He paused. "They're CIA, Marty."

"*Fucking* CIA?" Marty repeated, astonished. "Are you sure?"

"Sure as death and taxes."

"But why would the CIA be interested in me . . . or my father? I thought the FBI, not the CIA, was after the Mob."

Sinclair shrugged, reached for a stainless thermos, and pulled a packet of Sweet'n Low out of his pocket. "Gotta watch my waistline," he explained, patting his spreading middle as he tore open the packet.

Marty sat lost in thought for several long minutes. He'd thought the Mob was the enemy, but now, with this news about the CIA? What the hell was going on? He turned to Sinclair and abruptly asked, "Think you could find out what Kemper and Harper have been up to the past few years?"

"I'm way ahead of you. I already tried." Sinclair paused and looked Marty directly in the eye. "But I gotta go in the back door. It's classified."

"Classified? So we'll never know what the hell this is about."

Sinclair pulled an Almond Joy from his pocket and began unwrapping it. Obviously he'd already forgotten about his waistline. "I've got a source. But no guarantees." The detective took a bite of the candy bar and promised, "I'll give it my best shot."

Marty suddenly remembered something important. "I'll be out of town next week, in Central America."

"Business or pleasure?"

"Business. We're shooting a commercial down in Belize for a pharmaceutical client of ours—Isaac Arrow."

"It's probably best you're out of town for a while, anyway."

Marty frowned. He wasn't accustomed to having a cop be concerned about his welfare.

"Listen," Sinclair explained, "I think those CIA boys mean business. Hell, I imagine they've got us both under surveillance by now. Maybe even tapped our phones, our offices . . . shit . . ." He shrugged in frustration. "Who knows?"

Smiling, Marty shook his head. "I think you're overreacting, Sinclair." At the expression on the detective's face, he added, "Hey, maybe we both are. I mean, Jesus, I thought you were a goddamned hit man just now, following me."

"No, we're not overreacting," Sinclair retorted, eyes flashing. "This is fucking CIA we're talking about here, Marty. Those boys are a different breed. They're not like the feds. Truth, justice and all that flag-waving crap. Shit, they're not like your Daddy's guys in the Mob, either. They're a hell of a lot worse."

Marty started to protest, but Sinclair cut him off. "The game's different with the CIA. Don't believe all that public relations crap about a new, law-abiding agency. These guys can't afford to lose. And they'll do whatever it takes to win. You hear me, Marty? *Whatever* it takes, including killing."

Chapter 19

Reiki was asleep when Marty walked in, but he stopped in the bedroom long enough to lean over and give her a kiss. Her eyes fluttered open. "You're home," she said with a drowsy smile.

"Yeah." He kissed her again. "Long day."

"Guess what?"

"What?"

"I heard about the assignment in Rwanda."

"You did? And?" He sat down on the side of the bed.

"I got it. . . . I take off tomorrow morning for a week."

"Congratulations, Ms. Devane," he declared, forcing a smile. He wouldn't tell her that he'd planned to ask her to come with him to Belize. They each had their careers, after all.

"Thanks." She rubbed at her eyes. "How about Arrow?"

"We've got it covered."

"So then," she said, sitting up and propping the pillows behind her, "you take off for Belize on Tuesday, right?"

"Yeah, around noon."

She studied his face for a moment. "Any more visits from your agent friends?"

"No. And don't look so worried. The only thing strange that's happened since my office was redecorated happened just now, coming home." He wouldn't tell her about D'Angelo's call, about his growing suspicions. He forced a chuckle. "Can you believe I thought I was being followed?"

Her eyes widened.

"It was nothing . . . just that detective, Ford Sinclair." He shrugged. "Hell, my imagination's running wild."

"And we know you're one for flights of fancy," she declared, putting her hand on his arm. "Why don't you come to bed?"

He shook his head. "I'm not tired."

"I leave tomorrow. . . ." She smiled that inviting smile she always did when she wanted to make love.

But he wasn't in the mood, though he wasn't sure why; he pretended he didn't catch on. "I don't think I could sleep right now. Not yet anyway. I need to unwind."

He started to stand, but she held on to his wrist and didn't let go. "I know just the thing to help my man unwind," she said slyly.

"I know you do," he replied, a sad note in his words. He smiled solemnly and brushed her hair back from her eyes. "But I think I'll just go out in the living room and relax for a while." At her wounded expression, he kissed her lightly on the lips. "I won't be long."

"Is that a promise?"

"Cross my heart."

"Okay then," she said brightly—too brightly, he thought. "You're off the hook for now." She snuggled down into the blankets. "But remember . . . I'll be waiting."

Chapter 20

Visibility was close to zero at Meigs Field in the early hours of Monday morning. Sleet and snow pelted the tarmac, blurring the blue runway lights that rolled out in the distance.

Del Waters sat in his well-appointed Gulfstream jet, tapping his cigar on the ashtray. He'd been waiting for Roger Kemper for half an hour; his patience was wearing thin.

At last the door opened and the shivering agent stepped inside. Swearing under his breath at the cold, Kemper slapped a leather glove at the ice crystals clinging to his Burberry trench coat.

"What took you so long?" Waters barked. "What's the word?"

"The word is we've got a situation," Kemper replied, taking off his coat. "Looks like that cop talked English into working with a police artist to come up with some sketches of me and Harper."

"And?"

"Our boys intercepted this." He handed Waters a laser printout.

Waters's metallic eyes grazed over the artist's renderings.

"I'd say we've blown our cover, Del."

Waters looked up. "No. We're at the point now where I don't think this warrants putting somebody else on the operation. You and Max will be keeping your distance from now on. English won't be seeing you again." He knocked the ash off his cigar. "But what about that cop, Sinclair? Sounds like he's been asking a lot of questions."

"Our sources tell us Sinclair checked our files, talked to an agent in the Chicago office, black guy by the name of Jackson, Stone Jackson. All Sinclair got from him was that we're CIA, and there's nothing illegal about that. Sinclair won't get anything more. He'll hit a brick wall. Jackson's a desk jockey—he won't stick his neck out."

"I'm getting tired of Sinclair."

"So am I. But if we stay on him, maybe he'll lead us to the disc. That is, if English has it."

"English has it all right."

"Yeah, I think so. So unless you disagree, I'd like to give Sinclair a pass for now, give him a while longer." He smiled. "Until he's served our purpose."

Waters nodded and exhaled a thin stream of smoke. "Any progress on the disc?"

"D'Angelo's gorillas didn't find anything in English's office. I figure it has to be at his place, at the Astor. Hell, we've looked everywhere else."

At the mention of D'Angelo, Waters's fingers clenched around the cigar. "Keep D'Angelo away from the Astor," he snapped, eyes gleaming. "They did a half-assed job wiring English's office and tore the place up looking for the disc while they were at it."

"It's thanks to them that English started talking to the cops."

Waters sighed. He would've liked to have removed D'Angelo from the playing field, but for now that desire had to wait. "So, Roger, what's the plan for next week when he's out of town? Are you going to get into the Astor or is his girlfriend still in the way?"

"She's going out of town on assignment."

Waters smiled appreciatively. "That's convenient."

"I thought so."

"So then they'll both be gone. That should give you enough time to go over the place with a fine-toothed comb."

"If the disc's there, Del, we'll find it. And if it isn't, well, the fucking place'll have more wires than Con Ed."

"Just make it neat."

An arrogant smile flitted across Kemper's face as he stood up and put on his coat. "He'll never know we were there."

"Good. I'll be down in Escoba all week. Let me know if you find anything."

"And if we don't?"

"Then," Waters replied coldly, tapping his cigar in the ashtray, "we'll have to make other arrangements."

Chapter 21

It was still dark when Reiki climbed out of bed. "Where are you going?" Marty asked drowsily.

"Got to get up," she whispered. "My plane leaves at ten, remember?"

He leaned up on one elbow and squinted at the clock. "But it's not even five-thirty," he objected. He grabbed her arm and pulled her back into the bed, sliding his arm around her.

"Marty," she protested.

He drew her close and started kissing her neck. "Just a little while longer," he said tenderly.

"Come on . . . really. I'm serious, now."

"But I want you," he said huskily, leaning over her, pinning her beneath him.

"Not now," she said, struggling against his kisses. *"Please."*

"But I want to give you a good-bye present," he teased, taking her hand and putting it between his legs.

She pulled away. "I'm not in the mood now, okay?"

"But I thought you said you'd be waiting. . . ."

"Waiting?" She rolled over and turned on the lamp, and he shielded his eyes from the sudden glare. "Maybe it's your turn to wait for a change."

Frowning, he sat up. "What's that supposed to mean?"

"It means I've been waiting for you for *seven years.*"

So that's what all this was about. Reiki felt rejected because he hadn't wanted to make love last night. And now she was mad and was going to turn it into a major issue about something else entirely different. "That's not fair, Reiki."

"It may not be fair, but it's the truth."

"The truth is, I'm trying to make president of the agency. I'm working my ass off."

"And you're saying I don't? You think because I'm a woman I should just spread my legs whenever you whistle? Really, Marty, what a crock! I happen to have a job that takes me all over the world, but somehow I manage to find the energy to coddle your male ego. I guess I'm just not as creative as you are with the excuses. If it wasn't work, if you *were* president of Bergman, you'd just find some other reason not to hold up your end of this relationship."

She searched his face, her brown eyes welling up. "Is there somebody else? Is that it, Marty? Because if there is just let me know. . . ."

"There's nobody else."

"Then what's the problem? Why the hell can't you make a commitment?"

"I *am* committed."

"No, if you were really committed, you'd be married. You're putting success and material things before what's really important in life."

"That's not it at all," he protested, his voice rising. "I told you before, I'm just not ready for marriage."

"Not ready?" She shook her head. "Goddammit, Marty, I'm not your mother." She saw him wince but pressed on. "I'm not going to promise to stay with you forever and then leave. I won't do that."

"Like I said, I'm not ready." He glared at her. "And I don't like being pushed."

"Oh, so now I'm being pushy, is that it? I've been waiting for you to 'be ready' for seven fucking years, and now, just because I'd like a little stability, some direction in our lives, now I'm being fucking pushy? It just so happens that I want more for us than . . ." She waved around the room. "Than all this. I want a house in the country with friends and fresh air. Time's running out. We're not kids anymore. I want to have a family, Marty."

"We could always adopt."

She glowered at him. "You just can't handle this, can you?"

"I guess not." He shrugged defiantly.

"Well, neither can I—*anymore*."

"What the hell does *that* mean?" He sat up straighter.

She shook her head and started out the door.

"Well?"

"Never mind," she shot back. "Forget it."

"Are you telling me that if I don't marry you, you're going to call it quits?" The fact that she didn't answer infuriated him. "God, and here I thought you were a liberated woman," he yelled.

Shaking her head, she spun around. "Jesus, you're so god-damned good at bullshitting, you've actually conned yourself."

"You want to talk about bullshit?" He climbed out of bed. "Well, I'll tell you what's bullshit. All that crap you hand out about being a feminist. And about freedom. When it comes down to it, you're no different than all those other women you look down on all the time who grew up playing Barbie and Ken."

Trembling with anger, she turned on her heel. Regretting his words, he called after her, "Reiki wait . . . I . . . I'm sorry."

She turned around. "So am I, Marty," she said softly, tears streaming down her cheeks. "So am I."

They didn't call it blue Monday for nothing, but Marty thought this one was more miserable than most.

It wasn't just the way he and Reiki had left things between them—numb and distant, without resolution, with only a formal peck on the cheek to say they cared for one another—that had put him in a funk. No, on the one morning he wanted to be in the office bright and early, Chicago's well-oiled machine of urban commerce was moving in maddening slow motion. The sidewalks and pavement were glazed and treacherous, thanks to the steady sleet blasting through the city's concrete canyons, and Marty swore to himself as he heard the DJ on WLS say that the rush-hour commute from Woodfield to downtown was taking over two hours.

With only a few blocks to drive, it still took thirty minutes to get to the Bergman building. Wynn Bergman's parking garage was usually jam-packed by seven o'clock; this morning it was half full. But things would heat up soon enough, Marty reminded himself as he parked his car; this was the quiet before the storm. As usual, there were too many things to do and not enough time to do them, and today would be worse than most.

As he got on the empty elevator and headed up to his office, he looked at his watch again; he hadn't even gotten to his desk and he already felt under the gun. But then he wasn't exactly in top form today; he'd hardly slept all night, thinking about the disc, about his father. Hell, it was impossible *not* to think about it all. And now this thing with Reiki . . .

The elevator door opened on the third floor and Lee Wilde stepped in with a crisp clip of her stiletto patent-leather heels.

"Marty," she gushed. "Just the guy I wanted to see."

"I don't trust enthusiasm at this hour," he teased wearily. "Especially from you."

She laughed. "*This* hour? Where've you been? The day's half over."

"So I take it you wanted to see me?"

"That's right. First off, Arrow's *in* the Super Bowl. You heard me, they're *in* the game, Marty. Not before it, not after it. *In* it. And get this: They're in at the two-minute warning."

Sensing she wanted to flaunt her victory, Marty grinned. "So are you going to tell me how you managed to accomplish this miracle?"

"I was hoping you'd ask. You see, it just so happens that there's this beer company—"

"Uh-huh."

"—that bought into the Super Bowl. But to get an exclusive beer sponsorship, they had to buy four spots when they only wanted three."

"And one of your friends in network sales negotiated a buyout of the extra spot?"

She beamed proudly. "How'd you ever guess?"

"What's the price tag?"

"Are you ready?" She took a deep breath. "Two million."

"That's five hundred thousand more than anybody else is paying."

"I never said it would be cheap. I just hope Arrow doesn't balk."

"They don't care what it costs, remember?"

"I remember. I just don't believe it. Hell, I never believe a client. There's not a one of them that's as loyal as a dog in heat."

"You must have heard about NHP," he laughed. "But it isn't *their* loyalty that's in question. They're happy with us— it's Hexall that's the problem. Now that their buyout of NHP's a done deal, they're the ones pushing for an agency change."

She nodded sullenly. "Bastards."

Marty laughed again.

"Hey," she snapped, "unlike you, I don't find losing six hundred million in billings to another agency very humorous. Especially not to one like Todd, Gattwick, and Lorenz. Those fucking guys don't know shit about NHP's business." She paused. "And by the way, just for your information, Wynn is pretty nervous about this situation."

"I would expect him to be. But it's all in how you look at it, Lee. In your perspective. You're thinking of this as a problem, like it was the enemy."

"Well, isn't it?"

"No, it's an opportunity." If there was one piece of advice

Marty's father had left him with, it was never to take the defensive. If there's blood in the water, even if it's your own blood, go for the other guy's throat. Marty smelled blood on this deal. Forget saving NHP, that was just the beginning. He was going to do that *and* get Hexall in the process.

The elevator doors opened on the eighteenth floor. Intrigued, Lee followed Marty, her high heels clipping on the marble floor, into his office.

Marty walked behind his desk. "You're putting together that postbuy analysis for NHP, aren't you?"

"Yeah," she replied cautiously. "What about it?"

"Can you have it ready when I get back from Belize?"

"Sure," she said, sitting down. "But what's the point? It's just a formality. NHP already knows we do a good job."

"Just have it ready, okay?"

Lee's eyes narrowed. "What are you up to, golden boy?"

"Golden boy? Why, thanks, Lee," Marty teased. "I had no idea you were such a fan."

She put her hands on her slender hips and retorted, "Well, don't go getting too cocky. I may be a fan, but not everybody else is. In fact, at this very moment I think the entire Human Resources Department is creating a dartboard in your image."

"Why? What's going on?"

"You didn't hear? H.R. got a request from Isaac Arrow's security department, asking us to release the personnel files for everybody connected with their account. They want us all to sign off on background checks." Lee frowned. "And guess who's doing them?"

He stared back at her blankly.

"The U.S. State Department, that's who. Let's just hope nobody here at Bergman has any skeletons rattling around in their closet."

Marty nodded. On the surface he conveyed an air of unconcern, but beneath the facade he was stunned. He'd never been worried about having his real identity come to light. After all, his legal records had been sealed by the court; his past had been buried for years. But a background check by a sophisticated government agency was a different matter altogether. The State Department would find out who he was, all right. And when they did? His connection to Tony Inglesia would cause a hell of a scandal, probably kill the deal with Arrow's conservative board—and jeopardize his career at Bergman too. "Are you sure they said background checks by the State Department?" he asked lightly. "Really, Lee, that sounds sort of extreme."

"Yeah. I'm sure." She frowned. "Why the hell do you suppose they need a security clearance on all of us?"

He shook his head slowly. "I don't know," he replied thoughtfully. Nobody at Arrow had said anything to him about such elaborate security checks. Sure, the company was big on security—he'd seen that firsthand when he went down to the VR lab. But this? He wondered why they'd want such a thing. And even more, he wondered why the State Department would be involved.

"Human Resources is going nuts trying to get through all the red tape before you guys get back from Belize and start the photo shoot at Arrow. You think this could hold up production? If it does, we'll never make the Super Bowl."

"If there was a chance of that, Arrow would've mentioned it before."

"Well, I can't imagine this is something they do with every company they work with. Can you?"

"No," he replied, his thoughts racing. "No, I can't."

Marty ate a bagel at his desk and scrambled through the stacks of paperwork that always mysteriously appeared when he was scheduled to go out of town. Although he'd already checked his appointment book, he did it again, making sure he was clear for the rest of the week. He canceled a Wednesday night racquetball game with some friends from the gym. Rescheduled a haircut. Flipped through a few client files. Then he picked up the phone to call Reiki.

It was just eight-thirty: he still had time to talk to her before she left for the airport, although he didn't have the slightest idea what he was going to say, other than the routine "Good-bye, I love you, have a safe trip" crap. But that wasn't enough to make things right; he didn't want to leave things like they were. He didn't want her anger—or was it hurt?—just to lie there and fester until they were together again.

So what should he say? he asked himself as listened to the phone ring. Hell, why kid himself? He should tell her he loved her, that's what. He should say he really wasn't married to his work. That he wasn't afraid of commitment, either—no, that what he was really afraid of was failure. He let out a sigh as his thoughts drifted to his mother.

"Hello."

"Reiki?"

"The one and only." She sounded hurried, distant. "What's up?"

He hesitated. "Oh, just the usual craziness. I guess I was just wondering if you missed me." He frowned. Couldn't he do better than that? Hell, he was known for his up-front communication skills. For that direct, take-charge style he'd honed to perfection. But here he was acting like some tongue-tied kid.

"Missed you?" she replied softly. "I haven't even left yet."

For a moment he thought she might be warming up, that he'd found some opening of affection where he could wiggle in with a word or two about his feelings.

"I'm sorry, Marty," she went on, "but I've got a cab coming in ten minutes. I really can't talk right now."

His heart sank. "Sure," he said, forcing a happy tone. "No problem. I know how it is."

"I've go to go," she said, sounding distracted.

"Something wrong?"

"It's the doorman on the intercom, Marty. My cab's already here."

He knew he should say more, but all he could think of was: "Well, watch out for those Baptiste types in Rwanda."

"Will do," she promised crisply.

"I love you, Reiki."

"I love you too," she replied, a sudden tightness in her voice. "Bye."

Chapter 22

As he entered the impressive ivy-covered brownstone on West Wacker Drive that was home to Planetlife International, Marty felt as if he'd slipped back in time, back into a world inhabited by old-money blue bloods and tweedy pipe-smoking academia. The only sign of modernization in the director's office was a computer workstation on a carved mahogany desk. The style of the grandly appointed room was old-school traditional with heavy velvet drapes and heavy air that smelled of molding books and leather. There were a dozen antique globes stationed around the room. The walls were hung with faded, yellowing maps of faraway lands and rows of masks and headdresses, lending the impression that a great conference of explorers was underway.

But instead of Stanley and Livingstone, Carson Page and Frank Torello—along with another man Marty had never seen before, whom he assumed was the foundation's director, Arch Templeton—were seated around an ornate table, looking back at him from massive leather wingback chairs. Nearby stood a rolling cart, TV monitor and VCR at the ready.

"Marty, hello!" Torello exclaimed, running over to throw a brotherly arm around him.

From her place at the table, Carson Page toyed with her Mont Blanc pen. "Hello again, Marty," she said, smiling invitingly as she crossed her tanned legs, forcing her short skirt all the way up her thighs. "Looks like these meetings of ours are becoming a habit."

"A good habit," he quipped, pretending not to notice her come-on. But he had noticed, of course. How could any man not notice those long legs that went on forever? Hell, nothing beat a great pair of legs.

Torello turned Marty's attention to a tall, well-built man in wire-rims seated across from Carson. "Marty, I'd like to introduce Planetlife's director, Arch Templeton."

Marty smiled at the slightly balding man. Though he was dressed conservatively enough—gray flannel trousers, white shirt, rep tie, blue blazer—Arch Templeton looked more Marlboro Man than foundation director, thanks to his muscular physique and an old scar that sliced down one side of his deeply tanned face.

Templeton stood up and extended his hand. Marty saw it then: the sexual energy and charisma, the extreme confidence. The kind of confidence Marty recalled seeing in some of the combat-hardened guys in Vietnam.

"It's a pleasure meeting the man who's going to help us change the world," Templeton said cordially.

Carson laughed. "Arch will never be accused of underestimating the importance of what we're doing with Planetlife."

"No," Templeton allowed, shooting her a broad grin. "I may be accused of a lot of things, but underestimating you people at Arrow isn't one of them." His eyes slid admiringly over her voluptuous frame.

So that was it, Marty thought. Carson was fucking Planetlife's director. But then she seemed like the type who would go for a guy like Templeton, a man's man. And Arch Templeton was that, all right. The Gillette "Best that you can get" kind of guy. Probably an ex-Vietnam marine who could handle a machete as well as he could a straight edge. From the look of Templeton's weathered face and body, he could probably handle his fists and his liquor pretty well, too.

But Arch Templeton didn't seem like an eco-nut—definitely not your typical peaceful "save the rainforest" type or a Frank Torello nerd—a fact that made the warm relationship between Planetlife and Arrow all the more puzzling. From what Marty understood, the foundation's rainforest preserve and its wealth of medicinal herbs were the only links between the two disparate organizations.

"Carson and Frank have been singing your praises, Marty," Templeton continued. "They say you're going to do a great job."

"Nobody can do a great job without great clients," Marty said. God, the bull he had to hand out in this business. "Carson and Frank are turning out to be terrific clients."

"They also said you had all the right words." Templeton chuckled. "Have a seat; fill me in on what the three of you have cooked up for the Super Bowl."

"We've cooked up a winner," Marty declared, taking a seat next to Carson.

Nodding, she leaned over and poured him a glass of mineral water, exposing the outline of two full breasts pressed firmly against her fitted blazer.

"So, Marty," Torello boomed, "I take it we're all systems go for the Super Bowl? Got our ad in the big game?"

"Absolutely, Frank. Arrow will be at the two-minute warning. It's a beautiful position, too . . . and position is as important as being in the game. Maybe more so. We're lucky we pulled it off."

"*Lucky?*" Scowling, Templeton leaned forward in his chair. "I didn't know there was any concern about not being able to get an ad in the Super Bowl."

Templeton's affable manner was gone, replaced by the shrewd, commanding demeanor of a military man, and Marty suddenly wondered how Planetlife had gotten hooked up with Isaac Arrow in the first place. A not-for-profit that got to ride along on the coattails of a three-hundred-million-dollar ad campaign was unheard of; Templeton should've been kissing

Frank Torello's fat Elvis ass. But he wasn't doing that, not at all.

"I'd be a liar, Arch," Marty said, speaking very deliberately, "if I said there hadn't been some concern. The Super Bowl is always sold out by now."

Carson jumped in. "That's right, Arch. This wasn't the easiest thing to pull off. We're asking a lot from Bergman. I hope"—she shot a seductive smile at Marty—"we're not asking too much."

"Not at all. That's what we're here for," Marty said. "We do the impossible. That's our job."

"Well, you've certainly done that," Carson declared. "And your Media Department has done a great job, too. Which reminds me, I want your people to put together a formal media recommendation for the introductory campaign that follows the Super Bowl. Print, broadcast—you know, everything you recommended in your presentation."

"I've already got Lee Wilde working on it."

Torello shook his head appreciatively. "Is there anything you don't anticipate?"

"Thanks for the vote of confidence, Frank," Marty replied as he flipped on the monitor and put the video in the player. "By the way, I should warn you, you're going to see a few changes from the original concept, but I think you'll agree the spot's even more terrific than before."

"Well, let's take a look," Templeton urged. "I've only heard about the concept."

Marty hit the start button on the player. The animated visuals came up on-screen and Marty began walking them through the thirty-second announcement, point by point. By the time he was finished, they were beaming.

"Fantastic," Carson crowed.

"Wonderful," Torello agreed.

Templeton leaned back in his chair and crossed his arms. "I'm impressed, Marty. You and your agency are everything

Frank and Carson said you were—and more. That's going to be one hell of an ad."

"And it works perfectly with our packaging and print materials," Carson interjected. "I just love the way you used the shaman's arrow with the background vocals to seed the Arrow name."

"It's very clever," Templeton agreed. He looked over at Torello and grinned. "But I thought you were supposed to be in the spot, Frank."

Carson's arched brows knitted into her forehead. "That's right. Where's Frank?"

Marty was ready for this. "As you just saw, there isn't any on-screen talent in the revised concept. Frank will still be Arrow's spokesperson, of course. He'll just be the announcer instead of being on-screen."

So far so good.

"But why isn't there any on-screen talent?" Templeton demanded.

"The consumers we tested preferred the visuals of the lab and rainforest to seeing a talking head." He paused and smiled at Carson. "Even a talking head like Wendy's Dave Thomas . . . that sort of sales pitch just got in the way of the message and, even more importantly, it lowered the product's credibility in our target's eyes. You may have noticed in the spot that the shaman was the only person the viewer sees until we get to the lab segment. Then we see the chemists at work. From our research, the sight of scientists increased the target's confidence in the product. The focus groups judged Frank's voice as highly reassuring, so we'll be using his voice to explain Arrow's high-tech lab."

"I don't know," Carson said doubtfully. "What about the board? What do you think, Frank?"

"I think it's fine." Torello turned to Marty. "I'm comfortable with the ad being done like that. The board can do without my smiling face. They'll see the logic of what you're saying." He grinned and shrugged. "Besides, who can argue with research?" Torello paused, rubbing his fleshy palms together. "So what's this going to cost? If that's a fair question at this point."

"That's a fair question," Marty answered as he began passing out a series of embossed folders. "I think these estimates will answer that. If they don't, please tell me now because I need your sign-off on the budgets before we can start production."

Marty looked on as they dropped their eyes, studying the figures intently. Well, here they were, at the moment of truth. The time when a client put up or shut up.

Carson looked up first. "This looks fine to me, Marty. Frank, Arch, do either of you have any questions?"

Templeton looked up and took off his wire-rims. "Not now. My questions will come when we get down to Belize. I'm waiting to see how you film a thing like this."

Torello scratched at his head. "Well, I have a few questions, Marty."

"Yes?"

"Production for the spot is going to run approximately two million dollars? Is that right?"

"That's correct," Marty replied, scrambling to assess Torello's change in attitude and head off whatever objection he'd dreamed up. It couldn't be money; hadn't the Arrow people said money was no object?

"Isn't that high?"

"Yes, it is, thanks to the rush charges."

"And location, too, I imagine," Carson chimed in.

"Oh, I understand all that," Torello said with a wave of his hand. "The airtime in the Super Bowl's two million as well . . . so basically, we're spending four million dollars to be in a football game."

Marty smiled; sticker shock was common at times like this. "You're paying almost one hundred percent more for media and production because they're being purchased at such a late date. Keep in mind these figures are only estimates at this point, although I wouldn't anticipate any changes. The only missing link right now is the network's legal review. They'll be taking a look at the storyboards this afternoon. I don't expect any problems, but if Network did require some revisions, we can make them when we get back from Belize. Even so, you shouldn't see any change in the budget."

"That's good," Torello remarked, taking out a chewed-up ballpoint from his shirt pocket and signing the estimate, "because we wired an advance to your agency this morning." He passed the paper over to Marty.

"It was for five million," Carson explained, "so we're covered no matter what."

"That wasn't necessary," Marty said, trying to conceal his surprise. "Wynn Bergman's not a bank, but we don't expect full payment in advance, either."

"You'd better get used to it, Marty," Templeton chortled, "that's how the people at Isaac Arrow do business."

Torello nodded. "We think paying quickly motivates our suppliers to do their best work. Besides, you've done a great job pulling this together, and on such short notice, too. By the way, we want you to attend our Super Bowl party here."

"It's going to be a fund-raiser for Planetlife," Carson added. "Black tie. A thousand-dollar-a-plate dinner—of course you'll be our guest."

"It should be a hell of a party," Templeton added. "There's going to be conservationists, politicians, celebrities, the media. . . . You name it, they'll all be there."

"Along with Del Waters," Torello said, "the chairman of our board."

"Pardon the pun, Marty," Carson said coyly, "but it's going to be a great kickoff for Arrow's campaign."

"So then, you'll be there?" Torello demanded, looking at Marty expectantly.

"Wouldn't miss it for the world. . . . I'll have my tux ready," Marty vowed with feigned enthusiasm.

"So where do we go from here?" Templeton asked.

"To Belize," Carson said, keeping her cat-eyes fixed on Marty.

"Sounds good to me," Torello boomed. "Let's get packing."

They all stood up and started out the door while Marty lingered behind, clearing up his belongings.

"You have a minute, Carson?" he called out, closing his briefcase.

"For my favorite ad man?" She spun around and smiled. "Of course I do." She walked back to the table and purred, "How I can be of service?"

"I need to know what's going on with this security clearance thing. Human Resources is in an uproar."

"Security clearance?" She pursed her lips and frowned. "Oh, jeez, I'm sorry. I thought you knew about that. We check out everybody we work with. It's a board—"

"Directive?" he finished.

"You're catching on." She laughed.

"But why with the State Department? I mean, Arrow doesn't work with the government."

"No, we don't."

"So if you're not a military contractor," he pressed, "why do State Department checks?"

"A lot of our research has potential military applications. It's in the nation's best interest to assure their secrecy. That's why the State Department's involved. They've changed their focus from the cold war to industrial espionage."

"So that explains the State Department's interest in Arrow's suppliers, even the ones that aren't connected to the military?"

Carson studied him intently. "Does Bergman have a problem with that?" Her green eyes narrowed. "Or do you?"

"No," he replied, flashing his most disarming smile. "No problem. I just want to have my facts straight when I talk to Human Resources. They're gonna grill me on this one, for sure." He deflected the query skillfully. After twenty years in business, dodging bullets had become second nature.

"I see. You know, for a minute I thought maybe Marty English wasn't the man I thought he was . . . that maybe you had something to hide. But then if you do, our guys are really falling down on the job."

"How's that?"

"You already passed our security check with flying colors," she said, retrieving a plastic card from her blazer pocket and handing it to him. "I almost forgot to give you this. Use it when you go down to the VR lab for the photo shoot. Just be sure to call Dr. Bachmann first—he really hates drop-ins."

"Thanks." He tried not to look shocked. How could he have passed a State Department background check? Why hadn't they turned up something on his name? And what about his father? It didn't jibe.

"You don't seem very pleased," she remarked, leaning in to him. "Maybe our people missed something?" Her eyes met his. "Maybe I should investigate further?"

"I'm pleased," he insisted, putting the card in his wallet. "Actually, I was already on to another subject, thinking about all the work we've got to do in Belize before we even get to the photo shoot in the VR lab."

Frank Torello stuck his head into the conference room. "We've got to get going, Carson. Bachmann's waiting."

She nodded impatiently. "Be right there, Frank."

As Torello disappeared down the hall, she turned back to Marty. "I'm looking forward to Belize," she said huskily. "Who knows, maybe we'll have some time to get to know each other better."

"We're going to be pretty busy," he remarked, trying to sound offhand.

"Busy?" she exclaimed incredulously, arranging her pretty features into a frown. "Jesus, you've got to learn how to relax, Marty. A guy has to have a little fun now and then, you know. You can't be working every minute of the day. It's just not healthy." She sidled closer and lowered her voice. "You know what I think? I think you need to drop all this business crap and forget I'm a client for a little while. You know, let yourself go, have a good time." She put her hand on his and he felt a surge of arousal. "A few days in Belize are just what you need."

Chuckling, as if he didn't take her at all seriously, he gave her a polite, professional smile. "Is that what you think?" he asked, gently withdrawing his hand.

"That's what I think. And when we get there . . ." she paused and stared, inviting him to challenge her words, "I intend to prove it."

Chapter 23

In Marty's experience, catching a plane never went smoothly. There were the acrobatics through the parking lot and airport corridors that could easily win a guy the old O.J. slot in the Hertz ads. The high drama of bungled reservations and mixed signals that dogged you right through the gate and down the jetway to those cushy first-class seats your client had unwittingly purchased. But even then, securely buckled into your seat with a glass of wine in one hand and an upscale magazine in the other, you weren't really safe from last-minute catastrophe. No, you couldn't relax until the view outside your window turned to clouds and the seat belt sign went off. Then you could sit back, close your eyes, and unwind. Or at least try.

The TACA 727 jet engines droned on hypnotically as a serving cart, overflowing with fifths of Mexican tequila and rum, rattled down the aisle. The pilot announced that they were somewhere over the Florida Keys. Marty pulled his notebook computer from under his seat and opened it on his lap.

"What the hell are you doing?" Zak exclaimed. "Working?"

Kidman leaned around Zak and shook his head at Marty. "Hey, put that down. Relax, have a drink." He lifted a margarita. "These are great."

"I *am* relaxing," Marty replied, slipping his B. B. King CD into the drive.

They watched as he plugged in a set of headphones and put them on. "Have fun," he said, closing his eyes.

At the gripping beat of "The Thrill Is Gone," his thoughts turned first to work—then to Carson Page. A few days in Belize, some fun, a *good* time. Yeah, that's what Carson had said he needed. Hell, maybe she was right, maybe he could use a little R & R, after all. These past few weeks had definitely taken their toll.

But then, Carson wasn't talking about bird-watching; girl-watching was more what she had in mind. And he didn't think that Carson would be content to leave it at watching, either. No, Marty was pretty sure she craved some audience participation. Shit, he didn't need this problem with Carson Page— not now. It was tricky, like walking a tightrope, dodging a client's advances. You had to keep the account—and try to keep your self-respect at the same time.

Marty smiled to himself; it amused him to play the role of straight arrow. Still, he did have a few rules. Don't cheat on your lover was one. And, as his father used to say, "Don't dip your pen in company ink." Marty had gotten romantically entangled with a co-worker once, early in his career, and learned his lesson the hard way. Ever since, he'd made it a practice not to get involved with colleagues or clients. Who knew? Carson Page might be a good lay, but he'd never find out; he'd never let their relationship get that far.

"You asleep?" Zak asked, leaning across Marty to look out the window.

"Not anymore." Marty grinned resignedly as he pulled off the headphones. "What's up?"

Zak held up a travel guide to Belize. "Have you read this?" he asked excitedly.

Marty shook his head.

"Well, according to this, Belize is un-fucking-believable. Sounds like the goddamned Garden of Eden."

"Wasn't Belize a British colony?" Kidman asked, glancing up from a copy of *Rolling Stone*.

"Yeah," Zak replied. "But they didn't call it Belize then. They called it . . ."

"British Honduras," Marty offered.

"That's it." Zak nodded. "You know what else? It's nothing like the other Central American countries with their juntas and guerrillas and shit. Belize is different."

"What's the population these days?" Marty asked. "About two hundred thousand?"

"Hey, I thought you said you hadn't read this," Zak complained.

"He hasn't," Kidman shot back, giving Zak a wink. "Marty's an account guy, a suit. They know everything, remember?"

"Not everything." Marty laughed.

"Then maybe you should get a look at this," Zak said, handing him the guidebook. "Everything you ever wanted to know about Belize but were afraid to ask."

Marty looked down at the book in his hand. *Belize: Paradise on the Edge of the World,* the title read. He opened it and started reading.

Belize was located in the Caribbean, just south of Mexico's Yucatan Peninsula. To its west and south lay Guatemala. It wasn't a very big country; the mainland was just one hundred eighty miles long and sixty-eight miles wide. About the size of Massachusetts. There were over two hundred islands scattered along its rocky coastline, most of them hemmed in by the world's fifth largest coral barrier reef. The guidebook cautioned that the Belizean terrain was varied and rough, dotted with vine-covered Maya ruins, and filled with endless limestone caves, flatlands of jungles and mangroves, highland rainforests, and pine mountains.

The country's history read like a chapter from *Treasure Island* with a dash of roll-up-your-sleeves capitalism thrown in for good measure: lots of ruthless Spanish conquistadors, swaggering Long John Silver characters, smuggling rings, and greedy colonialist entrepreneurs. For the past three hundred years, Belize, thanks to its treacherous barrier reef, had been a pirates' paradise, a hideout for rogues and cutthroats.

Throughout that time, there was almost constant logging in the rich forests, and the Maya continued to practice their traditional slash-and-burn agriculture. For years, the nation's rainforests had been rapidly diminishing. But recently, thanks to a shift in thinking among the locals, as well as the efforts of the Planetlife organization, much of the deforestation had come to a screeching halt. Thus, the thousands of plants and hundreds of birds that flourished in Belize were safe for now. As were the scorpions, big cats, and—Marty's eyes stopped on the page—snakes.

Belize, he read, was crawling with snakes, many of them poisonous. The guidebook described dozens, the worst being a big, slithering, bad-tempered reptile called a fer-de-lance that didn't even coil to strike. At the vision of hundreds of snakes hanging languidly from trees and vines, Marty closed the book. He could handle culture shock—he enjoyed traveling to the hinterlands around the world—but the fer-de-lance?

The pilot came on. "Welcome to Belize," he said, first in English, then in Spanish.

Marty gazed out the window. Just below, the shimmering aqua sea lapped at a jagged coastline of rock and mangrove scrub. In the distance, tin roofs gleamed against the dark, barren landscape. So this was Belize, not a white sand beach or Maya ruin or rainforest in sight. From above it looked more mosquito coast than tropical oasis, and Marty glanced doubtfully at the guidebook. They were on the edge of the world, all right. But paradise seemed to be a long way off.

Chapter 24

Heat waves undulated from the runway as the passengers spilled off the plane and onto a tarmac surrounded by barbed wire and chain-link. Beyond, a military installation of drab olive bunkers and camouflage-green hangars stood at attention, lining a dusty road leading to nowhere. A shoddily constructed concrete-block building splotched with a chalky coat of cheap white paint welcomed the new arrivals.

"New terminal," Marty cracked as they strode past two swarthy Belizean security officers sputtering out "Welcome to Belize" over and over again from beneath thick black mustaches.

Zak surveyed the terminal's interior. "This place looks more like Hell's waiting room than a tropical paradise," he observed. He gave out a weary sigh and shifted his bulging carry-on from one shoulder to the other and back again.

"Well, get used to it, Toto," Marty teased. "We're not in Kansas anymore."

Grinning, Kidman swatted at a mosquito. "So what you're telling us, Marty, is the guidebook lied. It's not gonna get any better once we get out of here, huh?"

"Places like Belize don't come with a guarantee," Marty acknowledged. "They're an adventure, you know, an escape from all the crap you have to put up with back home."

"Oh, so that's it." Zak groaned. "This is supposed to be an adventure?"

"Aw, come on, Zak," Kidman soothed. "It'll only be a few days. What the hell? Besides, the rest of Belize has to be different than what little we've seen so far."

"Maybe," Marty replied with a hesitant smile. "Maybe not."

After retrieving their baggage and clearing Customs, Marty, Zak, and Kidman loaded their gear into a cab and climbed into the backseat.

"We're headed to the airstrip just outside Belize City," Marty called out.

"No problem," the cabbie replied. "You guys ever been here before?"

"No, this is our first visit," Marty answered from the backseat.

"Guess Belize looks pretty shitty, huh? At first glance and all. But don't go judging a book by its cover. I've been down here thirty years and, man, I can tell you there's no place in the world like Belize."

"Thank God for that," Kidman whispered to Marty.

"We're headed to a place called Escoba. Ever heard of it?" Zak asked to cover Kidman's snickering.

The cabbie looked at Zak in disbelief. "Are you kidding? Who the hell hasn't heard of Escoba? It's practically a national monument—"

"So, how far is it to this airstrip we're going to?" Kidman interrupted impatiently.

The driver smiled to himself. "Just got off the plane from one of those high-pressure jobs back in the States, huh? Well, take my advice: Go with the flow. And by the way, my name's Smitty and it'll be my pleasure to get you there." He paused and looked down at his watch. "The airstrip's about a half hour from Belize City. So, hmm . . . let's see now. It's nine miles from the airport to the city and then it's another thirty to the airstrip over on Western Highway. That's what—almost forty miles?"

"Great," Marty replied cheerfully and settled back for the ride.

The cab rumbled down streets more alley than avenue, dodging throngs of cheerful pedestrians, rusty bicycles, scooters, and smog-belching cars, while the gregarious cabbie pointed out what sights there were in the broken-down harbor town of fifty thousand.

Gradually, the sounds of daily commerce rose until they reached a deafening cacophony of honking horns, police whistles, and barking dogs. On street corners, a haze of exhaust and gritty dust hung over groups of idle men while above, on weathered porches, women balanced squalling children on rounded hips as they hung out the day's wash.

At the sight of a taxi carrying "gringos," barefoot boys rushed into the street to peddle souvenirs. "Made right here in Belize," they claimed. Smitty shooed them all away, explaining that closer inspection of the trinkets would reveal a MADE IN CHINA stamp.

As they wound their way deeper and deeper into the heart of the city, Marty found himself warming to the curious mix of urban squalor and Caribbean charm. The people he saw weren't wealthy, no question. They might even be called poor, but they weren't struggling in the grip of poverty like people did in Mexico City or Rio.

The Belizeans lived in whitewashed clapboard houses, not cardboard boxes and cast-off crates. They ate seafood and chicken and Yucatec fare and, it appeared from all the signs, drank a lot of beer and Cokes. For the most part, it seemed the Belizeans lived in simplicity rather than poverty, and Marty found himself drawn to that. As they continued on their journey through the city and he saw the relaxed smiles of the people's faces and heard their laughter, he found himself envying their peace.

*   *   *

After driving about five maze-like miles, Smitty turned down a sandy side street and pulled up to a clapboard shack. An illegible sign was nailed above the door.

"Welcome to Captain Larry's," Smitty announced, jumping out of the car. "Before we head out to the airstrip, you guys gotta have a Belikin beer and some of Captain Larry's famous granachos." He didn't wait for their reply, but ran up a set of rickety stairs. "Be right back," he yelled down as the screen door slammed behind him.

Marty turned to Kidman and Zak. "So how do you like Belize?"

"It's not getting any fucking better," Kidman said flatly.

"Some adventure," Zak agreed. "I'd say it sucks."

"You can't use an American yardstick to judge other countries," Marty replied, feeling suddenly defensive for the tiny nation. "You've got to look beyond the obvious, forget all those trappings of wealth we're used to . . . and look for the soul—"

"Here you go," Smitty interrupted, shoving three ice-cold bottles of beer and a clump of greasy wax paper through the window. "This may not be Margaritaville," he conceded as he climbed in and the cab coughed into action, "but I gotta tell you, there's nothing better in the whole damned world than a cold Belikin and a hot granacho." He paused. "Hell, don't just sit there listening to me go on—dig in!"

Smitty beamed with pleasure as they gulped at the beer, letting the cold liquid run down their parched throats.

"Best beer I ever had," Marty said gratefully.

Zak studied the bottle in his hand and then turned to face Marty. "Look familiar?" he asked, tapping at the peculiar hieroglyphic on the bottle's label. "Looks a lot like that thing on your disc, doesn't it?"

"Yeah," Marty admitted. "It sure as hell does."

"Hey, Smitty," Zak asked, holding up the bottle, "you got any idea what the hell this is?"

"That?" Smitty answered. "Oh, that's a Maya glyph. They

all look like that. Weird sons of bitches, aren't they? You'll see 'em all over the place. The Maya lived down here for thousands of years. There's even a few Maya around now. Mostly they're in Guatemala."

"Weren't the Maya the ones who were big on calendars?" Kidman asked.

Smitty's reply faded into the background as Marty's thoughts spun off in a maze of questions. A Maya glyph, so that's what it was. Hell, his father had never mentioned the Maya. Or shown any interest at all in Central America. As far as Marty knew, he'd never taken a trip down here, either, for business or pleasure: third world nations weren't exactly Tony Inglesia's style. It didn't make any sense. What possible link could there be between a Chicago Mob boss and some obscure hieroglyphic? Whatever it was, it had to be worth killing for.

"You all are going to Escoba, right?" Smitty asked as Belize City thinned out into flat mangroves.

His train of thought broken, Marty nodded, looking at Smitty in the rearview mirror.

"The owner of Escoba is probably the richest guy in Belize. Name's Del Waters. You know him?"

Marty frowned. Del Waters? Wasn't Del Waters the chairman of Isaac Arrow's board?

"I thought that Planetlife guy, Templeton, owned Escoba," Zak interjected, glancing back at Marty.

"Templeton's the guy meeting us at the airstrip," Kidman explained. "He's gonna fly us out to the jungle."

Smitty let out an appreciative whistle. "You guys didn't tell me you were goddamned VIPs. Last time I heard of Arch Templeton doing that was a couple of years ago. Some big shot from the U.S. Senate . . . Goode, that was his name."

"Steve Goode?" Marty asked incredulously. "The guy in charge of U.S. Foreign Security?"

"I don't know what he does in the Senate. We don't care too much about that sort of shit down here. But that's who it was, all right."

"What the hell was a guy like that doing in Belize?" Kidman wondered aloud.

"Hell." Smitty shrugged. "They all get down here to Escoba sooner or later. All the bigwigs."

Marty nodded thoughtfully. A successful organization like Planetlife naturally commanded attention. Hadn't Arch Templeton even said that their Super Bowl fund-raiser would draw all the big names? Arrow's connection to Planetlife was beginning to make sense. But how did Waters and Templeton get together? And in a remote place like this? "So tell me, Smitty," Marty asked, "what's the story behind Templeton and Waters? How'd they ever get hooked up?"

"Supposedly they were old military buds, went way back to the Special Forces in 'Nam. In the late seventies, Waters got a license for a soft drink plant in Belize and put Templeton in charge of running things. I hear Waters made a goddamned fortune. Then, about fifteen years ago, he sold the plant and bought three hundred thousand acres of rainforest. Hell, from what I hear, the guy could own the whole fucking country if he wanted to."

"So," Kidman prompted, "after he sold the plant, Waters started Planetlife?"

"I don't know much about all that." Smitty shrugged again. "I'm not a big fan of Waters or Templeton, but not many people down here are. Hell, this country's seen enough pirates over the years."

Marty frowned. Pirates? What did that mean? he wondered. He started to ask, but suddenly the cab driver turned on the radio and seemed to pull back. They drove on in silence. Kidman and Zak dozed off, but Marty sat upright, thinking furiously. How did Waters and Templeton fit in here? And why would some guys who were pumping so much money into this small country be so unpopular?

"That's the airstrip?" Kidman exclaimed in horror from the backseat of the cab. "Jesus, it's nothing but sand."

"That's right," Smitty agreed, twisting his head around to grin toothily at Kidman. "You afraid of flying?"

"No, but this isn't exactly modern aviation."

Smitty laughed. "Don't worry, Arch Templeton's got a hell of a reputation as a pilot and, from what I hear, Escoba's airstrip's nothing like this. Hell, it's supposed to be able to handle the big stuff. Besides, you haven't felt the thrill of flying until you've been up in a plane flying over a hundred thousand acres of rainforest. Scary, though. Going down in there, in the middle of nowhere? Shit . . ."

Smitty turned back to the road and lit another cigarette. "Let's just say you'd be in a world of hurt if you were with anybody *but* Arch Templeton. He may be a prick like Waters, I don't know, but I hear he's one smart son of a bitch. Supposedly the guy can live for months in the jungle with nothing but a pocketknife. They say he was one mean motherfucker in 'Nam. Killed a hundred gooks. Supposedly the guy has some, uh . . . 'spiritual' connection to the jungle. Wait'll you see the damned scar on his face."

"I've seen it," Marty offered. "And I'll make a bet he didn't get that falling off a bicycle."

"Not hardly." Smitty chuckled. "Supposedly he got it out here in the jungle, wrestling with a fucking jaguar. They say he killed it with his bare hands."

"When he was only three . . . just like Davy Crockett?" Marty laughed, shaking his head incredulously. He'd enjoyed most of the cabbie's ramblings, but this shit about Templeton was going too far. "I think we're talking about two different guys, Smitty. The Arch Templeton I know runs a major not-for-profit foundation. He's a Brooks Brothers type with a dash of off-the-rack Banana Republic thrown in. Not a G.I. Joe jungle guerrilla or Zen master."

Kidman and Zak broke out laughing, but Smitty didn't laugh, nor did he respond until they'd turned off the paved road and onto a sea of soft sand that rippled in waves around the tires, giving way beneath the weight of the old car.

"Laugh all you want, guys," Smitty retorted as he parked the car beneath a broad-leafed tree. "But you see that guy over there?" He nodded toward a man dressed in proper British white leaning in the shade of a Cessna, whom Marty recognized as Arch Templeton. "Well, he and Del Waters are in charge down here. And if I were you, I wouldn't forget it."

Chapter 25

"Do you two guys always ask so many questions?" Arch Templeton wanted to know. Zak and Kidman had been firing them off ever since Templeton had sat down behind that glistening row of flight controls. He turned to Marty and, above the roar of the plane's prop engine, demanded, "Where the hell'd that agency of yours find these jokers anyway?"

"That's a damned good question," Marty admitted with an easy laugh.

Templeton flashed a grin Marty's way, making the long scar slashing down his cheek retreat into the folds of his deeply tanned face. His eyes met Marty's for one moment and then shifted back to the endless rainforest below.

Marty smiled back, trying to figure out what was somehow off center about the man. Templeton's bush look wasn't off the rack, as Marty'd previously thought. He was wearing a crisp, white bush shirt and pants complete with military-style belt—the sort of style that implied rank and privilege, and made you think of gentlemen explorers and big libraries lined with trophy heads. But even with all the proper trappings there was a roughness, an edge, about him. Marty had seen a few mercenaries in his day, and he thought Arch Templeton fit the bill.

Still, it just didn't make any sense that the head of a respected ecological foundation would be, in reality, nothing more than a well-dressed gun for hire. Then again, Marty reminded himself, what did he really know about Arch Templeton? Smitty said the guy had been one mean motherfucker back in 'Nam, had faced death and won. That hadn't come as any surprise; Marty had guessed as much when he'd met the guy the first time. No, what Marty saw now in Arch Templeton was something else, something dangerous.

"You're the one I expected all the questions from, Marty." Templeton laughed, putting an end to his contemplation. "Why so quiet? Can't get a word in edgewise?"

Marty flashed a comfortable smile and shook his head. "No, nothing like that. I guess it's this view. It's breathtaking." "Breathtaking" wasn't a word he used very much, but it seemed to fit the scenery. "I'm blown away, Arch. Speechless." He paused and, hoping to learn more about Templeton, added, "I guess it takes me back, too . . . to when I took a chopper out of Lai Khe."

"Yeah, Belize is beautiful, isn't it?" Templeton agreed, ignoring Marty's remark about Vietnam as he put on a pair of mirrored aviators.

Too bad, Marty thought regretfully. He'd have liked to have had another chance to look into those vacant eyes. Marty returned his gaze to the lush monochromatic carpet of green beneath them. Perhaps Belize was a paradise after all, he mused. At least this part. "You know, Arch," he remarked, "this area of Belize seems pretty remote. From up here you'd think the rainforest went on forever."

"Unfortunately, it doesn't. But it *is* about as far away from the rest of the world as you can get. Which is just the way I like it." A bitterness filled Templeton's deep voice as he went on. "Hell, I'd be here full time if I could. But you know how it goes. Planetlife may be a foundation, but it's still a business. Somebody has to run it all. As it turns out, the man who bought all this land and turned it over to Planetlife decided that somebody would be me."

"You mean Del Waters?" Zak asked. "Sounds like he decides just about everybody's fate down here. Who does he think he is, Mr. Big?"

"Don't believe everything you hear," Templeton said sharply. "Del Waters may be the country's most powerful man, but he's also a hell of a nice guy. He's turning the Belizean economy around with eco-tourism. Hell, he's saving the country's ass. And you know what else? This Isaac Arrow herbal medicine thing he's doing—letting scientists come down here to study the rainforest and develop new drugs— well, that's going to save people's *lives*. As far as I'm concerned, that makes Del Waters one of the few heroes left in this world. And besides, who wouldn't want to be king of the hill? That's what Del is down here, you know."

"I'm looking forward to meeting him," Marty commented.

"You're going to be disappointed then. Del's a busy man. He's out of the country all week. . . ." Templeton's voice trailed off as he pointed toward a thick black cloud of smoke hanging over the horizon. "That's the Guatemalan border. The Indians are clearing the rainforest. They do it every damn year about this time. In a few weeks, you won't be able to see the sun for all the fucking smoke."

"God, that's terrible!" Kidman exclaimed. "Can't anybody do something about it?"

Templeton shook his head. "No, we can't do a goddamned thing about what they're doing over in Guatemala." Setting his jaw, he smiled coldly and added, "But we sure as hell can keep them from coming over here."

"Still," Zak argued, "someday they're gonna run out of productive land over in Guatemala and then they'll head for the Planetlife preserve and Escoba. Then what?"

"Then we'll kick their little red-skinned asses, that's what." Templeton gave an arrogant shrug. "Hell, we've done it before. In places like this, you don't really have a choice. You have to nip these problems in the bud. Let a bunch of ignorant people have their way and pretty soon they're taking over the whole goddamned country. We learned that lesson in Vietnam."

Marty tried not to look surprised; he'd never expected the guy in charge of Planetlife to be a bigot, but from the way it sounded, Arch Templeton could have been in charge at My Lai. All of the questions he'd had about Templeton came rushing back.

Templeton smiled again and Marty smiled back in return, but his stomach was in knots. Sure, he could kiss ass with the best of them—he did it all the time—but Marty found himself wishing that just once he could look at one of those ethnocentric, fascist bastards and tell them that, in his opinion, people like them were what was wrong with the world.

"The Guatemalan Indians have always thought Belize was theirs," Templeton continued. "But you're right, Zak, if they get desperate, they'll make a play for it. They're all rebels, you know . . . commies and wannabe dictators. It's just like the Sandinista shit in Nicaragua."

"Well, if that's the case," Kidman said, in his best country-boy drawl—the one sly southern politicians used, "I must be missing something."

Templeton frowned. "What's that?"

"Why would anybody put a resort in a war zone to begin with? Isn't Del Waters just asking for trouble?"

Zak grinned. "I think you mean 'Why is Waters asking to get his ass kicked?' "

Marty had to hand it to the two guys; Kidman had asked a damned good question. But what the hell were they thinking? For all intents and purposes, this man was their client. And as chairman of Arrow's board, so was Del Waters. Pissing Templeton off wasn't exactly the thing to do.

Marty had started to say something to soften Kidman's remark when Templeton retorted, an edge of anger in his voice, "Del's a very determined guy. He found a piece of ground he liked and he bought it. He isn't afraid of a fight. He never has been. And he never will be. He believes in democracy. Hell, he'd lay down his life right now for the red, white, and blue if he had to—"

"I hear that's why he was named chairman of Arrow's board," Marty broke in, trying to put Templeton at ease. He frowned over his shoulder at Zak and Kidman and added, "I doubt Del Waters is the kind of guy who'd back down from much of anything."

Responding to Marty's warning signal, Zak joined in, "Yeah, that's true. From what we heard, Arch, you and Del Waters are part John Wayne, part Tarzan."

At the compliment, Templeton's frame eased into the leather seat and he let out a laugh, his handsome smile returning. "Is that so? So not everything you heard about Del was bad?"

"Oh no, not at all," Zak replied with an ingratiating smile.

"Yeah, that's right," Kidman began, crossing his arms over his suspenders. "I'd imagine the governments of the industrialized nations recognize the importance of preserving the Belizean rainforest. I suppose it's ridiculous to think there'd ever be a problem at Escoba."

"As long as Del Waters is in charge," Templeton agreed soberly, "there won't be."

"It's a good thing there's guys like you and Waters around to make people understand the importance of trees and wildlife," Kidman said. "From what I've read, there's what— two thousand species of plants at Escoba and Planetlife?"

"Four thousand," Templeton corrected. "But it's not just plant life. Guests at Escoba see rare birds, too, maybe even a jaguar if they're lucky. It's a great place to live. You go to sleep to the sound of howler monkeys and wake up to thousands of chattering green parrots. You'll have to have one of our guides take you on a jungle hike."

Zak's eyes went wide. "Hiking in the jungle? Isn't that dangerous? I mean, aside from a man-eating cat or two, what about snakes?"

Templeton shook his head. "Jaguars are elusive; be happy if you see one. As far as snakes go, the guides will take care of you. You won't be in any danger. Most of our men have guerrilla warfare training—they know their way around the jungle."

Puzzled, Marty frowned. An eco-resort run by a mercenary, with guides trained in guerrilla tactics? What kind of place was that?

"Just watch out for the scorpions in your cabanas," Templeton went on, interrupting Marty's ruminations. "Those eight-inch suckers pack a nasty sting." At the looks of terror on Zak and Kidman's faces, he added, "You guys brought mosquito net and some insect repellent, didn't you?"

"Jeez," Zak moaned, "nobody said anything about scorpions."

"No problem," Templeton said. "We'll get you whatever you need. After all, we want your experience at Escoba to be more than work." He smiled broadly. "We want it to be memorable."

"Is that Escoba?" Kidman exclaimed, pointing to a clearing below.

"No," Templeton replied. "That's Del's little town, Top Dollar. That's where the workers live—fifty men and their families in all. From Top Dollar, it's another fifteen miles through the jungle to Escoba." He motioned toward the setting sun. "It'll be dark by the time you get there."

The plane took a sudden dip over the treetops and then made a pass over an intersecting maze of concrete runways lined by verdant jungle.

"Wow, get a load of that!" Kidman exclaimed.

The airstrip was even more impressive than Smitty had said. It looked just like a top-notch military airstrip you'd see back in the States. "You guys fly 727s into here?" Marty asked, thoughts racing.

Templeton smiled proudly. "This airstrip can handle just

about anything. Hell, we've even had the Eighty-second Airborne down here."

"Really?" Marty remarked in surprise. "What was the Big Red One doing down here?"

"Just routine shit," Templeton said with an easy smile. "You know, joint maneuvers with the British, that sort of stuff."

Marty nodded slowly. Joint maneuvers? He'd read that Britain still provided military support to Belize, but he'd never heard anything about U.S. involvement down here. What the hell was the U.S. government up to now? And at a rainforest preserve?

"What's that, way over there?" Kidman asked, pointing into the horizon.

"Coffee trees. Del's starting a small coffee plantation. He wants Top Dollar to be totally self-sufficient. The people here grow their own vegetables, corn, beans. Del's even been talking about growing some sugarcane, an orange grove or two, maybe even bring in a few hundred head of cattle."

Marty tried to suppress his astonishment; that kind of agriculture meant cutting down trees, draining wetlands. Why wasn't Templeton, a man in charge of protecting the rainforest, upset at the prospect of a thing like that?

"You can get a pretty good look at Top Dollar from this elevation," Templeton commented, making another pass over the small village.

The land surrounding the town was flat and green, but in the center there was a large hill rising incongruously from the landscape. There, overlooking a small town edged by vast rainforest, was a large estate.

"Hey Kidman, how'd we end up in Georgia?" Zak cracked. "Looks like we died and went to Tara." He pointed to the white-columned mansion.

"That's Del's place," Templeton explained. "He's got a hell of a spread."

Yeah, he sure as hell does, Marty thought as he studied the antebellum-style plantation home. It did look like Tara: You could just picture the dozens of servants jumping to get the Master a cool drink at the peal of a bell. Indeed, the mansion looked like it was inspired by some longing for a life of birth and privilege, for a return to the days when men were men and everybody else was either a woman or a slave. An enormous veranda circled the mansion's perimeter, giving its occupants a view in all directions. Clearly, like his buddy Arch Templeton, Del Waters had a hell of an ego.

"Check your seat belts," Templeton ordered. "We're going in."

As the plane arced to one side, a sudden movement on the mansion's veranda caught Marty's eye. It was a man, dressed in a navy blue blazer and khaki trousers, leaning on the balcony rail, a drink in hand. As they neared, the man walked hurriedly inside, closing the French doors behind him.

Was that Del Waters? Marty wondered. But hadn't Templeton said he was gone for the week? Why would Templeton lie about a thing like that? Maybe he was just covering for his boss; maybe Waters was some kind of antisocial recluse. Or maybe he was a snob who didn't want to bother with a few nobodies. Templeton might just be trying to spare them some social embarrassment.

But like everything else Marty had heard about Escoba since arriving in Belize, that didn't add up either. Arch Templeton sure as hell wasn't the kindhearted type who'd go out of his way to protect you from a snub; three guys from a Chicago ad agency didn't really mean shit to a guy like him. Why even bother to lie? The only thing that made any sense to Marty was that Templeton *wasn't* lying, that Waters really was out of the country and the man on the mansion's veranda was just one of those VIP guests Smitty the cabbie had been talking about.

Still, despite what seemed to be a plausible explanation,

Marty felt a strange uneasiness settle over him as the Cessna came in for a landing. And he resolved to do what all good Sicilians did at times like this: He'd live by the old mafia rule of *omerta:* He'd keep his eyes and ears open and his mouth shut. After all, you never knew what predator might be on the hunt in a jungle—snakes, scorpions, jaguars—or the two-legged kind: a millionaire with an attitude.

Chapter 26

I'll be here tomorrow for the TV production," Templeton said as he climbed back into the plane. "But tonight I've got some business to attend to in Belize City. Sorry I won't be the one to show you guys around, but you'll be in loyal hands with Che here." He shot a strange look at the Maya Indian standing nearby, at the ready, a look Marty could only interpret as some kind of warning. "Won't they, Che?"

The Indian nodded somberly.

As Arch Templeton flew off toward the east in his Cessna, Che turned to study each of them with the trained eye of a doctor. Marty wasn't at all put off by the scrutiny; hadn't Templeton said that Che had been well educated by missionaries, that he was a real, honest-to-god shaman?

"I see you are all very tired," Che finally said, speaking carefully, formally. "But please, take heart—tonight, at Escoba, you will rest." He smiled kindly and then said something in what Marty assumed was Mayan. "You are in God's hands in the rainforest," Che translated.

"That's a nice sentiment," Kidman remarked offhandedly.

Che looked at him in surprise. "That is not a sentiment. That is the truth."

Kidman nodded patronizingly and sneaked a look at Marty as if to say that this Indian guy was certifiable, as goofy as hell. One glance at Zak confirmed that he felt the same way.

But Marty didn't. He'd liked Che almost immediately. Maybe it was something in the man's eyes, or maybe it was his easy yet somehow regal gait, his gentle touch. Marty couldn't explain it—he just knew there was something that made him feel connected to Che, something strongly familiar that made him feel as if he'd known the man forever. It was odd, Marty noted in silent amazement, to feel that kind of thing with a stranger.

Che loaded their bags into the waiting jeep, handling them reverently, with all the care you would give priceless artifacts.

"So, now shall we begin our journey?" Che asked, taking his place behind the wheel. Climbing aboard, they nodded eagerly.

That was how their introduction to Escoba began: no fanfare or fireworks. Just a simple Indian guy wearing simple cotton clothes a size too big for his small, thin frame and a fifteen-mile drive through the jungle.

They rode in silence, Marty sitting up front beside the Indian while, despite the bumpy dirt road, Zak and Kidman nodded off in the back. The encroaching night dropped over the land and gradually the forest came alive with the sounds of chirping frogs, insects, and howling monkeys.

"The earth is alive, yet it sleeps," Che said abruptly. "And tomorrow it will all begin again. Life will be reborn with the morning star."

"With Venus?" Marty asked.

"Yes." Che nodded. "My ancestors, the Maya, considered Venus very sacred. Did you know that the Maya were great astronomers? Their entire civilization revolved around the cycles of the sun and moon and stars. Do you know much about the Maya people, Mr. English?"

"Marty," he corrected. "Please. Call me Marty." He paused, shaking his head. "I'm embarrassed to admit I don't know much about the Maya, but I'd sure like to know more."

Che smiled broadly, his white teeth flashing against his dark skin. "Good," he said, wagging his finger playfully. "Because I am a great one for teaching." He stroked thoughtfully at his chin. "Let me see . . . where should I begin?"

"At the beginning?" Marty offered.

"Yes!" Che agreed with childlike happiness. "The beginning is always the best place to start."

And indeed, Che did begin at the beginning, describing the Maya's roots in Mezoamerica, speaking with a deep reverence for his people and their past.

"The Maya built more grand cities and pyramids than the great Egyptian culture," Che said. "If you are familiar with the early Asians, you may see a resemblance to some of their structures, like the one they call Angor Wat, in Cambodia. The Maya were magnificent builders and architects—and great sailors, artists, sculptors, writers, priests, merchants, farmers. They were a deeply spiritual people who worshiped many gods and saw the creative force in all things. To the Maya way of thinking, a stone is just as alive as a stork or the sun. Everything has its place in the universe. Everything is sacred."

Che conjectured that this view of the universe had played a part in the Maya's decision to settle in such a hostile environment. Their range was a harsh one, he said. It encompassed few rivers. There was little topsoil, merciless climate conditions, and countless menacing beasts. Yet, somehow, despite those obstacles, a mighty civilization rose up from the ashes of cleared rainforests, flourishing for almost three thousand years. Then, for no apparent reason, the Maya vanished. "Like the smoke of the sacred incense, copal," Che finished.

"But how could they just disappear?" Marty objected. "They had to go somewhere. Where did they go?"

"No one knows. The Maya are the very essence of mystery."

"Speaking of Maya mysteries," Marty said, "do you know much about their glyphs? I came across one the other day, and I was wondering what it meant."

"Unfortunately, most Maya glyphs have not been deciphered. But I do know *un poco*—a little—about them." He looked at Marty searchingly. "Is this glyph important?"

"I think so. Well, at least it is to me."

Che didn't ask why it was important, and Marty was grateful for that; instead, Che asked, "And do you have this glyph with you?"

"No, I left it back home."

"Perhaps you could draw it."

"Maybe . . ." Marty shook his head and laughed. "Who am I kidding? I'm no artist. I could ask Zak to try, but it was pretty complicated."

"Maya glyphs are very complex. And they often have several meanings, depending upon the context in which they are used. But if you would have your companion make a drawing of the glyph, I would be happy to look at it."

"I appreciate that, Che. I'll have Zak do what he can. Thank you."

"No, *thank you* for allowing me to assist you. That is my purpose, to assist."

"Your purpose?"

"Yes. As well as my destiny." There was a proud lilt in the Indian's voice. "You see, I am a direct descendant of a great Maya ruler. As such, I have the task of sacrificing myself for others. It is a responsibility I bear with honor and humility."

A frown passed over Marty's face. The word *sacrifice* brought to mind visions of bloody chickens and trances. Or worse. Was this like Haiti? Did the Maya Indians do that kind of thing down here, in Central America?

As if divining Marty's thoughts, Che smiled. "Sacrifice is an honor and a privilege in many cultures. Like the Maya plumed serpent god, Kukulcan, Maya rulers were divine, embodying the creator's promise that people would conquer death, that they would be reborn into new life."

"So are there still Maya rulers?" Marty asked with a grin as he craned his neck to see the first signs of civilization—an illuminated clearing—just ahead. "Are you one?"

"No, I am not a ruler." Che chuckled. "Those days are long past. I am only a community leader and shaman. Of course, as I said, like my ruler ancestors, I have a purpose and destiny. And like them, I believe our creator made a perfect world, that all things are sacred—the plants and animals, the earth, the wind and water." He paused, his face turning somber. "As well as the blood."

Puzzled, Marty shook his head.

"The Maya believed that blood held the secret, the code, to all life. That is why it was considered sacred. The blood of the kings was the most sacred of all, which explains why a ruler often drew his own blood in public rituals and why he risked his life to play the sacred ball game."

"Sounds like a pretty serious ball game," Marty commented.

"Indeed. The Maya ball game was more than a metaphor for good winning over evil. It was the very heart of Maya mythology, with a special place in our creation story. Often it was played to the death with a Maya ruler taking on the role of the mythological hero who played the first ball game against the evil lords of the underworld. Maya rulers willingly suffered and did penance for their people so that their beloved children might be saved from death and destruction, very much like the Christian Jesus, I believe."

"That seems pretty harsh, Che. I mean, just because a guy's born a ruler he has to play a game to the death or slice himself up every so often and then be happy about it?"

Che smiled patiently. "You are making the concept of sacrifice far too simple, Marty. Have you ever served in a war?"

Marty nodded slowly and answered, "Yeah, Vietnam."

"Then you should understand. Men have always made heroes—and saints—of those who sacrificed their lives, who spilled their own *blood*, for others. Leaders of men must be willing to sacrifice themselves if necessary."

"So do the Maya still do that sort of thing?"

Che laughed aloud. "Do the Romans still execute men by nailing them to a cross? Times change, Marty. Of course men, Maya or otherwise, still sacrifice themselves. They just find different ways in which to do it now."

"That's good," Marty teased. "I was afraid you might have to follow your ancestors' example."

"I do follow their example of sacrifice. I just find other ways to express it. Things like giving of my time. Time is life too, you see. We have a limited supply of time on this earth, just as we have a limited supply of blood in our veins. Giving of one's time can be a great sacrifice for a busy man . . . say, a man like you."

"So you've given your time to Escoba and Planetlife . . . because it's a positive thing for your people?"

Che hesitated. "In the beginning," he said at last, "when Mr. Waters and Mr. Templeton came to me, asking for my help in bringing the people together in agreement with their idea, I felt the preserve would protect our land and our heritage." He smiled what Marty took as a rueful smile and added, "I thought Planetlife and Escoba would protect my people's future and give them a way to make a living without destroying the rainforest, without slash-and-burn agriculture. After all, the forest is our real home, not huts made of thatch. Without the forest my people would be truly homeless. I believed Mr. Waters and Mr. Templeton could save them both."

"Believed?" Marty's voice registered surprise. Was Che, like everyone else he'd come in contact with down here, going to leave him with more questions than answers about Escoba and Planetlife and the men who ran it? "I take it, Che, you don't feel that way anymore?"

Che averted his eyes, looking toward the glow of the light ahead.

"What about all this?" Marty gestured at the seemingly endless rainforest that lined the dirt road. "Isn't your land safe from loggers now? Doesn't Escoba draw tourists who care about the same things you do? And what about the new drugs the Isaac Arrow company is producing with herbs from this rainforest?"

"Sometimes what one sees are illusions." Che looked Marty directly in the eye and smiled. "In any case, I'm not so certain that such things as a rainforest or a village of Indians are your destiny. You have your purpose. I have mine. A man must do what he must do. But above all, a man must be clear on his purpose and must follow his path. I would think a man of your stature and import would agree."

Marty nodded thoughtfully. Evidently he was prying into things that Che felt didn't concern him; that's what the Indian was insinuating, wasn't it? An old movie with George C. Scott playing General Patton came to mind. Patton had believed in destiny; it had driven the eccentric man's life. Marty had always thought people who knew who they were and where they were going were lucky. Che was one of those lucky few.

"I'm sorry," Marty said, genuinely apologetic. "I guess I'm just sort of confused about this place. It seems full of contradictions to me."

"Contradictions. Illusions. Who can say? It is all a mystery."

"I imagine you don't need the opinions of a guy who doesn't even know what his destiny is," Marty conceded, deciding he'd save his questions for another time. At least he'd found someone who might be willing—and able—to answer them. "I guess I haven't spent too much time trying to figure it out . . . you know, with work and all." He paused, considering the statement he had just made. "Then again," he said tongue-in-cheek, "maybe work *is* my destiny. Yeah. Maybe I've found my path after all."

Che smiled kindly, but there was a doubtful expression in

his dark eyes. "You don't go looking for your destiny; your destiny comes looking for you. You'll know it when it comes calling and you'll have no choice but to answer."

"Like you?"

"Yes. Like me. And like my ancestors who spilled their blood for their people. They did that willingly and without question. Because, you see . . ." Che paused, his words becoming one with the sounds of the night, "that was their destiny."

Chapter 27

Like ancient Maya sentinels standing watch over tombs of
buried treasure, the giant cohune palms loomed majestically
over Escoba's plaza. Beneath them, their lights twinkling in
the humid air and evening shadows, a handful of wood and
thatched-roofed cabanas were scattered amid a wonderland of
lush tropical gardens. Exotic plantings of brightly colored
plumeria, bougainvillea, and hibiscus lined the meandering
paths leading from the cabanas to a central lodge. There, beneath a high, thatched roof and slowly revolving plantation
paddle fans, the guests gathered for meals, drinks, and cama-
raderie.

The mood in Escoba's lodge was light when Marty and his
road-weary companions walked through the door. A few of
the guests had already taken a seat at one of the two dozen
linen-covered tables and were quietly browsing through
menus, but, for the most part, everyone was standing around
a Polynesian-style bar, talking all at once, giddy with the
day's jungle adventures.

At the sight of the familiar faces of production crew and
agency staff, Zak's and Kidman's fatigue evaporated and—
with Zak's solemn promise to Marty to reproduce the glyph
as faithfully as his memory would allow—they hurried over
to join the party.

Marty paused in the entry, hanging back from the crowd. The lodge was right out of *Architectural Digest:* casual, elegant, with a J.-Peterman-meets-the-Four-Seasons look about it. But his thoughts weren't on interior design and ambience; they were on what Che had said earlier: Destiny knocked and you answered. So that was it? Just sit under a shade tree eating peaches and wait for your destiny to come looking for you? Could life be as simple as that? Marty didn't think so. No, that would be too easy. Life was supposed be a struggle. To get anywhere at all, you had to fight your way there. You had to make your own destiny.

"Hey, there . . . earth to Marty," Kidman teased, coming up alongside him. "Come on. It's Miller time, big guy. Everybody's over at the bar. Let's party."

"Forget it," Marty retorted as he fell in step with Kidman. "I'll party after the Super Bowl." His words trailed off at the sight of Carson standing among the other guests at the bar.

Kidman saw her too. "Wow." He gasped. "Who the hell is that?"

"That's Carson Page. Our *client.* So close your mouth and quit staring."

"*That's* our client? Really? Man, what I could do with a babe like that . . ."

Playing the boss, Marty shook his head at Kidman in disapproval. "Like I said, she's our client. Hands off."

Client or not, Marty had to admit, if only to himself, Carson did look stunning. Of course, he'd known she was a good-looking woman—only a blind man would have missed that. But tonight she was more than just good-looking; tonight Carson Page was hot.

She was wearing a tight-fitting camisole that clung to her breasts, emphasizing the erect nipples beneath. Around her tiny waist, she'd knotted a colorful silk scarf into a pareo. As she padded, barefoot, across the floor to greet him, it lifted like a feather, exposing a long length of sun-bronzed leg.

"Marty," she exclaimed playfully, locking her arm in his. "Glad you finally made it."

At her touch, Marty found himself thinking that she felt good against him and that she smelled good, too, intoxicating, like one of the heavy-scented flowers hanging from the vines outside the lodge.

Looking at Kidman, Carson's smile quickly faded. "God, I'm sorry. . . . Help me out here, Marty. Who's this?"

"This is Bill Kidman, the production manager on your account."

Turning on the southern charm, Kidman extended his hand. "It's a pleasure to meet you."

"The pleasure is mine," she said, flashing her sexiest smile.

Marty gave Kidman a look that said it was time to get lost.

"Well, guess I should be moving along now," Kidman drawled, taking the cue. "Hopefully, our paths will cross again."

"Hopefully," she agreed.

As Kidman ambled away, Carson leaned over to Marty and whispered, "You hungry? Dinner's lobster. I hear it's wonderful . . . fresh caught, right off the reef."

"Sounds delicious," he said flatly, taking a step back. This was his client, he reminded himself; he had to keep his distance.

She noticed his retreat and gave him a cool stare. "You don't seem very enthusiastic."

"Sorry, long trip. Guess I'm not going to be much fun tonight." He grinned, stifling a yawn.

"Well, I know just what you need," she declared brightly, taking his arm and pulling him up to the bar. "You need a Belikin." She handed him an icy bottle.

He nodded and took a long, slow drink of the Belizean brew. "Just what the doctor ordered," he agreed, setting it down.

"I usually know what a man needs," she purred, moving closer, her bare thigh pressing between his legs.

Carson's advance was unmistakable, and Marty's first reaction was to pull away, but for some reason he didn't. Instead, he felt himself responding, wanting her. She felt him
responding too, and she leaned back against the bar, exposing
a long curve of throat and neck, and smiled triumphantly, as
if to say she'd won.

It was the smile that did it—that made him come to his
senses. Get a grip, he told himself angrily. Carson might be
beautiful *and* available, but there was something about that
smile of hers that told him this was only a game, that she was
on the hunt. She was the kind of woman who liked a real challenge, and he was that, all right. But he'd never cheated on
Reiki, nor had he ever blown an account playing grab-ass
with a client. He wouldn't start now.

He averted his eyes, forcing his stare to the others around
the bar. "So, where's Frank?" he asked casually, fighting his
desire to look at her. He'd always been in the driver's seat
when it came to the opposite sex, but with Carson he seemed
in danger of losing control at any moment.

She smiled, as if sensing his emotional turmoil. "Frank?"
she asked, saying the name with all the enthusiasm of Morris
the Cat. Dropping her pose, she picked up her drink. "Oh,
Frank had to go back to his cabana and change." She made an
amused face and sipped at the foamy concoction in her glass.
"God, Marty, you should've seen him. Frank looked like such
a geek. You wouldn't believe it. He had on a jacket and a button down shirt and a pair of Sansabelt trousers. He had to be
melting in this heat." She giggled.

"Frank had a jacket on? Really?" Marty pretended to be in-
terested, but truth was, he could've given a rat's ass about
Torello's wardrobe. "He must have been sweating bullets.
Hasn't he figured out this is the tropics?"

Carson pushed a stray lock of red hair behind her ear.
"Frank's got this thing about always looking professional.
You know . . ." Her tone turned accusing, but she smiled.
"Like you."

"Afraid you've got me figured wrong this time," Marty objected. "It's not giving the *appearance* of professionalism that I'm about. I *am* a professional." He grinned. "There *is* a difference, Ms. Page."

Carson raised her glass. "Touché." She laughed. "Good for you. I, for one, have no intention of letting all that 'look professional' crap get in my way of having a good time. While I'm down here, I'm going native all the way."

She spun around, making the scarf float up her thigh again. "What do you think?" she demanded. "Am I native girl enough to get a city boy's attention?" She ran her fingers over the knot of her pareo as if considering a more daring option.

"Yeah," he said quickly, with studied seriousness. "You look fine, *very* native."

Her expression darkened. "Jesus!" she complained over the sound of laughter and reggae music. "You sound like an old man." She took a sip of her drink, her lips forming a sensuous pucker around the straw, and added slyly, "You need help, Marty."

"Help with what?" a friendly voice asked. Marty turned to see Frank Torello standing there, his fat cheeks gleaming with sweat. From the way Torello was dressed, it was obvious he'd made a little trip to the "place where America shops" before heading for Belize. His clothes were cheaply cut and poorly dyed and Marty tried not to gape. Replete with greasy hair, loud tropical shirt, and wide gold neck chain, Frank Torello looked like he'd just stepped out of Elvis's *Blue Hawaii*. All he needed was a pair of blue suede shoes and a guitar and he'd be off and running. At least in Vegas. How could a guy who dressed like this—and *looked* like this—have gotten to the top in his company? Marty was totally baffled.

"I don't think Marty needs any help, Carson," Torello chided. "He's the kind of guy who always has his bases covered."

Marty grinned, thankful for the reprieve from Carson's games. "That's right, Frank. I've got it covered."

"I'm glad to see you came down for the production. I like a guy who stays close to his work. We notice things like that at Arrow. Make sure our vendors are rewarded for it, too. Right, Carson?"

From beneath a fringe of long lashes, she looked up and nodded. "We open our checkbook."

Marty grinned. "I have to admit an open checkbook's a great motivator."

"You do a good job for us," Carson said huskily, "and you can have whatever you want." She punctuated the remark with a gentle squeeze of his arm.

Somewhere in Marty's brain a warning went off. This thing between them, whatever it was, was going too far. Experience told him to get the hell out of there. But he didn't; instead, he just smiled back at Carson, holding her fixed in his dark-eyed gaze.

It was crazy, looking at Carson that way—like playing with fire—and he knew it. So why the hell was he doing it? Was it his ego? Did he think that with just one look he could make her understand she didn't fool him? That her little double entendres hadn't gone over his head, that they just didn't work on Marty English?

Carson shot him an amused, haughty smile and then looked away. "Everybody's starting to eat," she remarked offhandedly.

"Let's have a seat," Torello urged. "I'm a sucker for lobster."

Marty nodded genially in Frank Torello's direction, like he was just dying to spend the rest of the evening with the guy. He'd need a good excuse to get out of this one, Marty thought as his eyes came to rest on Zak and Kidman, who were already seated at one of the tables across the room. They were being joined by Jules Benson, the guy they'd hired to direct the filming. Bingo: Marty had his excuse.

Turning back to Torello, he said politely, "I'd love to join you both, but . . . well, the truth is, I need to have a little pow-wow with our director, Jules Benson." He motioned toward Zak and Kidman's table. "There's a thousand details to go over."

"Isn't that Bill Kidman's job?" Carson demanded.

"Yeah, it is," Marty acknowledged with a grin, trying not to appear annoyed by her pushiness. "Don't tell anybody, but I've got it made at Bergman. I only have two jobs. One of them is making sure my clients are happy. The other is making sure they stay that way."

"Well, you don't have to worry about me," Torello declared, lifting his mai tai. "I'm as happy as a clam. But I do want to sample some of that seafood everybody's raving about. Why don't you go ahead and take care of business? We'll plan on dinner tomorrow night."

"Sounds great." Marty beamed, relieved to be spared an evening of Torello's backslapping and Carson's torrid looks, even if he'd have to face them the following night.

"Tomorrow night's fine with me," Carson agreed. "But I have to tell you, Marty, from what I saw earlier at the bar, your director, Mr. Benson, is wasted. I'd be surprised if you got much more out of him tonight than a few frat-house war whoops and adolescent belches."

"Wasted?" Torello exclaimed. "You mean drunk?"

"He's probably just enjoying himself a little too much," Marty said quickly. "You know how those brilliant creative types are. They're just a little bit wilder and a whole lot crazier than the rest of us. We only forgive them because they're so damned good at what they do."

Carson nodded. "We'll take your word for it, Marty. You know the guy better than we do. If you say Jules Benson is okay, then that's good enough for us."

Chapter 28

Marty made his way back to the table, his calm exterior masking a rising sense of panic. He knew Jules Benson from way back; Benson had done a short stint at Wynn Bergman over ten years ago and had earned a reputation as brilliant, but a major fuckup. If Marty had had his wits about him instead of being distracted by minor details like his old man's death, visits from phony FBI agents, and being tailed by the Mob, he would never have allowed this clown to be hired. But now that Benson was here, and apparently up to his old tricks, Marty was anxious to find out how badly off the guy really was. Then he could get on with damage control.

Seeing his boss approach, Kidman grimaced. "Have a seat, Marty," he said woodenly.

Zak forced a smile and pulled out a chair. "Yeah, sit down and join the party."

Kidman cleared his throat uncomfortably. "Jules says filming down here is, uh . . . gonna be tricky."

"Oh, yeah?" Marty glanced over at Benson and then back to Kidman. "Hell, every shoot's tricky. But there shouldn't be any surprises on this one. You guys went over everything."

"Sure we did," Kidman replied defensively. "A million times. But Jules says the humidity's gonna cause more problems than he expected. His crew's gonna have to constantly check their equipment to make sure it's operating properly. That's really gonna slow us down."

"Slow us down?" Marty exclaimed, giving Benson a wan smile. "I don't believe it! Since when did Jules Benson ever let anything slow him down?" Marty extended his hand. "Hey, buddy, good to see you." Like his father, Marty would assess things first, let the scene play out. Then he'd make his move.

"Good to see you, too, Marty," Benson bellowed, his words thick and stumbling. There was the smell of rum on his breath and the aroma of pot on his clothes. "Old man Bergman must be treatin' you pretty good . . . you're lookin' mighty fuckin' sharp. So how's show biz, Marty? The rich gettin' richer?"

"I don't know about richer," Marty replied. "But business couldn't be better. Bergman just came off its best year ever and it looks like this one's gonna be another record breaker."

"Bergman? Who the hell you tryin' to kid?" Benson taunted. "That motherfuckin' agency you work for has been headed south for ten goddamned years."

Marty smiled. "Since you left, you mean?" Sour grapes had been Benson's delicacy of choice for years.

"No, since *you* got there," Benson retorted with a wicked laugh. "Hey, don't go getting bent out of shape. . . . I'm just shittin' you, Marty." He paused and added, "Jesus, it's a good thing I got the fuck out of that son-of-a-bitchin' salt mine that prick Bergman calls an ad agency. Best goddamned thing I ever did." He smiled contentedly and patted his bulging middle. "Yep, life's been good these past few years." He nodded at Zak and Kidman and added, "Your boss here may be living in a vacuum, but you boys know what the skinny on Bergman is, don't you?"

"Do they want to?" Marty chuckled, wishing they could get on to another subject. "Hell, I would've thought you would have something more *riveting* to talk about than Bergman Advertising."

"Oh, this is riveting all right," Benson sneered. "And you of all people should be damned interested."

Marty was barely containing his temper. "So what's the point, Jules? You've got us on the edge of our fucking seats here. Come on, what's the word on Bergman?"

Benson leaned in and lowered his voice, "Let me put it this way: You guys are losin' NHP. By the end of the year, half of Bergman's people are gonna be on unemployment." At the expression on their faces, he smiled smugly. "That's the word on the street."

News traveled fast.

"What street have you been walking on?" Marty shot back. "You heard wrong, Jules. NHP's not going anywhere. Hell, they just increased their budget for the year. And layoffs?" He gave out an easy laugh. "Wynn Bergman hasn't had any layoffs in all its fifty years."

"You mean to say you really haven't heard about Hexall buyin' out NHP?" Benson studied Marty incredulously. "Shit, I thought you were more dialed in than that."

Marty saw Zak and Kidman exchange looks of alarm. He'd hoped this NHP problem would blow over before they ever got wind of it. They weren't used to the ups and downs of the business. A few doom-and-gloom rumors and Zak and Kidman might bolt and run. They wanted to keep their BMWs, their American Express cards, and their generous salaries. They wanted to be perceived as rising stars moving up in a hot agency, not losers on a downhill slide. Marty wasn't about to let a jerk like Jules Benson fuck with their heads.

"Go on, Jules," Marty encouraged, feigning interest, "tell us more."

"Well, Hexall's already got an agency, you know."

Marty cut him off with a melodramatic yawn. "You mean Todd, Gattwick? Yeah, I know. You'll have to be quicker than that, Jules. That's *old* news."

Benson frowned and drew himself up. "Well, try this one on for size, then: As soon as the Hexall buyout's sewn up,

Todd's gonna steal NHP right out from under you. You heard that one? Or is that old news too?"

"It's news to me," Zak exclaimed.

Kidman shook his head somberly. "Me too."

"I'd be talkin' to a headhunter when I got back to Chicago if I were you boys." Benson smiled maliciously. "The guys over there at Todd are saying Bergman's screwed. Hell, I got it straight from the horse's mouth."

"And what horse was that?" Marty demanded.

"Tim Bowles."

"Tim Bowles?" Amused, Marty shook his head. "If I were you, I wouldn't listen to a guy who can't hold on to a piece of business for more than six months. With Bowles it's been wham-bam-thank-you-ma'am with every account he ever got his hands on. Take-the-Money-and-Run Tim—that's what they used to call him in Atlanta before he went to Todd. And while we're on the subject, how many clients has Todd screwed over the years?"

"None as far as I can remember. Hell, they've got as good a rep as Bergman."

Marty smiled to himself; Kidman and Zak were about to find out that Jules Benson was nothing more than a big-mouthed drunk with an ax to grind. "Come on, Jules." He laughed. "Did all that rotgut booze you've been drinking fry your brain? Jesus, who knows better than you and me about Able Foods and what Todd did to them?" He turned to Kidman and Zak and explained, "Back when Jules was at Bergman, he and I worked on the Able account." He smiled over at Benson. "Able was our baby. Wasn't it, Jules?"

Benson nodded uncomfortably.

"Todd stole the Able account from us," Marty continued, "broke our fucking hearts, too. And then what did Todd do but take old honest Able to the cleaner's. Spent their money like it was water. Hell, Able even ended up suing Todd for mishandling their media. It was a big agency scandal, made all the trade pubs, even hit the national news. Real ugly. Hell, you would've thought Todd was ruined. But no, here they are, ten years later, trying to destroy another unsuspecting client. Guess there's a lot of short memories out there, huh?" He grinned at Benson. He had him right where he wanted him. "Right, old buddy?"

Kidman's and Zak's eyes turned to Benson, waiting for his reply.

"Yeah." Benson sighed resignedly. "Okay. Maybe Todd did screw a few clients over the years and maybe their reputation isn't that sterling. Shit, maybe it fuckin' sucks." Benson shrugged drunkenly. "I gotta hand it to you, Marty"—he let out a hoarse laugh and picked up his beer—"you play it by the book. Nobody'll ever catch Marty English screwin' a client. . . ." Benson's bitter words trailed off as his bloodshot eyes drifted to the other side of the room and he grinned lewdly. "But maybe you should reconsider, you know, give it a try. I know one client I'd be fuckin' if I were you." He tipped his head toward Carson Page. "Hell, the way she's been lookin' at you all night, I'd say she wants it bad. Or have you had her already? Come on, let us in on it. Is she any good?"

"I wouldn't know."

"You wouldn't *know*?" Benson snorted. "Oh, aren't we the professional! Still the same old Marty, huh?"

"Marty's attached," Kidman said defensively.

"Aren't we all? That never stopped me from gettin' a little action." Benson sat back in his chair, his red face suddenly grave. "Speakin' of action—and this time I don't mean the horizontal kind—you guys ever heard anything about this joint we're stayin' in here?"

"Like what?" Marty asked, his curiosity suddenly aroused.

"Like the fact it's CIA."

Marty nodded distractedly, as if barely hearing Benson's shocking pronouncement. But he had heard it and, suddenly, Harper and Kemper standing before his desk in their regulation trench coats, notepads in hand, came to mind, and he found himself wondering if maybe he and Sinclair had been off base thinking the CIA had been connected to his father. Maybe it was Arrow and their relationship with Planetlife that had gotten the government agency's attention. But what was so magical about a pharmaceutical company's ad campaign that the CIA would actually break in and trash a guy's office? What the hell were they looking for?

"CIA?" Zak exclaimed.

"Hold it down," Benson snapped, looking nervously around the room. "Yeah, CIA. You know, secret agents, mercenaries, all that spy shit. I got this friend over in the State Department . . . you know, my company does recruitment films now and then. And when I told him I was comin' down here, to this place, Jesus, you shoulda seen the look on his fuckin' face." Benson paused, shaking his head in disbelief, and then lowered his voice. "Get a load of this: This guy told me that Escoba's some kind of staging area."

"Staging for what?" Kidman demanded.

"Yeah," Zak argued, "what would the CIA be doing down here?"

"You remember the Iran-Contra shit, don't you? Who knows what they're up to . . . guns, drugs. . . ." Benson shrugged. "Fuck if I know what it is. But it can't be good."

"You know, Benson," Kidman taunted, "you've really gone off the deep end."

"Hey, I didn't buy it either 'til I saw the fuckin' airstrip they got out here. You guys saw it. Hell, you gotta admit you could land the mother ship on that son of a bitch. You may not see the possibilities, but I sure as hell do. And I think it's pretty fuckin' amazing." He stood up and grinned. "But you know what's gonna be even more amazing?"

Marty shook his head. "What, Jules?"

"Pullin' off this goddamned shoot tomorrow, that's what. Man, my crew's already bitchin' about the conditions down here. You guys just showed up tonight, but I had a chance to look around earlier today and, let me tell you, it's one fuckin' nightmare. Heat, humidity, bugs—"

"Don't give me that BS, Jules," Marty said, cutting him off. "You knew what the hell you were getting into when you agreed to come here in the first place." Marty knew a setup when he saw it. Benson was laying all the groundwork, giving them a list of excuses that would cover every possible production fuckup known to man.

"Jesus, you're mighty fuckin' touchy. What the hell's your problem? This business finally gettin' to you, Marty? Nerves aren't as steady as they used to be, huh?"

"I'm more concerned about how steady *your* nerves are these days."

"Oh, my nerves are just fine, thank you." Benson smiled, swaying noticeably. "How about another round? It's on me."

"We'll pass," Marty said flatly.

"Fine with me," Benson retorted as he headed toward the bar. "But from now on, you guys are on your own."

"Shit fire." Kidman groaned. "Look who's headed our way now."

Seeing Carson Page, Zak shook his head in despair. "I wonder what the hell she wants."

"Maybe they want the Beatles in the spot along with Elvis," Kidman needled. "That'll make your day, huh, Zak?"

Marty stood up. "Hi, Carson. How's your dinner?"

"Do me a favor," she said, her words pouring out in a dramatic rush, "tell me that wreck's not *really* directing our ad." She motioned toward Jules Benson, who was now standing at the bar. "I was worried before about him being wasted and all, but I was mostly just giving you a hard time. You're such a *consummate professional*"—she shook her head, underscoring the words with a roll of the eyes—"that I'd never really worry about a shoot under your direction. But Frank's been watching Benson all through dinner and now he's practically hysterical about the shoot tomorrow."

"Well, we don't want that," Marty replied.

"Yeah." Kidman nodded. "Just tell him everything's under control."

"You guys don't need to convince me," she said, smiling at Marty. "*I* trust you completely. You say there's no problem, there's no problem. But Frank?"

"You want me to talk to him?" Marty asked.

"No." She sighed. "I'll just get him another drink and tell him to let you do your job."

"That sounds like a good idea," Zak grumbled.

Carson gave Zak a perturbed look and then turned back to Marty. "Well, I'll let you get back to your dinner." She waved. "Bye, guys."

As they watched her stroll back to her table, Zak glared at Kidman. "Just what the fuck were you thinking, Red, hiring a drunk? Jules Benson's a total fucking loser. And he's set to take us down with him."

"That's enough, Zak," Marty said firmly. "Chill out."

Zak drew himself up. "Fuck *relax*. I'm way past that. You heard what Benson said about the conditions down here? All that bullshit about the humidity? If you ask me, he's just getting us ready for some screwup. Yeah, that's what the prick's up to—I'd put money on it. The guy's old and washed up. And now he's even got Elvis over there worried."

"I'll handle the client," Marty retorted. "You just keep Benson straight. If he's sober, he'll come through."

"Sober?" Zak exclaimed. "What difference would that make? The guy's a wacko. And by the way, what was that shit about NHP?"

"I have no idea," Marty answered; now wasn't the time for the truth. "It's probably just another barroom rumor. I'll check it out when we get back to Chicago—"

"Fine," Zak said, cutting him off. He turned to Kidman. "So tell me, smart-ass, what the fuck *were* you thinking when you talked us into hiring that bastard?"

Kidman slammed his fist on the table, making the salt and

pepper shakers rattle around in their chrome holder. "I'll tell you what I was fucking thinking, Mr. High and Mighty. I was thinking about *you*. And about getting the best fucking job at the best fucking price."

"Yeah, right." Zak snorted. "Thanks for your concern. What's Benson gonna use to film with—the bottom of a beer bottle?"

Kidman leaned over the table. "Hey goddammit. I heard the guy's been on the wagon for years. How the hell was I supposed to know any different?" He looked to Marty for support.

"Kidman's right, Zak. I heard the same thing. We were all misled on this one."

"Goddammit, Marty." Kidman moaned. "I'm sorry. . . . I really am. Shit, I never thought this would happen."

"It's not your fault. Maybe Benson's been sober for a while and just picked tonight to fall off the wagon." Solemnly, he stood up and pushed his chair under the table.

"Where're you going?" Kidman asked, panicked. "What are we gonna do about Benson?"

"Yeah, what if he's too fucked up to get the job done, Marty?" Zak asked nervously.

"I'm confident that won't happen."

Zak's eyebrows shot up in surprise. "You *are*?"

"Yeah, I am. I know you guys won't let this project go down the tube. That's why I'm leaving you both in charge of Benson. Get him out of here, keep him the fuck away from Torello. Take him over to your cabana and pour some coffee down him. Whatever the hell it takes . . . get him sobered up by tomorrow morning."

"Why the hell should I have to pay for Kidman's fuckup?" Zak objected. "I don't want Benson puking all over the place."

"Neither do I," Kidman snapped. "If Benson knows what's good for him, he'll stay the fuck away from me."

Marty's face darkened. "You listen and listen good," he hissed. "There's three hundred million dollars riding on Arrow being in the Super Bowl. Their measly half minute of advertising just happens to be the most important thirty seconds of your lives. And, in case you forgot, the clock's ticking—there's only twelve days 'til the game. I don't have time for your bullshit. You understand? Benson fucks this production up and I can guarantee you both a place in the unemployment line. It's not gonna be my ass. It's gonna be yours. I'll see to it. You get this campaign produced and produced right." He paused, eyes flashing. "You got it?"

There was a strained silence as Kidman and Zak looked at one another. "Yeah," they both replied soberly. "We got it."

Chapter 29

Marty had traveled in wilderness environments before—the Alaskan tundra, the Amazon basin, the Australian outback—but even so, he'd never encountered anything quite like the Belizean rainforest. He'd heard the Central American jungle swallowed up everything that dared venture into its domain and, indeed, as he turned down a dimly lit path and headed toward his cabana, all signs of human life vanished. The friendly glow of the lanterns in the lodge, the guests' laughter, and the comforting clinking of glasses were lost in the darkest night he'd ever experienced.

The path twisted through a labyrinth of dense foliage, taking him deeper into the jungle. There was little light to illuminate the way, just a few randomly placed solar lamps springing up from beneath towering firs and cedars. The scent of flowers drifted in and out of the breeze, and Marty suddenly realized he'd never smelled an air so fresh and alive as this.

There *was* a connectedness here between Man and the primal force of Nature, and Marty was profoundly conscious of it. He was as much a part of the cycle of life as the sun and sky and rainforest. And, for one split second, all of his suspicions and discomfort with this place fell away and he felt as if he could have turned his back on his ambitions and stayed here forever. Reiki would fit right into this dream. She would have loved Belize; her idea of being connected was being close to nature.

Marty sighed, his smile fading. Reiki wanted to live out in the country instead of the spacious condo close to work he'd chosen. He imagined she'd like the kind of place where neighbors borrowed cups of sugar and kids still went trick-or-treating. Where you had a big front porch with a swing and you actually sat there.

She wanted commitment and marriage, a home and a family. She'd certainly made that clear enough the other morning. Hell, he'd thought things were going along pretty well lately, too, that they'd gotten past the subject of marriage and on to just living each day.

She'd blindsided him, that's what she'd done. At least that was how he'd felt. But there was something else that had gotten under his skin: the idea he might actually lose her over this crazy obsession she had with commitment. Where was the free spirit he'd fallen in love with? Maybe, he mused, it was that biological clock thing that women were always talking about that had gotten her so fired up. Reiki had said time was running out, hadn't she? But then again, maybe it wasn't that at all. Maybe, as she'd said, that thing with his mother was still in there, eating at him, screwing with his head, and now it was screwing up things with Reiki.

Or maybe the whole thing boiled down to the fact that he was just too involved in his work. Had he chosen his career over a relationship with his father? Was he doing the same thing with her?

He didn't want to lose Reiki. But he couldn't imagine turning his back on his all-consuming career at Bergman, either. He'd worked ten years for a shot at being the agency's top man. How could he just drop his dream now that he was so close?

Reiki knew advertising ate you alive. After all, she had a career too. She knew that to make it to the top, you had to be-

lieve your job was more important than seeing your kid's first
steps or hearing your mother's last words. The thought suddenly occurred to him that maybe she didn't feel that way
anymore, that maybe he was alone, out there on a shaky
philosophical limb.

At the eerie laugh of a night bird overhead, Marty glanced
around nervously; in an instant, the rainforest had been transformed from a wonderland to an unearthly landscape. The
connectedness he'd felt was gone, and his anxiety, as well as
his countless questions about Escoba and Planetlife, had returned.

He looked down at the path at his feet. He could barely see
it in the darkness, and he remembered what the guidebook
had said about poisonous snakes in Belize being nocturnal.
Why the hell hadn't he brought a flashlight? He took one hesitant step forward, then another and another. Tired as he was,
the thought of a bed summoned energy from some hidden
inner reserve, and he started walking faster.

Stepping inside the cabana's screen door, Marty felt blindly
along the rough wood wall until his fingers bumped into a
light switch and he flicked it on, flooding the room with light.

"Wow!" he said aloud at the sight. He had a keen appreciation for beautiful surroundings. And the cabana was, indeed,
beautiful, like a hut in the South Pacific with its louvered windows and high thatched roof and overhead paddle fan.

The cabana was also nothing short of a modern construc-
tion miracle with hot and cold running water, a flush toilet,
and a shower complete with designer curtain. In the middle of
nowhere, such amenities boggled the mind. But the natural
beauty hadn't been sacrificed for the sake of comfort, either:
The rough wooden floors were covered in native sisal rugs
and the walls were hung with Maya art.

His gaze turned to the majestic plantation bed carved of native mahogany and draped with a canopy of natural gauze and
silk. He would've liked to have made love to Reiki there, on

that bed, on a warm jungle night like this one. They'd made love in Bermuda like that; the sweat pouring over their bodies, covering them with a sensual glaze and adding to the heat of their desire.

Marty looked away; he didn't want to think about Reiki now, about what she wanted and what he couldn't give.

He turned off the light and went out on the porch, collapsing into a wicker chair. He closed his eyes and Chicago came to mind, along with his father—and Ford Sinclair. He wondered if the detective had turned up anything. Maybe Sinclair was just blowing smoke, trying to put up a tough facade for a gangster's son.

Marty sighed, reminding himself that he had more pressing issues to deal with right here. Jules Benson, for one. At the image of the drunken director, Marty's thoughts turned to the man's assertions about Escoba and the CIA.

"Feels like rain, doesn't it?"

Startled, Marty turned to see Carson Page in the moonlight. "Sorry," she said. "Didn't mean to scare you." She smiled and held up a bottle and two glasses. "I thought you could use a little pick-me-up. But remember, beware of friends bearing gifts. . . . Isn't that what they say?"

"Something like that," he replied unhappily; entertaining Carson had definitely not been in his evening plans. No, those plans could be summed up in two words: Bed. Alone.

"Hey, what's wrong? I'm not gonna bite." She giggled. "I promise."

"It's pretty late," he remarked evenly. "To be honest, I was just getting ready to go to bed."

"Go to bed? Now?" Carson shook her head. "I don't think so. Let's have a drink and talk awhile." Sensing his hesitation, she frowned. "Well, aren't you going to ask me to join you? Or am I going to have to stand here all night and let a perfectly good bottle of champagne go to waste?"

Marty's immediate instinct was to put an end to this. If he did it quickly and gently, no one would get hurt. But then again, Carson Page was his client, wasn't she? She wanted some company. And although he knew he should make her leave, some part of him was rationalizing allowing her to stay. After all, entertaining the client was just as much his job as anything else. "Have a seat," he offered, forcing a smile.

She tiptoed up onto the veranda and knelt down in front of him, her hair falling around her face in a tousle of curls, and he suddenly remembered why his father had always counseled him to trust his first instincts. He started to tell her that he wasn't comfortable with her being there. That they were asking for trouble. But then, the silk pareo she was wearing slid up, revealing the curve of her hip and firm buttocks, and he stopped, entranced by the length of her legs, her skin.

"Service with a smile," she announced, filling the two glasses and handing him one. "Here's to a fantastic future between Isaac Arrow and Wynn Bergman Advertising." She clinked her glass to his.

"And Planetlife," he added. He was glad to be talking business, but he was also hoping that Carson might shed some light on Arrow's involvement with the mysterious foundation.

"And Planetlife," she agreed, taking a sip of champagne. "Not to change the subject, Marty, but I think I should warn you, Frank isn't very happy about Benson. He's decided the guy's an incompetent."

"You told him what I said. . . ."

"Sure. But Frank just loves to obsess. All he could talk about was why Bergman would hire somebody like Benson for such an important job." She paused, taking a pack of cigarettes out of an embroidered pouch.

"Like I said," Marty replied in a tone more irritable than he'd intended, "Benson may like to tip a few, but he's good at what he does."

"Now, don't get me wrong," she said, lighting a cigarette. "I don't feel that way at all. I just don't want your credibility going down in Frank's eyes."

"I appreciate that. But I'm not concerned about my credibility with Frank. I just don't want Frank losing any sleep over it." He paused, trying to let go of the tension that was slowly creeping up into his shoulders. "After all," he deadpanned, "losing sleep is supposed to be *my* job."

Carson laughed. "Well, believe me, you haven't got a corner on that. Jesus, Frank's always worried about something. Between you and me, Frank can't handle stress very well." She shook her head and drew on her cigarette. The glow of the ember illuminated her face, reminding Marty just how beautiful she was. "God," she went on, rolling her eyes dramatically, "I can't tell you how I hate that. Especially in management. And *especially* in a man. Handle a problem and move on, that's what I say. See an opportunity, hell, take it. Life's as simple as that. But not for Frank."

"Well, Frank's got his strengths," Marty said guiltily; he was uncomfortable sitting around bashing his client. "He *is* president of Isaac Arrow, after all."

"Yes, he is, isn't he?" she replied, a note of bitterness in her voice. "Actually, Marty, I'm a much better manager than Frank Torello. I should be president of Isaac Arrow, not him."

"You're pretty modest, aren't you?" Marty chuckled. But the truth was, he admired her drive and, for the first time since they'd met, he felt a surge of kinship with her. "Don't forget, Frank's got a few years of experience on you. Your day'll come."

"No," she countered, her glass tipping drunkenly in her hand, champagne spilling out. "No, it won't. The guys at Arrow don't know what I'm capable of. Hell, you know more about me than they do . . . and what do you *really* know?"

She edged closer to him, her face upturned and Marty struggled with an unexpectedly intense urge to kiss her. Instead, he took a deep breath and held out his empty glass. "Let's just say I know you well enough to say you can pick out a great bottle of champagne."

"It's Cristal," she said, filling his glass. "At Arrow, they don't even know that much. They just think I'm a pushy broad with good looks." She took a quick swallow of champagne and lit another cigarette. "And don't try to convince me there's any company in America that's any different, either. Because the truth is, it's the fact that I'm a woman that's the problem. And being smart and beautiful on top of it? That doesn't open doors, it just makes things worse." She exhaled a neat ring of smoke and raised one eyebrow. "Don't you agree?"

Caught off guard by the question, Marty replied quickly, "Of course you're beautiful . . . and smart."

"No, silly," she exclaimed with a laugh. "Not that. I wasn't asking if you think I'm beautiful or have brains . . . but I have to admit it's nice to know you think so." She studied him with an amused expression, and Marty suddenly felt foolish and angry at himself; he'd let her into his head with that remark.

"Oh," he said awkwardly, "I thought—"

"Forget what you *thought*. What I meant was, don't you agree that most women are held back just because they are females?"

Marty nodded and looked out into the surrounding jungle. They were talking business and that was what he wanted, wasn't it? So why did he feel so uncomfortable? For one thing, he didn't understand why she was talking so freely. It wasn't very smart politically to complain to an outsider about the circumstances in your company. Maybe it was the booze—she'd hit the bottle pretty good.

But then there was also the fact that she'd called him "silly"; he wasn't used to being called that, not by a client. "Silly" was the kind of word you reserved for intimates; Reiki called him that when he did things like refuse to try a cup of her weird herbal tea or climb in the shower with her when he was already dressed and a half an hour late for work. Carson's casual use of a word like that made Marty uneasy, like they'd crossed the line somehow.

He saw she was refilling her glass, and he thought he should stop her. She was already feeling pretty good; he didn't want her to get bombed. Things got messy when a woman drank too much. Christ, he'd learned that as far back as his high school prom night in '68. All sorts of things happened when a woman got loaded, most of them bad.

He started to say something about taking it easy on the champagne, but then had second thoughts; hadn't Carson just finished complaining about sexism? He'd keep his mouth shut.

"You know," she said, interrupting his thoughts, "men can get by just going along and playing the game. Most times they don't even have to know their ass from a hole in the ground. Take Frank, for instance. He doesn't have the slightest idea what Dr. Bachmann's lab is all about. And he doesn't even try to understand it. The only guy I know of besides Bachmann who understands Trinity is Del Waters."

She frowned and waved her hand. "Of course, that doesn't matter to the old boys at Arrow. No sir. Frank gets all the fucking credit—excuse my language—for whatever's happening at the company. It was my idea to turn over the give and take—the escoba—to Dr. Bachmann. *My* idea! Can you believe it?" Angrily, she smashed her cigarette on the porch floor.

"It was your idea that led to all this?" Marty exclaimed. "I'm impressed." At the look of skepticism on her face, he nodded earnestly. "No, *really*. I am. What made you think of getting Bachmann involved?"

She smiled with satisfaction, though Marty couldn't tell if she was more pleased that he was impressed or just proud of her ingenuity. She was getting a bit difficult to read, which made him nervous. He decided it was best just to give her the approval she was seeking, so he smiled back expectantly, waiting for her reply, ready to be a supportive, nonsexist male.

"Well," she began, "on one of my first trips down here I hooked up with Che—you know, the Indian guide—and we started talking about the escoba tree. What he said got me to thinking we should turn Dr. Bachmann loose on it. I suggested that to Del and . . ."

"Struck a gold mine," Marty said appreciatively. "I imagine you got his attention. Waters *is* the chairman of the board, after all."

"Oh, yeah. He thinks I can walk on water. But that's mostly because I took the time to get to know what the hell goes on down in the VR lab. I can almost run the Trinity software as well as he and Bachmann can."

She was still looking for some strokes. "Nobody will ever say you're not smart, Carson," he said. "I like that in a client."

"And in a woman, too, I imagine." She smiled seductively. "Better than dumb, right?"

"Hey, I'm serious." It was true; he found smart women extremely sexy. But whatever the reason, his warmth for Carson was suddenly growing. Like he'd guessed from the very beginning, they were a lot alike. Maybe too much for comfort.

"Hold out your glass," she commanded, bottle in hand.

He shook his head. "No thanks. I've had enough."

"You aren't serious?" She looked at the bottle and moaned, "It's still half full. Aw, come on . . . just one more."

"I think we've had enough for one night, Carson."

She looked at him in surprise. "Wow . . . did you hear that? You just called me Carson."

"I always call you Carson."

"No, you don't say it like *that*."

"Like what?"

"Hmm . . . sort of, well, *familiar*." She smiled dreamily and started to fill her glass.

The ball was in his court. But he was determined not to play. Besides, he had more burning issues to address. "So," he asked, "was it your idea to get Arrow involved with Planetlife, too?"

Smiling to herself as if she knew what he was doing, she shook her head slowly. "No, not entirely," she replied. "Del Waters and I came up with that idea one night over dinner."

Dinner, *alone*, with the chairman of the board. That wasn't exactly typical for a marketing director, Marty thought. But he didn't say what he was thinking; instead he said, with all the admiration he could muster, "Selling the board on such a big investment, and something so ecologically oriented, must've been a real challenge."

"Easy as pie," she declared smugly. "Del and Frank got the board intrigued with the idea that Arrow could make an impact on global affairs. And I put together a corporate plan suggesting we start out with something innocent." She smiled and added, "Like saving three hundred thousand acres of pristine Belizean rainforest."

"Something innocent? So that's not Arrow's real goal, then?"

"Of course not!" She tossed her head back and laughed wickedly. "But it looks so damned upstanding, doesn't it, taking care of good old Mother Earth?" She paused and added conspiratorially, "But that's just the first step in a grand plan."

Grand plan? Was this the champagne talking or was it Carson Page, pharmaceutical executive? "And this grand plan," he ventured with a grin. "It's *your* plan of course."

"Of course."

Marty suddenly realized that the champagne had indeed loosened more than her inhibitions. "So tell me more," he prodded.

"Well, most people think it's the politicians that rule the world, but they're wrong. More and more it's the big corporations that call the shots. The way I see it, someday Arrow's going to be one of them. And when that day comes . . ."

"You'll be right there," Marty interjected, realizing he'd underestimated her from the very beginning, "ready to sit at the head of that conference table."

"Exactly." Carson nodded emphatically. "Now don't get me wrong. Arrow's ambitions aren't purely self-serving. And neither are mine. What we're doing with Planetlife is going to prevent a huge disaster, like the one a few years back on the Mexican-Guatemalan border."

Seeing Marty's puzzled expression, she explained, "The Indian population up there grew too fast, which is exactly what's happening right now along the Belizean-Guatemalan border. The Indians clear a few acres of rainforest and, when the soil gives out, they move on to another piece of ground. If the population keeps growing, all that's going to be left is a pile of cinders and ash. It might not be so bad if there were only a few Indians, but now there're thousands. And do you think they'll listen to reason? Hell, no. They think nobody owns the land, that it's some kind of collective. Del and Arch believe that the industrialized nations have to wake up and take the driver's seat, that we shouldn't be afraid to protect our own interests." She paused, lighting another cigarette. "We can't just sit by and let the third world take over. As Americans, we have a responsibility to do something. And as a major pharmaceutical company, Arrow has to protect the hundreds of plant species in this rainforest that could save millions of lives. Don't you agree?"

Saving plants was fine, Marty thought. Of course he agreed with that. But he didn't agree with the tactics Carson was proposing they use, and he found himself wanting to say so. Badly. He wrestled with the contradictions rolling around in his head: the feelings of desire Carson had somehow managed to arouse in him just now, coupled with his outrage at hearing such an arrogant and—he thought—ridiculous political ideology.

Politics wasn't exactly pillow talk, and Marty was surprised the seductive beauty had brought up the subject at all. And even more surprised it hadn't dulled the attraction he'd been fighting ever since he laid eyes on her. If anything, Marty found himself more drawn to Carson. The haughty flashing eyes, the passion in her tone, the calculating mind—they all made her all the more appealing.

He could attribute her diatribe to the booze, if he wanted. Or blame it on the fanatical influence of Templeton and Waters.

After all, the two men had to be masterful schemers; they'd obviously bowled over Carson Page and her naive boss, Torello, as well as a whole goddamned board of corporate directors. But wasn't that just a handy rationalization to excuse a philosophy he deplored?

"Surely, Marty," Carson said, breaking in on his thoughts, "you realize that having a large population of people who contribute nothing to society is a problem for everybody? It can only get worse. People like these Indians are a danger to the balance of things. That's why the rainforest on the border of Guatemala and Mexico was devastated in under thirty years. And that's why Arrow's board of directors intends to make sure it doesn't happen again. Even if it means war."

"War? I don't think the Belizeans will be taking up arms to save a bunch of trees." Marty chuckled, trying to lighten the conversation. "I got the impression they're pretty easygoing."

"They are," she agreed in a tone he took as exasperation. "They're no different than the Indians. Lazy socialists. If nobody was watching, all of Central America would go to hell. All people care about down here is their next tortilla. Thank God for the British and American military. If there's a problem on the Belizean border, Arch and Del will be the ones who'll make it right. They learned everything there is to know about guerrilla warfare in Vietnam. They could go head-to-head with the Guatemalans any day."

Marty nodded. It was all starting to add up. Planetlife was right on the Guatemalan border. Templeton and Waters were former Special Forces. The guides here were trained guerrillas. Maybe the U.S. government was using the rainforest preserve as a cover. Maybe the Top Dollar airstrip had been bankrolled by the CIA. His thoughts suddenly leaped to Chicago and Planetlife's brownstone office. Maybe it was a cover too. Maybe that's where Harper and Kemper fit in.

He wondered if Carson was aware of a relationship between Planetlife and the CIA—and, if his theory was on target, about their intense interest in Arrow's ad agency. But then, if she knew that much . . .

Marty studied Carson for a moment, silently noting that the champagne had definitely had an effect; she was relaxed all right, and talkative. If he was ever going to get any answers, now was probably the time for questions. He'd just have to take it slow, work up to what he really wanted to know. "I understand," he said nonchalantly, "that Arch Templeton flew in the military?"

"Uh-huh," she replied, sipping at her champagne. "Arch is probably the best pilot south of the border. He and Del came down with the U.S. military about twenty years ago."

"So they came down to assist with the situation in Nicaragua?"

"No, the one in Belize."

Marty frowned, scanning his recollections of the U.S. military's involvement in Central America over the past twenty years. What situation in Belize? he wondered. "So when their stint in the military was over, I take it they decided to stay and Waters went into selling soft drinks?"

"Yeah." She nodded. "It's a real success story. Going from soldiers to international magnates! Now they even have presidents and heads of state coming here to see them."

"I guess that's why they built that huge runway at Top Dollar." He was pushing harder now.

"I guess," she replied, her voice trailing off as if she were suddenly bored with the conversation, and the thought occurred to Marty that Carson knew more than she was saying, but it was obvious his little fishing expedition was over—for now, at least.

"Hey," she said, throwing him a coquettish pout, "enough about politics. Let's talk about you. Is it true? Are you really *attached*?" She wrinkled her nose at the word.

"Yeah, I am," he answered, feeling suddenly stodgy.

"I hear she's a real beauty with brains . . . a photojournalist with credentials out the wazoo." At the look on Marty's face, she laughed out loud. "Your director buddy, Jules Benson, he's a real talker. Really, I think it's kind of sweet . . . a guy like you, a guy who could have any woman he wanted, settling on *just* one." She made a face. "Jesus. It sounds so boring. But then again, I don't really believe it."

"Believe it?"

"That you're such a straight arrow." She smiled and reached over to touch his hand. "I've seen the way you look at me, Marty." Her voice had lowered to a sultry whisper. "Come on, admit it. You've wanted me all along . . . haven't you?"

She had him and she knew it. "Like I said," he replied uncomfortably, "I'm attached."

"So?" She shrugged. "Most of the guys I know are involved with somebody. That doesn't stop them. Besides, if you were really committed, you'd be married."

Reiki had said those very words. "I'm attached, Carson, not blind," he objected. "You're a good-looking woman, okay? But this is business."

"Business!" she grumbled, standing up. "Thank God you can at least admit that you'd like to get in the sack with me. I was getting tired of all the games." She tossed her head back haughtily. "But now I see that you're a man—just like all the rest."

"Then you should know I'm just as boring and thoughtless as every other man."

"You'll have to do better than that." She shot him an amused glance. "What the hell, I guess you can play it any way you want. But I can tell you I'd never get that involved with somebody, not in a million years." She laughed a mocking laugh. "Not a chance. *Meaningful* relationships bore me. They always have. I guess I should've been a man. I like to play the field too much. And I like to be in charge. I haven't found a man yet that could keep me satisfied. Besides, who wants to sleep with the same guy night after night? Not me. I can fluff my own pillows, thank you."

Surprising himself, Marty laughed aloud. He had to hand it to her: Carson knew what she wanted and she went after it.

She took a few steps in front of him, stretching languidly, her damp, round breasts clinging to the fabric of her camisole. Even in the dark he could see her erect nipples. "Speaking of pillows," she said, "did you know Escoba's are eiderdown? They're made in France. All the linens come from Ireland. Every cabana's designed to create a special ambience." She padded across the porch to the doorway. "There's no two alike," she said, peering through the screen into the dark room. "How's your place decorated?" He saw her put her hand on the door.

"It's a real mess in there," Marty said quickly. "I'd be embarrassed for you to see it."

"Bullshit!" she retorted, turning back to the door. "If my ad man is a disorganized slob, I think I should know about it." The screen door creaked open and then slapped shut behind her.

Goddammit, she was in his room.

Chapter 30

The security system at Chicago's palatial Astor had been experiencing problems for almost a week. Jack Flannigan, the portly doorman, was tired of going down to the basement to reset the system. And even more tired of fielding calls from angry residents. When the alarm went off again that Tuesday night, he blew his stack and called Dorbett Security Systems, demanding they fix the problem *pronto*.

Flannigan was impressed with Dorbett's promptness and expertise; within thirty minutes—and maybe less, he asserted later—Dorbett's sedately painted beige vans arrived, their jumpsuited security team descending on the Astor's doorstep, arms loaded down with metal attaché cases filled with what Flannigan could only assume were the tools of their trade.

Fifteen minutes later, Dorbett's security supervisor, a man with a strangely wooden face, came down to the lobby to say they'd pinpointed the problem: The recent ice storm had created moisture along the cabling system and, thanks to that, three of the condos had faulty response systems. Dorbett's men would need a pass key.

The explanation made sense to Flannigan. It had been a wet winter, after all. He gave the Dorbett man what he wanted and let him get to work. And, for the first time in days, the Astor was quiet.

* * *

"Looks like ad men do pretty well for themselves, doesn't it? Get a load of this antique chest." Max Harper looked over his shoulder at his partner. "This remind you of anything, Roger?" He didn't wait for a reply. "Nineteen seventy-two, Jakarta, Indonesia." He grinned. "Now *those* were the days."

Kemper shook his head impatiently. "We don't have time to admire English's interior design talent." He turned to the other four men standing in the condo's hallway. "You three each take a room. You know what to do." They gave a nod and disappeared down the hall. The fourth man, a gaunt, balding fellow, shifted on his feet, waiting for Kemper's command.

Kemper ignored him, turning back to Harper. "What's in the chest?"

"CDs." Harper moaned. "Hundreds, thousands, of them. This is gonna take all night."

"Well, get going then. Test every fucking one of them if you have to. And remember, put them back just like you found them. Alphabetical, whatever. We don't want a thing out of place. Del likes a neat job."

Annoyed, Harper shook his head. "Jesus, give a man a uniform and put him in charge . . . how long we been working for Waters? Thirty years? I think I know what he likes by now."

Kemper chuckled and turned back to the other man. "Shelby, you come with me," he said. "I found the computer."

Chapter 31

Carson Page sat down on Marty's bed and smiled. "Jules Benson gave me his version of the Marty English story, so now it's your turn. Tell me, Marty, who's really behind those Foster Grants?"

Marty looked down at his watch.

"Forget the time," she said, giving his wrist a playful slap. "Let's talk a while."

"It's getting late, Carson. Tall tales take a long time. We should get some rest."

"You're throwing me out?" She pouted, lying back on the bed. She leaned up on one elbow and smiled seductively. "But I'm the client—you can't do that."

"No, I'm not throwing you out. But if you think today was a long one, wait 'til tomorrow. It's late, we should . . ."

She sat up and stretched, catlike, ignoring his remark. "God, I never knew silk could be so hot." She untied the pareo and tossed it to him. "What do you think?"

What did he think? Shit, she was sitting on his bed in nothing but a camisole and lace panties. What kind of question was that?

"About the scarf." She giggled, as if reading his mind. "It's Hermés. Think it was worth eight hundred bucks?"

"It's nice," he said awkwardly, looking down at the piece of silk that smelled of her perfume. "Eight hundred dollars?" He smiled stiffly and handed it back to her. "That was probably a fair price."

Frowning, she got up on her knees to face him. "Stop it, Marty. Let's not play any more games, okay?" She reached over and gave him a kiss. Her lips felt good, wet and warm; he would have liked to have kissed her back. She moved closer and he could feel her breath on his face. "We're both adults, Marty. Let's be honest—we both know what this is about." She started unbuttoning the tiny pearls running down the front of her top. "I want you. And you . . . want me." The camisole parted and her breasts tumbled out.

They were firm and high—just large enough to put his hands around, he thought—and Marty knew that she was right. No matter that he was attached, no matter that he despised the kind of bigotry Carson espoused. This had nothing to do with reason and everything to do with the desire he felt throbbing insistently between his legs. Yeah, he wanted to touch her. He wanted to mouth the nipples that jutted out at him invitingly. To taste them. To taste *her.*

Carson saw it in his eyes and gave him a knowing smile and took his hands and put them on her breasts, cupping them, moving them around until her nipples went hard beneath his fingers.

But at the sight of her arousal, Marty's discomfort returned. Jesus, he thought angrily, what the hell was he thinking? Or was his dick doing that for him now? He couldn't get it on with Carson Page. No way. "Carson . . ." he said huskily, withdrawing his hands.

Her mouth went over his, smothering his protest in kisses. "Let go, Marty," she whispered, unzipping his trousers. Feeling Carson's hand on the bulge there, Marty pulled back. "Goddammit, what's wrong?" she cried. Her face was flushed and she was breathing hard. "Is it me?"

"No. No, it's not you. You're beautiful. Maybe in another place, you know, another time . . . maybe things could've been different. It's just that . . ."

She groaned and fell back on the bed. "It's your fucking conscience, isn't it? That girlfriend of yours back in Chicago? Jesus, don't tell me I've hooked up with the only ad man with ethics. Really, Marty, I thought you were more together than that. Life's short. Play hard."

He stood up. "This isn't a good idea. Getting involved—"

"Involved?" she hooted. "Who said anything about that? I just want to feel good. You keep going on about me being your client. Well, isn't it your job to make your client feel good?" She glared at him like a spoiled child and sat up, easing forward. "You *do* want me to be happy, don't you?" she demanded, wrapping her hand around his throbbing length. Keeping her eyes fixed on his, she moved her hand slowly, up and down.

He felt himself responding, pulsing. For a brief moment, Marty stared down at the beautiful woman's upturned face. Then, unable to listen to the battle raging in his head and heart any longer, he pulled her to him and succumbed to his desire.

When Marty woke up, he was alone and it was still dark. The candle flame was flickering, fighting to stay alive in the cool breeze. At first he'd forgotten—the image was hazy, more dream than reality. But at the scent of a woman on his hands, the pillow, his mouth, he moaned.

Carson Page had won. He'd been a challenge to her, nothing more, and he guessed he should be glad for that. What had happened between them was about power, not love, so at least there wouldn't be a next step, some awkward tangle of miscommunication.

Marty sat up and lit one of the cigarettes Carson had left lying on the table. Reiki wouldn't approve of him smoking, he thought, turning the cigarette around in his fingers. He wished he'd brought his harmonica; it would've made a good oral stand-in. He smiled to himself. Reiki liked it when he played the blues. She said it gave him "dimension."

Reiki.

He sighed, exhaling a cloud of smoke. God, in seven years he'd never been with another woman. Not for any reason other than he hadn't wanted to. And that he loved Reiki. They'd had a thing about trust from the very beginning. Maybe because they'd both been burned before—or maybe they were just tired of relationships based purely on sex. Whatever the reason, they'd agreed to be up front with each other. After all, Reiki insisted, if you can't trust the person you live with, who *can* you trust? He thought she was right.

So what the hell was this thing with Carson? Hell, he didn't have any romantic feelings for her. She'd been good in bed, but that was all it was. Carson was a fuck, plain and simple. Would Reiki understand that? He shook his head ruefully. What woman would? No matter what they'd said in the past about honesty, he couldn't tell Reiki about this. When it came to cheating, confession was only good for the soul of the confessor. No, he'd just go back to Chicago and get on with it all, pretend nothing had ever happened. Hell, he was good at pretending, wasn't he?

The real reason he'd played along with Carson's little game was simple, and not very flattering. He knew she wanted him, so he just gave her what she wanted. He crushed out the cigarette. He was a whore just like everybody else, just another pilgrim looking for paradise.

He'd made his choice with both eyes open. But had he also chosen to give up the only woman he'd ever really loved? Or could he still turn back—before it was too late?

Chapter 32

Marty was dressed and out of his cabana by dawn. The past was the past—for now at least, he told himself, pushing his feelings aside. Right now he had to take care of the future; they had to get the Arrow spot in the can. And that meant getting Jules Benson in line, whatever it took.

Marty found Zak and Kidman sitting on Benson's porch, heads in their hands, looking about as useful as Beavis and Butt-Head. At his approach, they stood up and tried to look lively, like they'd actually been doing something besides pissing and moaning.

"Where's Benson?" Marty demanded as he stepped onto the porch.

"Inside," Zak replied, motioning behind him.

Kidman nodded somberly. "Dead to the fucking world."

"So what the hell are you two doing out here? Get in there and wake the son of a bitch up."

"Shit fire, Marty." Kidman groaned. "We *can't* wake him up. We've tried everything."

"Kidman's right," Zak jumped in. "Look, we want this shoot to go well just as much as you do, but short of a motherfuckin' miracle . . . well, in less than an hour and a half, the shit's gonna hit the fan."

Marty didn't shoot back a clever reply; he was looking up

at the sky. He'd heard a distant rumbling that sounded like thunder and, indeed, some dark clouds were rolling in. Hadn't Carson mentioned last night that there was rain in the air?

"Was that thunder?" Kidman asked, following Marty's gaze.

"Sure sounds like it," Zak answered.

Marty's wheels were turning now; if it rained, the shoot would be called off and they'd have a day to get things under control. That, he thought, would be divine intervention.

"A good rain day would save our ass," Kidman remarked wistfully, as if he'd read Marty's thoughts.

Zak shook his head. "From what I just heard back at the lodge, our resident Elvis won't see it that way."

"Torello's already having his Wheaties?" Marty exclaimed in surprise. He hadn't figured Arrow's president for the high-energy type.

"Yep. He and Carson Page are over at the lodge, having coffee as we speak. I heard him going on about how disappointed everybody's gonna be if it rains all week and we don't get the ad done."

At Carson's name, Marty inhaled sharply. He'd almost forgotten the gloom he was feeling about what he prayed had been a one-night stand. "Torello's just flapping his damn jaws," he said quickly. He didn't want them to panic, not after all that crap about NHP Benson had been shooting off his mouth about. "He's a compulsive worrier," Marty added. "Carson says he's like a dog with fleas when something gets under his skin. You know, dig, dig, dig."

"Maybe." Zak shrugged. "But he was talking Plan B with Carson just now. He said if they didn't get the new campaign produced they'd just have to run the old Endall spot, or maybe they'd just bail out of the Super Bowl and put off the new-product introduction until late spring or early summer."

"Hey, what about Lee's media schedule?" Kidman demanded, glaring at Marty. "I mean, she's been workin' her ass off to put that thing together." He shook his head. "I'm sure glad it's you, and not me, who'd have to drop that bomb."

Zak let out a sigh. "If Arrow dropped their media for first and second quarter, that'd sure fuck things up, wouldn't it?"

Yeah, it would, Marty thought. And the agency's cash flow, too. But he didn't let them see his concern. "Forget about it, guys," he soothed. "Nothing's going to fuck things up. First of all, it's too late for Arrow to dump out of the Super Bowl. Carson knows that. And besides, the network wouldn't go for that in a million years. Secondly, this isn't the rainy season in Belize. It's *not* going to rain all week. Okay? We'll get the spot in the can. But as far as today goes, well, you can pray like hell for it to rain today. We need to keep this problem with Benson under wraps."

"Did somebody say pray?" Kidman asked with a country-boy grin. "When it comes to connections with the Big Guy, you've come to the right place. Consider it done." Like a two-bit TV evangelist waiting for those phones to ring, Kidman folded his hands dramatically and gazed heavenward.

"So you've got your own highway to heaven just like Jimmy Swaggart?" Marty laughed, shaking his head doubt-fully. "Well, you're going to have to prove it to me." He stuck his hand out from under the porch ceiling. A large raindrop smacked him on the palm and he let out a whistle of surprise. "Damn, I'm impressed, Kidman." He held up his wet hand.

Kidman beamed with satisfaction. "What can I say? Ask and ye shall receive."

The rain started coming down harder.

"I can't believe it!" Zak exclaimed. "We've got ourselves a rain day."

"I'll go let the crew know," Kidman called out from the path; he was already on his way.

"Oh, before I forget . . ." Zak turned back to Marty and handled him a paper napkin. "Here's that drawing of the glyph you wanted. Sorry about the napkin—it's all I could find last night."

"No problem," Marty replied as he carefully unfolded it. "Wow, Zak." He looked up. "You must have photographic memory. It's a dead ringer for the one on the disc."

"Yeah, it is, isn't it? I was pretty pleased with it myself." Zak smiled that satisfied smile all art directors got when they knew they were good. "So, if you don't mind my asking, what are you gonna do with it?"

"I thought I'd show it to Che. You know, see what he makes of it."

"Good idea. Speaking of which, you got any good ideas about what we're gonna do about *him*?" Zak gestured toward the cabana.

Marty smiled coolly. "Forget about him. Nobody's indispensable. Not even Jules Benson."

"Marty!" Frank Torello called out from across the lodge dining room. "Over here."

Marty waved back and hung up the phone.

Carson was sitting next to Arrow's president, a changed woman. Overnight she'd dropped the native girl–seductress wardrobe and gone professional. Now she had Talbot's written all over her: She was decked out head-to-toe preppie with linen slacks, a tailored shirt, and a duck belt by Dooney & Bourke.

Carson had been dressing—and behaving—seductively since their first meeting. But apparently that had all been a costume, a prop, in a carefully orchestrated plot to get him into bed. At least Marty had learned how manipulative and ambitious she really was, even if he'd had to learn it the hard way.

When he got to the table, he pasted on a cheerful smile, sat down and said "Good morning" with as much enthusiasm as he could call up.

Carson handed him a menu and looked into his eyes. He pretended he didn't notice the glint of triumph there. "I hate to be the bearer of bad news," he announced, "but the shoot's been called. It's a washout for today."

"That's what we figured," Carson said, nodding at Torello. "Frank's already past thinking about today, though. He's worried about the rest of the week. Of course I told him not to give it a second thought; it *never* rains more than a day down here this time of year. I'm sure it won't this time." She put her cup of coffee to her lips, her eyes smiling over the rim.

Marty's head bobbed up and down in dutiful agreement. So aside from nailing ad guys to the wall, Carson Page was also an expert in meteorology. Oh well, he was in no mood to tangle with her again, particularly not so early in the morning. Instead he merely nodded at Torello and said, in a voice more confident than he felt, "Don't waste your time worrying, Frank. At Bergman we know these things happen. Hell, we *plan* on it. That's why the production guys always budget for a rain day. You know, for insurance, just in case."

"I appreciate that," Torello said, mumbling into his coffee. "I just wish I knew about the rest of the week."

"Take it easy, Frank," Arch Templeton said, coming up to the table. "By the end of the week you'll be begging for shade."

Torello frowned up at Templeton, towering above him. He'd been startled by the man's sudden appearance, and now he was annoyed. "Where the hell did you come from, Arch? Jesus, you're starting to sneak around everywhere you go. You know, life isn't one big combat maneuver."

Templeton laughed and shot a wink at Marty and Carson. "Well, now that we're past the friendly hellos, I think I'll sit down."

Torello put on a good-natured grin and pulled out a chair. "Have a seat."

"Thanks. Don't mind if I do," Templeton replied, sitting down and tucking his long legs under the table. Away from Chicago's skyscrapers and granite, Arch Templeton looked even bigger, even more Greystoke.

"So when did you get in, Arch?" Carson asked, passing a menu across the table.

"About an hour ago. It rained the whole damned way, too, from San Pedro to Top Dollar."

Torello let out an audible sigh. "Does that mean a storm front's coming in from the ocean?"

Templeton shook his head. "Relax, will you, Frank? This'll blow over as fast as it hit. It's not going to rain tomorrow. The forecast is for sun. Today's just a fluke, a good day to take a nap in that hammock hanging on your cabana porch. Why don't you just kick back and enjoy it?" Templeton didn't wait for a reply, but quickly turned to Marty. "So how was the ride in with Che last night?"

"The ride was great," Marty answered. "Che treated us like royalty. And he's full of stories—he really knows a lot about the Maya. I imagine he knows even more about the jungle."

Templeton nodded cautiously.

Marty looked around the table. "Since it's going to be a rain day, I think I'll ask Che to take me on a jungle hike." He was anxious to have Che take a look at Zak's drawing—as well as find out what was really going on down here.

Carson gave Templeton a look of alarm. "Is that a good idea, Arch? Che's an old man. Who knows what could happen to Marty out there."

"She's right, Marty," Templeton agreed. "Forgive me for saying so, but you're an ad man, not a jungle naturalist. And Che, well, he's a sweet old guy who gets confused about things sometimes. He has quite an active imagination, you know. He hasn't gotten lost out there yet, but—"

"I'm sure Arch can find someone more qualified than Che," Torello interjected. "Right, Arch?"

Templeton nodded. "If you're really dead set on going out, Marty, I'd recommend you take my man, Carlos."

They all stared back at Marty now, waiting for his reply. Obviously, Arch Templeton didn't want him alone with Che. But then if Templeton was aware of Che's feelings about

Planetlife and his employers, Marty couldn't blame him for wanting to keep him away from the guests. But maybe it was more than that: maybe Templeton was afraid of what Che might have to say about his little CIA project in the middle of a rainforest.

But what about Carson and Torello? They seemed pretty eager to keep him away from the kindly Indian, too. What were they so worried about? Puzzled as well as intrigued, Marty flashed an easy smile around the table. "I'm sure Carlos is an excellent guide," he said. "But I think I'll stick with Che." He turned to Templeton and added slyly, "That is, if you don't mind."

"Of course not," Arch replied with a careless shrug.

Hoping to diffuse Carson and Torello's mysterious concerns about the Indian, Marty explained, "Che and I hit it off right away. I'd enjoy spending a few hours in a rainforest with him, listening to his stories, even if they are nothing more than an old man's ramblings."

"I guess it's settled, then," Torello mumbled uncomfortably.

Nodding, Carson averted her eyes and picked up her menu.

"Before you go, Marty, a piece of advice," Templeton said, smiling icily. "It's a jungle out there—watch your step."

eyed the diner.

Chapter 33

ello Holley's was on Chicago's westside, where all-
night joints and stabbings went hand in hand. The diner's
burly owner, Holley Habacker, had a criminal record, including three charges of aggravated assault, that was as long as the
reptilian tattoo winding up his hairy arm and around his thick
bull neck until it came to rest, open-mouthed, at the base of
his oily James Dean duck's-ass. In spite of his jailbird history,
Holley was quick to point out that he was reformed now. It
had taken some determination, he admitted, but he'd become
an upstanding citizen, as well as a man of culture and style.

Despite its proprietor's questionable past, Hello Holley's
had become a home away from home for the men in blue. Indeed, the little diner was a cop's dream come true: Holley
kept them up to their asses in hot pastrami on rye and danish
and coffee. A rookie, new on the beat, had his first free meal
there. An old-timer, his last supper before slapping on that
tacky gold watch and heading for Sun City. Occasionally, in
his effort at "good relations," Holley even went so far as to
pass on a tip or two—in exchange for a pass on some health
code or green-card violation.

Down on Chicago's westside, everybody from cops to cons
thought Holley Habacker could walk on water. But appearances and free meals aside, Holley was no saint; thirty pieces

of silver were all that was necessary to buy his loyalty. More than one poor devil had taken his last supper at Hello Holley's and ended up lying in the weeds in a vacant lot.

It was still dark that Wednesday morning when Ford Sinclair pulled up in front of Hello Holley's and parked the family wagon. He sat there for a minute, shivering while he fiddled with the heater, trying to figure out why the hell he was freezing to death. Finally, he gave up and started wrestling with the key in the ignition.

"Goddammit," he grumbled aloud as he jerked it free of the rusting metal. His wife had complained she'd broken a nail on the ignition, but why hadn't she warned him about the fucking heater? Sinclair sighed. Crissie had been asking for a new car for months. He looked around at the depressing interior of the '86 Taurus wagon. In ten years the kids and that damned dog of theirs had made a real mess of it. And Crissie wasn't blameless, either. Hell, she hardly ever took it to the car wash. When he complained he hadn't gone to college just so he and his family could look like they were on welfare, she'd just laugh and toss back, "But baby, look at it. I mean, what's the use?"

What *was* the use? he wondered as he took a swipe across the dash with his gloved hand. He studied the coat of grimy dust on his leather-covered palm. Filthy, just like the rest of the rattletrap. Filthy and falling apart. The radio was broken. The automatic windows were broken. And the seats, they were torn up to hell. Crissie'd thrown fake sheepskin over the back and put those weird little wooden-ball things over the seats up front. They helped her back, she told him.

Well, maybe he'd surprise her; her birthday was coming up next week. Maybe he'd just go right down to Al Paemonte Ford tomorrow afternoon and buy one of those goddamned Eddie Bauer Explorers all the neighborhood women drove. Sinclair smiled, pleased at the prospect of a smiling Crissie behind the wheel of a shiny 4 x 4.

He put his hand on the car door and started to shove it open with his shoulder, but, noticing the headlights of a car gliding down the street toward him, he paused instinctively and held his breath, waiting for it to pass. Coming in from Lake Forest, Sinclair had noticed a car tagging him. He couldn't make out the model or make—it had hung three cars back in the traffic, maybe more.

He watched now as the car crept by and then turned down a side street. He didn't think it was the same car that had been following him, but then he wouldn't stake his life on it, either. Ever since he'd gotten involved with Marty English, somebody had been tailing him. It was definitely not his imagination, and it was starting to get on his nerves.

Resolutely, Sinclair forced open the creaking metal door and stepped out onto the icy curb.

Shivering in the cold, Sinclair glanced back and forth, up and down the length of the street and, seeing no one, shook his head. Shit, he was getting as bad as Marty. An image of the ad exec flitted through his mind, and Sinclair grimaced. Here he was, freezing his ass off, running all over God's green earth for the guy, risking his life, goddammit, trying to figure out who had killed Inglesia. And what was Marty doing? "Working" in some tropical paradise?

Hell, Marty was probably working all right—working some good-looking woman, sitting in the shade under a polka-dot umbrella and drinking a goddamned rum punch.

The vision didn't improve Ford Sinclair's mood. The weekend snow had melted but had been replaced by freezing rain that coated the sidewalks, roads, and highways in a treacherous glaze. Hell, even rich guys with Mercedes had trouble driving on that kind of shit.

Trying not to slip and fall, Sinclair stepped gingerly across the sidewalk, the salt crunching beneath his Totes. Yeah, he thought irritably, Marty was probably kicking up his heels in some Latin resort, doing the limbo and that hot, salsa shit. And here he was standing in front of a two-bit diner, trying to stay alive. Or at least avoid having his dick fall off from frost-bite.

The lights in the diner were low; Holley Habacker liked them that way, claiming bright lights reminded him of past interrogations. As Sinclair searched the bustling diner for Stone Jackson, he was grateful for the shadows. When Sinclair approached the red Formica counter, Habacker wiped his big hands on the greasy dish towel slung over his shoulder and waved. "What you been up to, Ford? Ain't seen you around." He grinned. "Got a lot of trouble with those rich fuckers in Lake County, huh?"

Sinclair chuckled. "Yeah, same old shit, Holley. One damned homicide after another. Mostly guys killing their wives because they caught 'em banging the tennis pro at the country club. You know, shit like that."

Laughing, Habacker slid a plate of sunny-side-ups and toast across the counter to a kid sitting on a stool. Sinclair hadn't noticed the kid until then and, as his trained detective's eye skimmed over him, he suddenly realized that something about the kid didn't jibe. There was a Walkman on his head and he was spinning on his stool in time—nothing strange about that. But as far as Sinclair could make out, the cassette in the player wasn't moving. And that *was* strange.

Sinclair edged closer, pretending to study the menu scrawled on a chalkboard overhead. No, the cassette wasn't moving. Or was it? He looked again. The cassette was spinning along inside the player, just the way it was supposed to. Son of a bitch. Now he was seeing things. Sinclair swore to himself. But hell, why not? He was being followed most of the time. And just yesterday, for no good reason he could come up with, his captain had closed the Inglesia case. Sinclair had hit the ceiling at the news, marched right into Captain Malone's office and demanded an explanation.

But Malone had just passed the decision off to a combination of Sinclair's lack of evidence in the case and the precinct being short on manpower; Lake Forest just didn't have the resources to run down blind alleys in some vain hope of figuring out whether a criminal killed himself or not. When Sinclair pressed harder, the captain turned stone-faced as a sphinx, and Sinclair, knowing that look well, realized it was no use.

Oddly enough given their heated discussion earlier in the day, Sinclair had been called back into Malone's office that afternoon and commended for his hard work. His reward, the captain announced, was a two-week vacation, effective immediately. The only time a thing like that happened to a cop was in his dreams. Something smelled to high heaven, Sinclair thought; he just wasn't sure what that something was, though he was intrigued by the fact that it had occurred on the heels of a phone call from his friend at the CIA, Stone Jackson.

When Sinclair told his wife that he questioned Captain Malone's motives, Crissie got a funny look on her face and suggested he stop by her office at Social Services to have a little chat with one of the counselors. He was acting goofy, she told him, and not a little bit paranoid. "Don't look a gift horse in the mouth," she commanded.

Sinclair decided to agree; she was right, he told her. He'd kick back for a while, watch a little TV in the morning, take a nap in the afternoon. Make love to her at night. Be on the job as a full-time husband and father for a change.

But while he *would* devote most of his attention to his family for a few weeks, he had no intention of turning his back on the Inglesia case. He'd told Marty he'd find out what those CIA boys were up to and he'd keep his word. He had his sources. Stone Jackson for one. Evidently, Stone had come through.

Sinclair's eyes swept back over the diner, looking for his old friend. At the sight of an impeccably groomed black man in an expensive leather coat, seated in a booth, Sinclair smiled. They went way back, him and "Sly"—all the way to their college days at IU. They'd first become friends over a common interest in law enforcement and, probably, Sinclair had to admit, because they were both black and shared the sting of prejudice. They'd both gotten involved in the King movement, although Sinclair had been drawn more to Malcolm X than Martin Luther. Malcolm told it like it was, Sinclair thought, not like he wished it would be. He and Stone used to argue about that sort of shit all night long. Those were the days of shaking your booty, Afros, and Funkadelics. The days when a guy with any balls at all admitted he inhaled.

But, slowly, things had changed. They stopped inhaling smoke and started blowing it; maybe it was just that they'd grown up. Or maybe it was just that one of them subscribed to Sly and the Family Stone's "Stand," while the other was a "Dance to the Music" kind of guy. In any case, their paths diverged; Jackson got recruited by the CIA and Sinclair went to the police academy. They still kept in touch, of course. Although these days things were so busy that their contact was limited mostly to Christmas, exchanging news in Hallmark cards.

Reaching Jackson's booth, Sinclair scooted across the red vinyl seat and held up two fingers at the waitress. She was new; he'd never seen her before. "Two coffees," he said.

"Sure thing, honey," she replied, wiggling away. She came back with the oily black brew before Sinclair even had a chance to say hello to Stone Jackson.

"Got some Sweet'n Low?" Sinclair asked her.

Nodding, she took a handful of the little packets from her grease-spattered apron pocket and laid them on the table. "Anything else I can get you fellas?"

Jackson shook his head solemnly at Sinclair.

"Guess not," Sinclair answered. He smiled and added, "Except maybe a few minutes' peace and quiet."

"I can handle that," she said, giving him a little wink as she moved on to the next booth.

Sinclair turned back to Jackson. "Sly, you aren't looking so good this morning. You're mighty pale." He grinned. "Aren't turning white on me, are you?"

Jackson didn't smile at the joke, and when he picked up his cup of coffee and took a sip, Sinclair saw that his hands were shaking.

Jackson put the cup down. "I think I stepped on it, Ford," he said hoarsely. "Yeah, I think I stepped on it real good this time."

Sinclair frowned. "But you . . ."

"Yeah, sure," Jackson said defensively, "I was glad to get you the dope on your boys, Harper and Kemper. Have I ever let you down? I got everything there was. Which wasn't much, I can tell you." Jackson slid a manila folder across the table and sighed. "Guess I never expected you to throw me a curve ball like this. It's big-time, Ford. Big time."

Sinclair picked up the folder and weighed it in his hand. He had his doubts; the file was, maybe, four, five ounces tops. "This is *it*?"

"Yeah. That's it." Jackson fumbled in his coat pocket and pulled out a pack of cigarettes. "Got a match?"

"No, I don't. And I don't have a lighter, either." He paused and frowned. "Since when did you start? You never smoked."

"When I read that fucking file, that's when. Like I said, Ford, this is big time."

"Big time?" Sinclair held up the file and laughed. "You call this big?"

"Go ahead, read it. Nasty things come in small packages, bro. And while you're at it, read between the lines. Those fuckers of yours aren't just your regular garden-variety home-boys shuffling a bunch of papers from one continent to the next. No, they're *bad*, Ford. Covert Operations, Special Forces . . . they're into it all. You name it, they've probably done it. The only reason they're probably not in prison is because they'll do anything the agency wants, no questions. *Anything*, Ford. Man, the agency loves guys like that."

Sinclair stared back at his friend. Was this the same guy who'd never even raised his voice once during the march on Washington? In all those years, Sinclair had never seen Stone Jackson worked up. This was a guy known for his cool; whatever was in the folder had to be dynamite.

A wave of anticipation surged through Sinclair as he flipped open the folder, but his face fell at the sight of a thin sheaf of faded photocopies.

"They're originals," Jackson continued. "I had to lift the entire file. I wasn't about to risk making copies. High-security documents can sound an alarm when they're copied on agency machines."

"Is that right?" Sinclair queried distractedly. He took a pair of reading glasses out of his shirt pocket and looked down at the open folder. "Don't think I ever heard of that before. Must be some kind of high-tech magnetic shit. What'll you guys think of next? Guess I shouldn't ask if we can make a quick stop by Kinko's . . . before you take this back?" He looked up to see Jackson shaking his head.

Sinclair looked back at the folder. The dossiers were both marked CLASSIFIED, EYES ONLY. One was on Harper, the other on Kemper. "I'm not gonna ask how the hell you got your hands on these," he promised, glancing up.

"Good. Because you don't want to know." Jackson's eyes darted around the diner. "Hey, don't take all day, okay?"

"Keep your pants on," Sinclair replied, his eyes skimming over the two pages.

According to the file, the agents' real names were David G. Robertson and Frank W. Slater, though they could've been the James brothers from what the dossiers said; they'd certainly stirred up enough trouble over the past thirty years. They were expert marksmen, explosives and electronics specialists, and extraordinary linguists. They got their training at Langley and their feet wet in 'Nam. But that was just the start of an illustrious career in brutalities sanctioned by the U.S. government—that was the unaccountable part of it.

In the sixties and early seventies, the two men served as covert military advisers in undeclared wars. Vietnam, Cambodia, Laos, Korea—they'd been to them all. They'd lived and worked with the locals, eaten in their huts, slept with their women. And then, when the time was right, they'd called in their buddies and proceeded to annihilate whole villages.

From Southeast Asia, the agents went on to work in the Middle East. They got in bed with a radical Massad splinter group that had infiltrated various Islamic factions in Lebanon and Cyprus, blew up a few buildings, knocked off a few Israeli enemies. They had no scruples.

In the eighties, they headed for Central America; Guatemala and Nicaragua were heating up and things had gotten shaky in Panama: Noriega wasn't playing ball. Pineapple Face's cocaine shipments to Miami were getting light; he was skimming, evidently. Once the renegades in the CIA got wind of that, it wasn't too long before Noriega had half the fucking U.S. Army using his balls as a teething ring and Harper and Kemper were on to their next *excellent adventure.*

Yeah, Mr. Robertson and Mr. Slater—if those were their real names—had been two busy fucking bees, all right.

Sinclair scanned the list of places they'd plied their commando talents. At the last, and most recent, country on the list, he caught his breath. *Belize.* The word ricocheted around in his brain like a .38 slug. "Why, I'll be a son of a bitch . . . that's where Marty is," he said aloud.

"Who?" Jackson asked irritably.

"Nothing," Sinclair answered, his eyes still fixed on the word *Belize*, his thoughts still racing. He slipped the two sheets of paper back into the folder and handed it to Jackson.

"So there you have it." Jackson sighed as he tucked the folder under his overcoat. "Satisfied?"

Sinclair smiled. "Of course not. Am I ever?" He took his glasses off and rubbed at his eyes. "You got any idea who they report to?"

"Somebody *high* up, that's for sure. And my guess is they have to have a liaison on the outside, too."

"Liaison?"

"Yeah, probably somebody out of the mainstream . . . somebody who can get things done."

Sinclair's eyes narrowed. "What kind of things?"

"Things they want to keep under wraps, things Congress would never in a million fucking years approve of."

"You mean like the Castro assassination plot in 'sixty-one?"

"That's exactly what I mean."

Sinclair nodded thoughtfully. "That was the Mob on the Castro deal. You think they're in on this, too?" He didn't wait for an answer. "That's what I think."

"The Mob?" Jackson glanced around the room and then back to Sinclair. "Let's go outside, okay?" He threw a ten-dollar bill on the table and started for the door.

"Whatever you say," Sinclair replied, grabbing his overcoat. As he passed the counter, Holley Habacker waved goodbye and called out, "Don't forget your old friends, Ford."

Habacker's smile disappeared as the door closed behind Sinclair. He wiped his hands on the greasy towel over his shoulder and then picked up the phone and dialed it. It rang one time and a voice said, "And the word is . . ."

"Love," Habacker said with a grin.

"Yeah? What's up?"

"We nailed 'em, Roger . . . bigger than shit," Habacker said, winking at his new waitress. "Shelby's girl, Carla, is just as good as you said. . . . She got it all on tape."

As he stepped out of Hello Holley's, a blast of frigid Chicago air took Ford Sinclair's breath away and he tightened the muffler around his neck and pulled on his gloves. He stood there, shivering, letting his eyes get used to the early morning darkness. Stone Jackson was already on the street, standing next to what Sinclair figured had to be a GSA motorpool car.

"What the fuck is this about, Ford?" Jackson yelled angrily.

Looking up and down the street, Sinclair walked closer. "Hey, come on, Stone, keep it down, will you?"

Jackson nodded fiercely and his voice went to a harsh whisper. "You asked me to get a little info on those guys and I did. Hell, I've done a few things for you before. *Small* things. But you were holding out on me on this one. This isn't fucking small—it's the agency tied in with the motherfucking Mob and . . . and who knows what else." He paused. "What's going on here, Ford? Am I in deep shit? 'Cause I think I am. And I think it was you who fucking put me there."

Sinclair let out a sigh and walked closer. "Hey, listen, Stone, I'm sorry. Goddammit, I wish I knew what the hell to tell you. But I don't. All I've got are a million fucking questions. And one mobster's corpse."

"Mobster's corpse?" Jackson frowned. "So you're saying these two guys, Harper and Kemper, were involved in a hit on a U.S. citizen? Forget the man they killed was a fucking criminal. You're saying an American, one of our own, was murdered under the orders of an agency of the U.S. Government? Is that where you're headed with this, Ford?"

Sinclair nodded uncomfortably.

"Who was it? Who'd they hit? Was it that little scumbag Saul Effron?" Not waiting for a reply, Jackson shook his head. "No, it can't be him. . . . Hell, Effron's nothing but a two-bit fence, and nowhere near important enough to get you this freaked out."

Sinclair didn't answer.

"Was it that New York boss, Carlo Caruso? I heard they put him under twenty-four-hour watch down in Marion. Did the long arm of justice reach down there, into a federal pen . . . well, did it?"

Sinclair shook his head.

"This is bigger than that?"

Sinclair looked away and, at a sudden realization, Jackson paled and slammed his clenched fist on the hood of the car. "You goddamned motherfucker. You're talking about Tony Inglesia, aren't you? That's what this is all about." Jackson paused, shock written all over his face. "So you're saying those two animals you had me pull the file on murdered Tony Inglesia? Is that right? Fuck." He shook his head ruefully. "But I thought the papers said Inglesia's death was a suicide."

Sinclair took a step forward. "Fuck the papers, Stone. Trust me, it was a homicide. I'd stake my life on it."

"I'm the one whose fucking life's at stake," Jackson hissed. "Shit, if what you're saying is true, then lifting this folder could do a hell of a lot more than get me canned."

"Maybe I'm wrong, Stone. Hell, Captain Malone sure thought I was off base."

"Yeah, well, your goddamned captain's probably on the take."

Sinclair nodded. "Probably. He closed the case yesterday, said I was chasing my tail." He paused and added bitterly, "Then the son of a bitch turned around and gave me a two-week vacation. Can you believe it?"

"It's a cover-up, sure as shit," Jackson agreed with a groan. He paused and looked down at the keys in his hand. "I've got to go," he said blankly. "Don't be calling me again, either, okay?"

"But you've got to help me get to the bottom of this, Stone."

Jackson looked up and shook his head. "I can't."

"But you've gone this far," Sinclair pleaded. "I promised Inglesia's son I'd get to the bottom of this. Can't you give that tree of yours one more shake?"

"No way, Ford. I've gone too far already. Like I said, I did this as a favor. I didn't know what I was getting into. This is where I get off." He put his car key in the door and started to open it, but Sinclair grabbed him by the arm.

"What is it, Stone?" Sinclair demanded. "What are you so

afraid of? Nobody's gonna know you took the file out. You'll have it back and be home free before those bosses of yours have breakfast."

Shivering in a sudden gust of wind, Jackson turned away.

"Jesus, Stone, I've never seen you this shook before. You talk about me holding back, but what about you? You know something you're not telling me?" Sinclair's eyes met Jackson's. There was fear in his friend's eyes, blind, dumb fear.

"No," Jackson snapped, shoving him away. "I don't know anything. Just drop it. Okay?"

"You're a goddamned liar! Who do you think you're talking to? This is me, Ford Sinclair, standing out here with you in this fucking icebox, not some CIA prick. It's me. *Ford.* Your friend."

Jackson opened the car door and climbed in. "Then take some advice from a friend," he retorted, "and leave this one alone."

"You know I can't do that. . . . Hell, it's too late for me to do that."

Jackson smiled bitterly. "The way I figure it, Ford, it's too late for *me*. Don't you be a fool—get out while you can, while there's still time."

Chapter 34

At the sight of the slight brown Indian waiting for him at the edge of the Belizean rainforest, Marty couldn't help but smile. Che looked more like the Budweiser bullfrog than a stately Indian, squatting beneath a tree, holding a giant palm frond over his head to block the rain.

"I hope you haven't been waiting too long," Marty apologized, noticing that Che's white shirt and trousers were dripping wet.

"Oh, I haven't been waiting," Che replied, his eyes twinkling mischievously. "Well, not for you, anyway."

At Marty's puzzled expression, Che motioned to the tree overhead. "This is our national tree, the ceiba. I think in America you call it the kapok. The Maya believe the ceiba was the first tree on earth and that it grows up from the center of the universe. It is considered sacred. I enjoy very much sitting beneath it, thinking about different things. Today, I was thinking about Ixobai, the beautiful forest seductress who has her feet on backwards. I was hoping she might come along and seduce me. Some people think Ixobai is a myth, but I don't know. I'm not so sure as they are." Suppressing a smile, Che looked back at Marty innocently.

Amused by the Indian's quirky sense of humor, Marty

laughed. "Maybe we should both have a seat and wait," he suggested.

"Not today. There is other business to attend to. You wanted to take a hike into the rainforest?"

Marty nodded.

"Then I will be honored to guide you." Che started walking down a muddy path that had been swept clean of leaves and vines. "Please," he coaxed, "come this way."

As they walked deeper into the lush rainforest, Che paused occasionally to describe the unique features of the jungle, relating the intimate habits of the invisible birds singing in the treetops or explaining the healing properties of various plants.

Reaching a tall, thin palm, its bark spiked with daggerlike thorns, Che stopped. "We call this the give and take," he explained. "The early Spanish *conquistadores* saw the Maya making brooms from the tree's fronds and so they named it the *escoba* . . . the *broom* tree."

"So this is what Isaac Arrow is using for its new line of herbals?"

"Yes. The thorns are quite threatening, aren't they?"

"What are they—three, four inches long?"

Che nodded. "If you were to brush against them you would experience horrible stinging . . . and very serious bleeding. That is where we Maya get the 'give' part of the tree's name."

"I hate to imagine what the 'take' part's about."

"The escoba tree teaches us the meaning of balance. It reminds all who pass that life takes . . . as well as gives. You see, God did not create life with only one side to its nature. There is duality in all things, what we call 'good' and 'bad.' It is the same with this tree. The escoba tree's thorns 'give' a painful sting, but by using its inner bark we can 'take' the cure and stop the pain and bleeding."

"That's amazing."

"Yes, it is. But then the escoba is a most incredible tree. . . ." Che's voice trailed off and he frowned. "*Without* any attempt by Man to make it better or different."

"You're talking about Isaac Arrow, aren't you? Why don't you approve of what they're doing with the escoba?"

"The ancient Maya believed that Man cannot improve on Nature," Che said matter-of-factly as he sliced open the tree's bark with his machete and pointed to a clump of fibrous inner bark.

Marty reached out to touch it and Che grabbed his arm. "*Never* touch the inner bark of the give and take," he declared fiercely. "Leave that to the shamans and scientists. This is a very powerful substance . . . and very dangerous."

"I thought you said the inner bark was a cure."

"It is, *if* it is handled properly. But it is also a blood coagulant which is very rapidly absorbed through the skin. In high concentrations a man's blood would thicken and clot almost instantly. His heart would struggle, of course. But it would be of no use. The blood would literally curdle in his veins. He would die . . . and quite painfully, it is certain."

"Thanks for stopping me. Dying would be bad enough, but having my blood curdle? I don't think I'd handle that with much dignity at all."

Che gave out an easy laugh and, slipping his machete back into its sash, motioned for Marty to follow him down the jungle path. "Tropical forests such as this one," Che began, "cover only a small portion of the earth. But half of the earth's plants and animals live in these forests. Did you know that the forests actually help make the world's rainfall, by producing moisture that forms clouds? They give off oxygen, they shelter our creatures, our healing plants. Scientists are finally learning what we Maya have always known: The forest and earth live in unity, each giving and taking from the other. Without the rainforest . . ." Che's voice cracked and he shook his head sadly.

"I guess I didn't know all that."

"It seems there are many things you don't know." Che smiled kindly. "But fortunately you also have many questions, so you learn."

"Which reminds me . . ." Marty stopped on the trail and pulled a paper napkin from his pocket. "I had my artist, Zak, draw that glyph we were talking about." He handed it to Che. "What do you think?"

Che studied the glyph intently. "I can't promise you I will be of any help in its translation, but I can assure you that I will do my best to try. May I keep it for a while?"

"Sure," Marty replied, unable to conceal his disappointment.

"We will see what we are meant to see, Marty," Che comforted as he carefully folded the napkin and placed it inside his waist pocket. "No more. No less. That is the way of the universe."

"I'm starting to think the universe wants to keep me in the dark about a lot of things," Marty remarked bitterly.

Che looked at him quizzically.

"I've been hearing some strange things about Escoba and Planetlife. . . ."

"Strange?"

"Yeah, like this place is some kind of staging area for the CIA. Is that true, Che? Are most of the people who come here more interested in preserving their economic stake in Central America than in preserving the rainforest and the Maya culture? Didn't you say so much yourself the other night, on the way in?"

A look of surprise and then a frown crossed Che's usually placid face, and he started walking again. "That is a question I do not wish to answer."

"I take it I'm right?" Marty said, hurrying after the Indian.

Turning to face him, Che sighed. "The people who came here in the beginning were very nice people. They were looking for tranquillity. But little by little things began to change. People started coming here for other purposes."

"People like Waters and Templeton?"

"Yes."

"So why did they come here?"

"To conduct business."

"Business? What kind of business?"

"I don't know, Marty. But things are different now. There's less talk about saving the rainforest and more about politics and money and the 'Indian problem.' There are more planes and more men in uniforms." Che paused. "And more cutting of the trees."

"*Cutting* trees? You mean in Top Dollar, for the coffee and oranges and cattle?"

"No. They are cutting deep in the forest. For reasons I do not understand."

"The people who run Planetlife are doing that? Are you sure?"

"Yes. But they are not doing this thing alone. There are others . . . Isaac Arrow, your U.S. soldiers, businessmen."

"But Carson said they were trying to keep the Indians from destroying the rainforest along the Guatemalan border. She didn't say anything about cutting any trees."

Che smiled. "Is that what she said? Ms. Page has an interesting way with words. It's true, of course, that the Indians did their share of slash and burn along the border of Guatemala and Mexico. But what Carson Page neglected to tell you is that the loggers came and harvested the trees. Not the Indians. The loggers were the ones who built roads and buildings. After they left, the ranchers and cattle followed. Now thousands of acres of rainforest are gone. I have seen in my dreams that, left unchecked, this harvesting of the escoba tree by Isaac Arrow will lead to an equal destruction. Not by the Indians, but by greedy white men from the north. This rainforest will have the same end as the one you spoke of . . . unless someone intervenes."

"And I take it you think that someone isn't Planetlife?"

Che let out a bitter laugh, then turned serious. "I used to think so, Marty, but not anymore. Planetlife is not what it appears to be. Contributions are small. Escoba only holds thirty guests. The rainy season is long so they close the resort from

June to October. Even when Escoba is open, it is usually only a third full. Sometimes weeks go by and no one comes."

"That doesn't sound like much of a profit center. It had to cost a fortune to build a resort down here. Big bucks. And the runway in Top Dollar?" He whistled. "I hate to think."

"Yes, it costs a large amount of money to run a place like this. The money is not coming from the resort. I believe it comes from other sources. For several years Mr. Waters and Mr. Templeton have flown cargo in and out of Top Dollar." Anticipating Marty's next question, he quickly added, "Unfortunately, I have no idea what that cargo is. However, the flights stopped some weeks ago, precisely when the harvest of the escoba tree began. Perhaps there is a great sum of money to be made with the give and take."

"They told me that this was a sustainable venture, that Arrow's scientists only needed cuttings from the escoba tree to make their new product."

Che shook his head. "Then they were either misinformed themselves . . . or they lied. Would you like for me to show you where they are cutting?"

Marty nodded.

"Then, please . . . come this way."

The only sign of the once-majestic trees were their severed trunks—fitting markers, Marty thought—left to rot in the Belizean heat and sun like so many sacrificial heads.

Dark eyes glazed, Che sat down in a heap on the muddy jungle floor. Marty crouched beside him and, reeling in shock, surveyed the destruction.

The loggers had left little behind except for a few stones and browning undergrowth piled high into mounds of sludge. The tracks of a large bulldozer led out of the clearing and disappeared down a rutted road cut into the dense foliage.

"This place is only an acre, but it was once the forest of kings," Che said at last. "Each time, they cut one acre. No more, no less. And then they move on. I do not know the reason."

"You're telling me that there are more places like this?" Marty exclaimed in disbelief. "Right here, in the Planetlife preserve?"

"Many more."

"But if the escoba trees are worth so much, why don't they just keep on cutting?" Marty looked around at the encircling forest, still lush and green. "Why do they stop? Why pick up and start all over again?"

"That is a riddle I cannot answer."

"God, I wish there was something I could do."

"There is. You can leave this place with an image of what you have seen here today. Leave here with it imprinted forever, in all its ugliness, in your mind. Go back to America and tell the world about this wrongdoing. About the hypocrisy called Planetlife."

Marty blanched. If he did what Che was asking, he was sure to lose the Arrow account.

"A man can gain the world yet lose his soul," Che said suddenly, making Marty wonder if the Maya shaman was adept at reading not only the signs of the jungle but men's hearts as well. "There's no need to reply, Marty. I understand. I had just hoped that this was not my burden to carry alone." The Indian sighed. "But it is, and I must face that fact. I was just hoping . . . for an ally."

"I *am* your ally," Marty retorted fiercely. He suddenly felt confused—angry and sad all at once. Angry at the man he saw reflected in the Indian's eyes. And sad, too, sad that that man had slowly become a stranger to him. "Is this my destiny, Che? Is that what you're saying? Because if it is . . . well . . ."

Che shook his head. "I cannot know any man's fate with certainty. No one can. Perhaps the day will come when your talents will be called upon to assist my people . . . perhaps not. Just because I am a shaman does not mean I can tell the future." He paused, a vengeful expression surfacing in his eyes. "But I can tell you this much: Many trees may fall beneath a man's knife, but in the end, that man will shorten his own life as well. That is an old Maya saying, Marty. And *that* is justice."

feature." He paused, a worried expression surfacing on his face. "But I can tell you this much: Mary does need it." He needs a battle knife, but in the end that man, with shoes this tight or well, had is an old man again, Mary . . .
to pieces.

Chapter 35

Neither Max Harper nor Roger Kemper was smiling when they climbed back into the beige Dorbett van that morning. They'd gone over Marty English's Chicago condo with the precision of surgeons, and still they'd found nothing. Their only comfort was in knowing Del Waters couldn't question their tenacity or their expertise; Waters knew Knute Shelby was the best computer man in the business.

Indeed, Shelby had spent hours in English's study hunched over the computer screen, banging away on the keyboard. But all he'd come up with was one clue: Someone in the English household had accessed the CD-ROM drive on January 9 at 2:36 A.M. And that was all they'd been able to learn. Despite Shelby's best efforts, they couldn't retrieve a file name or extension. They'd hit a wall.

Del Waters wasn't pleased. Even the scratchy telephone reception from Belize couldn't disguise that.

"So what's next, Del?" Kemper asked uneasily. He swiveled back and forth in the soft leather chair and then stood up to look out the heavily draped window. His room had a great view: from the twenty-sixth floor of Chicago's Ritz-Carlton at Water Tower Place, Kemper could see Lake Michigan. Like all the other fine hotels he and Harper had stayed in around the world, the Ritz-Carlton did things right: twenty-four-hour room service, minibar, exercise equipment delivered right to your door, overnight valet service. It was everything the weary executive, or international spy, could ask for.

"There's a vault at Wynn Bergman in the Finance Department," Del Waters said, interrupting Kemper's reverie. "Carson found that out when she was up there last week. English told her they lock up client discs for safekeeping. Maybe he put Inglesia's disc there before he left town."

Kemper shook his head mournfully. Now they were talking Watergate. "There's always the possibility English doesn't even have the disc," he ventured, hoping to dampen Waters's enthusiasm for the idea.

"He's got it, all right. He has to."

"What about the cop?"

"You mean Sinclair?"

"Yeah, maybe he's got it. Maybe he stumbled across it when he was snooping around Inglesia's house. Or maybe English passed it on to him."

"No. You've kept Sinclair under surveillance. If he had the disc, you'd know it."

"You're right," Kemper conceded with a sigh. "Sinclair met with Jackson over at Holley's place this morning. Carla got their entire conversation on tape. Sinclair didn't say a word about a disc."

"So Sinclair met with Jackson, did he? I wouldn't have expected Jackson to go out on a limb like that. But then I guess those blacks all stick together when it comes down to it, don't they? Too bad. What did our Agent Jackson pass on to Sinclair?"

"Just one file, from what we can tell. Not much. But more than he should have. Sinclair knows we're Covert Operations. He knows all about where we've been."

"And Central America? Belize?"

"Sure. All that. Of course he has no idea what the hell's going on down there. Or who we report to."

"But Sinclair could put two and two together with English being down in Belize and all."

"He could. But I don't think it's anything to worry about. We managed to get the word to his boss. . . . He's put Sinclair on ice for two weeks. From what little Sinclair got from Jackson I don't think he'll make the connection. To go from me and Max working in Belize to an alliance between Planetlife, Arrow, and Tony Inglesia's organization—that would be a hell of a stretch, Del."

"But English might figure it out."

"He might. If he gets a chance to talk to Sinclair when he gets back to Chicago."

"I know where you're going with this, Roger, but I want you to hold up on Sinclair. You've got me convinced he'll lead us to the disc."

"But you still want us to go ahead with Jackson?"

There was a pause on the line. "Of course."

Chapter 36

Marty and Che didn't talk on their way back through the jungle to Escoba. Even when they stopped along the trail and Che sliced open a dangling vine and they stole a drink of the cool, sweet water that dripped from the fibrous core, they kept their silence. But there was nothing left to say, really. And too much to think about to waste time with words. What Che had said about Planetlife and Escoba had been enough. It had left Marty stunned. And then—what was it he'd felt after that? Disbelief? Or was it fear?

Hell, he knew as well as anybody that one of the most important assets a pharmaceutical firm had was its credibility. Companies like Arrow, if they were smart, spent more money trying to look credible in the public's eyes than they did on research and development. That's because they knew that all the R&D in the world was worthless without the public's trust.

Consumers had to be convinced that Isaac Arrow upheld the highest scientific, ethical, and moral standards. If they weren't, Arrow's products would be about as sought after as a surgeon who didn't wash his hands. Companies like Dow Corning, Union Carbide, and Exxon came to Marty's mind. Along with images of PR hell and lawsuit heaven.

If what Che had said about Planetlife was true, then Isaac Arrow's relationship with the foundation would spell public relations disaster. At least it would if word ever got out about Planetlife's shady dealings. But things like that *always* came out; they couldn't stay under wraps for long. They were time bombs, tick, tick, ticking, making anyone who knew the ugly little secret go crazy waiting for the big bang.

So now what? The answer seemed pretty obvious: Marty had to take care of himself. And that meant he had to protect his client. They'd go ahead with the production, using the company he'd called earlier that day to replace Benson. They'd film everything they needed, get it all in the can. Then when they got back to Chicago they'd just tweak the copy a bit and edit out any reference to Planetlife and *voilà!* Instant TV ad. No problem. No blowup.

But that was the easy part. The real bomb would be the "little" Super Bowl soiree Isaac Arrow was throwing at Planetlife's headquarters. There'd be some big names at that party. Lots of media attention, too—which was great if you were looking to make a splash, but terrible if you had a stone around your neck like this Planetlife shit Che was talking about. Media attention drew naysayers, detractors, and the curious. Somebody from *The New York Times* could easily start digging around, and then, faster than you could say "Jiffy Pop," Planetlife's ugly little secret would be front-page news.

The way Marty saw it, if he stood by and let Arrow go through with the Planetlife party, he'd be letting them alienate just about every powerbroker on the planet. Arrow would be ruined. And he'd be out three hundred million in advertising.

But Marty was Tony Inglesia's son, not one of those spineless guys who just watched from the sidelines waiting for the fallout. He'd drop this bomb himself. Not on the whole world like Che might have wanted. Just on Frank Torello.

By the time Marty got to Escoba's lodge, it was dusk. The day's downpour had ended and the guests were gathering at the bar for their evening ritual of cocktails and Yucatec appetizers. Marty found Arrow's president sitting alone on the lodge veranda, a pair of binoculars pressed to his eyes, scanning the treetops, he imagined, for the elusive yellow-rumpled flycatcher.

Torello smiled and waved him over. "Want a look?" he offered, holding out the binoculars.

"No thanks, Frank. But if you've got a minute . . ."

"Sure." Torello frowned. "What's up? You're not smiling, Marty. Something go wrong on that jungle hike?" His eyes clouded over. "Dammit! It's the production, isn't it? Is there more bad weather on the way? Or is it that jerk Benson?" Torello shook his head ruefully. "I suppose he's got us over a barrel? Thinks he's indispensable and he's right? So what does he want? More money?"

Shaking his head, Marty gave out a chuckle. "Contrary to popular opinion, Frank, including his own, Jules Benson *is* dispensable. As a matter of fact, he's getting ready to find that out. I'm giving him the boot and bringing in another director, a guy out of New York by the name of Phil Gentry. Gentry's every bit as good a director as Benson, but he's young and idealistic . . . *and* hungry."

"But what about the production?" Torello exclaimed, shifting in his seat. "Won't we fall behind? My God, tomorrow's Thursday—we leave on Saturday. How can we get the ad done in two days?"

"Everything's going to be fine, Frank," Marty comforted, wishing the guy would just relax and let him do his damned job. If this was any indication—well, he had to wonder how Torello was going to react when he told him what Che had said about Planetlife.

Torello broke in on his thoughts. "We *are* still going into production tomorrow, aren't we?"

"Just like we planned, Frank. Gentry's flying in tonight. When the sun comes up tomorrow morning, we won't skip a beat."

"So if Benson's not the problem . . ." Torello looked at Marty quizzically. "What is?"

"To tell you the truth, Frank, I don't know if we should call this a problem or not. At least not yet."

Torello leaned forward. "Go on."

"I guess I should start with a question. You ever heard anything negative about Planetlife? Or Templeton and Waters?"

"Never," Torello replied in a tone that was oddly calm—almost studied—for someone so prone to hysteria. Marty had expected his reaction to be more along the lines of alarm, but to his surprise, Torello now drew himself up defensively and declared, "And why should I? The whole world loves Planetlife: the Sierra Club, *National Geographic*, the Nature Conservancy . . . hell, you name it. Planetlife's top notch in everybody's book. And as far as Arch and Del are concerned, well, they're tough guys with hearts of gold, the perfect image for an organization like Planetlife. You know, John Wayne meets Wild Kingdom. What more could the public ask for? Like I said, *nobody* I know has a bad word for those two guys. . . ." Torello's voice trailed off. "Nobody, that is, except for that crazy Indian guide you went out with today." His face flushed red and he leaped up from his chair. "*That's* what this is about, isn't it? That goddamned Che got you out alone and started shooting his mouth off, didn't he? I imagine he cried on your shoulder about his poor, downtrodden people, probably carried on about how Planetlife's cutting down all the trees, an acre at a time, too."

"Something like that," Marty admitted uncomfortably, reeling at the realization that Torello had heard it all before.

"Well, it's all lies, Marty. You hear me?" Torello was pacing now, flailing his arms around. "It's a pack of *lies*. Whatever that son of a bitch told you, just forget you ever heard it."

Marty nodded agreeably, but his thoughts were racing. What was with Torello? The guy wasn't the least bit worried about the allegations that his company might be involved with charlatans, or worse, which wasn't at all in keeping with his character. Hell, he was too busy defending Templeton and Waters even to ask what Che had actually said. But how could a man in Frank Torello's position afford to do that? How could he just ignore something that might impact his company's future—even if it was just a crazy rumor—without even checking it out? The way it looked, all Torello cared about was convincing Marty that Che was a liar.

But Che was no liar; Marty would stake his life on that. So why was Frank Torello so intent on painting him as one?

His heart skipping a beat, Marty met Torello's eyes. There was only one explanation: This man standing before him was in on it. Torello hadn't been played for a fool by the scheming Del Waters and his side-kick Templeton, after all. No, it was Marty who'd taken that role.

Fighting back a wave of nausea, he gave Torello an easy smile. Never let them see you sweat, he told himself. Right now he had to stay cool. And he had to think fast. He knew instinctively that he had to convince Torello that he believed he'd been duped by Che. He drew a deep breath and launched into the performance of his life.

"God, Frank," he exclaimed, shaking his head in feigned amazement as he collapsed into a chair. "I have to tell you I'm really shocked. I mean, this Che guy comes off as nice enough. Arch said he was confused and all, had a few tall tales, but I never figured he'd try to con me. But that's exactly what happened, isn't it? Che just wanted me to feel sorry for him so he could get a free ride to the States and a green card. Jeez, I should've seen that one coming a mile away." A sheepish look crossed Marty's face and, chuckling with embarrassment, he looked Torello square in the eye. "Dammit, Frank. I hate to admit it, but that old Indian really had me going. I'm sure sorry about all this."

"Don't go blaming yourself. From what I'm told, Che's been unhappy working at Escoba for some time."

"Looks like the U.S. Postal Service doesn't have a corner on disgruntled employees after all, huh?"

Torello let out a laugh, seemingly satisfied that Marty had swallowed the party line. "So now that we've got all that nonsense with Che out of the way, how about some dinner? It's snapper Veracruz."

"Sorry, Frank," Marty apologized, rising from his chair. "I've got a few loose ends to tie up before tomorrow's shoot."

Torello nodded. "I understand completely. We'll plan on seeing you bright and early tomorrow morning." He put his arm around Marty's shoulder. "And thanks for telling me about Che. Planetlife and Arrow have impeccable reputations, and we want to keep it that way. Right?"

Marty flashed his most sincere smile. "Right."

"Why, look who's here," Benson growled from within the evening shadows of the porch. He disappeared into the candlelit cabana, the screen door slamming behind him.

Marty followed, stepping inside.

From across the room, Benson held up a glass and a bottle of scotch. "How about a drink for old times' sake?"

"No thanks."

"You mean this isn't a social call?" Smirking, Benson lifted his glass in a mock toast. "Let me guess . . . you dropped by to say I've been replaced, that you don't need me anymore. Is that it? Well you're wrong, Marty. You do need me." He smiled arrogantly. "In case you forgot, I do a lot of work for Todd. And their client, Hexall."

Ignoring the director's veiled threat, Marty replied impassively, "The only thing I'm interested in right now, is that you don't work for *me* anymore. You're fired, Jules."

" 'Fraid not." Benson winked over his glass. "We've got a contract."

"Null and void. You violated our agreement when you got drunk and—"

Glaring, Benson cut him off. "Let's get this straight, okay? I wasn't drunk last night. It's not like it used to be. I went on the wagon a few years back, got sober. I can handle the booze just fine now."

Marty nodded solemnly. "I want you out of here first thing tomorrow morning."

"Whatever." Benson shrugged. "It's your fuckin' party. I guess it wasn't as much fun as you thought it would be, huh— seeing me bust my ass for you again, just like the good old days? That's the real reason you hired Benson Productions, isn't it? I imagine it'll make your fuckin' day to go back to Chicago and run me down, too. But I've got news for you, Marty. You won't screw me and just walk away. You'll never keep NHP now. Not with me in the mix."

"You've got it all wrong, Jules. Bill Kidman brought you on board because we figured you were the best man for the job. And as far as what's happened here is concerned, I intend to forget it."

"Forget it?" Benson cackled in disbelief. "If you forget anything, it'll be the paycheck you owe me for coming down to this hellhole. Shit, you big shots are all alike. You just stand in line to screw Jules Benson." He shook his head mournfully. "But this time I gotta hand it to you, Marty: you really fucked me."

"No, Jules," Marty retorted flatly, "you did that to yourself."

Chapter 37

When computer whiz Jeff Macy was killed on his way into work that Thursday morning in what Chicago police called a "senseless drive-by shooting," the Universal Lock and Safe Company went into a tailspin. In addition to dealing with shocked employees, grief-stricken family members, and the usual assortment of demanding customers, Glen Youngblood, Universal's company manager, was forced to scramble to find a replacement for the computer operations specialist.

With that in mind, Youngblood contacted a high-tech placement service—"utilized by the U.S. military, the Pentagon, and CIA," the man on the phone had told him—a service that specialized in providing high-security clearance personnel for sensitive projects.

It was almost ten o'clock that night before Youngblood's prayers were answered and Macy's replacement, a surprisingly personable older fellow by the name of Knute Shelby, arrived at Universal. The company manager liked Shelby immediately. He showed Shelby where the men's rest rooms were located, took him down to the break room, and bought him a cup of coffee from the vending machine. Then he escorted Shelby to Jeff Macy's office, apologizing the whole way about how it all had happened so fast they hadn't had a chance to straighten up the poor guy's desk.

Fortunately, the agreeable Shelby didn't seem to mind. He sat right down and got to work, impressing Youngblood all the more.

On his way back to his office, Youngblood stopped by to see Carl Gibson, his night supervisor. Every cloud had a silver lining, he told Gibson solemnly, even a tragedy like the one with Jeff Macy. He confided to Gibson he'd be recommending they bring Knute Shelby on full time. Shelby, Youngblood reckoned, was just the kind of guy they needed.

Knute Shelby had always been quite amiable—at least when he wanted to be. But then sociopaths always were. He'd managed to stroll right in to the Universal Lock and Safe Company, shake a few hands, kiss a little ass—namely Youngblood's—and then, without so much as a second look, had been given complete access to the Universal computer system.

Alone in Macy's office, Shelby cleared up a few old problems the dead guy had left, just to make it look good, and then applied his considerable genius to accessing Wynn Bergman's account. Shelby's fingers flew over the keyboard, tapping purposefully, until he smiled broadly and sat back in his chair. "Open sesame," he commanded, then chuckled as the amber screen blinked twice and Bergman's file menu came up. Three more taps on the keyboard and he was staring at the words

WYNN BERGMAN ADVERTISING

VAULT ACCESS SEQUENCE

THURSDAY 01-15

AUTHORIZATION: J. MACY 08294

DATE	TIME OPEN/CLOSE	PASSWORD
WED 01-14	07:00/17:00	prez is penny pincher? Honest Abe
THU 01-15	07:30/18:00	talker is under water? Parrot Fish

Shelby started tapping away at the keyboard, shutting out
the rest of the world. When he was done, he paused to look
over his handiwork and take a sip of cold coffee. Then he hit
Enter and grinned as a new line of instructions appeared on-
screen:

DATE   TIME OPEN/CLOSE   PASSWORD
FRI 01-16   03:30/04:30   who deserves a break today? Big MAX.

"You're a genius, Shelby, old man," he said aloud.

Now getting into the vault at Wynn Bergman Advertising
would be no problem for Max Harper and Roger Kemper. All
the two agents had to do was get past Bergman's security
guard, a head janitor, and his cleaning crew. And, of course,
punch in the right password within the allotted time frame.
And that, Shelby thought with a wry smile, should be no
problem at all.

It was Old Roy's lucky day. Had he known just how lucky,
Wynn Bergman's beloved head janitor of forty years would
probably have said to hell with it all, hung up his faded brown
uniform, and taken retirement right then and there. But the
grizzled old man with the dead battery in his hearing aid didn't
know how close he'd come early that Friday morning to
meeting his Maker. He had no idea that twice he'd nearly
stumbled on the two intruders and gotten his throat slit in the
process.

Harper and Kemper liked an easy job. And this would indeed be easy—and cleaner than the job D'Angelo's boys did
on English's office. But they didn't like getting in and out of
the place. There was too much glass and too many lights and
too many workaholics spending all night at their desks. The
agents were good, but they weren't invisible, Kemper would
later grumble to Del Waters. Still, they'd managed to jam the
security system and elude the drowsy security guard. They

slipped by in the shadows of the dimly lit lobby and then took the stairwell up to Finance.

Bergman's third-floor offices were dark; in the low light of a small computer screen, the vault's shiny steel door gleamed back at the agents invitingly.

"Just like Knute said," Kemper whispered as they walked over to the desk where the computer was stationed. The computer screen blinked and the message came up on-screen:

who deserves a break today?

The agents looked on as a digital timer appeared in the lower left-hand corner of the screen and began counting.

"According to Knute," Kemper said, "you've got thirty seconds to insert the password. Hurry up."

"What's the rush?" Harper chuckled as he typed in the password:

Big Max.

"This is a piece of cake." Harper grinned as the vault's steel door swung open.

Kemper directed his flashlight inside.

"What the fuck!" Harper exclaimed, peering over Kemper's shoulder. They hadn't counted on the staggering amount of material stored inside the vault. The space was enormous—twenty by forty—with floor-to-ceiling fireproof, gray metal cabinets.

The agents opened the first cabinet they saw on their right. Inside, they found old manila folders, filed alphabetically. They opened and closed twenty more cabinets after that. All of them housed old files. They went across the vault and opened more cabinets. What they found there took their breath away: There were hundreds of computer discs filed inside the cabinets, maybe thousands.

"Hopeless"—that's what they'd tell Del Waters. They'd tell him they'd have to find another way to get their hands on the Inglesia disc. With just two of them to get the job done, they weren't going to find the disc here—even if it was in the vault. It would take a platoon to go through all the crap stored in the Bergman vault. With the clock ticking, that was more time than the two thieves had. And so, as they'd planned, at precisely four-thirty that Friday morning, Max Harper and Roger Kemper closed the door to Wynn Bergman's vault, armed it, and headed out of the building.

In the summer, Chicago's Navy Pier reminded Stone Jackson of the midways and carnivals he'd seen in pictures of the Gay Nineties. The concrete structure extended three thousand feet into Lake Michigan, studded with gleaming pavilions of steel and glass. Along its length, flags flapped and snapped in the breeze, waving their fun-house colors at passersby while the enormous McDonald's-sponsored Ferris wheel, a silvery Hula Hoop a hundred and fifty feet high, spun up in the air, so high that it made your heart skip a beat just to look at it.

Navy Pier teemed with sweating tourists toting One-Step cameras and yuppie couples in khaki walking shorts, pushing strollers loaded down with their in vitro Baby Gap toddlers. At night, the crowd changed: the yuppies went home to their backyard barbecues and the tourists, pining for a Chicago-style deep-dish pizza, headed to Uno.

But that was in the summer. It was winter now. And tonight, as Stone Jackson drove down Navy Pier, the board-walk was entombed in deep drifts of snow. The Ferris wheel and carousel and carnival rides stood glazed and stiff, frozen in place, a junkyard monument of creaking ice and metal. It was way too quiet on Navy Pier for Stone Jackson's liking. Way too quiet.

When he got to the end of the pier, Jackson parked his car in front of the big warship anchor. He got out and stood there, fishing around in his pocket with his cold, bare hands, search-ing for the feel of cold metal. At its comforting touch, he smiled. He might have a desk job, but he wasn't a complete idiot; he'd brought along a handgun—just in case.

But even with a gun in his pocket, Jackson's heart was pounding as he walked through the snow to the heavy link chains scalloping the pier's perimeter. To calm himself, he took a deep breath and then another. Then he plopped down on a bench, stared out at the glistening lake, and began scanning the area. His back was covered, and his senses were on full alert.

What the hell was he thinking, listening to some stranger on the phone? Again he felt for the gun in his pocket. Why had he come down here, all alone, to meet some guy he didn't know, at four-thirty in the morning? Was he nuts?

Jackson sighed. No, it wasn't that—it was the name Tony Inglesia. That was what had gotten his attention. That was why he was here. To solve a murder. And because the mysterious caller who'd awakened Jackson and his wife, Doneeta, out of a sound sleep last night had told him that he couldn't afford not to come. Knowing what he did about the case, Jackson believed him.

At the crunching sound of dry, packed snow underfoot, Jackson gripped the gun tight in his hand and craned his neck to look. It was only a stray dog, bony and old, and he had to laugh at himself. Poor thing, Jackson thought as he watched the dog struggle up the boardwalk toward the distant city lights, looking for a place to sleep out of the wind and cold.

When the dog finally disappeared into the shadows, Jackson's attention returned to the lake, and he started thinking about Ford Sinclair, about when they used to come down to the pier late at night, goofing around. They'd had a great time back then. But of course, back then, they'd still had their dreams—even if they were stoked by a bong full of reefer.

He sighed and shook his head. Dreams were in short supply these days. He'd hit forty and had had to face facts: He wasn't going to be the next Quincy Jones or some big shot at the CIA.

Jackson smiled and gave out a long, low laugh, a laugh that kept him from hearing the shadowy figure creeping up behind him, kept him from noticing the gun aimed point-blank at the back of his head.

Yeah, truth was, he was no different, no more special, than anybody else; he was just another nine-digit number with a heartbeat.

A bitter chuckle escaped Stone Jackson's lips as the .22 bullet exploded in his brain. Then it was gone, muffled in the wind, lost in the frigid lake air.

When the call came from Chicago at five that Friday morning, Del Waters was asleep. He'd been dreaming in tortured fits and starts, harsh, brutal dreams of bloodthirsty Iranians looking to collect their money. At the jangling ring of the telephone, he nearly jumped out of his skin.

"Waters," he croaked into the phone.

"Hello, Del." The voice on the line was friendly, easy. Too easy, Waters thought, and he was instantly awake and on guard. "This is Roger," the voice said.

"I know who it is," Waters snapped back. Rubbing his eyes, he stood up and stretched. "So, did you get it?"

There was a pause. "We checked his car in the parking garage," Kemper began. "Didn't find a thing there. Got in the building no problem. And in the vault, too. Shelby did a bang-up job getting it handled. We had it wide open. . . . Hell, it was like a girl's cherry, just waiting to be popped."

There was a pause again and Waters lit a cigar. "Yes?"

"We didn't get the disc, Del."

"Are you telling me you got that fucking far and still didn't get it?"

"Believe me, Del, it was fucking impossible."

"Impossible?" Waters's face flushed and his hand tightened around the receiver. "You know as well as I do nothing's impossible. Nothing."

"Well then, let me rephrase that." There was an edge to the agent's voice. "It would've been *crazy* to try. How's that? Is that better than impossible? Crazy, impossible . . . any way you fucking cut it, Del, we would've needed a month to get through all the shit they had stored in there. There were thou-

sands of discs in there, Del. Every goddamned thing the
agency had ever produced, from ads to accounting. We would
never have found one lousy disc in all that mess. Never. A guy
would have to be out of his fucking mind to even try it. Or
have a strong desire to see the inside of a prison." Kemper
paused and then added sarcastically, "And as you may remember, I have a thing about bars after our little tour of duty
in Cambodia."

Waters nodded to himself. He remembered all right. How
could he forget? They'd all been locked up: him, Arch, Max,
and Roger. They were starving, forced to eat roaches, rats,
dirt, you name it. But it was those three months they spent in
that bamboo prison, before they'd managed to escape and kill
the enemy, that had made them what they were. Unfeeling.
Unstoppable. Unbeatable.

Waters sighed and nervously ran his hand through his
brush-cut hair. In all his life, in all the times he'd stared down
the barrel of an AK-47, in all those nights of lying on a cold
dirt floor feeling God knew what crawl over his bare skin,
he'd never felt this desperate. This out of control. "So what
about that fucking Jackson?" he demanded. "Was taking care
of him impossible, too?"

"Naw, we heard from that greaseball D'Angelo a little
while ago. He said doing Jackson was like shooting fish in a
barrel." Kemper chuckled. "Jesus, it's no wonder the agency
never bumped the dumb son of a bitch up from a desk job and
put him in the field."

"Yeah," Waters replied absently. "It's no wonder."

"Unless you've got some brilliant idea about how we can
find the disc in Bergman's vault, I guess that's all for now."

There was silence on the line.

"Hey, you okay down there, Del?"

"Yeah, I'm fine. Everything is fucking beautiful. What the
hell—"

"You'll be back when? Saturday morning?"

"Yeah," Waters said morosely, thinking that by then the Super Bowl would be just eight days away.

"There's just not much we can do at this point, Del. Not until English gets back on Saturday night."

"No, there isn't," Waters agreed flatly. He started pacing now, his voice going hoarse as his throat constricted with each word. "But the minute his fucking plane lands, we'll close in. You get D'Angelo and his goons lined up, put together the guys you need. I want English's ass, Roger. No more games. No more *excuses*. Marty English has that disc and I intend to get it . . . whatever it takes. You hear me? *Whatever* it fucking takes."

As he hung up the phone, Roger Kemper smiled coldly. That was what he liked about Del Waters: the guy's killer instinct. The last time he'd heard that craving for blood in Del Waters's voice, they'd ended up taking out two dozen Guatemalan civilians just on principle. But Del had felt better afterward. They all had. And as far as Roger Kemper was concerned, that was all that mattered.

Chapter 38

Reiki had always gone on about how places had "bad vibes," but Marty had never really gotten it. It sounded like mumbo jumbo to him. But now he knew what she was talking about: Escoba had bad vibes in spades. Despite that fact, he'd managed to stick with the program throughout Thursday's production with Gentry. He'd kept up the ruse: raved about Planetlife's preserve, pretended he'd bought Torello's story about Che. And he'd kept right on playing the doting account executive to Carson's marketing director, too. But the truth was, right now he'd rather be anywhere but here in Escoba. Unfortunately, that wasn't in the cards; this was Friday and he still had a full day of production ahead.

He let out a sigh and peered out of his cabana window. On the lawn, Bill Kidman was pacing back and forth while Zak, all decked out in a dashiki and seated in a director's chair, looked on at the thirty or so production people bustling about, setting up for the next shot. Marty turned back to his address book and hurriedly thumbed through the pages until he got to S. "Sinclair, Ford," he said aloud. He dialed the number and waited.

"Lake Forest Police Department," a woman's voice answered crisply.

"Detective Sinclair, please."

"I'm sorry, sir. Detective Sinclair is out on vacation."

"Vacation?" Marty exclaimed incredulously. "I was calling for *Ford* Sinclair. In Homicide. He was working on the Inglesia case."

"I heard you the first time, sir. Ford Sinclair. If your call is regarding the Inglesia case, that case has been closed."

"Closed? Are you sure?"

There was an impatient sigh on the line. "Yes, sir. I'm sure. Would you like to speak with someone else?"

"When do you expect Detective Sinclair back?"

"The twenty-sixth, sir."

Marty could hardly believe his ears. "The *twenty-sixth*?"

"Yes, sir," the woman said irritably. "A week from this coming Monday. You know, the day after the Super Bowl."

At the sound of the screen door scraping open behind him, Marty spun around to see Carson standing there. She hadn't left his side since yesterday morning, and he was starting to get annoyed. He'd wanted to find Che to warn him about Torello, but that hadn't been possible with her there all the time. Hell, he'd been lucky to shake loose and make this call. And now here she was again, standing in his room, sticking to him like Cling Wrap.

"Marty, Frank's asking for you," Carson said, giving him the once-over. "*Marty* . . ." she repeated insistently.

Fighting back his anger, he nodded and put down the phone.

"Hey, you hung up and didn't even say good-bye," Carson objected. "Is there a problem?"

Marty plastered on his best "bullshit-the-client" face, the one he'd been using ever since he'd had the conversation with Torello. "No problem. I just couldn't get through to one of my clients. I'm sure you know how it is."

"Yeah. Frustrating as hell."

"You got it," he said, the smile falling from his face as he followed her out the door and across the lawn to the production.

Yeah, that's what he was, all right. Frustrated. Frustrated as hell.

But it was relief he felt later when, just after midnight, Marty slipped out the door of his cabana. He had to talk to Che. That's all he'd been thinking about for two days now—that and Torello's strange alliance with Templeton and Waters.

He paused on the porch, letting his eyes adjust to the shadowy resort grounds and, for one brief, sensible moment, considered taking the well-lit walkway. But he quickly decided the cover of darkness was better suited to this adventure, even if he couldn't see the ground beneath his feet.

Gingerly, he picked his way through the heavy foliage dotting Escoba's lawn, past one cabana after another, making his way toward the dirt road Che had said led to the caretakers' huts.

At the sound of voices—voices he recognized—spilling out from one of the cabanas, Marty paused and folded himself into the shadows of the tall palms. From where he stood he could make out three silhouettes, one of them pacing back and forth in the glow of the cabana's lamp.

"Listen, both of you," a gruff voice demanded. It was Templeton, Marty was sure of that. "Relax. He doesn't have the slightest idea what's going on down here. Hell, Frank—he told you about Che, didn't he?"

"Yeah," Torello admitted.

"What does that tell you?"

"That he's loyal?"

"Loyal?" Templeton laughed out loud. "Christ Almighty, Frank, haven't you figured him out yet? The only loyalty he has is to his fucking pocketbook. That's all he cares about. He forgot that girl of his real quick when Carson came along with her big ad budget, didn't he?"

There was a woman's haughty laugh, a laugh Marty recognized as Carson's. "You can say that again," she declared.

Marty's stomach turned: It had all been a setup.

"Okay, Arch. Maybe you're right," Torello conceded. "Maybe it's not loyalty that motivates the guy. But he's no fool. Marty's his father's son."

His father's son. The words hit Marty like a punch in the gut and he swayed on his feet for a moment, leaning back against the palm tree for support.

"Calm down, Frank. I'll talk to Del," Templeton snapped back irritably as the three silhouettes moved across the floor of the cabana and out the door into the night. "But I already know what he's going to say."

"Yeah," Torello said solemnly, his voice trailing off as they headed down the walkway toward the lodge. "So do I."

Marty stayed in the shadows, paralyzed with a mixture of fear and shock, as Torello's words hammered in his brain. *His father's son.*

What did the Mob have in common with an eco-foundation scam and a pharmaceutical giant? Where was the connection? Marty's thoughts ran back, free-associating over the chain of events these past weeks, picking up link after link: the Arrow presentation, his father's murder, Escoba, the Maya, the glyph—

The disc. Marty caught his breath. That was it—that was the connection.

Carson had been pumping him that day in his office when she asked where he stored his discs, hadn't she? Marty shook his head and groaned under his breath. And what had he told her? He'd told her about the agency vault down in Finance, that's what.

At the sudden realization that he'd put his father's disc in that vault before he left for Belize, Marty's face drained of color. "Fuck," he said in an exasperated whisper as he started walking, then running, across the damp grass toward his cabana. He had to get that disc out of the agency vault. And he had to do it *fast.*

*   *   *

The tension of waiting was excruciating. The phone rang ten times, maybe more; Marty lost count by the time Lee Wilde finally picked up and moaned, "Hello."

"Yeah, Lee, this is Marty," he said breathlessly, struggling to calm himself. His heart was still pounding. "You asleep?"

"That's what most *normal* people do after midnight," she shot back sarcastically. "Last time I checked it was called bedtime."

"You got that research report on NHP done?"

He heard her grumble to herself. "What the hell time is it down there, anyway?" she demanded irritably. "I thought we were in the same time zone. Or did you start working the graveyard shift?"

"Same time zone, but hell, you know me." He forced a chuckle. "Work, work, work."

She let out a weary sigh. "Yeah, I know you, all right."

"So did you finish the report or not?"

"Of course I did. And, if I say so myself, it's good, damned good. But hell, you know my reports."

"Yeah, they're great," he acknowledged. "Well, be sure and bring it along when you pick me up at O'Hare, okay? I want to look it over on Sunday. And while you're at it, do me another favor, too. Go by Finance first thing tomorrow morning and pick up a data disc they're holding for me in the vault. It's dated Tuesday, January thirteenth."

"Oh, shit, Marty. I almost forgot. Reiki called and said she'll be picking you up."

"Reiki's back? Her job's finished in Rwanda?"

"You don't sound very happy."

"Oh, it's not that. . . ." He'd wanted a few days to get himself together before Reiki came home and he had to look her in the eye. "I just didn't expect to see her so soon."

"Reiki was surprised too. I guess when she got to New York she found out there'd been a mix-up. She said that's never happened before."

Marty frowned. Maybe it wasn't a mix-up; maybe someone had wanted Reiki out of town. Maybe they'd wanted him out of the way too. Was that what this trip to Belize was about? The disc? At the thought, his heart began to hammer in his chest. "Listen, Lee. . . . You have to get that report and disc to Reiki. You understand? Make sure she brings them with her to O'Hare. Don't forget—be sure and tell her to do that. Okay? You got that?" His voice sounded more strained, more demanding, than he'd intended.

"Hey, I'm not senile yet," Lee objected. "I'll take care of it." There was a hesitation on the line. "Are you all right, Marty?"

"Sure. Why wouldn't I be?"

"Well, okay then." Lee didn't sound convinced. "You need anything else?"

"No. That should about do it. Thanks."

"Anytime, golden boy. Sweet dreams."

"Yeah," he mumbled, "sweet dreams." He hung up the phone and fell back onto the pillow. As much as he craved sleep, what he longed for most was escape. He closed his eyes and, within minutes, he succumbed to the comforting darkness.

In the dark cabana, Marty could just make out the indistinct shape hovering above him. There was a soft, fluttering sound, like the rustling of feathers, and he started to reach out and turn on the lamp. But instead he froze, hand barely outstretched, as the shape slowly lowered onto his bed. He felt a sudden weight on his sheets, followed by an undulating movement as it slid silently, thick and heavy, over his feet, and up his legs.

Numb with terror, he lay perfectly still, scarcely daring to breathe, as his thoughts raced helplessly in endless, pointless circles. It was gliding up his torso now; soon he would come face-to-face with his fear. He struggled to hold back a gasp.

Suddenly, a flash of light cut through the night, followed by a drawn-out sibilant noise, like air being let out of a tire, then a shudder. Marty felt the weight go limp, then dissolve into the darkness.

The door of his cabana opened and closed. In the split second in between, Marty thought he glimpsed a familiar face. But he couldn't be certain; hard as he struggled, he couldn't fix it in his mind. All he recalled was the whispered word "Kukulcan." And the rustling of feathers amid beating wings.

Marty squinted into the glaring morning sunlight. It had all been so vivid, so tangible—could it have really been just a dream? What about the face he saw in the doorway? That had been real. Hadn't it? And what about the word—what was it? Kukulcan? Trembling, he sat up, trying to shake off a growing sense of dread, trying to recall. . . .

But try as he might, he couldn't re-create the vision in the daylight. Still, he couldn't shake the terrible feeling that something—or someone—had been in his room. He was sure of that.

Marty glanced around uneasily and began throwing his clothing and belongings haphazardly into his suitcase. Suddenly he couldn't wait to get out of the small hut.

At the sound of fluttering wings outside his cabana door, Marty turned to look and, in a rush of cold terror, the dream flashed in his mind's eye, flooding him with terrible clarity. In that instant, he remembered: *Che*. Che had been in his room last night. Che had saved his life—hell, maybe his soul, for that matter—from some unspeakable, nameless evil.

A deep sense of unease settled over Marty and he shuddered, glancing around the room. Hurriedly, he zipped his bag and threw it over his shoulder. He was leaving Escoba in less than an hour. He had to find Che.

Chapter 39

Marty was hurrying down the road toward the caretakers' huts when he realized that Carson and Templeton were coming up behind him.

"Marty, wait up!" Carson called out.

Heart pounding, he stopped and waved, concealing his mounting anxiety behind a smile. After what he'd overheard last night, he knew he couldn't afford to arouse their suspicions. He couldn't show the slightest fear. Nor could he let them see just how anxious he was to get the hell out of Belize and back to Chicago. If he slipped up, if they suspected that he knew what they were up to—well, he had to figure there was enough at stake that he wouldn't make it back to Chicago at all.

Chill out, he told himself. As Carson and Templeton neared, he took a deep breath and smiled. Hell, hadn't Torello said it himself—that Marty was his father's son? Yeah, that's who he was, all right, his father's son. And right now Marty wasn't going to forget it.

"Where in the world are you going?" Templeton demanded.

"We've been looking all over for you, Marty," Carson complained. "The going-away party's back there." She pointed toward the lodge. "Frank's all excited; he wants to make a toast in your honor before you leave. You wouldn't want to disappoint him."

"Sorry about that," Marty apologized. "I wanted to take one last look around." He smiled earnestly at Templeton. "It really is beautiful here, Arch. I've hardly had a chance to take it all in. But from what I've seen, you've done a fabulous job. I'm going to miss it . . . the parrots in the morning, the smell of this air."

Templeton nodded agreeably, but he wasn't smiling. "Well, you're headed in the wrong direction for a nature walk. This is the way to the caretakers' village, which isn't exactly a wilderness hideaway."

Carson wrinkled her nose. "The Indians tend to be dirty."

"Caretakers?" Marty exclaimed, feigning confusion. "I thought this road led to the river." He scratched at his head and looked around. "Don't tell me I'm lost."

"You sure are," Templeton declared, the easy smile returning.

Marty shook his head in chagrin. "I guess things look a lot different in the rain, huh?"

"That they do," Templeton agreed.

Carson slipped her arm through Marty's. "This way, Tarzan," she said, leading him back toward the lodge. "You've got a plane to catch."

"We're not letting you out of our sight again," Templeton declared. "Who knows what trouble you might get into? More than one man has walked out in this jungle and never been heard from again. You wouldn't want to be one of them"— Templeton's eyes met Marty's—"now, would you?"

As the jeep sped down the road toward Top Dollar's airstrip, Marty's heart sank. He might be getting out of Escoba, but he hadn't wanted to leave without seeing Che.

It would probably be impossible to find someone in Chicago who could decipher an obscure Maya glyph. Without Che's help, he might never know what the glyph meant. Or, for that matter, who killed his father. And Marty was certain now that they were all connected: his father's murder, the disc, the glyph, Arrow, and Planetlife.

Marty glanced over at the young Maya Indian at the wheel of the jeep. He certainly couldn't expect any help from Carlos. The guy was a predator, probably trained by Templeton and Waters. With his camouflage clothes, pistol, and machete slung on his hip, Carlos reminded Marty of a Cong sniper. Or a hired killer.

As the jeep came to a stop beneath a lone tree near the runway, Marty had to remind himself that in a matter of minutes he would be out of here. But even that wouldn't be soon enough for him.

"Your plane is here, gentlemen," Carlos said, nodding up at the clouds.

"There it is!" Kidman shouted, pointing to the Cessna above.

The four-seater prop's wings tipped to the left and then to the right as it swooped over the runway. Touching down, it bounced and shimmied, its rubber wheels squealing on the hot asphalt until, at last, it skidded to a stop.

"Time to go," Carlos announced as a red-faced man with lank, greasy hair and a cigar dangling from his mouth stuck his head out the plane's window and waved them over.

"*That's* our pilot?" Zak exclaimed, grabbing his bags. "He sure as hell doesn't look like a pilot to me."

"What were you expecting?" Kidman snorted as they started toward the plane. "Chuck Yeager?"

At the sound of a horn honking insistently in the distance, Marty turned to see a jeep racing down the runway. He stood there, intrigued, until it screeched to a halt alongside him. "Che!" he exclaimed.

"Would you leave without this?" Che said, jumping out. He held out a paper napkin and smiled.

Marty glanced nervously across the runway at Carlos.

"We have to go," Kidman called out. "The pilot's ready to take off."

"Tell him to wait a minute," Marty ordered, pulling Che aside. "We're being watched, Che," he whispered.

"I have no time for Carlos," Che replied sharply as he unfolded the napkin. "I know this glyph, Marty. In fact, I felt very foolish after we parted and I had time to sit down and study it more closely. As you know, we Maya have many gods. This is one of them. But this one is quite special. You see, it is one of three gods who are almost always shown together, playing the sacred ball game. They are called the Palenque Triad. We call them the triad brothers. Or as archaeologists fond of cataloging things say, God One, God Two and God Three."

"And which one is this?"

"This is God Three, the god of the underworld, the powerful one who rules over death. He is the sun in the night."

Marty stared down at the glyph. God of the underworld? His thoughts raced ahead. Underworld: that was another name for organized crime. It was no coincidence his father had had this glyph in his possession. "What do the other two gods look like?" he asked.

"I'm afraid it is difficult to describe things so peculiar as these glyphs. It is simpler perhaps to explain their purpose and meaning. God One is the ruler of the sun, the first of all. God Two is the great smoking mirror, the god of illusion, of things different than appearances. The three gods were often depicted playing the sacred ball game against the mythological hero."

Distracted by the pilot's impatient calls, Che looked over at the waiting plane. "You must be going." He clasped his hands around Marty's and smiled into his eyes.

Marty steeled himself for what had to come next. He had to warn Che about Torello, he had to try to explain why he'd talked to Arrow's president in the first place. He couldn't leave without doing that. "Che, there's something else. . . ."

The shaman looked at him expectantly. "And what is that, my friend?"

Marty struggled with his feelings of shame and embarrassment—and fear. "Che, I had a dream last night. I think you were in it. And . . . and there was a word too. Kukulcan."

Che smiled. "Ah, Kukulcan. The feathered serpent of the Maya. It seems you have been blessed." Che held Marty's puzzled eyes with his steady gaze. "Many times Nature calls upon the dream state to show us that evil may surround us even in the most beautiful settings."

Marty was nonplussed. Was Che telling him that he actually knew what had happened, that he hadn't been dreaming after all? It felt like the ground dropped away beneath his feet and, suddenly, Marty knew with terrible certainty that the terror and the presence that had filled his room in the darkness, that the thing that had slid over his feet, was no dream. Che *had* been in the room.

From Marty's very core came a flashing image of something that crawled and coiled, its smooth, cold length representing an entity he feared even more than the death it could so swiftly inflict. Somehow, in body or spirit, Che had been there, protecting him. Or was he there to show him something? Was there something Marty was supposed to see, to understand? A searing pang of guilt accompanied the realization that he had betrayed this man.

Marty cleared his throat, struggling to find the right words, but Che shook his head. "It is best left unsaid, Marty. There are no apologies in life, only right action. As in the sacred ball game, good always triumphs over evil in the end. For the hero, death is the final play."

Che smiled solemnly, looking at him as if he were trying to fix those words forever in Marty's memory. As if they held some clue to that destiny they'd talked about. And Marty had only to find it.

Chapter 40

As Marty trudged up the long jetway at O'Hare with Zak and Kidman at his side, he tried to steel himself. Despite the whirling maelstrom of suspicions—and their accompanying questions—he now had about Planetlife and Arrow, his thoughts were largely focused on how he was going to act when he finally came face-to-face with Reiki. She was probably the one person in the world he'd never lied to. But then, was it really a lie if you said nothing and simply kept the truth to yourself?

The truth was a funny thing. Although you might claim to be telling the truth, you could still stretch it, shade it, color and hide it. But when it came right down to it, there weren't really any good excuses for lying, unless, of course, you were an ad man or a copywriter. Then, the term "creative license" could be applied. And they'd put your face on the cover of *Ad Age* or *Time* and call you a genius.

For the past four hours on the plane, Marty had tried to convince himself that seeing Reiki wasn't going to be any different than the hundreds—hell, probably thousands—of times he'd looked clients in the face and lied out his ass. But his attempts at self-persuasion didn't work; this *was* different. A lot different. This was Reiki, not some corporate stranger with a fat budget to whom you handed a line just to snag his account.

And, too, wasn't Marty the same man who'd voted against a presidential candidate because of his steamy "extracurricular" activities? He'd done that not because he was a prude but because, as he'd argued with friends over dinner one night, he thought it said something about a guy's character if he didn't have a problem betraying the person he had to wake up with every morning and look in the eye. Marty didn't think a guy like that would think twice about cheating the American public. He didn't think that made for a good president. And he knew it didn't make for a good life partner, forget about husband.

Marty was still trying to figure out how he was going to look Reiki in the eye when he saw her, standing among the crowd of friends and family waiting for loved ones among the herd of tired passengers in wrinkled clothing who were streaming into the terminal. He studied her face, that open, honest, intelligent face, from the doorway. It was safe to look into her face now. From where he stood she wouldn't be able to read the guilt in his eyes, even if their eyes met.

When they'd last talked, Reiki had been distant. Suddenly the thought occurred to him that maybe he could do the same tonight; maybe he could use their argument as an excuse to avoid looking her in the eye. That way he could sort of slip into their relationship slowly, get used to the discomfort. She'd just think he was sulking. She'd be annoyed, but wasn't annoyed better than . . .

Yeah, that's what he'd do, Marty decided. He'd play it that way. That would work. For a while. But hell, a damned smile and a bear hug wouldn't cut it, now would they? No, he'd go for the withdrawn look.

But then, he reminded himself, most guys got away with cheating because they either didn't love the woman in the first place or they'd convinced themselves they hadn't done anything wrong. He sure as hell was convinced he *had* done something wrong. And he knew he loved her. That was two strikes against him already. Yeah, no question he'd fucked up. He suddenly wondered if he could really pull this off.

But maybe it wouldn't matter. Maybe she'd read the guilt in his eyes right away and that would be that. After all, both Reiki and her camera lens had a talent for exposing the truth. What if she saw it, the "little" lie that would dog him now for the rest of their relationship? What then?

Hell, he knew the answer to that one. She'd leave him, that's what. And she'd have every right to.

He saw her wave from the crowd and he put on a smile and waved back, his stomach doing a slow, nauseating flop. He didn't want to lose her.

"How was the trip?" she asked with what seemed like forced cheer, giving Zak, Kidman, and Marty the same polite, almost formal smile. She didn't throw her arms around Marty like she usually did. Usually she hugged him like he'd been gone for a year at sea. So he wasn't going to have to play Mr. Detached after all, he thought uneasily. No, Reiki was doing a fine job at that all by herself. And she wasn't looking at him either. No eye contact. Maybe he should have felt relieved, being off the hook like that. But he didn't. Her behavior was throwing him a curve. "The trip was great," he replied with false enthusiasm. "You bring that stuff from Lee?"

She nodded. "Yeah, it's in the car, in your briefcase." She turned to Kidman and Zak. "You guys need a lift?"

"No thanks," Zak replied. "We're heading over to Rush Street for a while. You know, no rest for the wicked."

"I guess that goes for you, too, Marty," Reiki remarked as Zak and Kidman ambled off down the concourse. "No rest for the wicked, I mean. Ford Sinclair called right before I left home, said he has to see you tonight. Right away."

"Good. I tried to get ahold of him from Belize, but they told me he was on vacation. Can you believe it? At a time like this, the guy took a goddamned vacation?"

"Well, he didn't sound like he was having much fun to me. He sounded pretty upset."

"Upset? Upset like 'mad' upset?"

"No. More like he was uptight." She pursed her full lips together thoughtfully. "I don't know. Hmm . . . scared, maybe. Yeah, he sounded scared."

Marty frowned. Scared? That didn't sound like the Ford Sinclair he knew. He'd figured the detective for a pretty together guy—and he sure as hell wasn't the type to cry wolf. Evidently something had happened here in Chicago while he was out of town, something that had spooked Sinclair.

But then, Marty reminded himself, things had been pretty spooky everywhere. Chicago didn't have a corner on that. Hell, what about Escoba? He was looking forward to getting the detective's take on what he'd learned down there. "So where's Sinclair want to meet?" he asked.

"At your father's place at ten."

Marty glanced at his watch. "Well, it's just after seven. Why don't you come along and we'll grab a bite at Portello's on the way?" He put his arm around her shoulder and gave her a warm hug, but she stiffened. "It'll be a nice ride," he coaxed. He wanted to tell her about Che and what he'd learned about the glyph, but that was all he intended to tell her about Escoba. At least for now.

"If you don't mind, I'd rather not. I'd really appreciate it if you'd just take me back to the Astor and then head out to Lake Forest. Okay?"

He dropped his arm from her shoulder and looked at her. She wasn't looking back. "Sure," he said thickly.

And that was all they said the entire way to the parking garage. No questions about how his trip had been—or hers. No pretense of sociability. Nothing. Marty started wondering if somehow she'd found out about Carson. He quickly discounted that idea and speculated that Reiki must still be mad about their fight the other morning.

They got in the car and headed down the Kennedy Expressway toward the city and still they didn't talk. It was unnerving, so he took a stab at making conversation.

"Looks like you got some snow while I was gone, huh?"

"Eight inches," she said flatly, like some TV weatherman. She continued to stare straight ahead.

He was starting to get annoyed. Didn't she know that he was tired, that he wasn't up to dealing with this kind of crap right off the plane? He let out a sigh. "All right, what's going on?"

She bit her lip and looked out the side window.

"Goddammit, Reiki. Come on. You're giving me the silent treatment, and you know how I hate that. Come on. Talk to me."

"I guess I don't have anything to say." She didn't turn back from the window.

"You still mad about the other day?"

She turned to face him now and he saw the pain there, rising up in those autumn brown eyes of hers. "No, I'm not *mad* about the other day, Marty." Her words were flat, empty of emotion, as if all the feeling had been wrung out of them long before they'd come together tonight. Her chin quivered. "No," she said resolutely, "I'm not mad. I'm sad."

He didn't know what to say.

"Since you've been gone, I've been thinking a lot about us, about where things are going."

"And?" His heart skipped a beat. Where was she headed with this?

The emotion broke through the tough veneer now, and Reiki's eyes welled up and her words came tumbling out: "The truth is, Marty, whether I want to believe it or not, we're headed nowhere. Nowhere." She swallowed hard and took a deep breath. "I love you, Marty. God, I've loved you from the first time we met. Hell, maybe I've loved you too much." Her voice cracked. "Or maybe I've just been afraid to face the fact that I've thrown away so many years of my life. I know now I shouldn't have stayed so long, waiting for you to want me the way I want you." She smiled back at him through her tears and shrugged. "But hey, I'm a big girl. Right? I should have known better."

He stared back at her, not believing what was happening.

"I can't go on pretending that someday things will change," she went on. "That *you'll* change. I know there're things that happened in your past . . . things that still hurt. But dammit, Marty, that's the past. You keep letting all that old stuff into your head. It's getting in the way. You're making choices, Marty. The kind of choices that set a person off down a road by themselves. You have to go forward and leave the past behind."

Reiki searched his eyes; she was waiting for him to say something. "We could have had so much, you and me," she said finally. "But all you can see is what you don't have."

He went on the defensive. "Like the agency presidency, you mean?"

She nodded, holding back her anger. "Yeah, like the agency presidency. And all those other ladders you think you have to climb. I can tell you right now they're not going to fill that empty space in your heart, Marty. The only thing that's going to do that is love. And trust. If you'd just realize I'm not like your mother—you don't need to be afraid that I'll leave you."

He turned onto Walton Street and threw her a bitter smile. "But you are, aren't you? Isn't that what you're telling me now?"

"It's time we moved on, Marty, got on with our own lives." A tear ran down her cheek and she wiped it away.

"But I don't want to move on," he objected. He pulled into the drive at the Astor and parked the car. "What I want is you, Reiki," he said softly. "That's what I want."

"You may want me, but do you *need* me?" She shook her head. "I already know the answer to that question: No, you don't need me. You've got power and money and status—those are the things you need. They're what's important to you—"

"That's not true," he snapped, cutting her off.

"No, I'm right . . . and it's taken me seven years to accept that fact. Seven years of being reminded every day that some fucking company on Michigan Avenue is more important to you than I am. Do you have any idea how that feels?"

Marty thought of his father. Yeah, he knew how it felt. Seventeen years of living with a man who wouldn't even tell you what he did all day? Who never once made it to your Little League game or school play? What did you call that? He thought the word *rejection* fit the bill pretty well.

"I'll tell you how it feels," Reiki said, opening the car door. "It hurts, Marty. Being rejected day after day like that. I guess . . . I just can't deal with it anymore." She set her jaw. "I've got most of my stuff packed. . . . I found a little place around the corner."

She was moving out. His throat went dry as sandpaper. "Jesus, Reiki, don't do this. Can't we talk about it? My God, I love you. Hell, there's never been anybody else but you." He felt a twinge of guilt. But he decided he wasn't lying: he *didn't* love anyone else. And as for Carson Page? Well, she'd been a meaningless one-night stand that he'd regret for the rest of his life. "Reiki," he said softly, almost pleading now. "I love you."

She stepped out of the car. "I know you do. But you don't *need* me, Marty," she said, starting to sob. "Maybe if you did . . . well, maybe then things would be different. But you don't, so I've got to go."

The night was clear and cold and moonless and, though Marty was speeding down the highway toward Lake Forest, it seemed to him as if everything had stopped. But he *did* need her, he told himself. He needed her level-headed assessment of this situation with Arrow, Planetlife, and his father. Who else could he trust? How would he figure it all out with the ache of losing her so strong in his heart? Reiki was wrong. He needed her—now more than ever.

Okay, so maybe he did obsess over making agency president. He'd had that same lecture from other women before. Women he'd left behind as he'd marched forward, climbing up that corporate ladder to success. Was it happening again? Would he go back home tonight and they'd start dividing up the CDs and forks and knives? What was he supposed to do after that? Just say "See you around" and start all over, going to fucking fern bars and buying strange women Long Island teas? Shit, he didn't even know what the hell a date was anymore.

Marty couldn't remember the last time he'd wanted to cry, the last time he'd felt this knot in his throat. The knot that kept growing until you could hardly breathe.

As he pulled into the recently plowed drive at his father's estate, Marty searched the road ahead, looking for Sinclair's car. It wasn't there and he was suddenly glad for that; he needed more time. But time for what? he thought angrily. To feel sorry for himself? Because that's what he was feeling. Yeah, he was a sorry son of a bitch. Maybe it was the fact that he'd never thought his life would turn out like this. Not now, not at this point.

He'd spent seven years with Reiki. And now, just like that, it was over? He was supposed to forget about all those tender moments and sweet-nothing whispers and deep-throat kisses with the Chinese carryout waiting for them, getting cold in those weird little boxes, on the table? Sure. He'd just toss all that aside and "move on"?

If he did that, what would it mean, all that time together? He swallowed hard, trying to make the knot in his throat go away. Was it all for nothing?

He couldn't accept that.

But enough about feelings and meaningful relationships, he told himself as he parked the car. He was here to meet Ford Sinclair. It was time to be a man. And suck it up.

Chapter 41

Del Waters turned back from the wet bar, his vacant blue eyes shifting to the three men sitting before him in his suite at Chicago's elite Athletic Club. He smiled at them, a thin, cruel smile, Nordic eyes gleaming.

It was the end of the line, Waters mused—at least it was for Marty English. He took a seat in a hefty leather chair and smiled again as the image of Marty English's body, mutilated and decaying in some remote Illinois cornfield, surfaced in his imagination. English would get what he had coming soon enough, Waters thought.

Del Waters had always hated being held captive by another man's whims—and for a while, Marty English had had him. But not for much longer, thank God. Yes, the tables were about to turn. Waters smiled again, more broadly this time, and lit his Cohiba cigar.

"So then," Waters began, his voice nearly betraying his eagerness, "English is supposed to meet Sinclair out at Lake Forest tonight?"

Harper nodded; in Waters's presence he always looked more like an obedient pup than a mercenary killer. Kemper, however, tried to maintain his machismo around their boss, and he spoke up now, saying, "Yeah, that's what Knute and his boys got off the wire. Sinclair called, talked to the girl, set it all up for around ten."

"Perfect." Waters smiled and clasped his well-manicured hands together with unabashed pleasure. "I didn't like the idea of taking him at O'Hare anyway . . . too public for my taste. Besides," he added, one eyebrow raised as he went back to puffing on the cigar, "this way we get two for the price of one."

"It's time we got Sinclair out of the picture," Kemper grumbled.

At the mention of Sinclair's potential demise, Waters caught Mike D'Angelo in his gaze. "Speaking of which, Mike, I hear those oafs you call enforcers finally got something right." He smiled, his dislike for D'Angelo coming through. "Stone Jackson must have been an easy target."

"Yeah, he was," D'Angelo admitted, glaring. He'd grown to hate Del Waters these past days; unlike Tony Inglesia, he wasn't highly skilled at interpersonal deception.

Waters tapped his cigar on the ashtray and said offhandedly, "English won't lay down while some goon puts a bullet in his brain. And Sinclair? He may be out of Lake Forest, but he's still a cop."

"That's right, Del," Harper agreed. "Holley says Sinclair's good. Not the average dick. He'll have a gun on him, for sure."

"Well, don't fuck around," Waters commented evenly, sounding like he was discussing the price of kumquats at the A & P. "Take Sinclair out first thing. Then go after English. Just remember, I want English alive. I don't want so much as a hair on his pretty-boy head out of place. You understand? Not until we know for sure we have the disc. And that it works. Then we'll dispose of English." The vision of the Illinois cornfield returned, and he smiled.

"What if English won't cooperate?" D'Angelo asked tentatively.

Waters gave D'Angelo a skeptical, haughty look. "If that

happens, Arch Templeton will be forced to have a little talk with him."

Kemper and Harper smiled and gaggled nervously at one another. They'd witnessed more than one of Templeton's little "talks" with the uncooperative—what they could stand to watch, that is. Basically, it was torture shit, stuff Templeton had picked up from the gooks in 'Nam, and horrible beyond belief, too, even to two guys who'd seen just about everything and had more blood on their hands than some Nazi prison guards. As terrible as it might be, they admired the way Templeton threw himself into his work. Arch Templeton was a very creative guy; sometimes he just let those nightmares in his head come to life. That's when he was at his best—and his most persuasive.

"So"—Harper grinned—"you've got Arch on call for a little persuasion session with English?" He crossed his arms and leaned back in his chair. "That should be interesting."

"I don't think that'll be necessary," D'Angelo said quickly, more quickly than he'd intended. "I think we can get English to listen to reason . . . maybe not at first, but he'll come around. I know him. He'll hand over the disc."

Waters sneered arrogantly. "What kind of fucking Mob guy are you, Mike? Guys like you ram cattle prods up guys' asses, for Christ's sake. Or do you prefer to use something warm-blooded for that?"

D'Angelo glared. "I don't mind strong-arming a guy," he growled, ignoring the insult. "I just think Marty English will cooperate without anyone having to resort to extremes. Like I said, I know how he thinks. He'll listen to reason."

"Reason?" Harper cackled. "What the hell difference does it make to you, anyway? I mean, the guy's as good as dead."

D'Angelo shrugged in studied nonchalance. "Sure. But I'd rather make it quick. You know . . . clean."

"I think you mean *painless*," Waters snarled, like a wild dog protecting a bone. Some Mob fucker wasn't going to steal his moment of pleasure; he wanted Marty English for himself.

"Sounds like you're feeling guilty, Mike," he accused, "now that we're down to the wire and we're gonna have to pop the kid. Trying to salve that conscience of yours with a 'clean' murder, is that what this is about? Well, guess what? Dead is dead." Waters paused and exhaled a ring of smoke before adding sarcastically, "But then again, maybe that Mob squad of yours doesn't know the fucking difference."

"When the time comes," D'Angelo bristled, "me and my boys'll handle the job."

Waters shook his head. "No. I don't think so. You're soft on the kid. I saw it right from the start, up in the Sears Tower. For all I know, you might have a change of heart." He looked over at Harper and Kemper. "Which is why I'm sending Max and Roger along with you tonight. I don't want any fuckups. I want this done right. And just so we've got this straight, when the time comes, I'll be the one taking care of English—not you and your no-neck thugs."

Red-faced, D'Angelo started to protest, but before he could, Waters crushed out his cigar and stood up. "You guys know what to do," he said, flashing a vicious smile in the direction of Harper and Kemper. "Now go do it."

Chapter 42

The sprawling, Tudor-style house loomed ahead, a brooding castle sealed off from the rest of the world.

As he walked up to the door of the dark house, briefcase in hand, Marty realized he couldn't push the vivid memory of his dead father away, and he stopped on the sidewalk for a moment. He didn't want to be here.

The house was darker than Marty had ever seen it; there'd always been a light in one of the leaded-glass windows this time of night when his father was alive. When he reached the front door, Marty started to put his key in the lock, but at his touch the heavy door groaned and swung open. In an instant of cold terror, he stumbled backwards, slipping, nearly falling down the icy steps. But he didn't fall; instead he managed to grab hold of the iron railing and steady himself.

He took a very deep breath. His heart was racing, pounding, almost as fast and hard as it did when he jogged through Lincoln Park. He craned his neck, looking around. There was no other car in the drive. No sign of Ford Sinclair. He studied the drifts of snow leading up to the door. In the dark he couldn't make out any other footprints. But he couldn't be sure. Was he alone? Or did somebody just want him to think he was? Heart hammering in his chest, he edged through the open door. One step at a time, he told himself. One step. He halted, listening—for what he didn't know—and then took another step. One step at a time. That wasn't so hard. That was all he had to do. He was in the foyer now. One more step and—

A rod of cold metal found his ribs and gave him a hard nudge. It was a gun. Fired, its bullet would travel through his back and directly into his heart. He froze, his knees turning to Jell-O. Cold sweat broke out on his face and neck.

"Okay, buddy, party's over. . . . Hands up."

It was a husky, deep voice with not a small amount of authority, and Marty recognized it instantly as Sinclair's. Weak with relief, his knees went to Jell-O all over again.

"Sinclair . . . it's me, Marty," he exclaimed, not moving. He was still afraid to move, afraid he might spook the detective and get himself killed for nothing. His voice cracked with the strain of so much fear and relief all at once. "Dammit, Sinclair, will you put that goddamned gun away before somebody gets hurt?"

The gun left his ribs. "Marty?" Sinclair flipped on the lights and stared at him. Brown eyes wide, he shook his head angrily. "Jesus H. Christ, boy, what are you doing sneaking around here like that? You about gave me a fucking heart attack."

"*I* gave *you* a heart attack?" Marty glanced at him indignantly. "What the hell do you think you did to me?"

Sinclair shrugged. "How was I supposed to know who it was, sneaking in here like that? How come you didn't walk right in and turn on the lights like a normal person? This *is* your house, you know."

"Hey, the door was unlocked. Which isn't exactly normal. I thought it might be smart not to make a grand entrance in case one of those CIA types was hanging around. Besides, you asked me to meet you here at ten, didn't you?"

"Well, you're early. It's just now eight-thirty."

"Didn't you see my car pull in? Jeez, you know my car. I

can tell you, I could've done without that red-carpet welcome you just gave me."

"Sorry about that," Sinclair said, genuinely apologetic now. "But I was back by the kitchen, checking things out. The door was open when I got here, too. . . . I didn't like the looks of things. When I heard your car, well, I figured you were one of those CIA bastards. I wasn't about to take a chance."

"CIA bastards?" Marty laughed uneasily. "You're getting a little shaky in your old age, aren't you?" He studied the man's tense frame; the detective looked as tight as a spring.

Sinclair's face turned somber. "I'll take exception to the 'old' part, but damned straight I'm shaky." He glanced outside and then, hands trembling, quickly closed the door. "Think there's any coffee back there in that kitchen?" he asked, putting his gun back in its holster. "Man, I could sure use a cup right now."

"So could I," Marty agreed. "It's been a long day." He wouldn't tell Sinclair just how long or bore him with the details of his problems with Reiki, but he did want to get the discoveries he'd made in Belize off his chest.

In the kitchen, Marty made a pot of coffee while Ford Sinclair leaned against the granite counter, looking on.

Sinclair broke the silence. "So how was Belize?"

"It was strange, Sinclair. Real fucking strange. That's how it was. Hey, maybe I'm paranoid, but I'm beginning to think there're conspiracies everywhere I go. There's something going on between my client and the conservation group they're working with. I know it sounds crazy, but I think they're tied in with the Mob and my father's murder. . . . I think it's all connected."

"Connected how?"

"Well, you see, Arrow—that's my client—is using a rainforest tree, the escoba, for its new herbal product line. According to Planetlife, the conservation group that runs the preserve down there, the project is supposed to be sustainable, at least that's what the commercial that's running eight days from now in the Super Bowl is going to claim."

"Makes sense to me. They're ecologists, right?"

"Yeah, they're supposed to be, but that's not what's happening, Sinclair. They're cutting the rainforest down. I saw the clear-cuts myself."

"I'd say that's pretty strange."

"It is. And it would be a hell of a PR nightmare if it ever got out that Arrow was involved in something like that. So I decided to talk to Arrow's president about it. And you know what? The guy went crazy on me. Hell, he defended the Planetlife people like they were gods." Marty paused and looked into the detective's eyes. "And unless you call Special Forces guys *gods*, I'm missing something."

"Special Forces?" Sinclair's face went ashen.

"That's right. Turns out that Planetlife and Escoba are run by some former Special Forces guys. One of whom just happens to be the chairman of Arrow's board."

"Your little CIA friends, Harper and Kemper, were Special Forces too. And, according to my sources, the last place they hung their hats was in Belize. Think they know your chairman fella?"

"I'd say it's a good possibility. There's a rumor Escoba's some sort of staging area for a covert CIA operation. Hell, the place is right on the Guatemalan border and it has a fucking airstrip that could handle C-130s." Marty paused, lifting his cup to his lips. "So what do you think, Detective Sinclair— coincidence or conspiracy?"

Sinclair shook his head. "If there's one thing I've learned over the years working on Homicide, it's that there's no such thing as a coincidence. You'll be interested to know that since you've been gone I've been working up a little conspiracy theory of my own. I think Harper and Kemper were the ones who poisoned your father, Marty. And I think they did it under orders of somebody high up in the CIA. But how this shit with Planetlife and Arrow fits in, hell, I don't get it. I mean, why would the CIA and an ecology group cut down a rainforest? And what would all that have to do with a pharmaceutical company and the Mob? I see the tangle, I just don't see the knot."

Marty started to tell the detective about the disc. After all, it was the knot that tied it all together, the one thing they all had in common. But instead he suddenly went on guard; maybe he'd said too much already. He shook his head uneasily. "I don't see it either, Sinclair."

Sinclair's eyes narrowed. "Well, whatever their connection is, my gut tells me it's big."

"Maybe your gut's paranoid." Marty smiled, suddenly eager to change the subject. "Speaking of which, I didn't see your car out there in the drive. What the hell did you do with it? You getting so paranoid that you left it down the street and hoofed it here?"

Sinclair shook his head. "I traded the old family junker in, got my little Crissie a brand-spanking-new one. I didn't have the heart to drive it through all this salt and crap on the roads—it's so shiny and new and all. I got one of the guys from the office to drop me off."

"You're really something, Sinclair. You know that?"

Ford Sinclair frowned into his cup, swishing the liquid around. "Yeah," he said bitterly, "I'm something, all right. I'm one selfish son of a bitch, that's what I am." Their eyes met. "You know that guy I said would help me out on this case?"

"Your friend from the CIA?"

"Yeah. That's the one. Only now he's my dead friend."

Marty put down his cup. "What are you talking about?" he demanded, his voice barely audible.

"I got him killed, Marty," Sinclair said, looking like he was going to cry. "The motherfuckers went after him. Took him out on Navy Pier just the other night. Blew his face clean off."

Sinclair's hands began to shake around the coffee cup and he looked up at the ceiling, swallowing hard, trying to pull himself together. "Shit, I knew Stone Jackson for more than twenty years. We went all the way back to the seventies. And now, all because I wanted some motherfucking file, now he's dead." He looked back at Marty. "Poor fella left behind his wife, Doneeta, and three great kids. Kids were smart as a whip, too. They were supposed to go to college—that's what Stone was busting his ass for." He smiled bitterly. "Not much fucking chance of that now . . . with him gone."

Reeling, Marty sat down at the table. "You're telling me that this friend of yours got killed because he was snooping around on my father's case?"

"Jesus," Sinclair growled impatiently, "do I have to fucking spell it out?"

"That's why you wanted to meet right away . . . tonight? To discuss this, this . . ." Marty searched for the right word, an impersonal word. "This *incident*?"

"Yeah, partly. I thought you should know what you're dealing with here. These boys do more than kick ass when they get pissed off."

Marty nodded. He wasn't sure he wanted to ask his next question. "What was the other thing you wanted to talk to me about?"

Sinclair sighed. "Your father's case has been closed."

"I know. I tried to call you. They said you were on vacation."

Sinclair let out a cynical laugh. "Oh yeah, my vacation. I've been having a fucking ball all week. First my captain closed a hot case for no good reason, gave me some time off I didn't ask for, and put me out of commission. Then the only friend I ever had was shot down like a dog." Sinclair jerked out a chair and sat down. "So what do you say, Marty? Think it's time we had a little heart-to-heart?"

Marty looked down at his half-empty cup of coffee and turned over his alternatives. It was time to let Sinclair in. He picked up his briefcase and put it on the table. He'd show the detective the disc with its glyph, tell him what Che had said. Maybe together he and Sinclair would be able to make some sense out of it all. "I think I know what they're after," he began as he opened the briefcase. "And when I say *they*, I mean the Mob, the CIA, Isaac Arrow, Planetlife—all of them." He took out the two identical B. B. King CDs and, after locating the scratch he'd made on one of the crystal cases, held it up. "They're after this," he said simply.

"B. B. King?" Sinclair let out a snort.

"This isn't a music CD, Sinclair. It's an image file."

"What kind of image?"

Marty handed Sinclair the printout of the glyph.

The detective examined the strange image. "This?" he exclaimed incredulously, smacking the paper with the back of his hand. "Are you telling me this is what's on that disc? Those guys are killing people over this?"

Marty nodded. "It sure looks like it."

"Well, what the fuck is it?" Sinclair demanded, passing it back.

"It's a Maya glyph. I talked with an Indian down at Escoba and he told me it's one of three gods in something the Maya call the Palenque Triad." He motioned to the image. "This one is the god of the underworld."

Ford Sinclair's mouth dropped open. "Underworld? You're shitting me."

"'Fraid not."

Intrigued, Sinclair pulled his chair in and leaned closer. "Did you get anything from that Indian on the other two gods?"

"Yeah, one of them is the god of the sun. He's the top dog, so to speak. And the other is the god of illusion, the one that isn't what he appears to be."

Sinclair stood up in exasperation and, shoving his hands deep into his pockets, started pacing back and forth across the tile floor. He suddenly stopped and looked at Marty in bewilderment. "What the fuck is this about?"

"I wish I knew. But I don't . . . not for sure, anyway. But take a look at these numbers." Marty pointed to the printout. "I think they're some kind of code."

Sinclair bent over the table. "The one up top there—I don't know about it. But this down here, on the bottom." He tapped at the paper. "My guess is it's a bank routing number."

"Can you find out for sure? Maybe check it out, trace it, see where it goes?"

"Yeah. We could have that in a few hours," Sinclair said, hurriedly scrawling the numbers down on his notepad while Marty looked on.

"But Sinclair," Marty objected, "you're on vacation, remember? How can you—"

"Hell"—Sinclair waved his hand, discounting the question almost before Marty had it out of his mouth—"there's a secretary at the station who thinks I hung the moon. Rhonda'll give me a hand. You watch, Marty." He smiled broadly. "We're going to get to the bottom of this."

Sinclair grabbed up his rumpled coat with one hand and took out his cell phone. "It's nine-thirty. I'm going to call my police buddy and have him swing by and give me a lift home." He poked at the numbers and put the phone to his ear. Sinclair spoke rapid-fire into the phone to someone and then, with only a "See you in a minute," slipped it back into his pocket.

"What's the hurry?" Marty asked, holding up the pot of coffee. "Sit down, have another cup. I even have more Sweet'n Low."

Sinclair grinned. "You're a good host, Marty. But no thanks. No time to chew the fat right now. I want to get on this thing pronto. I intend to nail those sleazy bastards to the fucking wall. Two murders, breaking and entering . . . shit, who the hell knows what else."

Eyes burning black like fiery coals, Sinclair paused and looked down at his hands, which were balled up into large, tight fists. "When I'm through with them," he vowed, voice trembling with hatred, "those sons of bitches won't see the light of day for the rest of their fucking lives. In the meantime, don't let that disc out of your sight." He threw on his topcoat and hurried toward the hallway. "I'm out of here, Marty. I've got some fish to fry." He smiled. "And I do mean fry."

Marty roamed around the big empty house for a while after Sinclair left. He went upstairs, poked around in the bedrooms, sat on his old maple bed.

His bedroom was just as he'd left it—the old mono record player in the corner, the forty-fives, the guitar—back when he was seventeen, that momentous night in the summer of 1968.

He lay back on the bumpy white chenille bedspread and studied the walls. They were covered in the same funky wallpaper, a mix of plaids and thoroughbreds, his mother had picked out years ago.

He'd never liked the paper, and over time he did a little papering of his own: two of the room's walls were covered in pennants and shelves lined with his high school golfing trophies. The other two were plastered with an eye-popping assortment of black light posters and psychedelic pop art.

Yeah, it was just like he'd left it. And it was clear to Marty now, as he surveyed the room, that he'd been pretty damned conflicted back then. In fact, to say he'd gone through an identity crisis seemed a comical understatement. Split personality was more like it: Jimi Hendrix meets Arnold Palmer, somewhere in the Twilight Zone. He was glad he'd finally grown up. Glad he'd never have to go through it all again.

He got up and wandered around the house some more, opening drawers and looking inside, rummaging around. He wasn't looking for anything in particular, except maybe a few memories. But when he came across an ancient pack of Trojans in the old man's drawer, he suddenly felt like a trespasser, and he turned off the lights and headed downstairs.

Marty was in the kitchen, putting on his coat, when he thought of the library. He hadn't gone in there tonight. He was looking for memories, wasn't he? Hell, the library was a walk down memory lane. Taking deliberate, measured steps, Marty walked into the library. Fumbling in the dark, he found a lamp and turned it on. When he did, his eye caught a reflection in the mirror behind the bar and he let out a gasp. Then, realizing it was his own reflection, he laughed out loud.

It was a hollow laugh, and he saw that his hands were still shaking skittishly, shaking like the hands of one of those winos he always bumped into over on the westside. Get a grip, he told himself as he looked around the dark-paneled room. A frown passed over his face as the familiar sadness came rushing back. Once again he was a boy hiding behind the one-way mirror in his father's library. The boy who listened. The boy who heard things he didn't want to hear.

Marty suddenly wondered what voices echoed there now, behind the mirrored panel and, curious, he walked behind the marble-and-brass counter and put his hand on the mirror. It was cool to the touch, like he'd remembered, and he ran his fingers lightly over the surface until he felt the ridge of beveled glass that told him he'd found the spot. He raised one finger, typewriter style, and gave it a gentle tap. Soundlessly, a mirrored door swung open on silent hinges, gaping like an open mouth, bidding him into the dark cavity.

Marty switched on the light and the small room came aglow in the cold, fluorescent-blue glare of the tubes of light positioned overhead. It was an unforgiving light. The perfect ambience, Marty thought sardonically, for an inquisition. Or a dental extraction.

He was surprised to see that the room was no bigger than an ordinary walk-in closet; he'd remembered it being much larger. But then, he reminded himself, the last time he'd been here he was a scrawny little kid just getting his first zit.

His eyes swept over the room; it didn't look anything like he recalled. His father had had an old safe, some dented metal filing cabinets. A beat-up desk and chair. Not much else. Nothing exciting. But it looked like things had changed: obviously, his father had gotten into the electronic age in a big way. The old desk and chair were gone, replaced by an ebony leather chair and an arty chrome model that reminded Marty of one of those surgical tables in *ER*. A slick new TV monitor and VCR were perched atop its shimmering surface, standing at the ready. Nearby, a state-of-the-art video camera, tape in place, had been mounted on a sleek tripod and its lens directed through the one-way mirror into the library beyond.

Stacks of videotapes, encased in shiny black-vinyl boxes with carefully printed labels on their sides, littered the gray-carpeted floor. There were more videotapes on the walls, crammed into steel shelves that seemed almost to groan beneath their weight.

"What the hell is this all about?" Marty muttered to himself as he took the tape out of the camera. Unlike the others, this one remained unlabeled.

What the hell? Was his father shooting home movies? Then suddenly, Marty caught on.

His father had been secretly recording his visitors. Yeah, that was it: He'd been putting it all on tape. Tony Inglesia, Mob boss, probably had more dirt right here in this little room than the entire FBI. If that was the case, there would be enough evidence on these tapes to put half of Chicago behind bars, maybe all of America's underworld.

Marty looked down at the tape in his hand, and his heart skipped a beat. Trembling with a mixture of fear and anticipation, he sat down at the desk. As he turned on the monitor and the VCR, he took a deep breath, trying to make his heart stop racing. Then he put in the tape.

For a moment he faltered, his finger poised over the Play button. Did he really want the truth? Maybe the voices recorded on this tape were the ghosts of some nightmarish past.

Hell, no maybe about it, *they had to be*. And like that boy long ago, Marty wasn't so sure he wanted to hear what those voices had to say. They were, after all, secrets—dark secrets. Perhaps they were better left that way.

"You need fifty-two cards to play the game"; wasn't that what his father had been fond of saying? Right now, Marty had only half a deck. And so, despite the fear that gripped him, he took another deep breath and hit Play. All the cards would be on the table now. But even so, he sensed that, somehow, the game was just beginning.

Marty wasn't sure how long he'd been sitting there, reeling, his thoughts frozen in numb shock, as he stared back at the snowy monitor. It could have been thirty seconds. Or an eternity. But it didn't matter. In an instant, in a few feet of spinning videotape, everything had changed. Destiny had come calling. And, like Che had said, Marty had no choice but to answer.

Of course, he shouldn't have been shocked by the tape's revelations. With his background, he should have been able to guess what he might see, but nothing had prepared him for the horror that played on the screen before him. Stunned, he rewound the videotape and played it back, trying to let it all sink in. But even then it was hard to believe. And he rewound it and played it all over again just to make sure.

And there it was right before his eyes, the truth, in living color: Del Waters meeting with his father. Carson Page and Frank Torello spinning their little web. The details of their collaboration over the years, in their own incriminating words. Words that echoed now, hollow and sinister, from the monitor speaker.

"That's the beauty of it, Tony," Del Waters had said. "Who would ever think that Isaac Arrow, the world's most respected pharmaceutical giant, and Planetlife, a rainforest foundation full of bleeding-heart liberals, would be tied up with rogue CIA agents and the Chicago Mob?"

Yeah, who would think a thing like that? Marty shook his head. And who would ever believe they had four hundred fifty million dollars in an account somewhere? And all you needed to get at it was a B. B. King disc? Yeah, like Frank Torello had so smugly asserted during the meeting, the public would never believe anything so preposterous—even if they saw it in black or white.

Or in color. Carson Page had laughed when she'd said that, and Marty had felt overcome with nausea, sickened as much by his own part in the ugly plot as by the memory of his night with her.

He fast-forwarded the tape to eleven-thirty that same night. Knowing what was coming, it was hard, almost impossible, to watch.

Mike D'Angelo had murdered his father.

The hidden camera had had a perfect view of D'Angelo stirring the poison into Inglesia's drink. A perfect view of D'Angelo ignoring the dying man's piteous pleas for help. And a perfect view of D'Angelo, cruel smile on his traitorous face, raising his glass in toast over the man's mottled corpse when it was over.

"Salud," D'Angelo had said. At those words, Marty's heart turned to stone.

He sat there as the screen went to snow and the voices from the past went silent. Silent except for one lone voice whispering in his head. The voice of a father, whispering an eerie, unsettling message to his son from the grave: "Friends take care of friends."

In his mind's eye, Marty saw the Mob boss on the videotape smile coldly, heard him say, "Enemies get taken care of."

Dark eyes gleaming in the light of the monitor, Marty nodded to himself and smiled his father's smile. Yeah, and double-crossers got what they had coming, too. And Marty was going to see to it. Personally.

Chapter 43

Their headlights off, two nondescript Fords eased up the long brick drive until they came to a stop a hundred yards away from the house. A '63 Jaguar was parked near the door. Inside, the lights were on.

From the backseat, Mike D'Angelo muttered out of the corner of his rubbery mouth, "It's English."

Up front, Harper and Kemper were checking the clips in their Berettas, but at the remark they looked up, puppet faces pulled into broad grins of anticipation.

"Where's the fucking cop's car?" Harper asked, peering into the night. "I don't see it anywhere."

"That's because it's not here," Kemper replied, a note of exasperation in his voice.

Harper shook his head angrily. "Fuck. Is Del gonna be pissed or what?"

D'Angelo shrugged. "Hell, we can't help it if the guy's gone," he said, pulling his .22 from its shoulder holster.

"Right. First things first," Kemper agreed. "We'll take care of Sinclair later."

The three men stepped out into the frigid night and stood in a huddle on the pavement. D'Angelo waved to the car behind him and six goons got out, guns drawn, and started trampling toward them over the crust of ice and salt.

"Spread out around the house," D'Angelo ordered. "He may try to run. Remember, shoot *only* if you have to . . . and only to stop him. Fuck up and kill him and you'd just as well go ahead and shoot yourself while you're at it."

Harper and Kemper turned away, shaking their heads. D'Angelo and his bull-necked goons were stupid fools for not realizing that Del Waters was merely using them. Warfare always required the grunts. When Waters was done, when this job was finished—well, Mike D'Angelo and his greaseballs would be, too.

D'Angelo didn't notice the agents' contemptuous expressions; he was too busy watching his men scatter and disappear into the inky night. He didn't make a move toward the house, not until he could no longer hear their footfalls scratching through the snow crust and he knew they were finally in position. D'Angelo had already decided he wasn't going back to Del Waters empty-handed; he'd have Marty English one way or another. There was more than his pride at stake here. There were millions, no, billions, of dollars to be made.

"Okay," D'Angelo said finally. "Let's get this over with."

Smiling cruelly, the agents fell in behind D'Angelo, walking purposefully up the drive toward the house.

Marty had just rewound the videotape and taken it out of the VCR when he heard the noise: a crashing sound, like a rifle crack through a window, shattering glass into a million pieces.

Instinctively, he turned off the bank of blue lights and rushed to the mirrored door and sealed it shut. The hidden panel made a slight gasping sound as it closed, the sound a vacuum-sealed can makes when you open it, and Marty prayed that it had only sounded loud to him, fixed as he was in the moment. Breathing hard, almost panting, he leaned against the wall and peered through the one-way mirror. Waiting. Seconds, minutes. It wasn't very long—it only felt like it—and then he heard voices, angry voices, coming his way, and suddenly D'Angelo, Harper, and Kemper burst into the library.

They were huffing and puffing, their faces cold, white slates chapped red across the cheeks. At the sight of them, guns in hand, Marty's nostrils flared with fear and then alarm. *Shit*; he'd left his briefcase, the disc neatly tucked inside, right under the kitchen table.

"You ever heard the word *quiet*, D'Angelo?" Harper chided scornfully. The agent glanced around the room as if half expecting someone to be standing there, listening, and behind the one-way mirror, Marty's heart raced faster. Could they see his shadow behind the mirror, was that possible? He took a step back.

"Hey," D'Angelo retorted, his irritation showing, "I didn't see the coffeepot on the edge of the table, okay?"

Harper laughed.

"Shut up, both of you," Kemper snapped as he strode across the room and walked behind the bar. He paused, inches from the mirror, and looked directly at his own image, smiling his familiar wooden smile. It felt to Marty as if their eyes had met. On the other side of the wall, he caught his breath, watching in terror, afraid Kemper might actually hear his heart pounding.

Admiring his reflection, Kemper adjusted his necktie and then turned back to his companions, his keen eyes examining the perimeter of the room. "Anybody check in here?" he asked.

D'Angelo shook his head. "Not yet," he replied, looking around with what Marty took as a nostalgic expression on his face. Probably having memories of his last moments with his mentor-boss, Marty thought savagely. "But there's no reason to," D'Angelo continued, "he's not in here."

Behind the mirror, Marty smiled.

Harper walked over to the fireplace and squatted down, staring up into the dark chimney. He let out a cough. "Yeah," he agreed resignedly, "there's no place to hide in here."

"Maybe we should go through the house again," D'Angelo suggested. "Maybe we missed something."

"Missed something?" Harper exclaimed in surprise. "I thought you said you knew this place."

"I do," D'Angelo shot back defensively.

"Well, where the hell is he, then?" Harper demanded.

D'Angelo shrugged. "I don't know. Shit, we've looked everywhere I can think of. I don't get it."

"Think he left with the cop?" Kemper ventured.

"No," D'Angelo replied. "Marty wouldn't leave the lights on. He's here. He has to be."

"Well, if he is we'd better find him," Harper declared, his usually calm, flat voice sounding shrill, almost panicked. "I'm sure as hell not going back to Del without him. You've seen Del—he wants that goddamned disc . . . bad. We'd better fucking deliver."

"*Relax*," Kemper snapped. "Hell, even if English gives us the slip we'll still have the girl."

"Well, we don't have her yet." Harper shook his head ruefully and slumped against the wall. "I knew we should've gotten her before we came out here."

"You heard what Del said. He wanted us to pick up English first," Kemper growled, losing his patience. "We'll get the girl."

We'll get the girl. Marty went weak-kneed, steadying himself against the mirrored wall. He suddenly understood what they intended to do. Understood that he was Reiki's only chance. That she would probably be dead before sunrise if he didn't get out of there and save her.

"Can we get going now?" Harper demanded impatiently.

Kemper nodded. "Let's split up. We'll each take a section of the house and make another pass at it. We know English is around here somewhere."

They vanished down the hallway and Marty groped around in the darkness for his coat and slipped it on. Regrettably, it was light, a soft, expensive cashmere. At least it was black; he wouldn't be easy to spot. But his shoes? Tasseled slip-ons from Italy with leather as thin and fine as a glove; they would be a problem in eight inches of snow. He shook his head; not exactly regulation gear, he thought bitterly. And that would've been nice right now. After all, it was below zero outside; he wouldn't be able to make it if his body temperature dropped. That meant he couldn't roll around in snowbanks and get wet or waste precious time hiding in some damned ditch, up to his ass in ice cubes. No, he'd have to keep moving if he wanted to survive.

Marty went to the mirrored panel and slowly eased it open, inch by unbearable inch, feeling vulnerable in the growing glare of the light beyond. Taking a deep breath, he stepped out into the library, fell to a low crouch, and shoved the door closed behind him. He couldn't turn back now. But then he didn't want to. He checked his watch, went over his plan one more time. Whatever happened, he knew he couldn't leave without his briefcase.

He started to move, but then, at the sound of the men's voices in the distance, he froze, listening. They were upstairs, he decided; but they'd be coming down soon. He had to get out of there—now.

Still in a crouch, he moved rapidly down the hallway. When he got to the kitchen, he peered cautiously around the door and into the room, his eyes searching desperately for the briefcase. At the sight of it, still under the table, he smiled in relief.

But when he heard the voices—closer now—the smile faded. They were on the staircase now, descending, coming toward him. It would be only a matter of seconds and they'd be on him. It was time to pull out all the stops, it was time to—

Move, soldier! a voice in his head commanded.

Marty bolted into the kitchen, grabbed the precious briefcase and crashed though the back door, knocking down one of D'Angelo's men as he went.

"He's getting away!" the thug yelled as Marty raced across the snow-covered lawn and scrambled up a high stone wall.

Smack. He heard the dull thud of a bullet hitting the icy snowbank below, and he went down in a squat on top of the wall. He looked over his shoulder, his eyes sweeping the surrounding landscape.

Ping. Another bullet struck the stone at his feet, sending splintered shards of rock in all directions. He squinted through the blackness to the ground below and started to jump, but then hesitated; it was a long drop, at least eight feet. But he knew a third bullet wouldn't miss so he threw his briefcase down and jumped after it, landing, with a painful jolt, on his feet.

Kneeling, breathing hard, he glanced around hurriedly in the darkness. He had the advantage of knowing the grounds: That's what would help him make it, he told himself. Two hundred yards ahead, through a dense stand of hardwoods and pine, he knew there was a street.

At the sound of footfalls and shouts from the other side of the wall, he snatched up the briefcase and sprinted through the thick underbrush lining the woods, tearing past the low pines, shoving away the branches as he ran. A hundred yards in, he stopped, panting, trying to get a fix on his pursuers' position. He could hear them rushing toward him, could see the narrow beams of light that told him they'd gotten flashlights and found his tracks in the snow.

He started running again, his breath expelling in deep, frozen bursts. Ahead, a streetlight glowed. He planned to take off through old man Collins's place across the street, dive into an old root cellar he'd stumbled on as a kid. They'd never find him there. It seemed like a good plan.

Even the best-laid plans didn't always work, Marty reminded himself when he saw two of D'Angelo's thugs standing under the street light across from the Collins estate. Of course all good plans also had to be flexible, so Marty switched to Plan B.

He stood up and ran.

As he turned and headed through the woods toward a side street, crashing through the underbrush, he tripped over a fallen limb and tumbled down a slippery embankment, landing, briefcase still clutched to his chest, in a clump of prickly evergreens. That's where he was, lying there, wind knocked out of him, trying to get his bearings, when he looked out at the street and saw the yellow cab pull up to the stop sign. He allowed himself a smile; it looked like Plan B was going to pay off after all.

Gripping the briefcase under his arm, Marty darted from the bushes and into the street. Almost instantly, he heard the thugs behind him give out a shout, heard their footsteps, moving faster and faster, running toward him through the heavy snow. A sudden flood of light crisscrossed his path to the cab, illuminating the face of its driver, his eyes wide with fear.

There were more shouts, and then a round of gunfire. A bullet struck the cab door with a *ping*, then another, and the cab's engine let out a roar, followed by the whirr of tires spinning helplessly on icy pavement. The cab was Marty's only chance—in seconds it would be leaving him behind.

He hurled himself onto the hood, coming face-to-face with the terrified cabbie behind the wheel. Their eyes locked through the windshield as the cab screeched forward, jerking crazily to the right and then to the left and back again as the cabbie struggled desperately to disengage his unwanted passenger.

Suddenly, there was the *crack* of shattered glass and the cabbie's eyes bulged in his head as a bullet exploded through his temple, spewing bone and brain and gristle in a bloody streak across the front seat. Out of control now, the cab lurched forward onto the curb, throwing Marty to the pavement.

D'Angelo's men were almost on him now. Time was running out. Dazed and bruised, Marty grabbed his briefcase, scrambled to his feet, and lunged at the car door. As he struggled to wrench it open, a bullet caught him in the hand. Wincing in pain now, he shoved the cabbie's grisly remains aside and jumped behind the wheel, wrestling the car off the curb and back into the street. Another bullet shattered the rear windshield and whizzed past his head as he slammed the accelerator to the floor. A hail of bullets followed.

The shouts of his pursuers were still ringing in his ears when Marty sped off down the street and disappeared into the night.

The bullet had only grazed his hand, but even so, the wound was bleeding—and it hurt like hell. Marty thought a visit to an emergency room would be prudent, but the cabbie's dead body lying in the seat next to him ruled out prudence.

Knowing that Chicago's finest tended to ask questions when they saw blood-spattered windshields, Marty turned off the interstate and took the seamy, poorly lit backstreets into the city, the places where, when you needed a cop, they were nowhere to be found. Fortunately, cops didn't want to risk their lives either.

He couldn't waste precious time trying to talk his way out of a murder charge right now. The clock was ticking, and it was close to midnight. He had to get to Reiki—that was the first order of business. The second was to dump this car and its contents. Cautiously zigzagging up and down the narrow streets, Marty kept the speedometer at thirty. When he got past the old ethnic neighborhoods, he picked up speed, doing forty-five as he threaded his way through a maze of tenements and warehouses, until, at last, he came to an abandoned rail yard on the near westside.

After maneuvering the cab over the abandoned tracks and across the snow-covered weeds and gravel, he killed the engine. Then, letting out a heavy sigh, he slumped over the wheel and closed his eyes. He stayed like that for only a moment before he sat up, poker-straight: alert, adrenaline flowing. He had to warn Reiki. Hurriedly he wiped down the car with his handkerchief and closed the door.

As he picked up his briefcase, he paused, studying the bloody body slumped in the front of the cab. The dead man's eyes stared up at him, open and milky white with shock.

"Sorry, fella," he said softly. And then he turned and ran.

"Hello," a tired voice answered.

"Reiki, it's me," Marty whispered. He didn't know why he was whispering; he was in the middle of nowhere, near the Domino. Nobody gave a good goddamn about some guy freezing his ass off in a phone booth in this part of town. Or about what he had to say, for that matter.

"Marty!" Reiki exclaimed. "Where—"

"I don't have time to explain. Just listen," he ordered. "Mike D'Angelo killed my father. And those phony agents, they're in on it too. And so are the Planetlife and Arrow bigwigs. They all want the disc and they're prepared to kill for it. They're after me, Reiki. And they're coming after you. They'll be there any minute." He heard her gasp. "I want you to get the hell out of there. Take your laptop and go to the lily pad. You hear me? The lily pad. Wait there. You got that?"

"Uh-huh. The lily pad." She sounded dazed, frightened. "Are you okay?"

"I'm fine."

"Is there . . . anything else?"

"Yeah," he said, his voice dropping tenderly. "I need you."

Reiki Devane was a very methodical, level-headed woman. In the five minutes that elapsed after talking with Marty, she'd brushed her long hair up in a neat ponytail and thrown on her Levi's and a bulky fisherman knit sweater. Then she stopped by the bathroom and put a small bag of toiletries into a tote along with her passport and some travelers' checks and cash she still had from her aborted trip to Rwanda. In the foyer, she stuffed her socked feet into a pair of Frye boots and slipped on a camel-hair coat, matching gloves, muffler, and beret. Then she picked up a leather computer case and slung it over her shoulder. Not quite the right wardrobe for Bermuda, she thought as she opened the door and hurried down the back stairwell and out into the night. But then again, she was in a hurry. Marty needed her.

on a continuous note; machine blowers muffled and soft.
Then she picked up a leather summer coat and slung it over
her shoulder. Not done: the right way to take the demands; she
thought, as she spotted the door and moved down the hall,
stairwell and dip into the night. She thought she could
hurry to her needed her.

Chapter 44

Like most places where the poor congregated, Chicago's
westside was invisible, except to those who lived there.

So were all the vacant lots littered with Cyclone fences and
rusty barbed wire and a thousand other pieces of disposable
junk. In the winter, the neighborhood streets iced over and
rutted up like the ridges on a Ruffles potato chip, forcing the
few cars that ventured down them to move slowly, drivers
looking down at the road to avoid potholes and paying little
attention to what was going on around them.

Nobody gave a fuck about the westside except the junkies,
pimps, and whores who hung out there, scratching out a living among the homeless and the winos. If a guy wanted to
drop out of sight for a while, he just dropped down that sewer
pipe of a neighborhood and got dirty with the rest of them.
Then he was invisible too.

Marty had never been to her place before. But he knew where
Suzy Q lived; he'd seen the middle-aged whore with the
retro–Farrah Fawcett hair, hot pants, and platform shoes lead
more than one guy up the stairs of that sagging tenement.

At his knock, Suzy didn't throw open the door right away;
she was cautious, unlocking the door, leaving the chain on, as
she peered, hollow eyes devoid of makeup, through a narrow

crack, assessing her caller. Seeing Marty standing in the dingy hallway, his coat over his shoulder and clutching a battered briefcase, Suzy's face registered surprise, then concern.

"Can I come in?" he asked quickly, gingerly slipping his wounded hand into the pocket of his blazer. He preferred not to have to explain a bullet wound right now, while he was standing in the hall. He was still trying to figure out how he was going to explain why he was there in the first place.

"Sure." She nodded, frowning, as she hurriedly unlatched the chain and opened the door. "Come on in."

While Suzy scurried around in a pink bathrobe and matching fuzzy slippers, turning on lights and plumping pillows, Marty surveyed her apartment. He'd expected something more along the lines of red-flocked Mediterranean, black wrought iron, cheap gaudy carpet, some gold-veined mirrors, perhaps. But instead the two-room flat looked more like a shrine to the early seventies than a den of iniquity. The carpet was a green shag, smashed and worn almost flat in places. The walls were paneled in dark sheets of fake-grained wood. On one she'd hung a poster that said SOCK IT TO ME in giant, Crayola-bright letters. Faded geometric-print drapes were drawn at the windows, and a curtain of plastic beads swayed in a doorway leading to a kitchen filled with ancient avocado appliances.

"You didn't come here for business," she said matter-of-factly as she motioned for him to have a seat on a swaybacked sofa draped in a crocheted afghan.

"No, I didn't," he confessed, taking a seat. He turned his attention to her and, bewildered, said, "You know, you look different tonight."

She laughed and pulled a worn beanbag chair across the floor and sat down. "You mean *normal*, don't you? You mean I'm not wearing those shitty grab-ass pants and trailer-trash hair you always see me in? All that crap on my face?"

She had him there; that was exactly what he'd been thinking. "Yeah," he admitted cautiously, a sheepish grin creeping over his tired face. "I guess that *is* what I mean."

"Well, for your information," she declared without a trace of offense, "I wasn't always a worn-out whore. I used to have some real looks." She nodded dreamily. "Did I ever tell you I was Miss Fort Wayne back in high school?"

He shook his head.

"Well, I was. After that, I went to college at Purdue for a couple of years."

He hid his surprise.

"But it was the sixties," she went on. "You know how they were. I got sidetracked, partied too much, flunked out. My old man and I got bored with all that 'Give peace a chance' shit and decided to go for bigger thrills than smoking pot and taking hits of speed on the night of an exam. It was high times, life in the fast lane, for a while. I did coke in the early seventies, but it gave me the jitters, made my heart pound real bad. So then I turned on to smack." She shrugged. "That's all she fucking wrote, after that. Hey, when a girl's got a habit, she's gotta work."

Marty suddenly felt embarrassed, like a voyeur, peeping through a window into a stranger's life.

"But of course," she said quickly, "I'm not using anymore. A few years back, the old man OD'd. That did it. I got straight. But easy money is easy money. Where else can a girl make eight hundred bucks a week, tax free?"

She paused to pour coffee from a battered metal percolator, and Marty suddenly wondered where the hell all that tax-free money had gone.

As if reading his mind, Suzy smiled. "Did you know I'm saving up for a place in Florida? That's where I want to go, to Daytona Beach, away from all this city crap. I'm tired of the cold." She shivered and pulled her robe around her.

"Maybe I should be going," he said awkwardly.

"Hey, it's okay. I know I'm not your type. But it's nice having some real company for a change. Guess I don't have too many friends." She nodded at his blazer pocket. "And from the looks of things, right now neither do you."

Marty looked down and saw that it was splotched with fresh blood. Wincing, he withdrew his hand. Suzy was right. He was on his own now, on the run. Still, she had to be wondering why he'd turned up bleeding on her doorstep at three in the morning. If she did wonder, she didn't ask. People didn't ask questions on the westside. Like mobsters and ministers, Suzy Q kept her eyes and ears open and her mouth shut. She listened. She knew the difference between someone *in* trouble and someone who *was* trouble, and she knew Marty English was a member of the first group. She'd been in bad spots before, and she had the decency and guts to help someone who was where she'd been on too many occasions.

Suzy tended to Marty's hand, gave him a pillow, and, pointing to the sofa, told him to get some sleep. "Whatever you gotta do, sugar," she said reassuringly, "it'll wait 'til tomorrow."

Chapter 45

Del Waters hadn't slept all night; patience, after all, had never been one of his virtues. After his three visitors had left earlier that evening, Waters had made a martini and turned on CNN. But there were no stories of war, disaster, or other entertaining events, so he got up and started pacing around his suite, going from room to room until, itchy and weary of waiting for news of Marty English, he went out for a walk in the cold Chicago night.

When Harper, Kemper, and D'Angelo finally arrived at his suite in the Chicago Athletic Club, it was after seven o'clock on Sunday morning. Waters had already read the *Tribune* and had a steam and a light breakfast. Almost twelve hours had passed since the men had left for Lake Forest, and in all that time Waters had heard nothing on their progress. And now what he heard from them was the story of a world-class fuckup.

"So what you're telling me is English outran nine men? Men with guns, I might add?" Waters glared at them and then added contemptuously, "You did take guns, didn't you?"

"Shit, Del, come on, give us a break here," Harper grumbled. "Hell, it was dark out there. We just fucking lost him in the woods and when he popped up again it was too late. He jumped in a cab and took off." The agent paused and then added, almost as an afterthought, "We fired a couple of shots, nailed the cabbie, hit English, too. Shit, you would've thought he'd given up right there . . ."

"But he's one tough bastard, Del," Kemper added.

D'Angelo nodded. "Hell, he's Tony Inglesia's son."

"What about Sinclair?" Harper asked. "We could move on him."

"Don't touch the cop," Waters snapped. "You stick on that asshole like toilet paper. Hell, shake the piss off Sinclair's goddamned dick if you have to—just stay on him. He'll lead us to English. I'm sure of it."

Harper nodded solemnly.

Waters's jaw clenched methodically, up and down, as he looked toward the window. He could have lost it right there, killed the three of them and enjoyed every fucking minute of it. But right now he needed them. He wasn't going down on this one by himself. Calmly, he turned to face them. "Perhaps I should make this as clear as possible," he began, "so there won't be any misunderstanding. Seven days from now, at precisely eight P.M. on Super Bowl Sunday, I am meeting at Planetlife with a small group of very unforgiving Iranian arms dealers to whom, it just so happens, I owe the sum of one hundred fifty million dollars."

D'Angelo's swarthy face drained of its color.

"A small amount in the past, no problem at all." Waters shrugged. "But unfortunately, a situation recently arose which changed the complexion of things." He glared at D'Angelo. "Tony Inglesia's untimely death has left me in a very awkward position. Without his disc, you see, it is impossible for me to retrieve that money. And without that money . . . well . . ." He smiled bitterly. "The men I deal with are quite humorless."

They stared back at him.

"Find English," Waters ordered. "No loose ends."

Chapter 46

At the sight of the Old One, its muscular shoulders undulating as it padded noiselessly across the dark Belizean jungle floor, Che's heart leaped in his chest. He could hardly believe his eyes. Only once in his life had he seen the elusive jaguar, but he had no recollection of that event: He had been just an infant at the time, unnamed and fresh from the womb.

For most of his life, Che had walked the rainforest hoping to catch just a glimpse of the Old One—that was what people called the great cat nowadays. But seeing the jaguar had always remained only a dream until now, and Che's excitement was so great he almost dropped the broom he'd been using to sweep Escoba's trails and gave himself away. But he didn't; he was a shaman, after all, a man of wisdom who knew this jaguar standing before him was a sign from the heavens.

As the regal creature gave out a yawn and curled up in a patch of dappled sunlight, Che, heart pounding, knelt behind a ceiba tree and looked on. What had brought this great jaguar to him, at this time?

At the sound of the crackling of leaves on the ground, the jaguar raised its massive head, peering golden-eyed into the forest, its gaze coming to rest on Che. *I am another one of yourself,* the eyes said, using the Maya greeting.

The leaves crackled again and Che glanced over his shoulder. He was surprised to see Arch Templeton standing there, with Carlos at his side.

"What are you doing, Che?" Templeton demanded.

Che looked back into the jungle; the Old One was gone. He picked up his broom and stood up. "Nothing, sir. I will get back to work now."

"Put the broom down, Che," Templeton ordered.

Che looked at him in surprise. "Is there something else, Mr. Templeton?"

"We've discussed these conversations you've had with guests in the past, haven't we?"

Che felt his hands trembling around the broom, but he kept his voice steady. "Yes, sir. We have."

"And after you talked with Marty English and took him out into the rainforest, didn't I tell you never to talk to him again?"

"Yes, sir."

"But you did that anyway, didn't you? You openly disobeyed my orders. Isn't that so?"

Che cast a disparaging look at Carlos. "Only to say good-bye, Mr. Templeton," he replied. "Only to wish him well . . . nothing more than that. It was quite harmless, I assure you. I never intended to show you any disrespect."

"Disrespect?" Templeton snorted. "What about an outright lie? Do you expect me to believe you only said good-bye, that you and Marty English didn't talk about Planetlife and Escoba?"

"We said good-bye, that is all."

"Well, that's not what Carlos here tells me. He says you did more than that. He says you gave Marty English something before he got on the plane. A paper of some kind."

Che hesitated. Why would Arch Templeton be interested in a drawing of an old Maya god scribbled on a paper napkin? From Templeton's demeanor, it had to be important, perhaps worth the price of Marty English's life. "Carlos is mistaken, sir," Che replied evenly. "As I said, I only gave Marty English a handshake good-bye."

Carlos shook his head at Templeton. "I know what I saw, Mr. Templeton."

"You're lying, Che," Templeton said coolly. "What did you give Marty English? Don't protect him. You saw how much he cared about you. The first thing he did was run to us with that little sob story you gave him."

"Marty only did that out of ignorance," Che objected. "He did not know he would be doing harm. As I said, I gave him nothing."

Templeton's face turned strangely placid and he drew his revolver and pointed it at Che. "You're a liar," he said flatly, firing into the Indian's chest.

At the force of the bullet, Che's small frame wavered on the spot like a reed. He clutched his hand over the bloody hole in his chest and steadied himself. "No sir," he repeated softly, smiling defiantly. "I am not a liar. I am Balam Che." He slumped to his knees. "I am a shaman and a leader."

"Is that so?" Templeton jeered, giving Carlos a nod.

Che looked up to see the young Maya withdraw a machete from his sash. So, Che thought, now he knew why the Old One had come to him today. Now he knew what his fate was to be.

Carlos grabbed Che by the hair, bending his neck back, exposing the veins throbbing there, and looked into his victim's eyes. *I am another one of yourself,* the eyes said.

Still, even with the eyes of the old man staring back at him, it was simple enough. Just as Carlos had done with the pigs that ran about on his farm, he sliced the shaman's throat from ear to ear. Che gasped in shock as blood spewed from the gaping wound on his neck. A gurgle of blood foamed on his lips and he struggled to lift his head to look at Carlos. Indeed, all things were one. He could not hate this man, nor could he fight destiny. And just as his ancestors had done before him, he would give the ultimate gift: He would give his life to protect Marty English.

Che hoped that would be enough. Hoped he had followed his destiny with some measure of wisdom and courage. His dying wish was that Marty English would be able to do the same.

Chapter 47

Marty's eyes flew open with a start, smacking his consciousness into the night. Heart racing, he tried to remember the dream.

He'd been in the secret closet, looking through the one-way mirror. But it wasn't his father's library he saw there; instead it was his own office at Bergman. Agent Kemper was standing before Marty's desk, adjusting his necktie. "Suicide," Kemper said, smiling into the mirror.

"Lies," Marty shouted, watching as the agent tugged at the Howdy Doody smile, peeling it off like a rubber mask. And then he saw it wasn't Kemper at all, but Mike D'Angelo lifting a glass in toast. *"Salud,"* D'Angelo said.

"Salud," Marty replied, and the office was gone, replaced by the Belizean rainforest, where Del Waters stood in a clearing, holding a chain saw. He gave Marty a sly wink and started it up, and the shiny-toothed saw flashed before Marty's eyes like the gaping, hideous mouth of a jack-o'-lantern. The mouth shrieked mechanically, words hissing out like hornets around a nest. "Who would think it? Who would believe it? Even in black and white."

"Or in color." A shadowy woman laughed as she handed Marty a videotape. It burned his hand at its touch and he struggled to hold on to it. "Looks like a fumble at the ten yard line," an announcer's voice declared. "Can our hero hold on?"

There were cheers and then suddenly everything went still and Che was standing in front of the mirror.

The Indian fixed Marty in his steady gaze. "Good triumphs over evil in the sacred ball game," he said simply. "For the hero, death is the final play."

The final play. The final play. The final play. The words sprang forward in Marty's mind and then rewound, playing over again and again until he couldn't stand it anymore and he clasped his hands over his ears. *The final play.*

He sat up in the dark, trying to get his bearings, shivering in his sweat-drenched clothes as the haunting dream played in his head. And then, at last, he looked down at the briefcase, lying on the floor, and smiled. Now he knew what he had to do.

At the sound of a key turning in the latch, Marty went on alert, watching as the door swung open and Suzy Q tiptoed in.

"It's okay, I'm awake," he said softly. He hadn't been able to sleep since the dream.

She flipped on the light and smiled. "So the sleeping prince finally decided to join the living? Hell, I was starting to wonder if you'd ever wake up."

An alarmed expression crossed his face as he suddenly thought of Reiki. Had she made it to the airport, landed safe and sound in Bermuda? There was no way to know, he thought ruefully. "How long have I been out, Suzy?" he asked.

She shrugged. "Forty-eight hours, maybe."

"Shit. Are you serious? What day is it?"

"Tuesday." She laughed. "You were pretty tired, huh?"

Marty nodded. He'd been exhausted, all right. Hell, he hadn't had a good night's sleep for days. Evidently, the stress had finally caught up with him.

"I don't think you moved an inch the whole time," she remarked as she hung a furry coat of questionable heritage in the closet.

"Where you been?" he asked.

She looked at him in disbelief. "Working. What else does a working girl do?"

"Oh, I thought since I was here . . ."

"What? That the rent would stop? Just 'cause I'm not turning tricks up here in the apartment doesn't mean I closed up shop. Hell, men don't care where they do it . . . the car, the sidewalk—most of 'em are like dogs." She laughed and then, thinking he might be offended, added, "But not all men, of course."

"Of course," he said with a quick nod.

She frowned and sat down on the beanbag. "All right," she began, the maternal tone he'd heard earlier returning. "I don't usually butt in, but hell, you're a friend, so I gotta ask. You in trouble, Marty? You need to get out of town?" She searched his face. "You just tell me how I can help." She winked. "Or as I would normally say, 'Tell me what you want.'"

He looked into her eyes. "I need a favor, Suzy," he said simply, without apology.

"You name it, sugar . . . you got it."

Chapter 48

At 9 A.M. sharp on Wednesday morning, Frank Torello and Carson Page arrived at the offices of Wynn Bergman Advertising. They had an appointment with Marty English, Carson explained to the attractive receptionist, watching with pleasure as the color fell from the poor woman's face and she picked up the phone, spoke a few hushed words, and then hung up.

"It'll be just a moment," the receptionist offered apologetically.

Carson and Torello nodded and smiled and stood there, calm and collected, as if they were totally unaware the agency was swimming in chaos thanks to their VP of domestic operation's recent disappearance.

Within moments, an agency escort appeared to usher them to the conference room on the eighteenth floor. Before leaving the two executives, the escort showed them to comfortable swivel chairs, poured two cups of coffee and offered a platter of danish, which they politely refused.

"Is something wrong, Mr. Bergman, Ms. Wilde?" Carson asked bluntly as the agency president and media director entered the conference room.

Nodding, Wynn Bergman said, without hesitation, "I'm afraid there is." He waved his hand to minimize the importance of his next words: "But only a slight problem. Unfortunately, Marty's been called out of the office on some unexpected personal business."

"We're expecting him shortly," Lee said quickly.

Frank Torello and Carson Page looked disappointed but, to Lee and Wynn's relief, seemed satisfied with the explanation.

"Can we still see our ad?" Torello asked hopefully, pushing his tinted aviators up the bridge of his nose.

"Of course you can!" Lee exclaimed, flashing that disarming smile she saved for the difficult ones.

"We'll need your approval in order to run it," Bergman added.

It took less than ten minutes to review the ad and rave about how great it was. Frank Torello gave his approval for its airing in the Super Bowl and, thinking they'd pulled it off, Wynn and Lee smiled and smiled. But ten minutes later they were still sitting around the conference table; Frank Torello had announced that he wanted to wait for Marty's return.

"We really should thank him personally," Carson agreed.

Wynn and Lee glanced at one another. It was dog-and-pony time. Twenty more minutes passed, twenty minutes of chitchat and bullshit. Twenty agonizing minutes that Carson Page and Frank Torello enjoyed immensely.

"Where on earth is Marty?" Torello exclaimed at last, an irritable note in the words. "Doesn't anybody in this place know for sure when he'll be back?"

"We could have Marty contact you as soon as he returns," Lee offered.

"And when do you think that will be?"

Lee and Wynn looked back at them blankly. They didn't have the slightest idea, but of course they wouldn't say that. They'd say something witty or clever. The only problem was they couldn't think of anything.

Frank Torello proceeded to go into one of his infamous fits while Carson looked on, suppressing her amusement.

"After paying millions of dollars, I think I deserve the courtesy of seeing my account manager," Torello declared.

Wynn nodded sympathetically and lit what was probably his hundredth cigarette that morning. "Of course you do, Frank," he agreed. "But it looks like that's just not going to be possible right now."

It took another twenty minutes of high-level convincing and ass-kissing before the Arrow executives, pretending to be pacified if not satisfied, finally left the agency.

Back in his office, Wynn Bergman vowed to kick Marty English's ass all the way to China.

"You'll have to take a number," Lee retorted. "It looks like it's gonna be a hell of a long line."

That afternoon, Suzy Q borrowed Harry Chong's car, a brand-new black Lincoln the Chinese laundry owner wrote off on his taxes thanks to a magnetic sign he plastered on its door that read: FRESH BREEZE CLEANERS. WE PUT THE "CLEAN" IN DRY CLEAN.

Chong was nervous about loaning his pride and joy to someone his insurance carrier wouldn't exactly rate as a good risk, but Suzy swore to God she'd take good care of it: When she was done, she'd run it through a car wash, fill up the tank, too. That seemed to satisfy Chong and so, without further fanfare, Suzanne Cameron, aka Suzy Q, headed for Michigan Avenue.

A good whore is a good actress, Suzy had insisted when Marty first told her about his plan. He needn't worry; she'd pull it off. The residents of the Astor might have plenty of attitude, but she could lay on that snobby bullshit just as thick as they could. Indeed, Suzy could have won an Oscar for her performance. She had it knocked: the hair pulled back into a smart French twist, the pink tweed Chanel suit trimmed in black and gold. The black patent pumps with toes capped in pink, and a quilted handbag. The gold—and then more gold—

accessories to match. Luckily, Marty still had a few travelers's checks left over from his trip to Belize; designer clothes cost an arm and a leg. But Suzy had cushioned the blow to his wallet by reminding him that it was expensive to look rich.

The doorman at the Astor, Jack Flannigan, never for a moment doubted that the attractive woman who strolled up to the Astor was, indeed, well off. And her assertion that she was a private style consultant for Ms. Devane seemed reasonable, too. She was returning several items, Suzanne Cameron explained politely, nodding to the black leather garment bag over her shoulder, and had been instructed by Ms. Devane to pick up a few more. Of course, she had Ms. Devane's key, she told Flannigan, but would he be so kind as to give a lady a helping hand?

Jack Flannigan knew the condo's rules, but spending a few more minutes with the pretty woman sounded rather inviting. And so he gave her a gentlemanly nod, slung the heavy garment bag over his shoulder, and ushered her up to English's place. He looked on as she opened the door, thinking how he would've liked to have hung around, gotten to know her better, but he had already broken the rules by leaving the lobby door unattended.

Suzy did exactly as Marty had instructed. He'd warned her that they—though he hadn't said who *they* were—probably had the place wired and were listening. She had to move about as quietly as possible. Even if they didn't hear her at first, they would soon enough, he'd said; she could count on ten, maybe fifteen, minutes. Suzy had to get in and get out. But she was an expert at that. Ten minutes for a hand job. Five minutes for oral sex. Three, at the most, for intercourse. No problem, she'd told him.

Not pausing now, she walked into the bedroom and opened the walk-in closet. When she found the tuxedo and charcoal gray pinstriped suit Marty had requested, she took them out and hung them neatly in the black leather bag. Then she gathered some shirts, shoes, a belt, and a tie. They'd had a lot of discussion about the tie. Marty also needed another briefcase. There was one on the top shelf, he told her. She got it down and threw in some underwear and socks she'd found in the bureau drawers. Then she put it all inside the leather bag and hurried out the door.

As Jack Flannigan held open the door for Suzanne Cameron, he tipped his cap. She was a real looker, he later told the boys down at the lodge as they played their Wednesday night game of pinochle. Yes siree, a real looker. He should've asked her out for a cup of coffee—*something*, he lamented. Hell, she'd liked him; and a man could always tell a thing like that. But then, after all, he knew his women, Flannigan said. And no question, this one was a peach.

Chapter 49

Roger Kemper and Max Harper had been staking out Ford Sinclair's house for days: the detective hadn't left home since Monday. By the time Thursday morning came around, the agents were eager for a change of scenery.

It was just after 6 A.M. when the bleary-eyed agents walked into Hello Holley's. All the regular breakfast crowd was there—the shift workers and off-duty cops—clustered around the red Formica-topped tables and booths. As usual, Holley Habacker was stationed behind the counter, a grease-spattered towel slung over his shoulder. When he saw them come in, Habacker tipped his head slightly in the direction of a tramp seated at a booth. "Sloppy Joe's hungry," he said, giving them a knowing wink.

"That's what we heard," Kemper replied, glancing in the tramp's direction. He grimaced in disgust.

Joe Jergens, or "Sloppy Joe" to the locals on the westside, was just fifty-five, but he looked every year of eighty. The loose skin that hung like translucent paper from the tramp's skeletal frame glowed gold, the color a man's skin turned when his liver had been pushed to the brink by rotgut booze and poor nutrition.

At the agents' approach, Sloppy Joe broke into a nervous, cockeyed grin. "Hey boys, how ya been?" he said, sounding jittery.

"Good," Harper replied with an easy smile as he sat down next to the tramp. He wrinkled his nose distastefully and looked at his partner; Sloppy Joe stank to high heaven, like a combination of vomit and sweat and smoke and booze. Harper lost what appetite he'd had right then and there—amazing, given the fact he and Kemper hadn't had a decent meal since Sunday night.

Kemper smiled with amusement and slid into the seat directly across from the tramp. "How about you, Joe? How's it going? Bad winter, huh?"

"Cold." The tramp nodded, lapping at his coffee. He paused, shivering beneath his thin, frayed coat, and looked at the agent.

"You hungry?" Kemper asked, almost gently.

Yellow eyes gleaming with anticipation, Sloppy Joe licked the spittle from his lips and nodded.

"Hey, Holley!" Harper called out. "Can you get this guy some breakfast over here?" Harper looked back at the tramp. "How about some steak and eggs?"

Sloppy Joe smiled. "With hash browns?" he asked weakly.

"Sure," Harper said.

Kemper nodded. "No problem."

Holley ambled over. "What'll it be?"

"Steak and fried eggs and hash browns," Kemper replied. He grinned at the tramp. "Right, Joe?"

"Right," the man agreed, liver-spotted hands trembling around his cup.

"And some coffee for us," Harper added.

"Coming right up," Holley called out over his shoulder as he headed back to the counter.

The agents' attention returned to the man in their booth. Kemper went first, his voice lowered an octave. "So what's the story, Joe? Holley said you have some news . . ."

"About a guy we're trying to locate," Harper finished.

Sloppy Joe hesitated. He'd seen Marty English around the blues joints for—what? Twenty years now, maybe more. English could always spare a bum a dime. Or a ten-spot, for that matter. He'd liked the kid. But Holley Habacker had said that English wasn't such a nice guy after all. He was in trouble with the law, that's what Holley'd said. Wouldn't he be doing his public duty now, the tramp reasoned, telling the agents what he knew? Besides, this was the westside, not fucking Barrington or Oak Park. You had to take care of yourself here. So screw Marty English.

"Here you go, Joe," Holley declared, sliding a heaping plate over to the tramp. "I threw in some whole-wheat toast and grape jelly," he added, giving him a wink. "Got to put some meat on those old bones, you know."

The tramp sniffed at the food like a starving old hound and threw Holley Habacker a smile snaggled by rotting and missing teeth. He watched the diner's owner walk away and then picked up a fork and poked it into the hash browns. "They're awful greasy," he muttered, looking up at Kemper with a frown. "Grease plugs up your ar'treys, you know."

Roger Kemper glowered. He'd slept four hours in the last seventy-two. He was running out of steam—and patience. "You want to talk or not, Joe?" he growled, glaring across the table at the tramp.

"Sure. Sure I wanta talk to you boys," the man replied uneasily, gumming at his steak with what few teeth he had. A sudden calculating glint shown in his dim eyes. "But I got a feeling this is kinda important, you know, a kinda touchy situation."

Kemper frowned. "What's that supposed to mean?"

"Nothing, really," the tramp replied, shrugging his bony shoulders. "I've just been thinking that five hundred dollars and a Greyhound out of town would be mighty nice right now. My daughter, Lucy, lives out in Phoenix."

Kemper nodded and, though his blood pressure was soaring with impatience and frustration, said coolly, "Those things could be arranged."

But Sloppy Joe was in no hurry; ignoring his patrons, he

turned his attention to his plate, shoveling the food into his mouth. Finally, he smacked his lips together and pushed the plate away. It was slick, cleaned to a shine. "That's what I like about you boys," he said, "you know how to treat a fella."

Kemper noticed that Sloppy Joe was steadier now. Sometimes food worked better than booze to loosen an old bum's tongue.

"Word on the street has it," the tramp muttered over his cup, "that English is shacked up with some whore here in the neighborhood."

"That's it?" Harper exclaimed in a mixture of outrage and disbelief. "That's your big fucking news?"

The tramp nodded eagerly. "So when can I get that ticket—"

"Do you have any idea how many whores live on the westside?" Kemper demanded, cutting him off.

Sloppy Joe shrugged timidly. "Plenty, I guess."

"Yeah, that's right," Kemper exclaimed. "Plenty. Don't you have any idea what the whore's name is, what street she lives on?"

Nervous now, the bum fumbled in the pocket of his grimy shirt for a cigarette butt. His liquored-up brain had long ago lost its quickness. "I don't know," he said, striking a match on his brown thumbnail. "I see her hooking down around Halsted. That's where she hangs out mostly. Doesn't have a pimp, she's a loner. Looks good, too, like a brunette Farrah Fawcett." He inhaled deeply on the cigarette stub and wheezed, hacking out a phlegm-filled cough. "Nice ass, too," he sputtered.

Harper's face flushed red and Kemper threw him a warning look.

"Think, Joe," Kemper insisted, "come on now. *Think*. What's her name?"

Sloppy Joe shook his head and sucked harder on the cigarette. "Hell, I should know it. . . . I see her all the time, showing off her stuff."

The two agents studied the tramp coldly.

"Think," Kemper demanded.

The tramp's waxy face suddenly lit up. "I got it!" he exclaimed, snapping his tobacco-stained fingers with a bony crack. "They call her Suzy. Yeah, that's it. They call her Suzy Q."

Their strategy was straightforward and simple: On Thursday morning, Carson Page and Frank Torello would, as Del Waters had suggested over breakfast at the Ritz earlier, walk softly into Wynn Bergman Advertising, carrying a very big stick. They'd put the pressure on the agency president—who surely had some clue as to English's whereabouts—using their three-hundred-million-dollar advertising budget for leverage.

As planned, at ten o'clock sharp, Carson Page and Frank Torello stormed into Wynn Bergman's office, demanding to see Marty English. When the agency president couldn't produce the account manager, Frank Torello threatened to pull the Arrow account.

Like his idol, Dale Carnegie, Wynn Bergman had always preferred to win friends and influence people. The concept had stood Bergman well, made him a very rich man. Even so, he wasn't a pushover; he didn't like intimidation and he liked threats even less. Isaac Arrow was locked into the Super Bowl, Bergman icily informed Ms. Page and Mr. Torello. But after that, if they wanted to pull their account from the agency, so be it.

Chapter 50

As the yellow cab nosed through the slush-covered Eisenhower Expressway toward the corporate offices of Hexall International, Marty studied Lee Wilde's research report for the fourth time in as many days. He smiled to himself; as usual, he had it down cold. He closed the spiral-bound document, put it back in his briefcase, and flexed his aching hand.

His hand looked fine now, almost like new. He would be able to shake hands with conviction. Thank God for that, he thought as the cab turned in to Hexall's headquarters. And thank God for Suzy, too. She was a hell of a nurse. And, he had to admit, grinning down at his gray pinstriped suit, she sure knew how to pick out a tie.

Appliance and electronics giant Hexall International was spread out over thirty choice acres of Oakbrook real estate. The neatly landscaped property was spare and modern in design. A dozen identical, low-rise steel structures with enormous black windows encircled the company's campus. Marty thought they looked like giant kitchen stoves. Appropriate, he supposed, for a company that had made its fortune largely off of women tied to one.

His briefcase in hand, Marty strode purposefully through Hexall's steel doors and into an immense lobby bustling with activity. He stood at the back of a crowded elevator, going over his strategy one last time. On the fifth floor, the doors opened and he stepped out.

When he saw the sign MARKETING AND ADVERTISING, Marty's pulse quickened with anticipation. It was like being back in high school when he had a hot date. Heart racing, he walked through a set of double doors and up to a reception area.

"Good morning," welcomed the young woman behind the chrome counter. "Marty English, right?" she ventured, flashing a warm smile.

"That's right," he said, smiling back as he assessed the situation. Receptionists and secretaries always—always—mirrored their boss's attitude. He interpreted the woman's friendliness as a sign of things to come. Two points for the good guys, he thought with pleasure, thinking of Jules Benson.

"Mr. Bryant is expecting you, Mr. English," she said, guiding him down the hallway and into the marketing director's office, a space as sleek and minimalist as the building's exterior. It was chrome and black with a pleasant expanse of windows overlooking a courtyard centered around a steel sculpture. All very tasteful. Very Euro austere. *Budget conscious.* Marty filed that in his memory bank as he turned to meet Hexall's marketing director.

John Bryant, a conservatively dressed man of fifty plus, strode around his desk and gave Marty a warm, almost eager, handshake. He's ready to play ball, Marty silently observed.

"So I finally meet the man who claims he can make me a star," Bryant declared with a grin.

Marty laughed an easy laugh. "Did I say that, Mr. Bryant?" he teased.

"Call me John, please." Bryant grinned again. "Well, whatever you said, you got my attention. Let's have a seat," he suggested, motioning toward a grouping of leather chairs.

Marty smiled to himself. So there wasn't going to be any of

that "sit behind the desk and play big shot while the ad man grovels," he mused. He figured that was two more points for his side.

"I got a look at that report you had messengered over," Bryant began, "and I have to tell you, I'm impressed."

"I'm glad to hear that. As you know, Wynn Bergman has an impressive track record. But we also have an eye for our client's bottom line. We get the job done"—he chose his next words carefully, throwing out the bait—"with *no frills* and *no fat.*" Bryant leaned forward ever so slightly, clearly intrigued. Like every good fish Marty had ever known, Hexall's marketing director couldn't resist checking out the bait. "And you feel confident you can pull this off?" Bryant asked, eyes shining now. "You really can increase our market share by five percent while lowering our overall costs? Trim our production dollars back and throw the ones we save over into media? And *still* reach our audience effectively?"

Marty nodded confidently. "Absolutely. If Hexall joins the Wynn Bergman family, I guarantee you'll get more 'bang for your buck.'" He threw out the old cliché, knowing it would play well.

Bryant nodded and then, as if some other thought had surfaced, averted his eyes.

Marty's guard went up immediately.

"There is another matter we need to address," Bryant said uncomfortably. "And that's the issue of Jules Benson."

Marty tried to conceal his surprise.

"You may, or may not, be aware of the fact that our current agency, Todd, Gattwick, and Lorenz, has Mr. Benson's production company under contract. Jules Benson has been producing our television ads for some time now."

"I seem to recall hearing that rumor." Marty smiled.

"Well, we've also heard a rumor here at Hexall," Bryant remarked, his face suddenly impassive, maddeningly unreadable. "Is it true you fired Benson and took him off the Isaac

Arrow account right in the middle of production down in Belize?"

Marty nodded calmly, maintaining his confident manner. He'd play it hardball. "That's right, John." He smiled. "But we weren't just in the middle of production, we were on deadline for a spot in this Sunday's Super Bowl."

Bryant looked impressed. "That must have taken some nerve," he remarked with a note of admiration, "firing Benson like that, and at the eleventh hour on top of it."

Marty looked back at Hexall's marketing director. He'd thrown out the bait, gotten the guy interested. How could he set that hook now and still get around this Benson shit? Bingo: "Actually," he began modestly, "it didn't have anything to do with nerve. It had to do with good business. Our client, Isaac Arrow Pharmaceuticals, couldn't afford incompetency. And, I'm sorry to say, Jules Benson is incompetent and unreliable." He looked Bryant right in the eye as he said it. The hook was set.

Bryant studied Marty for a moment and then nodded. "I'm glad to hear you say that. You're aware Hexall is buying NHP, of course. When the dust settles, we're going to need an agency that will look out for our best interests, not one that indulges some prima donna who thinks he's Cecil B. DeMille.

"Our current agency just doesn't seem to have the business sense to fire Jules Benson. And with over a billion and a half dollars in advertising at stake now, that's what we need . . ." Bryant's voice dropped passionately, "people with guts *and* brains."

Marty smiled. It was time to reel this one in. "Then I'd say Wynn Bergman Advertising is the agency for you."

"So would I," Bryant replied warmly. "Let's just see if my board of directors agrees."

Chapter 51

That Thursday had been the most eventful in recent memory, at least to Jack Flannigan. In all his years as a doorman, Flannigan had seen plenty of strange things. He'd held the door for everybody from medics to media, but he'd never seen so many law enforcement guys come in and out of one place in a single day. It got so incredible that Flannigan even went so far as to call his brother-in-law and ask him to check out his police radio scanner to see what the hell was going on. But according to him, there wasn't anybody squawking on the scanner about anything that Thursday. Jack Flannigan found that hard to believe.

First thing that morning, two DEA guys had come by the Astor, flashing badges and asking questions. Then there were some Customs guys asking more questions, most of them about Marty English. That afternoon the local cops dropped by, said they needed to look around, had some reports of a break-in in the neighborhood.

By the end of the day, when two FBI agents cornered Flannigan in the Astor's lobby, the condo employee had little left to tell anyone. He'd been pumped all day.

Flannigan told the agents that only one stranger had passed through the Astor's doors on Wednesday—a woman. But she was just some personal stylist, a pretty lady who wouldn't hurt a fly.

"What did she look like?" the agents asked.

Flannigan thought for a minute and then, with perfect seriousness, replied, "Like Princess Grace. Nice clothes, one of those Chanel numbers. Real class."

"Did you get a look at what she was driving?"

"A black Town Car, real sharp. Like I said, she was all class."

"Did she say who she worked for?"

"No," Flannigan answered, "but the car had a company name on the side door." He wrinkled his ruddy forehead thoughtfully. " 'Fresh Breeze Cleaners. We put the *clean* in dry clean,' that's what it said."

"Did you happen to get her name?"

"Suzanne Cameron," Flannigan said quickly.

"You have a good memory, Mr. Flannigan," one of the agents complimented.

"You have to in security," Flannigan said, pleased as punch with himself. "But I guess you guys already know that, huh?"

From the Curandero import warehouse on Goose Island, Mike D'Angelo commanded his troops. He had two dozen goons posted around the westside, checking out neighborhood dives, asking questions, turning the whole area inside out in their search for the whore called Suzy Q.

Late Thursday, one of D'Angelo's men finally caught a break, coming across a corner druggist who claimed that a woman matching their description had come by on Tuesday and bought some antiseptic and bandages.

According to the owners, she came in the store pretty regularly—buying rubbers and K-Y jelly, a pack or two of Juicy Fruit. She usually wore hot pants and tube tops and platform shoes. And what was her name? D'Angelo's men asked. "Suzy Q," the druggist replied. "You know, like the song."

As nightfall settled over Chicago's westside, a Ford van loaded down with surveillance equipment parked around the corner from Harry Chong's Fresh Breeze Cleaners. Del Waters's men had located the black Town Car earlier in the day, parked in the alley, minus its magnetic sign. There was no woman fitting the description given by Flannigan.

At 2 a.m. Friday morning, Holley Habacker got a tip from a low-life clown by the name of Hector, a cross-dressing pimp who was resentful of the stiff competition from local whores. Hector told the diner's proprietor that Suzy Q was usually on the street later than most working girls; she didn't hit the pavement 'til sometime after 1 a.m. She turned what tricks she needed to get by and was off the sidewalk by three, three-thirty, at the latest.

To show his appreciation, Holley Habacker turned Hector on to one of the diner's patrons who was looking for a quick blow job. Then he picked up the phone and called Kemper and Harper. The agents were on the Sinclair stakeout, bored as hell. Habacker figured this tip would liven things up; they were going to owe him a big one when this was over.

As they sped down Madison toward Halsted, the agents put in a cell phone call to Del Waters. The whore would talk, they'd make sure of that, Kemper assured Waters. It was almost 3 A.M. They were closing in.

Chapter 52

Suzy Q struck her usual pose, hiking her red leather miniskirt up to her crotch, thrusting one fishnetted leg forward, tilting her pelvis provocatively. Men liked that bad-girl shit. Several cars glided by and she waved and called out. But they kept on going, not even bothering to slow down, and suddenly she felt old and tired. She might as well admit it, guys didn't stop like they used to; no, lately they passed her up in favor of one of the younger girls.

Suzy looked at the watch inside her locket; it was just three. If everything went like Marty had planned, Ford Sinclair would be cruising by at any minute. It was all arranged; she had some time. Nervous, she took out a Marlboro and started to light up, but then, at a sudden gust of frigid air blasting through the street, she clutched her white rabbit fur chubby coat over her bare cleavage and started dreaming about that sunny beach in Florida.

When she got her place in Daytona, she'd sit on the beach every day, reading romance novels and eating as many Little Debbies and Ding Dongs as she wanted. And she'd have a tan, too—she always tanned real nice.

A dark van with tinted windows was suddenly alongside her; it pulled up to the curb. She struck a pose as the window rolled down. "What you looking for?" she asked through her Juicy Fruit.

"A good ad."

She smiled and leaned in the window. "Detective Sinclair?"

Something had gone wrong, terribly wrong. Marty felt sure of it, and, pale as milk, he lifted the edge of the musty curtains and looked out onto the street below, hoping to see the big-haired brunette strutting up the sidewalk. But there was nothing but a streetlight flickering in and out of life, just like all the other times he'd looked out since Suzy had left to meet Sinclair.

He should never have let her go. It was too dangerous, he knew that. Hell, he'd told her that, too, said he'd just have to find some other way to arrange to meet Sinclair. But she wouldn't listen.

The way Marty figured it, if they nabbed Suzy, they'd make her talk. Once they knew where he was, they wouldn't waste any time. Marty's eyes darted around the small apartment. If they came for him here, he'd be trapped. His heart started hammering again. He wouldn't stand a chance.

Marty lifted the curtain. A gray cast was in the sky now. It would be light soon. He'd never make it then. He let the curtain drop. He had to get out of here.

Nobody paid much attention to the ragged bum stumbling down the staircase of the rundown tenement. Like all bums, he was invisible. No heads turned when the bum with the rusty shopping cart piled high with rags and aluminum cans and fluttering newspapers made his way through the neighborhood, pushing the rickety cart ahead of him, slowly, purposefully, its rubber wheels wobble-weaving over the icy sidewalks.

Nor did anyone notice when, as dawn rose over the Chicago skyline that Friday morning, the bum thrust his cart through the double doors of the Holy Bible Mission and asked for a place to stay. The bum, like all the rest, was simply invisible.

Chapter 53

Originally, the massive athletic stadium called Soldier Field had been built to honor those killed in World War I. Its neoclassical architecture of Doric columns, twin colonnades, and pedimented pavilions was intended to mirror the ancient Roman playing fields where gladiators fought to the death in front of cheering crowds. Now, some seventy years later, Soldier Field was the home of the Bears football team. But spiked balls, cannonballs, or footballs, it was all the same: Somebody had to lose.

Marty had told Suzy Q to have Sinclair meet him in the stands by the stairwell on the east side of Soldier Field at two on Saturday morning. He couldn't have been more specific than that, Marty thought now in mounting frustration. But where was Sinclair? The detective couldn't have run into trouble getting into the deserted stadium; budget cutbacks had made Park Security pretty thin these past few years. The only obstacle a guy faced here was a chain-link fence. Shivering, Marty held his watch up in the moonlight. It was after two-thirty.

Marty's throat went tight as he considered the very real possibility that Ford Sinclair wouldn't show. Despite Suzy's disappearance and the obvious fact that something had gone wrong last night, Marty refused to give in to the nagging fear that she and Sinclair might actually be floating facedown in the Chicago River.

If Sinclair didn't show, who else could he turn to? Marty laughed bitterly under his breath. That wasn't any mystery. He'd be out on a very short limb all by himself. But what the fuck, he'd been there before. Right? He sighed and muttered, "Yeah, right, goddammit."

"You talking to yourself now?" a voice said from behind him.

Marty spun around. He could just make out Ford Sinclair standing in the moonlit bleachers. "You know, you have a nasty habit of sneaking up on people, Sinclair." Marty gave him a weary grin and silently cheered: He's alive.

"It's the getting away part I worry about." Sinclair chuckled, but his eyes were deadly serious as he sat down.

"I was beginning to think you'd lost your touch in that department."

"You and me both." Sinclair nodded, his eyes running over Marty's threadbare attire. "You out slumming, huh?" he asked drolly.

"It's the latest in the Emperor's new clothes," Marty replied with a grin, "wear these and you're instantly invisible." He paused, his smile fading. "What happened last night? Suzy never came back."

"Things kind of went to hell in a handbasket last night," Sinclair began. "I picked Suzy up right on Green Street. She filled me in on how you were doing, said you got fucking shot the other night after I left. . . ." He frowned, glancing down at Marty's hand. "She told me you wanted to meet here tonight. Hell, we got it all squared up in five minutes flat, but I'll be damned if we weren't a block down the street when I stopped at a light and those buddies of yours, Harper and Kemper, pulled up beside us. I'm pretty sure they've been shadowing me all week." He glanced nervously over his shoulder. "Anyway, it was a damned good thing I borrowed my neighbor's van last night. It has those goddamned tinted windows. I hate those sons of bitches, but that's what saved our ass. They couldn't see us."

Sinclair shook his head in relief. "Well, I kept right on driving, went around the neighborhood a few times. Pretty soon it came to me the entire westside was crawling with secret agents and thugs. I figured they were looking for you . . . maybe Suzy, too. Hell, I couldn't just throw her back out on the street. Who knows what they'd have done to her? I'd say somebody in the neighborhood squealed."

"So where's Suzy now? She's okay, isn't she?"

"Don't you think I can protect a citizen? Sure she is. I put some money in her pocket and got her on a bus to Kentucky. She's staying in a Marriott right over the Ohio River, off I-Twenty-four. I told her to sit tight 'til she heard from one of us. I don't think she'll get any bright ideas and come back. She was pretty shook up by the time I got her on that bus, poor kid."

"Good plan," Marty remarked absently.

Sinclair's brow furrowed. "So you got something more to tell me?"

"Yeah, I do. After you left the other night, I took a look around the house. You know, for old times' sake. I ended up in the library . . ."

"Where we found your father?"

"Yeah. I never told you, but there's a hidden closet in there . . . behind the bar, where the mirrors are, but they're really one-way mirrors. I used to hide in that closet all the time when I was a kid."

"I take it you decided to check it out?"

Marty nodded, his words coming out in a rush: "My father had a hidden camera in there. He was videotaping all of his meetings. There were hundreds of goddamned tapes . . . hundreds."

Sinclair let out a low whistle.

"I only had time to look at one of them before Harper and Kemper showed up with Mike D'Angelo."

"They were *together?*" Sinclair exclaimed. "Your father's right-hand man and the CIA? It was just like we thought."

Marty nodded. "Before they showed up, I watched the *last* tape, Sinclair, the last one my father recorded before he died."

Sinclair swallowed hard. "I'm listening."

"Mike D'Angelo murdered my father. . . . He was poisoned, just like you said. It's all there, on tape."

"What about the other guys? Where do they come into the picture? Were they on the tape too?"

"The people from Arrow were—Frank Torello, the president and Carson Page, the marketing director. And Del Waters. He's the guy who runs Escoba and Planetlife."

"The chairman of Arrow's board you mentioned before?"

"Yeah, and just like we thought, he's CIA too. I'd bet he's the one Harper and Kemper report to."

Sinclair shook his head. "So you were right. Arrow really is in bed with the Mob and the CIA. Jesus H. Christ. What the hell are the bastards up to?"

"I think I know now. In their meeting they talked about how my father had been assisting the CIA in a dope smuggling operation for the past fifteen years. Everything must have been going along fine until Waters came up with a new scheme. That was what the meeting was about . . . Waters's little plan to use a rainforest tree . . ."

"The escoba?"

"That's right. With it, they plan on producing a new street drug designed at Arrow's labs . . ."

"A drug ten times more powerful than cocaine," Sinclair finished as his meeting with the forensic chemist two weeks before came to mind.

"Waters's plan was to cut out the Colombian cartel. My father wasn't a fool; he didn't want any part of that. But D'Angelo did, and my guess is that's why he murdered my father. From what I can tell, Arrow, Waters, and my father shared a joint bank account and divvied up the profits every so often. When my father died, the other partners were left out in the cold. Evidently they need his disc to access the account."

"That's right. Without it, they're screwed." At Marty's puzzled expression, Sinclair pulled out his notepad and grinned. "Thanks to a little help from the FBI, the American Banking Association, and Interpol, I figured out what that series of numbers is all about. Turns out it's a bank routing number that links up to a Geneva account. To access it, you need three different security codes. Each one is unique, like a fingerprint."

Like a fingerprint. The words echoed in Marty's ears. Zak had said the very same thing when they first looked at the glyph. He'd said the numbers were an identification code, that you needed them in order to reproduce the image exactly. Marty nodded eagerly at Sinclair. "One code for each partner. Right?"

"Right. There's a pretty unusual security feature, too: All three security codes have to be entered from separate locations within an hour of each other."

"Which explains why they need my father's disc."

"That's my guess." Sinclair shook his head. "Jesus, there must be a ton of money in that account."

"Enough to kill for."

"More than once."

They fell silent.

"We've got to get that tape to the Justice Department," Sinclair suddenly declared. "And we need to get you some fucking protection, too." He paused, fists clenched. "We have to bring 'em down, Marty."

"No, revenge is a solitary sport, Sinclair. You've done enough."

"Don't tempt me," Sinclair said, smiling wryly, "or I might just get the hell out of here right now . . . pretend we never met." He paused, the smile dropping from his face. "But I can't do that. Remember what I said about your father that night we met? I said your old man had his own kind of honor, that I admired that."

"Yeah." Marty nodded slowly, his thoughts spinning back.

"Well, maybe I'd like to think that I have *my* own kind of honor."

Marty looked into Sinclair's eyes and said softly, "I think you're probably the most honorable man I've ever met, Sinclair."

Suddenly moved, Sinclair looked away, turning his solemn face toward the dark sky. "It's really something, isn't it?" he said at last. "You and me sitting here like this. A black man and a white man. Talking just like they were friends."

"We *are* friends." Marty realized that he no longer thought of Sinclair as a cop. Right now, he trusted Sinclair more than anyone.

"Move and you're dead," a voice growled.

They jerked around to see Harper and Kemper standing on each side of them, their Berettas drawn and ready to fire.

"Okay, hands in the air . . . hands in the air," Kemper demanded, motioning upward with the gun. "Get 'em up."

Sinclair shrugged. "Hey, buddy, what's the prob—"

"*I said*; raise your fucking hands," Kemper repeated with a hiss. "Now. Before I decide to blow your brains out."

"All right, all right," Sinclair grumbled as they both raised their hands. "Keep your pants on."

"Okay," Kemper said. "Now stand up real slow. . . ." They started to stand. "I said *slow*—and keep those hands up where we can see them."

Harper held the gun on them while Kemper ran his hands over Marty's body.

Wordlessly, Sinclair's eyes burned into Marty's.

No, Sinclair, Marty's eyes replied. *Don't try the hero bit. No.*

Kemper's hands stopped and he reached inside Marty's pocket, pulling out a B. B. King CD. "I'll be a son of a bitch," he exclaimed. "Lookee here, Max." He turned and held it up.

Harper's eyes flitted toward his partner. "Why, what do you know," he said. "It's the fucking disc."

Sinclair saw his chance and, with one swift motion, pulled his .38 from under his coat. "Run, Marty!" he yelled, firing two shots at Max Harper.

For an instant, Marty stood stock still, his world reduced to slow motion, and then, seeing Kemper raise his gun toward Sinclair, he lunged at the man, knocking him to the ground.

"Let's get the hell outta here!" Sinclair shouted.

Marty looked over his shoulder and Sinclair yelled, "I'm right behind you, buddy."

Marty hurled himself at the railing. *Smack.* He heard a gunshot behind him, then another. *Smack.* He didn't look back, plunging over the iron rail, landing with a bone-jarring thud on the concrete floor below. A bullet struck close by, and he dropped and rolled into the shadows as it ricocheted off the concrete walls. Out of sight, he stood up, panting, heart pounding, and scrambled down a stairwell, disappearing into the guts of the cavernous, deserted stadium.

Kemper looked down at the disc in his hand and his wooden face cracked into a smile. Then, with an eye skilled at taking body counts, he surveyed the grim scene.

Ford Sinclair was on the ground, jerking around in a pool of blood, feet drumming out an involuntary death dance, and, at the sight, Kemper smiled coldly. He'd nailed the cop with the first shot. The second had pretty much put an end to his life. Hearing a groan, Kemper turned his attention to Max Harper. His partner had taken a hit to the leg, another to the shoulder. For a cop, Ford Sinclair had been a hell of a bad shot. But even so, the damage to Harper's leg was massive. Pieces of bone contrasted with the bright red blood spurting, with each beat of his heart, from his wound.

"Roger," Harper called out with a moan. "We gotta get the fuck outta here."

Never leave your buddy behind, soldier.

Roger Kemper nodded. "Sure thing, Max," he said as he pointed his gun point-blank at Max Harper's upturned face and pulled the trigger. The face went cottage-cheese mushy, skin and skull and brains splattering out all over. Kemper pulled the trigger again and the face was shattered beyond recognition.

For a moment, Kemper stood there impassively, looking down at the place where the face had been. There had been practicalities to consider. He'd had no choice in the matter. No loose ends: that was Del's mantra.

No loose ends. Kemper's thoughts leaped to Marty English and a frown passed over his vacant face; he'd never find English now, not here. But what did that really matter? Kemper pulled the disc out of his coat pocket and smiled. They had the disc.

Chapter 54

From the backseat of the limousine, Del Waters trembled with anticipation. His hollow, hungry eyes drilled impatiently through the early morning fog that hung over Goose Island.

He had the disc. An irrepressible smile spread over his tired, gray face. Of course Waters knew the game wasn't over. He hadn't won, hadn't brought the enemy to its knees. There'd been no surrender. Not yet. But soon enough, Waters comforted himself. Soon Marty English would be his. Then . . .

At the thought, Del Waters trembled again and smiled more broadly, the rich, sunny smile of forgotten youth. And what of afterwards? After he was done with English? Then his enemy would be tossed into a ditch and left to rot like a piece of inconsequential roadkill.

But for now, first things first: the money.

The limousine turned onto a gravel lot and crunched to a stop in front of a ramshackle metal warehouse. CURANDERO IMPORTS, the weathered sign said. Waters frowned; he despised this place and everyone connected with it. But as his driver opened the car door and Mike D'Angelo strode quickly toward him, Del Waters's smile returned, quivering eagerly on his lips. *He had the disc.*

"Everybody's here, Del," D'Angelo said excitedly as he escorted Waters inside and took his coat. "They're waiting in the office."

Waters gave a nod but didn't reply. At the sight of the immense warehouse, skids piled high with herbs and shipping crates, his thoughts had turned to the future and what lay ahead: wealth, power, international influence. Of course he had all of that now. But then who could ever have enough?

At the back of the warehouse, Waters paused in the doorway leading into the office. The heavy steel security door was the only way in or out, a feature that always made the one-time POW claustrophobic. But Waters was a master of self-discipline, so he concealed his anxiety now, putting on an easy smile as he walked into the room.

The office was spacious, lab-coat white. Sterile, like the behavioral research facilities Del Waters enjoyed visiting at Bethesda and Stanford. But unlike those labs, which smelled all chemical fresh with their caged rats and formaldehyde and shiny clean dissecting knives, Curandero's office stank of decay, of dead fish, and of the filth that drifted past Goose Island in the Chicago River.

It was a smell that reminded Waters of rice paddies and rot and bamboo prisons, of things he wanted to forget. And, for a split second, his anxiety returned. But it retreated as his icy Nordic eyes came to rest on the large Formica conference table with a computer monitor stationed at its head.

Frank Torello and Carson Page were seated there, looking up at him expectantly. D'Angelo sat down beside them. Along the empty white walls stood Roger Kemper and Knute Shelby and eight of D'Angelo's goons.

"Del, he's still out there somewhere, right? English is still on the loose?" Frank Torello said, his voice shrill, like a woman's.

Waters frowned. "It would appear so, Frank," he replied flatly, without apology. His eyes fixed on the man as he added, "Are you concerned that I can't handle the situation?"

The color drained out of Torello's face. "Oh, of course not, Del," he said, shaking his head until the curl in his greasy hair drooped and fell over his aviators. "Hey, you got the disc. That's the most important thing." He looked around at the others. "Right, folks?"

They all nodded in unison.

"From what's happened over the past few days, Del," Carson said, throwing him a feline grin, "I'd say it's pretty clear you can handle anything that comes your way."

Around the room, heads nodded in agreement, while all eyes followed Waters as he strolled to the head of the table. He paused, taking the CD from his pocket with a dramatic flourish, and held it up before their eyes, like a priest charged with sanctifying a Sunday sacrament. They held their collective breath as he reverently removed the disc from its case, slipped it into the drive, and clicked the mouse. Then they waited, still breathless, listening in anxious silence to the whirring sound of the drive processing.

Waters smiled to himself. Super Bowl Sunday was just thirty-six hours away; he didn't like to cut it so close. But in any case, the Iranians would have their money. And he'd have his life. Heart racing, he leaned forward over the screen expectantly.

From the computer speakers, the voice of B. B. King belted out "The Thrill Is Gone."

Del Waters stared back at the computer screen with the empty eyes of a dead man. His face was oddly vacant, unsettlingly void.

"What the . . ." Torello blurted, his hand going to his chest like he was going to have a heart attack.

A bitter chuckle came from somewhere within Mike D'Angelo's thick lips. "English switched the discs on us. That's what."

Del Waters turned off the computer, his face as blank as the screen. His throat constricted, choking back any words he might have spoken. His brain throbbed against his skull, throbbed and throbbed—and the horrible, forgotten images of the bamboo prison returned, flashing in his mind's eye. It seemed like an eternity before it all sank in, but finally Waters understood.

He'd been had.

Then the haze cleared and, with all his will, like the wounded soldier who'd escaped that bamboo prison long ago, Del Waters drew himself up and said simply, evenly, "I'm giving you thirty-six hours to find English." It was a dangerously innocent tone, one only Roger Kemper had heard before, a tone reserved to lull those Waters intended to kill momentarily.

"Thirty-six hours," Waters repeated, his icy eyes boring through Kemper. "Get to our friends at the law enforcement agencies. Talk to Customs, the DEA, FBI. It's time to call in some markers. And while you're at it, pin those two murders at Soldier Field on English. . . . I want the local and state police in on this, too. I want the biggest fucking manhunt this city's ever seen."

"Will do," Kemper said weakly. Del Waters had offed plenty of guys for a whole lot less than the fuckup he'd committed; Kemper knew where he stood. He had only one more shot; he'd be as good as dead if he didn't deliver Marty English's head on a platter.

"We'll mobilize every man," Knute Shelby jumped in. "By noon we can have at least a hundred men on the hunt."

"I'll have my boys stake out the airports and highways," D'Angelo added. "We'll turn up the heat on the westside, too."

"What about the girl?" Carson demanded. "If we had Reiki Devane, we'd have an ace and, I can assure you, the disc. English won't turn his back on her."

"That's a good idea," Waters agreed. "Get in touch with the on-line services, Shelby. The Devane girl took her laptop, right? She has to use it sometime. Check out wire transfers, credit cards, national, international hotel reservations. Wherever she is, she has to eat and sleep."

Knute Shelby started to speak but, at the expression on Waters's face, backed down.

"I don't want excuses," Waters warned. "I want the girl."

Shelby nodded resignedly.

"In the meantime, Del," Carson suggested, "why don't we call English's bluff, make him think we've already got the girl? Mike's guys can put the word on the street that unless Marty English hands over the disc by the Super Bowl's two-minute warning, his girlfriend is history."

A flicker of admiration for Carson Page passed over Waters's face, and he nodded at D'Angelo. "Get the word out *pronto*."

"Consider it done."

A frown crossed Frank Torello's face. "What about the Planetlife party tomorrow night, Del?" he mumbled.

"What about it?"

"When does Arch get back in town? Maybe we should call the party off."

Waters scowled at Arrow's president. "Call it off?" he hooted. "That party's the cornerstone of a very carefully constructed and expensive cover, Frank."

Carson cast a disparaging look at Torello and then smiled earnestly at Waters. "Whatever it takes, Del," she vowed, crushing out her cigarette, "you know Arrow will hold up its end."

"And so will we," D'Angelo promised. "We'll find English. You won't be on the hot seat tomorrow night at the Planetlife party. You can count on it."

They all nodded.

Del Waters broke into a thin smile, his eyes slicing over them like a surgeon's scalpel. "Count on it?" he cried, giving out a nerve-wracking, manic laugh that sent a chill through the room. "It would seem that you, my dear friends, are under the mistaken impression that I am the only one here in jeopardy. Allow me to enlighten you. To put it bluntly, I have no intention of meeting the Iranians after the Super Bowl with nothing but a football score. But should I find myself in that predicament, I won't be taking the fall alone."

Their faces blanched to chalk.

"As you all know," he continued, "I'm a sociable creature by nature. A man who prefers companionship to solitude . . . team play to one-on-one. So of course it's only natural that I would want each of you to join me in the icy depths of Lake Michigan."

He paused and smiled cruelly. "A fate that, I can assure you, the Iranians will be most happy to accommodate."

Chapter 55

The official crime-scene tape wound around the hundred-foot column of Soldier Field, looking like a yellow-ribbon message tied on an oak tree for the returning soldier.

After the grounds crew's discovery of the victims of a brutal double homicide around dawn that Saturday morning, area law enforcement swooped down like storm troopers on the site, combing the enormous stadium for clues. By 8:30 A.M., Captain Bill Malone of the Lake County PD arrived on the scene and solemnly confirmed the identity of one of the victims as Lake County homicide detective Ford Sinclair. The other body remained unidentified due to the fact that his wallet was missing—as well as most of his face. Fingerprints were taken and sent out to the crime lab for local matchups and transmissions to the FBI.

Captain Malone gave the Chicago Police Department a statement, saying that Officer Sinclair had been on vacation for the past two weeks. What brought the detective to Soldier Field in the middle of the night (the coroner put time of death at somewhere around 3 A.M.) the captain couldn't imagine. And so far as the other man was concerned, if that's what he was—who could tell from his face?—Malone said there'd been no reports of any missing persons in his county.

By nine o'clock that Saturday morning, three Chicago-area

law enforcement agencies, as well as the Cook County Sheriff's Department and Chicago Park District, had united, setting up temporary headquarters inside Soldier Field.

Ensconced at Planetlife's wood-paneled office, Del Waters laid out his strategy: Using the pretext of an international terrorist alert, he would bring in eighty-four CIA agents and put them out on Chicago's streets—fourteen strike teams of six men each. These men in the field would report to a painstakingly efficient Roger Kemper, who clearly understood that far more than his job was at stake. Waters would also contact Washington and ask for an additional five communications experts to assist Knute Shelby in his electronic surveillance.

Without a doubt, this would be the boldest operation of Del Waters's career; he only hoped it wouldn't be his last.

The ink on Saturday's early editions of Chicago's morning newspapers was barely dry when the word about Marty English's girl was circulating on Goose Island and making its way down Kingsbury Street toward the Merchandise Mart, passing from one mouth to the next like a cheap bottle of wine: "The guys in the Mob have a message for Marty English. He's to hand it over by the two-minute warning. Yeah, that's what they said, *it* . . . or his girl's a goner." Nobody asked any questions. Nobody dared. They were a conduit, an underground pipeline, and nothing more; like a sewer, they just carried the shit.

Chapter 56

Marty spent what was left of the night in a cheap hotel in the Loop. Like an armchair quarterback watching from afar, he went over the next play.

In his heart, he knew Ford Sinclair was dead, and that Waters and his men would be out there, looking to make him their next victim.

Marty imagined that if life had a two-minute warning, his whistle was blowing right about now. After Del Waters discovered his men had fallen for the oldest trick in the book—that Marty had switched the discs—Waters would be more determined than ever to find his nemesis; he'd throw a net over the city and he'd have the help of D'Angelo's Mob to do it.

And if they nabbed Marty now? What then? Hell, a few clever words and a good sales pitch wouldn't save his ass. No, there wasn't any ancient Chinese secret to this game. They were playing for keeps. He and Del Waters knew the rules. And they both knew only one of them would be standing when it was over.

And what if Marty lost? What would his legacy be then? Hell, the answer to that question was easy: His legacy would be thirty seconds of sight, sound, motion, and emotion: thirty seconds in the Super Bowl.

*　*　*

It was just nine-thirty on Saturday morning when Marty walked into the Ugly Duckling Car Rental on Wells Street and rented an '84 Olds from a sleazy little old-timer named Vinnie wearing a glen-plaid hat and a polyester all-weather coat. Business had been slow lately, and Vinnie was as lonely as the Maytag Man. He wanted to shoot the breeze, but Marty wanted to get down to business. Marty paid cash for a three-day rental package and slid an extra hundred to Vinnie under the table to forget about taking his credit card number and driver's license.

Vinnie never hesitated; he pocketed Ben Franklin, took a set of car keys off a pegboard, and, with a conspiratorial smile, handed them over the counter. It was nine-forty-five when Marty drove out of the Ugly Duckling Car Rental with a full tank of gas and a complimentary ice scraper.

Chapter 57

During a midmorning breakfast of pancakes at Hello Holley's, three of Roger Kemper's boys got a hot tip: A guy matching Marty English's description had been spotted over at the Holy Bible Mission.

The agents rushed right over, and were told by the husband-and-wife do-gooders who ran the place that a tramp they'd never seen before had wandered in early Friday morning.

They wouldn't have thought much about the guy, the couple said, except for two things they found peculiar. For one, the tramp didn't take his gloves off until dinner that night, and when he did, they noticed his hands and nails were immaculate, not exactly typical for a guy who would've been using his fingernails to scratch everything from his ass to a match.

"What was the other thing?" the agents asked.

"The guy said he just got in from Memphis."

"What was so peculiar about that?"

"Why, everybody knows," the do-gooders said, "that no self-respecting tramp goes north in the winter."

The Saturday before the Super Bowl was always wild for Chicago's bookies; every amateur gambler and his grandmother wanted in on the action. But today was wilder than most. Today the bookies had more than spreads and handicaps to pass on.

"The guys in the Mob have a message for Marty English," they whispered as they went from place to place. "He's to hand it over by the two-minute warning. Yeah, that's what they said, *it* . . . or his girl's a goner." And what were the odds on English doing that? their customers wanted to know. Two to one, the bookies said. Two to one.

Chapter 58

Early Saturday afternoon, Marty bought a Coke and two Italian beef sandwiches at Portello's and promptly devoured them on the way to a hole-in-the-wall video and music store on Clark Street. Blockbuster it wasn't. Inside this place day and night became one, like Las Vegas, where there was never enough darkness to serve as cover for all the kinky things people wanted to do and see done, so somebody had the bright idea to just make it nighttime all the time.

Marty stood in line at the checkout, loaded down with a stack of music CDs and twenty-five blank, long-play videotapes with snap-lock storage cases, while nervous old men and teenage boys, porn tapes in hand, stared back at him. He paid an aging salesman, a guy with an embarrassingly large Italian Stallion complex and a bald spot to match, seventy-eight dollars in cash.

From there, Marty drove south to Washington and then over to the Federal Express office on Wabash, where he picked up twenty-five airbills, pouches, and small FedEx boxes from a middle-aged woman with a Betty Crocker smile and a nose for other people's business.

"Working on the weekend?" Betty Crocker pried.

"Doesn't everybody?" he replied as he headed out the revolving doors to a pay phone across the street.

* * *

Marty stood shivering on the sidewalk in front of the phone, trying to collect his thoughts, before he used his agency phone card to call the Raleigh Beach Resort in Bermuda and asked for the Lighthouse Cottage.

There was a pause on the line and then a tentative, cultured voice said softly, "Hello."

"Reiki . . . it's me. Marty." He thought he sounded breathless, just shy of fearful. He didn't want to sound afraid or out of control; he didn't want to scare her. "Hi there," he said, struggling at cheerfulness. "You okay?"

"Of course *I'm* okay!" she exclaimed in a way that made him wonder if she was mad. But then he heard her stifle a sob. "What about you? Are you okay? God, I've been going crazy over here. You know how weird it was sneaking around, getting out of that damned city? I started thinking there were hit men on every corner."

He let out a bitter laugh. "There are."

"Ha ha ha. Listen, it's been a week since you called me in the middle of the night and told me to run for my life. I've been sitting here in this damned little cottage, waiting all that time. Wondering what the hell happened. Wondering if you were dead or alive. I wanted to call somebody, wanted to find out something—"

"You didn't?" he interrupted.

"No, but it's been hell, Marty. Not knowing." She paused. "It's pretty bad, huh?"

"Yeah," he admitted. "And it's only going to get worse. . . . Things are really starting to heat up. And my guess is it's about to get a hell of a lot hotter."

"You're scaring me, Marty."

"*I'm* scaring Reiki Devane?" He forced a chuckle. "That devil-may-care photojournalist who dodges bullets and cavorts in cantinas with bandits?"

"I'm not scared for *me*," she corrected, her voice dropping. "It's *you* I'm worried about."

"Well, don't be," he ordered. "Now be quiet and just listen. I can't talk much longer."

"All right. I'm listening."

"After we hang up I want you to go to the Bank of Bermuda on Front Street in Hamilton and ask for a Mr. Everitt Peeler."

"Peeler?"

"Yeah, remember? Peeler's the guy who handled some overseas transfers for us. He's vice president of offshore and European accounts. He's kind of stuffy, but he's nice enough. Ask him to open a numbered account for you with the Swiss Bank Corporation in Zurich. He won't ask questions: the bank prides itself on being discreet. After he's opened the account, he'll give you three sets of numbers: an account number, a routing number, and a PIN."

"Account. Routing. PIN," she repeated. He could imagine her nodding, her tawny hair shining around her face. "Okay, I can do that. So then what?"

"Then go back to the Raleigh, plug your laptop's modem into the phone jack, and wait to hear from me."

"On E-mail?"

"No, we can't risk E-mail; they can trace on-line services."

"Sounds like they're pretty sophisticated."

"They are, so they probably wouldn't expect us to use a fax. Besides, I'm going to need a hard copy. I'll fax you direct from my computer when I'm ready for you to send me the numbers, but you should know it's going to take a while."

"No problem. I'll be waiting."

"Good. Now remember, go straight to the bank and come straight back. I don't think they know where you are, but we can't take anything for granted, not with these guys."

"I take back what I said a minute ago. I guess I am afraid for *us*, Marty."

"I was afraid for us too—*before*—when I thought I was losing you. But I'm not going to let that happen, Reiki. We're going to make it through this together. You hear me? *Together.*" He swallowed hard, and continued in a softer tone.

"I'm talking about forever, Reiki. *Commitment.* You know, the white dress, two cats in the yard. And babies, too, if that's what you want. All we have to do is make it through the next twenty-four hours and we'll be home free. I'm going to take these guys down. They're going to pay. And then you and I . . . we're going to find our own little corner of paradise." He paused. "I love you, Reiki."

"I love you, too. . . ." Her voice cracked. "But . . ."

"But?"

"But you should know, none of that, that house-in-the-country stuff . . . none of it means anything without you. Be careful, Marty. I won't breathe easily until you're by my side—safe and sound."

Chapter 59

With its romantic architecture and the hundreds of officers, helicopters, dogs, and cars, Soldier Field was a dramatic setting that winter afternoon. And, being a master at public relations, Chicago's mayor, Walt Camden, knew a good photo op when he saw one. Because of that, and despite the bitter cold rolling in from the lake, he'd insisted on having the two o'clock press conference held outside, in front of the stadium. Saturdays were slow news days, so the mayor intended to get maximum coverage.

The emotions of both the mayor and the superintendent of police were high that afternoon—they were both in fine political form—as they described for the press the grisly double homicide at Soldier Field. The phrase "fallen soldier" was used several times in referring to the murdered officer, Ford Sinclair. And vows were made to learn the identity of the other victim by sundown.

Mayor Camden promised to provide Police Superintendent Murphy's department with every available resource in the effort to bring the fugitive cop-killer to justice. Chicago, the mayor declared, was about to witness the biggest manhunt in its history.

*　*　*

Pike Stevens didn't watch the news; he watched *Sea Hunt* instead. The Chicago news was depressing, after all, and more than anything, Pike wanted to escape depressing Chicago. He wanted to sail right on down the Chicago River and out into Lake Michigan and never look back. Sail around the world, look for sunken treasure, maybe. Dive the great reefs, too, if his sinuses didn't kick up.

So far, the closest the old Swede had ever come to realizing that dream was when some crooked union guy paid him to haul a load of garbage, paint cans and batteries, mostly, down the Chicago River late at night in his little tug, *Annie*, and then dump the whole mess into Lake Michigan.

Mainly, Pike scraped by, working at the Burnham Park Harbor marina. Set off Lake Shore Drive, the marina was frequented largely by the wealthy maritime set. To pay for *Annie*'s slip, Pike performed odd jobs or donned his antiquated scuba gear and scraped the scum off other people's yachts and sailboats. Most of the guys who came through Burnham Harbor were either old sons of bitches who liked to throw their weight around or snot-nosed little bastards. Most of them except Marty English, of course.

Whenever Marty was down at the harbor on his ad agency's yacht, the *Wynner*, he took the time to come around, say hello, maybe pass along a sailing magazine. Pike liked Marty a lot. So when the old man saw Marty hustle up and down the dock three times late Saturday afternoon, carrying a shitload of stuff to the *Wynner*, he waved enthusiastically, pleased to see him even on this miserable, gray day.

Marty waved back, but he didn't stop like he usually did. And that worried Pike Stevens. He decided to make it his business to see what was up.

"Need a hand, Marty?" Pike asked, catching him on his fifth trip to the yacht.

"No thanks, Pike," Marty answered, putting down a stack of FedEx materials and fumbling in his pocket until he pulled out the Robusto cigar he'd picked up downtown. "Thought you might enjoy a smoke tonight when you're watching *Sea Hunt*," he said, handing him the cigar.

"Why, gee-whiz . . ." The Swede smacked his lips. "You know old Pike's got a soft spot for a good cigar." He closed his faded blue eyes and sniffed at the stogie, his sun-leathered nose wrinkling appreciatively.

"So what you got going on the burner for tonight?" Pike asked as Marty started toward the yacht again.

"Fish," Marty called out over his shoulder.

As he shook his head, a brief chuckle escaped the old man's lips. For an ad man, Marty English was a hell of a comedian.

At six o'clock at Soldier Field, the Chicago Police Department held their second press conference of the day. Police Superintendent Murphy told the somber gathering that the second victim in the slayings had been identified as one Maxwell Harper, a decorated Vietnam veteran, currently employed by the Central Intelligence Agency as a specialist in foreign smuggling operations.

"As many of you may recall," Murphy said, his voice eloquently outraged, "this is the second slaying of a CIA agent in as many weeks. The first involved agency clerk Stonewall Jackson, who was found brutally gunned down on Navy Pier."

The superintendent paused and hands flew up in the audience, but he went on. "Both the Chicago Police Department and the Central Intelligence Agency have concluded that these murders are connected. Therefore, I am here with CIA representative Richard Taylor to announce that, effective Saturday, January twenty-fourth at six o'clock P.M., Central Standard Time, the Central Intelligence Agency, an agency of the federal government, has officially joined the Chicago Police Department's investigation of what the media is calling the Fallen Soldier Slayings."

Richard Taylor stepped forward now and, looking directly into the TV cameras, said, "We are asking the public to assist us in apprehending the individual or individuals responsible for this tragedy. Persons having information regarding these crimes should contact either the CIA or the Chicago Police Department."

Again the hands flew up and reporters shouted out questions, but Superintendent Murphy held up his hand. "Mr. Taylor and I will take no questions at this time."

"When can we expect some news?" a reporter yelled.

"When we have some," Murphy replied soberly.

Chapter 60

Wynn Bergman had fallen for the luxurious 143-foot Oceanco yacht while visiting a client in Fort Lauderdale. Though it had been love at first sight, what had really caught the agency president's eye was the yacht's state-of-the-art high-tech wizardry—and the fact that, with a twenty-nine-foot beam and four staterooms, it had plenty of room for more.

As he had with the agency's offices and its Gulfstream jet, Bergman envisioned the yacht as a technological wonderland, a sort of floating showpiece for his company's cutting-edge style. Bergman bought the yacht on the spot, and a few weeks later she was christened the *Wynner*, and docked at Chicago's Burnham Park Harbor.

Of course that was just the beginning; the electronic gadgets Bergman so adored had to be installed. And installed they were. When it was over, the *Wynner* might not be able to transport its passengers to the planet Vulcan, but nobody questioned the fact that the agency's magnificent yacht was about as close to the starship *Enterprise* as a guy could get.

Marty English was one of three people in Wynn Bergman Advertising with access to the agency yacht, a perk he wished he could enjoy more often. But then this wasn't exactly a pleasure cruise he was taking now, Marty reminded himself as he pressed the keypad combination that unlocked the door to the yacht's elaborate electronics suite.

Once, during an agency cocktail party, Marty overheard Wynn jokingly refer to the suite as the war room, a fitting moniker, he thought at the time, for something that looked more like a military helicopter cockpit or battleship's bridge than a media room on a luxury yacht. Now, as he methodically turned on the computer workstations and the monitors crackled on, flashing like little blue soldiers snapping to attention, those words returned. *The war room.* And with them, Marty was transported back in time. Back to the blue-flash glare of enemy artillery in a cloudless night sky. Back to the agonizing *snap-crack* of blue-hot bullets hitting home.

Marty took a deep breath. *The war room.* Well, he was prepared to come out fighting. He steeled his shoulders and loaded five blank videotapes into the recorders lining the wall.

He loaded them one after the other, mechanically, as if he were loading slugs into a clip, until they were all in place in the racks. Until they stared back at him, gleaming metal and black plastic, neat, like weapons at the ready.

Then he opened his briefcase and took out the videotape of his father's last meeting. He stood there, staring down at it, for what seemed like a long time, letting its contents replay in his mind, letting the truth sink in. Feeling the familiar hatred gnawing at his gut, feeling the hunger for revenge rise up inside him all over again.

Enemies get taken care of, the voice in his head whispered.

Marty smiled the smile of the soldier-hunter whose prey is at last in his sights, and then, eyes gleaming in the cold blue light of the monitors, he slid the tape into a slot marked ORIGINAL SOURCE TAPE. And hit Record.

It was eight o'clock at night—Marty checked his watch just to make sure—when the videotape machines' Record lights went off and he took the last five videotapes out of the racks and began stacking them on the table next to the other twenty he'd already copied. Slowly, deliberately, like a man savoring his last meal, Marty placed the tapes in their snap-lock cases and then packed each one in a Federal Express shipping box, addressed, in neat block letters, to twenty-five of the nation's most prominent law enforcement officials, congressmen, and media.

It was just after eight-thirty when Marty finally heard the gratifying *kaplunk, kaplunk* of twenty-five boxes dropping into the FedEx drop box stationed across the street from Burnham Park Harbor. Most Monday mornings were probably a little short on entertainment as far as his recipients were concerned, Marty thought dryly. But the little scenarios on these videotapes should remedy that.

As he hurried back to the safety of the yacht, Marty smiled to himself. And to think he'd only just fired the first shot.

Chapter 61

Bing Valentine, aging wannabe actor and full-time pornographic video salesman, wanted to be "connected." Thus, when three of Mike D'Angelo's faithful followers had swaggered into the video store where he worked on the previous Thursday looking for some dude named English, Valentine had been devastated; having nothing to report, he figured he'd lost his one chance at the big time.

Valentine brooded the rest of the week, but then Saturday morning came and his luck turned when a man walked into the video store and bought twenty-five blank tapes and snaplock cases. It was usually pedophiles and other perverts who bought that many tapes at once. Bing Valentine took a second look and—jackpot! The dude looking back at him fit English's description to a T.

After the man left, Valentine stewed, furiously trying to determine whom to pass the information on to. Finally, that night, he put in a call to a tough guy he knew who wore a lot of gold jewelry and worked at the track. To Valentine's immense satisfaction, word traveled fast in the underworld and, later that evening, Lady Luck smiled. The tough guy called him back and, as a thanks from his boss, gave Bing Valentine a tip on a sure thing.

*　*　*

From what Roger Kemper's boys were able to learn from the flamboyant desk clerk at the ratty Hotel Arcade, Marty English had spent the early morning hours Saturday in the Loop. The clerk told them that a guy who sounded a lot like the one they were looking for had gone out for a while and then come back, looking real wild-eyed, at around three o'clock Saturday morning.

The guy had been dressed like a common bum when he'd signed in late Friday night, but when he left the next morning at around eight, he was dressed real sharp, like one of those stud movie stars, the clerk said: leather bomber jacket, tight jeans, boots. And he was carrying an expensive-looking briefcase and a black leather garment bag, too. Yeah, it was some transformation, the clerk remembered, sighing deeply. But then, he said, he'd always known clothes made the man.

When the whore in the red fox coat wiggled into the Cook County Sheriff's Department sometime around nine-thirty that Saturday night and said she wanted to make a statement regarding a murder at Soldier Field, she got the royal treatment. She'd expected as much, of course. D'Angelo's boys had warned her about all the uproar she'd be causing. But they'd paid her well enough for her time, so she didn't mind. If anything it was kind of exciting; hell, what whore didn't like to be the center of attention?

After being plied with a cup of black coffee, a Krispy Kreme jelly doughnut, and a cigarette, she proceeded to part her heavily lipsticked mouth and tell the detectives in the rolled-up shirtsleeves everything they wanted to know. Her story was that she'd had a john early that morning over at the Hotel Arcade in the Loop. "The guy acted real strange," she said. "Carried on, crazy-like."

"Did he say what got him so worked up?" the detectives asked.

"Sure did." She nodded, enjoying the way she had them on the edge of their seats. "Said he just got through icing a 'nigger cop'." She watched their faces as she lit a cigarette. Then she threw them a sly smile and added, "At Soldier Field."

"Can you give us a description?" they asked excitedly.

"Sure can." She winked. "Right down to the hairs on his ass."

By the time the ten o'clock news came on that Saturday night, every newspaper rag and TV station in the city had a picture of what police were calling the leading suspect in the Fallen Soldier Slayings.

All they needed now was a name.

For fourteen hours, Knute Shelby had hardly moved from the desk in his suite at the Ritz-Carlton, what Roger Kemper was irritatingly calling "home base."

Shelby had been glued to his telephone and computer all day, drinking buckets of coffee and eating snatches of crème brûlée while barking out orders to his men in the field and hammering away on his keyboard, searching for any sign that a Ms. Reiki A. Devane had recently used a credit card or an on-line computer service.

It was ten o'clock now and Shelby was exhausted, empty-handed, and bored. He stood up and, giving out a yawn, flipped on the television. At the news of the Fallen Soldier Slayings and the composite drawing of the suspect, Shelby chuckled to himself; Marty English didn't stand a snowball's chance in hell.

But according to the reporter standing in front of Soldier Field, microphone in hand, law enforcement officials weren't as confident as Shelby was; they still needed a name to go with the face. They needed the public's help and, to that end, they'd set up a hot line to take calls from potential informants.

Knute Shelby sat down at his keyboard and smiled; he couldn't shirk his duty now. He'd always considered himself something of a public servant.

*   *   *

"It was him on the news just now, wasn't it, Wynn?" Lee Wilde demanded, her hand gripping tightly around the telephone. "It was Marty."

There was a pause on the line.

"The rendering had a vague resemblance," Bergman agreed.

"Vague? Are you fucking kidding? My God, Wynn, could it really be him?"

"Of course not!" Bergman snapped.

"He must be hiding, that's why he's been gone all week," Lee ranted on. "Dammit, I knew we should've called the police when he didn't show up at work on Monday and I couldn't find Reiki anywhere."

"No," Bergman said quickly. "We did the right thing, keeping the goddamned police out of this. Besides, we didn't want to panic a three-hundred-million-dollar account."

"Like that made any difference."

Bergman ignored her sarcasm and went on. "There's got to be an explanation that makes sense, Lee. . . . We just haven't thought of it yet."

"A better one than Marty English is a murderer, you mean?"

"That's exactly what I mean."

"Well, I sure as hell can't think of one . . . can you?"

"No, I can't," he admitted. "But that doesn't mean one doesn't exist."

"On the news they said the police are looking for a name—"

"Leave it alone, Lee," Bergman said brusquely. "Marty's no murderer. You know that as well as I do."

"Well, he sure as hell's acting like one. Why doesn't he just turn himself in? I mean, if he hasn't done anything wrong, why's he hiding?"

For the first time in his illustrious career, Wynn Bergman was totally mystified. "I wish to God I knew."

Chapter 62

If the Maya Indians had been more than mere ballplayers, if they'd actually elevated the art of warfare to a sacred game, then they had also been brilliant strategists. Blood sports, after all, weren't for the fool. Games of life and death were for the clever, the astute. The exquisitely brutal. The artistic. The Palenque Triad was all that and more, Marty thought now, his heart pounding with excitement as he studied the glyph from Harvard's Tozzer Library he'd just downloaded onto the yacht's graphics computer.

It was just like Che had said it would be: three glyphs in one. The god of the sun, the god of the underworld, the god of illusion: They were all there together in a perfect death dance called the ball game.

Now all Marty had to do was take them apart.

Marty was sitting at the yacht's graphic workstation when Reiki's fax came in. The slick paper rolled out like an ancient papyrus scroll into his waiting hand. He tore it off and held it up in the blue light of the computer monitor.

DATE 01.24   TIME 23:04   PAGES 1 OF 1

TO: THE FROGMAN
FAX: 312.427.3618

FROM: THE LILY PAD
FAX: 441.233.5421

Marty paused, a brief smile flitting across his tired face; nobody would ever accuse Reiki Devane of being unprofessional, despite those goofy amphibian names she'd had to use
to disguise their identities.

The smile disappeared as his eyes continued down the
page.

FROGMAN, HERE YOU GO.

SWISS BANK CORPORATION, ZURICH
ROUTING NBR. 062007755
ACC. NBR. 357-9ES-549
PIN NBR. 10848.

TAKE CARE. LOVE FROM THE LILY PAD.
TWO CATS WOULD BE NICE, BUT CAN WE HAVE A DOG, TOO?

"Yeah, you can have a dog," he said softly. "And an ele-
phant, too. If I make it out of this . . . alive."

Over the next hours, Marty separated the Palenque Triad
glyph into its three parts. He put each image in a separate
computer file and matched its format size and resolution to
the glyph on his father's B. B. King disc.

Like all computer images, each god in the Palenque Triad
comprised a unique number of computer bits. If Marty's guess
was right, that number was one of three security codes he'd
need to get into the central account. He plowed ahead resolutely, keenly aware that time was running out.

It was after two in the morning when he was finally finished. On the table before him lay three shimmering discs,
gleaming like silver bullets waiting for a gun.

Chapter 63

After the composite drawing of the suspect in the Fallen Soldier Slayings aired in the ten o'clock news, the police hot line was swamped with callers. The regular telephone lines at the station were jammed too; nobody could get through to 911. Reports on the suspect were as common as raisins in a box of bran. And about as reliable as sightings of UFOs. They were getting nowhere fast.

Then, sometime around three o'clock Sunday morning, the Chicago PD got a break when an all-night disc jockey at WLS saw the E-mail icon blinking on the station's studio computer. He clicked it and was stunned to find the message:

TO: WLS RADIO
FROM: A FAN
RE: FALLEN SOLDIER SLAYINGS

         THE MAN POLICE ARE LOOKING FOR IS MARTY
         ENGLISH AKA MARTINO INGLESIA, SON OF
         RECENTLY DECEASED CHICAGO MOB BOSS, TONY
         INGLESIA.

When the DJ called the Chicago Police Department and read the message to the chief of detectives, the cops went wild. They had a name, all right. A hell of a name.

Pike Stevens hadn't said no when a husky-voiced man had called around midnight and asked him to take a run upriver for a pickup. His little forays into the world of waste disposal added a bit of excitement to an otherwise dull existence. Aside from this shady dumping business he'd fallen into over the past few years, Pike Stevens had never so much as jay-walked.

It was after three-thirty Sunday morning, and dark as an underwater cave, when the *Annie* made her way past the Lake Michigan shoreline. The tug turned up the Chicago River, chug-chugging beneath a dozen bridges, past Marina Towers, Wolf Point, and acres of warehouses and railroad tracks, until Pike Stevens cut the engines at a broken-down dock on Goose Island.

It was always the same; they had it down to a science. Four burly men, stevedores by day, Pike imagined, loaded the tug's holding tank with those Hefty trash bags with the yellow lock strips and then hustled away, climbing into a waiting car that rumbled into the night.

That was when the husky-voiced man stepped out of the shadows and, handing Pike a couple hundred bucks for the job, whispered, "Keep your nose clean."

Pike would always say "Aye, aye, Captain," just to lighten things up, and that would be that. They'd both be on their way.

It had gone the same tonight, until they got to the part where the husky-voiced guy stepped out of the shadows. Tonight, as the man handed Pike the money, he whispered instead: "Spread it around. . . . The guys in the Mob have a message for Marty English. He's to hand it over by the two-minute warning."

"It?" Pike asked, his mind racing with a thousand questions—like how they could possibly know he knew Marty English, for one.

"Yeah, that's what they said—*it* . . . by the two-minute warning. Or his girl's a goner."

"Aye, aye, Captain." Pike Stevens nodded, trying to still the pounding in his chest. He wouldn't ask any questions. He was just the messenger, after all. But he couldn't help but wonder if that fish Marty had been fixing to fry was going to be too big for the ad man to reel in.

Chapter 64

Creating a TV commercial could be as simple as "Lights, camera, action" or as complicated as "Let there be light."

But no matter how exciting the photo shoot or how great the footage, in the end it came down to editing, the most monotonous part of the monotonous production process, to Marty's way of thinking. Yet it was in the tedious editing process that a creative director took that lump of clay called footage and breathed life into it. Until then it was all just cheap talk and high-priced film crews.

Frankly, the editing process had always put Marty to sleep. Until now. Now, as he sat in the yacht's electronics suite and edited the videotape of his father's last hours into a thirty-second television commercial, the sound of the videotape running back and forth, back and forth in the machine as he selected the most incriminating scenes reminded Marty of Vietnam and the sound his breath had made when he'd looked through the sights of his gun at the enemy. The sound of his breath, in and out—slow, slow, then faster and faster. Hypnotic, that's what it had been.

But no one else was pulling the strings this time. This time Marty had the enemy in his sights. And he knew what to do.

Squeeze the trigger, soldier.

He hit Record. Rewind, fast-forward. Hit Record.

Marty sat, entranced, his gaze fixed on the enemy, as the videotape rushed by in a garbled nightmarish cartoon of sight and sound.

Del Waters. Fast-forward and rewind. Fast-forward. Rewind. Hit Record. "Who would ever think . . ."

The whirring, whooshing of tape was the only sound he could hear. And then it was fast-forward and rewind all over again.

Mike D'Angelo. Hit Record. The whooshing of tape. Carson Page. Frank Torello. Hit Record. Fast-forward, rewind. Tony Inglesia. Fast-forward, rewind. Hit Record. Again and again and again. Until it all came together in one continuous thirty-second creation.

Marty played it back. Looked it over. And then realized that tonight he had paid the highest possible tribute he could have made to his father: He'd made him the focus of a masterpiece.

Marty had never fully appreciated the agency's satellite communications capabilities. Oh, he'd used them, of course, countless times, talking to some ramrod executive in Frankfurt about how to advertise faucets or attending an Asian conference on chips via linkup. But even so, he'd never really considered all the possibilities. A simple tweak of an ISCI code here, a few new traffic instructions there, a little tapping on a computer keyboard until you were locked in on, say, a certain time and—presto! a guy could change the course of history.

Indeed, the possibilities for abusing the agency's satellite capabilities were dizzying, and in the wrong hands, even devastating. And now, as Marty sat before the yacht's satellite console and slid his thirty-second video creation into a slot in the rack and locked it in, he couldn't help but smile.

He was going to send a two-million-dollar bombshell out a

hundred miles into space and then let it bounce right back
down from the network satellite and onto millions of TV sets.

In less than twelve hours, the whole world was going to
meet a man named Del Waters. Marty didn't think they would
like what they saw.

Chapter 65

It was dawn Sunday morning and still a bit foggy, and Pike Stevens, having just dumped his latest toxic cargo into the depths of Lake Michigan, was thinking about how he was going to spend the rest of the day as he navigated his little tugboat into its slip at Burnham Park Harbor. First, he'd high-tail it over to the *Wynner* and pass along the husky-voiced man's message to Marty English. Then he'd settle down to some biscuits and gravy on *Annie*, turn on his Goldstar TV, maybe even light up that fancy cigar. And of course the Super Bowl would be on later. He wouldn't want to miss that.

Pike sighed. It sure didn't sound very exciting, but what the hell—when you were eighty years old what could you expect? Not much, that was for damned sure, Pike chortled, peering out into the harbor. It was then that he saw the three men standing on the dock, looking out at him.

They were cops, Pike was sure of that, and he suddenly wondered if this was it: The big bust—that's what they called it on TV. Maybe the cops had found out about his little night job dumping garbage and they were here to cart him off to jail. Did they put old men like him in prisons? He didn't think so, but then again, he wasn't so sure the long arm of justice gave a good goddamn how old you were.

"What's doin' old-timer?" the taller of the three called out from the dock.

As Pike eased his tug into the slip, he shrugged and grinned his best befuddled-old-man grin through the light fog. "Aw, me and my *Annie* here, we always go out for a few little runs on Sundays." He shivered in a gust of wind. "Keeps the blood flowing, if you know what I mean."

The man nodded and Pike saw him wink at his two companions. So they thought he was an old fool, did they?

"My friends and I have a few questions we'd like to ask you, sir—if you don't mind." The three men flashed their badges and smiled like a row of schoolboys. "We're with the Chicago Police Department. Detectives, Homicide."

"I see," Pike said thoughtfully, like he was letting it sink in. Homicide? At least he knew he was off the hook. He'd only dumped a few deadly substances in the public water; he hadn't actually killed anybody. It was a technicality, perhaps, but an important one.

"Can we come aboard, Mr. . . . ?"

Pike smiled, all friendly and crooked-toothy. "Stevens. Pike Stevens. Real name's Gustaf Stevens, but I like Pike better." He paused and shook his head. "Forgetting my manners, aren't I?" He waved them down. "Come on aboard, just watch your step."

The tall detective and his two companions clambered onto the tug. "Well, Pike," he began, his eyes scanning the boat, "you live on here, do you?"

Pike nodded cautiously. "Uh-huh. It'll be forty-five years this spring."

"You have a TV on board? You watch the ten-o'clock news?"

Pike thought that was a peculiar question. "I have a TV all right," he replied, pulling his frazzled red knit cap down snug over his ears. "But can't say I watch the news. *Sea Hunt*, that's my favorite show. It comes on at the same time as the news."

The detective held out a drawing. "We're looking for this man. His picture was on the news last night. We believe his name may be English, Marty English. We're pretty sure he's in this vicinity. You seen him around the harbor?"

With one steady gloved hand, Pike took the picture. His face was the picture of innocence. And his hands weren't shaking at all—it was just like he was one of those sneaky guys that Columbo fellow always questioned on TV, all cool and collected—and Pike congratulated himself on his nerve. He didn't think these guys were as smart as Columbo; yep, they'd be fooled by a nice old man for sure.

Pike squinted, studying the drawing for a minute, and then, his nerves under control, he looked back up at the detective and shook his head guilelessly. "Nope. 'Fraid I can't say I've seen this fella around." His hands still steady, he gave the detective the picture back and said indifferently, "What's he done, anyway?"

"He killed a cop and a CIA agent over at Soldier Field the other night. On TV they're calling it the Fallen Soldier Slayings. He may have killed another agent last week, too. We don't know for sure yet."

"Sounds like a bad one," Pike remarked, his red-rimmed eyes going wide. "So that's what all that fuss was about over at the stadium yesterday morning?"

"Yes, sir." The tall detective nodded grimly.

Pike looked him square in the eye and said earnestly, "Well, I wish I could help you out, but I can't say I've seen that fella you're looking for. If I do, though, I'll be sure and call you"— he paused and grinned—"lickety-split."

"Maybe you should take another look," one of the other detectives suggested. "Do you wear reading glasses, Mr. Stevens? Maybe you should put them on."

Offended, Pike bristled like a banty rooster. "Now, lookee here, son," he retorted testily. "I've been on this earth probably fifty years more than you and I may need my cheaters now and then to read the racing sheets, but I'd know if I'd seen that man you're looking for and I'd remember it, too. Just because you're young and got everything working right doesn't mean I'm a blind old fool, you know."

"No sir, of course not," the tall cop said quickly, shooting a warning glare at his companions as he climbed back onto the dock. "Thanks anyway, Mr. Stevens," he said. "You have a nice day. And if you do see anything suspicious, you be sure and call us."

"Lickety-split." Pike nodded, throwing them a cheerful wave good-bye.

As the detectives walked back to their car, they started to laugh. "Old fools," they said to one another, shaking their heads. "They're all alike."

Pike waited until the detectives had been gone for some time before he ambled down the dock to the *Wynner*. He carried a bucket and mop, just to make it look good, and he took his time getting there, too. When he finally boarded the *Wynner*, Pike stopped and glanced nervously over his shoulder, his milky blue eyes shooting toward the parking lot as he rapped his wrinkled knuckles on the door.

"Who is it?" a voice from the other side demanded.

"Pike," he replied. He lowered his voice. "Just wanted you to know, those fish of yours are starting to smell."

Marty opened the door a crack.

"Let me in, quick, and don't ask questions," the old man whispered. "You got trouble, son."

Chapter 66

F ive hours had passed since law enforcement officials had learned the identity of their suspect in the Fallen Soldier Slayings. It was Sunday morning now, and they were running out of steam. For all their effort and wasted gas, there'd been no sign of their man. Then, around eight that morning, the Chicago Police Department got a break. A Federal Express employee called the hot line, said English had been in the downtown FedEx office on Saturday, asking for a bunch of mailing labels and boxes. He drove off in a gray '84 Olds, the caller said, just like a car she used to have.

It was the lead the cops needed. Their man English was probably driving a rental car since his Jag had been found abandoned at the Inglesia place in Lake Forest. The word went out from police Dispatch, spreading across the city like wildfire. In fifteen minutes, every rental car agency in three counties was bombarded by squad cars loaded down with cops and detectives.

At Ugly Duckling Car Rental, a salesman named Vinnie had initially brightened at the prospect of having some company for a change, but when the detectives showed him the artist's rendering of their suspect, he suddenly got tongue-tied, went brain-dead right on the spot, and swore he couldn't recall much of anything that happened the day before. But a flash of green in front of Vinnie's eyes, placed there by a street-smart undercover cop, refreshed his memory. Within seconds, word went out over the squad car radio: They were looking for Illinois license plate number UDR-661.

By noon Sunday, Chicago was under siege. The mayor and superintendent of police held another press conference, informing the public they were confident their suspect, now identified as one Marty English, would be behind bars by nightfall.

Shortly thereafter, the Chicago Police Department and the Cook County Sheriff's Department mobilized their men for a united blitzkrieg on the city's downtown area. By one o'clock, marked and unmarked cars, their glacier-blue lights throbbing, were screaming across the city, racing from one hot tip to the next. Detectives in trench coats were canvassing the city's downtown area, interviewing everybody from parking lot attendants to wannabe snitches and housewives. By two that afternoon, state troopers had thrown up roadblocks north and south and west while cops in patrol cars eased up and down the maze of city streets.

It was five o'clock and already dark when two policemen on dinner break pulled into Burnham Park Harbor and their headlights came to rest on a gray '84 Olds, license number UDR-661. Bingo: They'd found their suspect's car. Now all they had to do was find their suspect.

As Pike Stevens guided his little tug through the harbor, his eyes stayed fixed on the dozen or so police cars now descending on Burnham Park Harbor. The lights on the cops' hoods were flashing like a Christmas parade, but their sirens were eerily silent—a bad sign, the old man thought. Sure as hell they were planning a surprise attack, just like they did on *Matlock* now and then.

When he eased the tug alongside the *Wynner*, a shadowy figure dropped onto the deck with a thud and Pike quickly opened the door and whispered between clenched yellow teeth, "Go below and stay there . . . 'til I tell you different."

There was no reply, just a shadow gliding past, disappearing into the hold.

"They're like sand fleas, there's so many of them," Pike said aloud, barely above the tug's chugging engines. "They're climbing all over that damned car of yours. . . ." His voice trailed off. "Aw, shit . . . look's like there's some cops back on the dock, waving me over. . . . Shit."

As the tug got closer, Pike recognized the tall detective and his two companions. "Hey there, fellas," he called out with all the bravado he could muster. "What's all the ruckus?"

"Some officers spotted our suspect's car, Mr. Stevens, here in the parking lot," the tall detective yelled. "You seen anything out of the ordinary?"

Pike shook his head. "Nope. Can't say I was watching, though. *Sea Hunt* was on." He smiled at the detectives through the darkness.

"Well, if you do happen to see anything, let us know."

"Lickety-split," Pike called out above the *chug-chug* of the tugboat engine. He nodded. "Yes siree. I'll let you boys know . . . lickety-split."

Chapter 67

As Del Waters ascended the winding staircase, he paused to survey the hundreds of glittering guests amassed on the marquetry floor below. At the sight, he smiled a thin, self-satisfied smile; he'd been pleased to find that a little diversion like a local manhunt hadn't dampened the enthusiasm of Planetlife's illustrious party-goers. He'd arrived late; the party was in full roar, a herd of distinguished guests clustered around buffet tables laden with exotic fruits and cheeses, caviar, pâté, shrimp, Oysters Rockefeller.

They were all having a hell of a good time; and the stellar turnout guaranteed that the press would be tremendous. In his mind's eye, Waters could see the headlines: PLANETLIFE FOUNDATION SCORES BIG DURING SUPER BOWL.

Waters smiled broadly at the vision. It was going just as he'd planned. The pundits and politicians and producers were all here, martinis and Manhattans in hand, each one vying for the title of largest contributor to the Planetlife Foundation, each one eagerly awaiting the Super Bowl's two-minute warning and the moment Isaac Arrow's TV ad built around Planetlife's credo would flash onto the enormous TV screens positioned around the ballroom.

He took one last look at the noisy throng gathered below, his blue eyes sparkling out from his weary gray face like a youth who'd just witnessed his first rocket launch at Cape Canaveral or gotten his first ten-speed, and then continued up the stairs.

Waters was still smiling as he made his way down the corridor, his patent-leather footsteps slippering noiselessly over the heavy Tibetan carpets as he passed through the French doors leading into Planetlife's executive office. When his gaze fell upon a morose Arch Templeton seated at the conference table, bow tie dangling loose around the neck of his tuxedo shirt, Waters smiled again.

Templeton assessed him sullenly. "You don't look like a man who's getting ready to die," he remarked, lifting a glass of scotch to his lips. Waters didn't reply; he looked on, smiling happily, as Arch Templeton gulped at the amber liquor, gulped like a fish gasping for air, Waters thought, or a desperate fool.

For the first time in his life, Waters was disappointed in his friend; Arch Templeton had obviously underestimated him. He wouldn't forget this lapse of faith, but any retribution he might mete out would have to wait for another day.

"I hope you weren't waiting long, Arch," Waters said politely.

Templeton set the glass down and stared back at Waters in disbelief; the man's tone, as well as his cheerful demeanor, implied a total lack of awareness for their dangerous predicament. "No, I just got here," he replied curtly. He nodded at a chair. "Have a seat, Del . . . and let me in on the fucking joke."

"No joke," Waters said flatly. "And if you don't mind, I'll stand. We really shouldn't be away from the party very long. After all, we wouldn't want our guests to feel abandoned, now would we?"

Templeton scowled and then looked down at the glass in his hand. "I'm sure Carson and Frank can hold things down for a few minutes," he growled, taking another drink.

"I don't think Frank Torello knows how to hold his own

dick"—Waters snorted in disdain—"much less handle a room full of statesmen and millionaires."

Waters started to laugh and Templeton stared back at him quizzically, scrutinizing his friend with a jaundiced eye. He'd known Del Waters for over thirty years—they'd been together in more than their share of foxholes and tight spots—and in all that time, Del had never lost it, never gone hysterical on him. Hell, Del Waters had always been the coolest customer around. "The Iceman Cometh"—that's what they all called Del Waters.

"I'd say we're fucked, Del," Templeton said abruptly and without emotion. He picked up his drink and sipped at it gravely, watching Waters over the rim, hoping for some reaction that made sense. "The cops were all over Burnham Park Harbor a little while ago," he added in the way of explanation. "And no fucking English in sight."

"And no disc," Waters added nonchalantly.

Templeton leaned forward in his chair, glaring now. "You do know what that means, don't you, Del?" His deep voice had taken on a high-pitched, nervous tremor. "It means we're not going to have the money for those friendly Iranian arms dealers of yours when they show up tonight."

Waters nodded vacantly and then, despite the fact that he hadn't slept in days, his eyes began to shine with an inexplicable mischievousness.

"Okay, Del," Templeton snapped. "You've had your fun. Your little motherfuckin' game's over. What the hell's going on? We both know those goddamned bastards are gonna be here in less than an hour."

"No," Waters said matter-of-factly. A smile crossed his thin lips. "No, they won't."

Templeton slammed down his glass. "Let's get back to goddamned reality here, okay?" he shouted. "The Iranians are going to *kill* us. You got that? Do you hear me, Del? Our fucking number's up."

"No, Arch," Waters said simply as the cheerful sparkle in his eyes transformed to a sinister glint. "No. We're going to kill *them*."

Templeton shot Waters a look of amazement. "What the hell are you talking about?"

Waters didn't reply. He smiled conspiratorially, walked over to the desk, and picked up the phone. Templeton watched in frank fascination as Waters dialed.

"Roger," Waters said into the phone, "get on the horn. Call the police, the feds, hell, you know the A-list. Tell them that those Iranians—you remember the ones I told Washington about? Well, tell the cops that you and Knute just located them a few minutes ago . . . at the Drake Hotel. Tell them Knute's surveillance team picked up that they're planning to blow up half the free world's leaders and celebrities at a charitable foundation called Planetlife. Make the authorities understand that these Iranians are dangerous cutthroats who don't mind dying for Allah. Tell them because of that you're going to need an army of well-armed marksmen. Yeah, make sure you get plenty of backup, a couple of SWAT teams. Hell, get more, if you can."

A wide smile broke over Arch Templeton's face and he whispered to himself, "Why, I'll be a son of a bitch."

"I want those bastards, Roger," Waters continued into the phone. "Dead or alive. Preferably dead. But if you manage to take them alive, hit them up with some Thorazine before they get a chance to talk to anybody and then lock them up in the county jail. I'll come by later and handle it from there." He paused. "Hopefully, that won't be necessary."

Templeton was beaming now, shaking his head appreciatively. "Goddammit, Del, you're a motherfucking genius."

Waters looked over at Templeton and waved his hand, dismissing the compliment. "Now remember, Roger, there's five of them. You know their names, right? You got some ID on them?" Waters listened for a moment and then nodded. "Good. Like I said, they're staying at the Drake. Yeah, you're right. I imagine they'll be heading to Planetlife anytime now."

Waters looked down at the elegant brass clock perched on the desk, and as he did, the blue light of the computer screen caught his eye. He froze, a shocked expression washing over his face. The phone dropped from his hand and fell to the floor with a clatter.

"What is it, Del?" Templeton cried. Waters uttered a strangled gasp and Templeton hurried over to his side. "What! What is it?" Templeton's eyes went to the screen, and then he understood everything.

CURRENT TIME: 19:10:00
TIME REMAINING UNTIL TRANSFER: 50 MIN. 00 SEC.

CENTRAL ACCOUNT DISBURSEMENT

LOCATION	SECURITY	ROUTE TO	ACCOUNT	PIN	STATUS
PLANETLIFE	AUTHORIZED	TRANSFER PROCESSING			ACTIVE
CURANDERO	IN-ACTIVE	ACCESS DENIED AT THIS LOCATION			IN-ACTIVE
I. ARROW	IN-ACTIVE	ACCESS DENIED AT THIS LOCATION			IN-ACTIVE

Unable to speak, Waters stared at the screen fixedly, as if staring at it would somehow make it go away. But it wouldn't, he knew that. Marty English had actually accomplished something he had never been able to: Marty English had broken the "unbreakable" Triad code.

The room began to spin. Suddenly warm, Waters put his hand to his forehead and swayed dizzily on his feet. His heart was thumping, drumming against his rib cage, and he thought for one brief instant he might vomit or faint or go insane. But he didn't. Instead, at the returning vision of the Illinois cornfield and English's body lying in it, rotting beneath a winter sun, Waters steadied himself and looked back at the screen.

Yes, it was all clear, though it hardly seemed possible: Marty English had somehow gotten into Planetlife and then walked right in to this very office, without raising so much as an eyebrow. And, even more astonishing, English had gotten into Trinity, accessed Waters's account, and activated the transfer.

The words GAME OVER flashed like pinball lights in Waters's mind, and he swayed again.

"But when the hell did he get up here, Del?" Templeton croaked at last, his normally tanned face now as colorless as a pane of glass. "And for Christ's sakes . . . *how?* How did the son of a bitch get past everybody—"

"It probably wasn't hard at all," Waters cut him off, his voice almost inaudible. "Not for English. I imagine he put on a tuxedo and waltzed right in. He received an invitation, you know. So he had that. And besides, English looks the part. Mingling with a room full of power brokers and millionaires wouldn't be a problem for Marty English. Hell, he's one of them. But in any case, it really doesn't matter *how* English did it. All that matters is that he has the disc—and knows how to use it."

Templeton nodded thoughtfully as Waters turned back to the computer screen. From the time he activated Planetlife's disc, English only had an hour to complete the transaction. The time on the screen had begun counting down; there were forty-nine—no, forty-*eight*—minutes left. English still had to activate the other two locations before he could make the transfer.

Waters's heart started to race. There was still time! He could still stop him. Marty English still had to go to Curandero and Arrow. All Waters had to do was intercept him somewhere along the way. The words GAME OVER flashed in Del Waters's mind again, but this time he pushed them aside and started running toward the door. "Call that dumb little cocksucker D'Angelo!" he yelled. "Tell him English is on his way to Goose Island, planning to break into the computer. D'Angelo has to stop him."

"Any way he can?" Templeton asked, the question coming out swiftly, with the precision of a sniper's bullet.

Waters spun around. "There's only *one* way to stop a man like Marty English," he hissed, his face taking on the chilling expression of a china doll staring out from behind a toy-store window. "Kill him."

Chapter 68

The *Annie*'s running lights were off and the engines were idling halfheartedly. The tug's stout chugging was now a raspy cough that was echoing, in what Pike Stevens thought was an irritatingly loud manner, across the black waters of the Chicago River.

The old Swede stood on the tug's shadowy deck, a shivering silhouette in the night, shifting from one rubber-booted foot to the other and then back again. The last time Pike Stevens could remember being this cold was fifty years ago when he'd found himself swimming in the icy waters off the coast of Normandy. But it wasn't the cold that put goose bumps on the old Swede tonight. Tonight it was the waiting.

Marty had said he was going to crash a party. Pike shook his head. Now, what kind of crazy tale was that? But then maybe it wasn't a tale after all. Maybe the reason he'd been waiting so long was that Marty had gotten caught; maybe the kid wasn't coming back.

Pike squinted down at his watch to see just how long it had been, but it was too dark for his faded blue eyes to make out the time through the scratched-up crystal of his old Bulova. He figured it must be around seven-fifteen, which meant he would miss pretty much all of the Super Bowl. But Pike didn't mind. This was a lot more exciting than watching some damned football game or TV detective. Hell, this game was for real, and by God if he wasn't helping carry the ball. Old men didn't get to do that very often.

At the sound of feet running over pavement, Pike jerked around, craning his neck toward the Chicago River shoreline, his old eyes sorting through the light and shadow like they did when he sorted through a hand of cards.

"It's me, Pike," Marty panted out breathlessly and clambered aboard.

"What took you so long?" Pike grumbled, though he was more scared than annoyed.

"Oh, just a few small details," Marty answered with a grin. "Like making it past a couple hundred party guests, a few dozen cops . . . that sort of thing."

Pike's eyes widened. "Anybody get a good look at you?"

Marty shook his head at the quivering old man. "Don't worry, Pike. Nobody recognized me. I went through a service entrance, ran into a few caterers . . . but they were too busy to pay attention to one more guy in a tuxedo."

"Who was walking around like he owned the place," Pike finished with an admiring nod.

Marty let out a weary chuckle. "Don't kid yourself, Pike. It was slow going. And nerve-wracking as hell." He glanced hurriedly down at his watch. "And it's not over yet. Let's get out of here. I've only got forty-five minutes."

"Aye, aye, Captain," Pike said as he put the engines in full throttle. Forty-five minutes for what? he wondered, but he didn't ask, just like he didn't ask what Marty was doing going to a party at a time like this. Or why the hell he wanted to go to a dump like Goose Island. As the tug chugged upriver, Pike gave Marty a good once-over, like he'd seen that detective Columbo do with those suspects of his, hoping to get a few answers that way.

Marty might have just gone to a party, but there wasn't a damned thing festive about his mood. No siree Bob, Marty was as tight as an alley cat. Those dark eyes of his had been sweeping back and forth, back and forth, like a damned lighthouse beam, the whole way up the shoreline, keeping an eye out for the cops, Pike figured.

But of course Pike didn't know that for sure. Marty hadn't filled him in on what was actually going on. Pike only knew what he'd seen back at Burnham Park Harbor. And what those detectives had told him. Pike could play, but this wasn't his game, which meant he wasn't supposed to ask any questions. But really, there was only one that mattered.

"Did you kill those fellas, Marty?" Pike asked, the words tumbling out before he could stop them. "You know, like they're saying on the television?"

Marty smiled. "I'm the good guy, Pike," he said, putting his arm around the old man's shoulder. "Remember?"

Pike nodded sheepishly. "Sorry," he mumbled. He fell into an awkward silence and started navigating the tug toward a leaning dock just ahead. "Welcome to Goose Island," he announced, happy to change the subject. He cut the engines and gave out a snort. "Don't look like much, does it?" He grinned. "Looks even worse in the daytime."

"I know," Marty said, scrambling off the boat and onto the rotting dock. The old timbers sagged and groaned beneath him.

"You sure you don't want me to wait?" Pike asked hopefully. "You know, I'm not like you young fellas, always having to go nowhere fast."

Marty smiled. "I'm sure, Pike. You just go on home now, get on back to the harbor."

Pike nodded slowly, but even in the dark Marty could tell he was disappointed. "You know, the Super Bowl's still going on," Marty prompted as he started walking up the dock. "I bet if you hurry, you can make it by the two-minute warning."

"Hell, the game's as good as over by then," the old man grumbled.

"Not tonight, Pike," Marty called out softly. He was on the shore now and the old Swede could see only a silhouette. "Tonight, at the two-minute warning, it'll just be starting."

Chapter 69

Marty stood in the shadow of an abandoned rail platform and stared across the empty street at Curandero. The warehouse, its corrugated metal walls gleaming like a dull buffalo nickel beneath the streetlights, was just ahead, twenty yards away.

At the glow of a car's approaching headlamps, Marty's stomach did a quick flip and he dropped down behind a pile of plastic trash bags and ice-spiked weeds. From there, he watched—his apprehension growing by the second—until he saw with relief that it was just an old Camaro and not some slick, black Town Car with a thug behind the wheel. The rusted-out car rumbled by, its stereo pounding out the beat of a heavy, bone-shaking bass guitar.

When the car turned the corner and disappeared, Marty stood up slowly and peered across the street. Curandero was dark and its parking lot empty, which meant that no one was there. Thank God for that, he thought with relief. That had been his biggest concern when he'd hatched his plan: what he would do if the place was crawling with D'Angelo's men. He'd tried to cover all the bases, but try as he might, Marty had been unable to come up with any brilliant ideas for that little hitch, at least any that weren't suicidal.

But now that it looked like he wouldn't have to face any

of D'Angelo's goons, Marty realized he had a bigger problem than dodging a few bullets. And that was the issue of time. The fact was, he didn't have much. He looked down at his watch. Seven-twenty. His heart skipped a beat. Forty minutes left to make the transaction, and the clock was still ticking.

And then there was Del Waters. If by chance he had discovered Marty's little foray into Planetlife—well, there was just no way he'd sit on his hands. Del Waters would declare all-out war. This game was for keeps. Hopefully Waters would be too busy pressing the flesh to wander upstairs to Planetlife's computer. Marty was betting on that. Otherwise . . .

Shivering, he glanced across the street. Getting into the warehouse wouldn't be a problem; it was getting out that had him worried. There was a silent alarm in there somewhere; years ago, he'd overheard his father and D'Angelo talking about Curandero's security. Once he stepped through that door, the countdown would begin. He had to hurry.

Standing in the warehouse doorway, Marty slipped a set of keys from his pocket and looked back nervously over his shoulder. He was good at a lot of things, but breaking and entering wasn't one of them. Fortunately, Mike D'Angelo hadn't considered the potential usefulness of his father's keys and taken them at the funeral.

Marty turned the key in the lock, opened the door, and stepped inside. He was instantly struck by the fact that the air in the warehouse smelled just like the Belizean rainforest: It was moist and heavy with the earthy perfume of plant life.

He stood there for a moment, just inside the door, letting his eyes adjust to the darkness. A shaft of light spilled in through the crack of the door, illuminating a tunnel of skids that stretched into infinity. Marty gave out a low whistle of amazement; the skids were stacked all the way to the ceiling with pink-fiber bales. There was enough give and take here to make tons of Brown Sugar. He smiled bitterly. Certainly enough to kill for.

At the thought of the silent alarm, he started half walking, half running, groping his way rapidly through the darkness, down the tunnel of skids until he came to a steel door that led to the office at the back. He paused, hand on the knob. He could almost hear the shrill alarm, ringing somewhere far away, alerting the enemy.

They would be coming for him soon.

He felt the fear again as the words hammered against his temples, throbbed inside his brain with each beat of his heart. Chill out, he told himself and took a deep breath and shoved the door open. His eyes hurriedly scanned the room until they found a computer monitor on a credenza behind a large conference table. He rushed over, slid into a chair, and flipped on the monitor. Instantly, the room was bathed in amber light.

Hands trembling with anxiety, Marty took a disc from his coat pocket and slipped it into the drive. He waited, staring at the screen for what seemed like an eternity. *Hurry*, his brain screamed. *Hurry*.

They would be coming for him soon. The screen blinked once, then twice. *Hurry*, he silently shouted, a terrible sense of apprehension growing in him with each passing second.

At last, there was a *beep* and a dialogue box appeared on-screen with the message:

SECURITY AUTHORIZATION PROCESSING

The screen flashed once and then went blank. There were two more *beeps* and then the flashing words:

AUTHORIZED AUTHORIZED AUTHORIZED

Marty watched anxiously as the words disappeared and the screen went blank again. Nothing happened for a moment and he held his breath. Goddammit, *Hurry*.

The computer gave out three *beeps* and Trinity's logo appeared. He was in! A broad smile broke over his face and, weak with relief, he slumped back in the chair.

CURRENT TIME: 19:25:47

TIME REMAINING UNTIL TRANSFER: 34 MIN. 13 SEC.

CENTRAL ACCOUNT DISBURSEMENT

LOCATION	SECURITY	ROUTE TO	ACCOUNT	PIN	STATUS
CURANDERO	AUTHORIZED				IN-ACTIVE
PLANETLIFE	AUTHORIZED	TRANSFER PROCESSING			ACTIVE
I. ARROW	IN-ACTIVE	ACCESS DENIED AT THIS LOCATION			IN-ACTIVE

Marty sat bolt upright in the chair and then leaned over the keyboard. His fingers started flying over the keys, tapping wildly. But at a sudden warning beep, he froze. Heart pounding, Marty watched in horror as the screen started flashing off and on. Something was wrong. Something was very wrong.

COMMAND DENIED

At the words, Marty caught his breath. Goddammit, he'd hit the wrong key somehow—he must have.

Hurry.

He frantically studied the screen. He had to do something. He had to. Beads of sweat broke out on his forehead.

They would be coming for him soon.

In a frenzy, he started punching at the cursor on the keyboard. The screen went black. Panicked, he punched at them again and the screen flashed off and on.

COMMAND DENIED

COMMAND DENIED

COMMAND DENIED

"Fuck," he swore aloud. What now? He suddenly thought of Che. Something the Indian had said came back to him now. "The beginning is always the best place to start." Yeah, that was it: he had to start over.

Marty yanked the disc out of the drive and exited the system. Then he put the disc back in and rebooted.

Hurry. Hurry. Marty's eyes stayed fixed on the screen until the Trinity logo came up again.

This time when the bank transfer information came up on-screen, he was more careful; he tapped precisely, cautiously, at the keys, putting in the routing, account, and PIN numbers he'd gotten from Reiki.

CURRENT TIME: 19:27:21
TIME REMAINING UNTIL TRANSFER: 32 MIN. 39 SEC.

CENTRAL ACCOUNT DISBURSEMENT

LOCATION	SECURITY	ROUTE TO	ACCOUNT	PIN	STATUS
CURANDERO	AUTHORIZED	062007755	357-9ES-549	10848	IN-ACTIVE
PLANETLIFE	AUTHORIZED	TRANSFER PROCESSING			ACTIVE
I. ARROW	IN-ACTIVE	ACCESS DENIED AT THIS LOCATION			IN-ACTIVE

The computer gave a beep, signaling it was waiting for a final command, and Marty smiled. He started to press Enter, but at the squeal of tires in the street outside, his hand fell to his side and his stomach turned. *They were here.*

He ran over to the window and lifted the dusty old venetian blind in time to see a sleek black Lincoln screech to a halt in the parking lot. Mike D'Angelo and two of his thugs jumped out of the car. D'Angelo motioned them around back.

A cold terror swept over Marty. He had to get out of there. Now.

He raced to the computer and hit Enter. The words TRANSFER PROCESSING and ACTIVE appeared in the Curandero status field.

Hurry.

Grabbing the disc out of the computer, Marty bolted from the office, knocking over a chair as he went. He darted into the warehouse and ducked behind a row of skids just as D'Angelo walked in the door.

"Okay, Marty!" D'Angelo yelled into the darkness. "I know it's you . . . you keyed the door. Burglars don't use keys. And I know what you're up to, too, but it's not gonna work. Hell, it's over, Marty. You understand what I'm saying? Over." The lights in the warehouse flashed on and Marty suddenly felt naked, crouched behind the skid in the bright light. He slipped the disc into his pocket and stole a glance out from behind the skids. D'Angelo was standing in front of the door. He had a gun drawn and was obviously aching to use it.

"There's only one way out of here, Marty," D'Angelo declared. "And that's through this door. You can go for it, but you won't make it. And that's a goddamned promise."

For one split second, Marty was paralyzed with fear, gripped with the same kind of terror he imagined an animal caught in the jaws of a trap must feel. But he didn't have time for such emotional luxuries, he told himself as he glanced down at his watch. He had thirty minutes left to make the transaction. He had to get the hell out of there. Now.

He eased swiftly around one skid and then another and another, silently padding across the concrete floor until he was a few feet away from Mike D'Angelo, on the other side of the skid.

Marty looked on, heart thumping wildly, as D'Angelo fingered the trigger of his gun and stepped closer to the skid; the mobster was so close now that the heavy, cloying scent of his cologne filled Marty's nostrils with its nauseating sweetness.

"Let's not make this any harder than it has to be, Marty," D'Angelo coaxed. "Come on out now. I'll do what I can to help you. You have my word."

Marty stifled a bitter laugh. His word? What the fuck did D'Angelo take him for?

"Don't forget, Marty, you'll always be Tony's boy to me . . . and you know that stands for something."

You know that stands for something? At the words, Marty felt his venomous hatred for D'Angelo rise up inside him and he sprang forward with a guttural shout, giving the stack of bales a shove, toppling them over onto the mobster.

Marty didn't wait to see what happened to Mike D'Angelo. Right now he didn't have time for revenge. He didn't even have time to say *"Salud."*

Marty jumped into D'Angelo's Lincoln and reached under the dash, fiddling with the wires. He'd been just fourteen—and his father had hit the ceiling—when D'Angelo had taught him how to hot-wire a car, insisting that "it might come in handy someday." Now Marty smiled to himself at the strange irony of it all.

As the engine turned over, Marty saw D'Angelo's two thugs running toward the car, their .38s raised menacingly. There was a thunderbolt of light through the darkness and then a *ping* as a slug hit the car door and ricocheted off. Another *ping* and then a *crack* as a slug torpedoed through the window and past his head. Adrenaline pumping in his veins, he ducked and slammed the car into gear.

For a moment, the tires spun sickeningly in place on the loose gravel and it felt as if the whole world were in slow motion, but, at last, the car lurched forward across the parking lot and out into the street, throwing gravel as it went.

Marty glanced at the dash. D'Angelo would be calling Waters now; the cat would be out of the bag. There were just twenty-five minutes left on the clock. But Marty was out front, inside the ten-yard line. All he had to do was make it to the end zone.

Alone in the warehouse, Mike D'Angelo struggled against the fluffy bales pressing down on top of him. His eyes were open, but he couldn't see; the give and take, as soft and downy as he imagined an angel's hair might be, had blanketed his face and mouth in its smothering softness.

D'Angelo's lips felt strangely numb and he licked them and instantly felt his tongue go floppy and loose in his mouth. He gasped with fear and swallowed, and a searing pain shot down his throat and then—nothing. His throat was numb, too.

Gripped by fear now, D'Angelo gasped for air and then felt his lungs go hot in his chest. He was suffocating in the soft pink shroud of poison, that was it. He opened his rubbery mouth to scream for his men, but nothing came out. Not a word. Not even so much as a whisper.

He flopped and flailed away at the fibrous pink bales, but his arms and legs quickly went limp and useless with the effort. Soon they went numb and wouldn't move at all. Paralyzed, D'Angelo lay there, panting in fear in the pink darkness.

At the sensation of warm drool oozing down his chin, D'Angelo suddenly realized he was hemorrhaging, drowning in his own blood and life juices, drowning from the inside out. Raw terror shot through him like an electric current and he began to cry, babbling noiselessly, senselessly, through his thick tongue like a baby.

Then, as quickly as it had started, the warm ooze stopped. For a moment, D'Angelo thought it might be over, that by some miracle he had been saved. But then his throat went suddenly tight and an excruciating pain shot through his brain, a horrible, stabbing pain that drilled right into his eye sockets and his temples and bored into his skull like beetles gnawing into a rotted tree.

It was then that Mike D'Angelo understood: It was his own blood that was pounding in his brain. The give and take had absorbed through his skin; his blood was slowly thickening. Soon it would curdle like sour milk and clot in his veins. D'Angelo felt a searing pain sweep through his body, and he shuddered involuntarily. With each beat of his heart the pain grew more unbearable. Hotter and hotter it grew until it burned inside his chest, his brain. Eating, gnawing.

Mike D'Angelo opened his mouth to scream, to beg to die. But no sound came out. And he didn't die.

In fact, Mike D'Angelo didn't die for quite a while.

Not until his blood turned to a hard, hot goo in his veins. Not until he realized that Tony Inglesia had been right all along: Friends take care of friends. And double-crossers get what they have coming.

Chapter 70

Like all good predators, Del Waters had always been able to sense his prey's presence. It wasn't just a sound. Or a smell. It was a *knowing*. A knowing that burned like desire in his groin, demanding the kind of release that could only come from the slick feel of hot blood on his hands.

It was that knowing, and its attending ache for the kill, that washed over Waters now, making him shiver with desire, making his sea-blue eyes turn otherworldly sapphire in the green glow of the VR lab computer monitors.

As he loosened his bow tie, Waters stretched back in the chair and kicked up his patent-leather shoes onto the desk. He hadn't been this pleased with himself since his escape from that Cambodian prison camp. He was good, all right—damned good. And obviously, from what he'd seen so far today, he hadn't lost his touch. The Planetlife party had been successful beyond his wildest dreams; the Iranians were surely out of the way by now; and, at any moment, Arrow's thirty-second TV spot would be airing in the Super Bowl, dispersing his brilliantly constructed lie to over one billion people around the world. With that, his operation's cover would be complete. And he'd be on easy street.

"A thing of beauty, if I say so myself," Waters chortled as he lit a Cohiba. He smiled, puffing away happily at the cigar.

Then, abruptly, the self-satisfied smile froze on his lips. Unfortunately, there remained one more small detail to attend to:
Marty English.

The image of his enemy slumped in defeat brought a
sparkle to Waters's flat blue eyes. No doubt about it, this
was going to be a very special day. He only hoped he would
be able to hold it in his memory forever. Hold the sight of
Marty English, on his knees, begging for mercy, pleading
for his life.

Of course Del Waters had no intention of just making
English grovel. He had more entertaining things in mind for
Tony Inglesia's precious son than that. Trembling with anticipation, he let out a dejected sigh. By its very definition,
anticipation meant one had to wait; he'd never been good at
that. But he wouldn't blow it now. Not when he was this
close. After all, he'd been waiting for this moment for how
long? Waters exhaled a raft of smoke and a long sigh escaped his thin lips. Forever, it seemed. At least as long as he
had hated Tony Inglesia, had longed to put him in the
ground.

But the wait would be well worth it, Waters thought now,
his angular face softening, taking on a dreamy quality, even if
Marty English had to stand in his father's place. After all,
what more could a man ask for than to finally meet the perfect
enemy, to come face-to-face with an opponent who was worthy of one's best? Surely he could wait for that.

With a shudder, Waters closed his eyes, his thoughts drift-
ing back in time to the Cambodian hellhole his captors had
called a prison and the night of his escape. For hours he'd lain
on the damp earth, coiled like a viper, waiting to strike. Waiting for the sound of the enemy's booted footsteps and the
scent of black market cigarettes and pungent rice wine waft-
ing out before them.

At the memory of the wonderful massacre that followed,
Waters's heart began to pound wildly in his chest and the ache
of desire returned. He could wait this time, too: for the ex-

quisite pleasure of watching Marty English writhing in a perfect, beautiful death. Yes, for that, he could wait.

But only for a while.

Waters's eyes flew open and he pulled himself to attention. He'd be taking care of English soon enough; right now there was other business to attend to. He didn't want to miss one second of the advertising launch of his "grand plan" in the Super Bowl. He scooted the twenty-inch Sony Trinitron around on Dr. Bachmann's desk so he could watch the door of the VR lab and still see the football game.

Over the cheering fans, the play-by-play man was shouting excitedly: "We're nearing the end of the fourth quarter, folks. There's ten minutes left on the clock. It's first and ten, ball on the thirty-five-yard line. This one's gonna be a screamer."

A screamer? Waters tapped his Cohiba in the ashtray and hit the Mute button on the remote. He wasn't about to tip off English with a bunch of screaming footfall fans; he intended to use the element of surprise. He checked the Beretta lying in his lap and then looked up from the chair, smiling expectantly at the doorway. Marty English would be surprised, all right. He'd make sure of it.

Marty had no trouble getting into Isaac Arrow; he just sauntered up to the security guard and, like he'd done all his life, used his charm to get what he wanted—that and the security pass Carson Page had so thoughtfully provided.

Even so, as he strode across the empty lobby toward the elevators, Marty found himself trying to shrug off a growing sense of dread. But what was there to worry about? Of course Mike D'Angelo wouldn't waste any time alerting Waters to his break-in at Curandero. Upon hearing the news, Waters would certainly run upstairs to check out Planetlife's computer. It wouldn't take a genius to figure out that Marty's next stop would be Arrow. But by then it wouldn't matter. Because if his calculations were right, Marty had about a fifteen-minute headstart on Waters. Granted, it wasn't much, but it

was enough time for Marty to get to Arrow, make the transaction, and then get the hell out of there before Waters and his
men arrived.

With a little quick maneuvering—and a lot of luck—he just
might pull this off, Marty thought as he walked up to the elevator and hit the Down button. The doors slid open and he
stepped inside. He was almost there.

As the elevator doors closed, Isaac Arrow's security guard, Ed
Parry, picked up the phone and dialed. "He's on his way
down, Mr. Waters," Parry said impassively, his eyes never
leaving the game on TV. "Of course I'm sure. It's him all
right." Parry rolled his eyes. Parry knew how important security was in a big-time outfit like Isaac Arrow, but this guy Waters was plain obsessed. "He's on his way, Mr. Waters. Should
be there any minute now."

At the click on the other end, Ed Parry shrugged and turned
his attention to the little Sony Watchman beside him. With a
two-hundred-fifty-dollar bet riding on this game, security
would just have to wait.

At each floor, Marty watched anxiously as the bank of numbers above the elevator doors flashed off and on and a star-
tling electronic beep crackled in a loudspeaker. The elevator
paused momentarily, shimmying slightly on its cable, threatening to stop. Marty's heart pounded in his chest as he surveyed the four gleaming brass walls around him. He was
trapped here, he thought ruefully, suspended in a goddamned
metal box. His stomach started to go into knots, but then,
abruptly, his expression turned fierce at the recollection of his
battlefield lieutenant's words: *Get mad. Get crazy. But whatever you do, soldier, get the fucking enemy.*

At the memory, Marty was suddenly eager to get on with it,
to get the whole thing over with, but time was creeping now,
and the floors passed by with a nerve-wracking tediousness.
He looked down at his watch. Seven-fifty. Under the best of

circumstances, making the transaction was going to be tight. And he still had to get out of there. "Come on," he snapped, glaring up at the illuminated numbers. "Move it."

As if on cue, he felt the distinctive drop and lift of his stomach signaling that the elevator had come to a stop. His heart started racing. *What if he was wrong?* What if he'd miscalculated? He wasn't going to take any chances; as the doors parted, Marty flattened himself against the side wall and waited, listening. Hearing nothing, he peered out.

Finding the hall deserted, he edged out into the open, moving slowly up to the steel security door. For an excruciating moment, he stood there before the door, heart thundering, wishing he could just turn around and go back upstairs, get into D'Angelo's Town Car, and forget the whole damned thing. But he couldn't. Not now. He set his jaw and ran his security pass through the scanner. The light turned green and he hurried through.

He sidled down the corridor, stopping now and then to still his heart, which felt like it was rattling like dice in a cup, listening for any sounds that might say he'd blown it, that they knew he was here—that he wasn't alone. But only his own heavy breathing interrupted the shroud of silence hanging over everything and, as he continued down the corridors, he was filled with apprehension. Arrow's halls were too still, too empty. Even for Super Bowl Sunday.

He began panting heavily, almost hyperventilating. Chill out, he commanded angrily. This was *his* game, now. And *he* had the ball. Not Waters. He'd been to Planetlife, hadn't he? Lived through an encounter with Mike D'Angelo and his goons? This was it. This was the final play. The door to the VR lab was just around the corner. He was almost there. He was one step ahead of them.

Suddenly, Marty frowned, freezing in place. From around the corner, he heard them: marching, purposeful feet. Footsteps. Coming his way. Closer. Louder.

The footsteps abruptly stopped and, risking exposure, Marty peeked warily around the corner, scouting the hall. Just ahead, maybe thirty feet away, a company chemist stood at an office door. Quickly, Marty drew back. Now what? The last thing he needed was this. He didn't have time for lengthy explanations or a social visit. Marty looked down at his watch. Only eight minutes left.

He peered cautiously around the corner. The chemist was still standing there. What was the guy waiting for? Why didn't he go inside? Had he, like Marty, heard footsteps as well? Marty stood stock still, his feet glued to the floor, afraid to move or breathe. At last the man opened the office door and disappeared inside.

It was the break Marty needed. *Move, soldier!* a voice shouted in his head and, instinctively, he shuffled silently around the corner and down the hall, all the while wondering what the hell he would do if the chemist walked out.

When he got closer to the door, Marty's senses were assaulted by a familiar smell and he crinkled his nose, searching his memory. Suddenly, he smiled wryly, almost letting out a laugh. Popcorn. The guy was making goddamned popcorn.

Abruptly, the door swung open and Marty ducked behind it, huddling against the wall. If the chemist turned just one inch, he'd see Marty. If he went back the way he came . . .

With a magnetic click, the door closed and Marty watched, his fear slowly receding, as the man strolled back down the hallway and past the VR lab. Marty stole a glance at his watch. Seven fifty-four. He only had six minutes left to make the transaction. It was now or never.

Breathing hard, the acid taste of fear in his mouth, he bent forward halfback-style and charged down the hall toward the VR lab. His legs were heavy, his muscles aching hot flares. But they didn't let him down. He made it.

At the door to the lab, he paused, heart racing. There was

no turning back now. Whatever lay beyond this door had to be met head-on.

Steeling himself, Marty took a deep breath, gripped the knob with white knuckles, and pushed it open. Across the shadowy white room, the emerald light of the VR lab computer monitors cast an eerie glow, spilling out from the doorway and across the tile floor, rolling out like a carpet to his feet.

His heart drilled against his rib cage and he had to remind himself that he was almost there. He heard the voice of the battlefield lieutenant, shouting in his memory: *Left, right, left.* That was it. That was all it took; all he had to do now was put one foot in front of the other. Fear wrenched at his gut as he eased across the floor.

At the doorway, he stopped and gingerly reached around the corner, patting the wall, fumbling for the light switch. Then, floating out from the room, he was suddenly struck with the unmistakable odor of a cigar.

Marty froze. Fuck. *He was wrong.*

"Well, well, well . . . if it isn't Marty English," Del Waters purred as the lights flashed on. He smiled out from his chair. "Or should I say Martino Inglesia?" The smile suddenly turned to a smirk.

Marty stood in the doorway, immobile, his eyes fixed on the enemy. He felt the man's eyes run over his frame, saw the pupils shining glassily as they sized him up.

"Don't be shy, come on in," Waters coaxed.

Marty didn't move.

"I *said* come in," Waters repeated with a hiss. The smile disappeared and he took dead aim with the gun. *"Now."*

Eyes locked on the Beretta, Marty nodded solemnly and eased slowly into the room.

"That's better," Waters said, the strange, sunny smile returning. There was a sarcastic note to his voice as he added, "So at last I meet Tony Inglesia's brilliant son. My, my, but it *is* a pleasure."

"The pleasure's all mine."

Waters frowned and surveyed Marty coldly. "Hmm . . . I see you're just as arrogant as your father." He stood up. "But I suppose you have a right to be. I've got to admit even I admire your guts . . . and your brains, too. Tell me, how did you do it? How did you figure out the code?"

"Sorry," Marty replied, shaking his head firmly, "that's a trade secret."

Waters smiled. "I understand. But then, I'm sure so do you; nothing ventured nothing gained. A man has to ask. Right? In any case, I'm impressed. You do good work."

"I try," Marty shot back as his gaze shifted to the TV. According to the game clock, the two-minute warning was just seconds away. In his mind's eye he saw the yacht's satellite console. Saw the network satellite a hundred miles out in space, waiting to drop his thirty-second bombshell. And he felt a strange quiver in his stomach at the nauseating realization that he probably had three, maybe four, minutes left after the whistle to complete the bank transfer. His eyes darted from the TV to the nearby computer workstation.

As if reading his captive's thoughts, Waters declared haughtily, "No. I don't think so. I'll be taking that disc now. You've had enough fun for one day." He pointed at Marty's tuxedo pocket with the Beretta. "Okay, let's have it."

Marty dug his hand into his pocket.

"Slow," Waters ordered. "Take your time." He waved the gun. "I *said slow*. You hear me?"

Marty nodded.

"I want to see what you've got in your hand . . . you got that? Okay, okay . . . I want to see your hands now. *Slow*."

Cautiously, Marty held up the disc.

"Good. Now give it to me."

Marty handed the disc to Waters, who studied it for a moment, then, raising one eyebrow, scowled at Marty skeptically. "What do you think? Should I trust a man who's already proven he has a talent for trickery?" Waters shook his head. "I don't think so. I think it would be wise to check this disc, to make sure it's real. Don't you?"

"Hey, what the hell." Marty shrugged. "Knock yourself out."

Gun still trained on his prisoner, Waters slid the disc into the drive. When the Trinity logo came up on screen, he shook his head and gave out a wistful sigh. "Do you have any idea how long I've been trying to break this code? Did you honestly think I could allow one man to bring it all down in an hour?"

Marty didn't reply, and Waters tapped at the screen. "In any case, it appears you're running out of time, Mr. English . . . literally." Gloating, he walked over to the VR workstation and booted up the system. "Are you familiar with Isaac Arrow's computer system? It's the world's most advanced technology, you know. With Trinity here, there's nothing we can't do. We've even improved on nature." Waters grinned. "Hell, we've beaten nature."

Marty glared back him. "You can't do that. It won't work."

Waters let out a chillingly maniacal laugh. "Oh yes we can. In fact, we already have." He smiled grimly and started tapping on the keyboard. "You were in Vietnam. How much do you know about psychological warfare?"

"Enough."

"Did you know that with just the press of a button we can now make a man go insane?" Waters smiled broadly as he hit a key and a red light started flashing inside the empty VR chamber. "From what I'm told, this VR psychosis thing Bachmann's dreamed up is one goddamned awful trip—and highly effective at disarming the enemy. Hypothetically at least. You see, Bachmann still hasn't tested it on a living human being." Waters smiled eagerly, like a child waiting to unwrap a birthday present. But then the smile dropped away and he shook his head in disgust. "You know, all those ethical questions . . . they always get in the way of progress." He let out a sigh. "Actually, I hate to do this. Putting a man like you in this chamber, it's a sacrilege. Believe it or not, Marty, I've actually come to respect you. You really are a worthy adversary. Not many of those left these days. I would've preferred that we'd fought on the same side. But unfortunately it's too late for that now. You seem to have made your choice." He waved Marty toward the chamber.

Marty didn't move.

"Come on now," Waters coaxed, his voice chillingly gentle. "Don't be afraid. We both know it's a shame to have to end it this way. But then your sacrifice will be in the name of science. I'd think that would give you some comfort." He smiled coldly and fingered the Beretta. "Now move it."

Thoughts racing, Marty walked slowly toward the chamber.

"Think what a wealth of information you'll be providing," Waters suggested. "Of course, I'll say it was a tragic accident."

Marty suddenly stopped moving; his eyes locked on the TV. From the look of the fans on screen, the whistle was blowing, signaling the two-minute warning. The bomb was going to drop. It was just a matter of seconds.

"I said *move it*," Waters growled nervously, his eyes darting to the TV set and then back to Marty.

Marty smiled at his captor disarmingly. "You want to see what two million dollars buys in the Super Bowl these days, don't you?" Marty's smile was growing broader, brighter by the second.

The smile told Waters something was wrong and, without taking his eyes off Marty, he leaned over, picked up the remote, and aimed it at the set. At the sound of B. B. King belting out "The Thrill Is Gone," his face drained of color and his gaze went to the nineteen-inch Sony.

At that same instant, around America, millions of eyes fixed on millions of TV sets. Faces registered astonishment, then slowly twisted into disgust, then horror, as Marty's thirty-second bombshell exploded across the screen and the words *ten times stronger than cocaine* blasted into living rooms everywhere.

At neighborhood dives, loud, beer-bellied men playing Foosball and darts froze in place. Riveted to TV screens hanging over mirrored bars, they hung on every word.

Cocaine will be history. It'll be obsolete.

They'll call it Brown Sugar.

We'll make billions.

As the seconds ticked by, their eyes grew wider and wider, looking like they might pop out of their meaty heads at any moment, until, at last, the mobster on-screen declared, *Who made sure for the past thirty years that the CIA had all the fucking money it needed for its dirty work?*

The revelers gulped angrily at their beers and, like good, taxpaying citizens everywhere, clenched their fists in outrage at the realization that the American public—hell, the whole damned world—had once again been played for suckers by some arrogant government asshole.

Meanwhile, at the Super Bowl, a hundred thousand cheering football fans stopped midwave, transforming into a petrified forest of faces, arms upstretched. Mouths gaping, they stared in mute shock at the enormous TV screens suspended around the field.

Now, thanks to the masterful creative talent of Marty English, they knew that bad guys did more than squeeze a roll of Charmin and lie about Isuzus. Now they knew what bad guys really looked like; they even knew their names.

On the stadium's wide-screen TVs, larger-than-life Frank Torellos rolled ten-foot eyes. *The public would never buy it*, he chortled at them from all directions. *Even if they saw it in black and white.*

Or in color, a colossal Carson Page added with a cackling laugh. Her words bounced off the concrete walls, reverberating again and again:

or in color,

or in color,

or in color,

striking the stunned onlookers like a shower of enemy bullets, ricocheting around the field, echoing through the stands. Echoing until there were no words left.

Lee Wilde was sitting in Wynn Bergman's office, sipping on a martini, when the Arrow spot came on. Emitting a garbled cry of surprise, she coughed a spray of gin and vermouth across the conference table.

Bergman didn't notice; he was too engrossed in the commercial playing on the stylish chrome TV positioned before them. At Carson Page's words *The advertising campaign at Bergman will be part of our cover*, his cigarette dropped from his hand and began smoldering on the polished slate floor. "What the hell's going on here?" he yelled, slamming his fist on the table. "Is this Arrow account bogus?"

"I . . . I have no idea," Lee stammered, swiveling around in her chair to face him. "That may be Carson Page and Frank Torello there . . . and they may be from Isaac Arrow . . . but that's about as far as the resemblance to what we produced goes. *This* sure as hell isn't what we sent to the network." She followed Bergman's eyes back to the screen. "Oh my God! Isn't that that gangster? What's his name? Tony Inglesia? And who the hell is that?" she demanded, pointing to Del Waters.

Bergman's typically ruddy face flushed deeper and, not taking his eyes off the screen, he lit another cigarette. "You have any idea who the hell's responsible for this, Lee?"

Dumbfounded, she shook her head.

"Well, I can tell you one thing, we're in big fucking trouble here. The FCC's gonna have our ass in a goddamned sling." Incensed, Bergman set his heavy jaw. "I didn't spend fifty years building this company to have some bullshit like this bring it down."

At the strains of B. B. King reverberating from the TV, Lee's face went ashen. "Oh my God . . . Marty."

"Marty? What about him?" Bergman's bristle-cone brows shot up in puzzlement over his bifocals. Then, suddenly understanding, he exclaimed, "Are you saying Marty did . . . *this*?"

"It has to be Marty, Wynn. Marty loves B. B. King. Everybody knows that. My guess is he found out what these Isaac Arrow bastards were up to and didn't have any choice but to go on the run. He probably decided the best way to bring them down was to produce his own little home video—complete with music bed."

"But how the hell did he get this thing past the network and on the air? It would take a goddamned genius to pull that off."

"At the very least, somebody brilliant," Lee remarked drolly. "Somebody who could get ahold of the ISCI code and figure out how to jam the network's signal so they could insert another spot in place of the one the agency sent. Then all they'd have to do is use a network satellite linkup—"

"Like the one on the agency yacht," Bergman broke in.

She nodded. "Why, I'll be damned!" She flashed a cynical smile Bergman's way and chuckled. "You have to admit the spot's well done, Wynn. The edits are beautiful. Hell, who knows? Wynn Bergman Advertising might even win a Clio for Marty's little masterpiece."

Scowling, Bergman clicked the TV remote to Off. "Well, if the FCC has anything to say about it, all we're gonna win is twenty-five years in a federal prison."

At the sight of their esteemed hosts and a gangster *together* in a TV commercial, a confused murmur rose up from the assembled Planetlife glitterati. On-screen, Del Waters was talking; they all pushed forward, craning their necks for a better view, eager to hear what in the world the chairman of Isaac Arrow Pharmaceuticals could have to say to a Mob boss.

Who would ever think that Isaac Arrow, the world's most respected pharmaceutical giant, and Planetlife, a rainforest foundation full of bleeding-heart liberals, would be tied up with rogue CIA agents and the Chicago Mob?

There was a collective gasp of shock in the dimly lit room—the sound of a balloon deflating—and then dozens of Baccarat glasses dropped from jeweled hands and shattered into a million glittering pieces, scattering across the floor.

Abruptly, the lights came up and the wide-screen TVs went to black. With a rustle of her red satin gown, Carson Page, flushed with anger, marched forward, leaving a stunned Frank Torello leaning feebly against the wall behind her.

"This is an outrage, a total outrage," she declared shrilly, waving at the empty screens. "Obviously, *someone* . . . someone intent on destroying us all is out to sabotage Isaac Arrow's partnership with Planetlife. I'm sure we'll learn soon enough that this . . . this *commercial*—if that's what we can call it—is nothing more than the act of some attention-grabbing kook, some eco-terrorist's pitiful attempt to ruin our plans to save the Belizean rainforest and bring new pharmaceuticals to market."

Carson paused to survey her audience. Her passionate sales pitch had clearly left them unconvinced: A sea of skeptical, almost threatening, faces stared back at her and, anxiously, she looked back at Torello. Chalk-faced and paralyzed with fear, Arrow's impotent president would be of no help.

Going on the defensive, she turned back to the audience and drew herself up. "Do you people understand what I'm saying here? What you saw never happened. It's sleight of hand. A sleazy trick. Like all those presidents in that *Forrest Gump* movie. It wasn't real. I can assure you of that." There was a sudden note of desperation in her voice and she added, "And I can also assure you that we won't waste any time getting to the bottom of this travesty."

A tense silence fell over the room. And then, from within the menacing throng someone cried, "Bleeding-heart liberals? So that's what we are?"

"Do you take us for fools?" yelled another.

A unified rumble of agreement rose up in the ballroom, followed by an angry roar: "Somebody call the police!"

Reiki Devane was sitting in front of the TV in her Bermuda hotel room, nibbling on a jumbo shrimp, when Marty's thirty-second masterpiece erupted onto the screen. She dropped the half-eaten appetizer into the bowl of cocktail sauce and gasped. "Oh my God!"

Hands clasped over her mouth, she watched in cold terror, mesmerized, as the images paraded by. Tony Inglesia. Del Waters. Carson Page. Frank Torello. Mike D'Angelo. The drink. *Just like you like it; not too much ice.* Marty's father grabbing his chest, crashing to the floor, pleading with his assassin. *Mike. Don't do this.*

She sat in rapt attention, her eyes welling up with tears. "Marty, Marty," she murmured, pulling her tanned legs up to her chest, hugging them, rocking back and forth. "You were right. It was Mike D'Angelo all along. He killed your father just like you said." She looked on, stifling a sob, as D'Angelo lifted a glass over the dead mobster and declared, *Salud.*

Then it was over and, smiling through tears, Reiki lifted her wineglass in a toast. "Bravo, Marty," she whispered. "You did it. You brought them all down. And it only took thirty seconds." She swallowed hard, choking back her fear. "I only hope you don't go down with them."

In the glow of the computers, Del Waters's face was blank, unreadable. Vacant of emotion. Just as it had been years ago when he'd watched as his men, standing before the Cambodian firing squad, were shot down, one by one, in a storm of searing bullets. Now that horrifying memory had come back in the rush of an instant. In less than thirty seconds.

He could hear the order "Fire!" Could hear the terrible hiss of bullets piercing the heavy Cambodian air. In his recollections now, they possessed a singular voice—and Waters suddenly shuddered at the realization that it was the voice of Tony Inglesia that he was hearing. With perfect precision, it shot out at him from the TV screen, mocking him from the grave.

Fire: *You guys at the CIA came up with a hell of a cover for this operation.*

Fire: *That sham of a resort in Belize.*

Fire: *Friends take care of friends. Enemies get taken care of.*

And then Waters heard his own voice, a lone, self-inflicted bullet that pierced his skull and ricocheted around in his brain, exploding with the words *Who would ever think?*

Marty saw Del Waters's thin lips moving silently, as if he were chewing those shocking words, saw Waters's hands drop to his sides. It was only for an instant. But it was enough— and Marty pounced, knocking the gun from Waters's hand and shoving him into the chamber.

With a hiss of air, the door sealed shut and the flashing light inside went from red to green. Behind the glass windows, Del Waters's face registered fear. And then he smiled a smile Marty had seen before in his dreams: the hideous smile of a gap-toothed jack-o'-lantern.

"Who would ever think?" Waters cackled over the chamber's loudspeaker. "Who would ever think? Who would ever think . . ." His voice trailed off and his face went strangely blank and then he crumpled to a mute heap on the floor.

Marty ran to the Trinity computer. His eyes raced over the screen but stopped when they came to the time. He only had nine seconds left. And at that realization, his dream returned: "Looks like a fumble at the ten-yard line. Can our hero hold on?"

"Yes. Yes," Marty declared aloud, urging himself on. He was too close now to drop the ball. His fingers began flying over the keys.

CURRENT TIME: 19:59:53
TIME REMAINING UNTIL TRANSFER: 0 MIN. 07 SEC.

CENTRAL ACCOUNT DISBURSEMENT

LOCATION	SECURITY	ROUTE TO	ACCOUNT	PIN	STATUS
I. ARROW	AUTHORIZED	062007755	357-9ES-549	10848	
CURANDERO	AUTHORIZED	TRANSFER PROCESSING			ACTIVE
PLANETLIFE	AUTHORIZED	TRANSFER PROCESSING			ACTIVE

Marty frantically scanned the screen and then, taking a deep breath, hit Enter. To his horror, the screen went blank. "No!" he hissed, fists clenched, at the screen. A message came up:

TRANSFER SUCCESSFULLY COMPLETED

"All right!" he shouted, forgetting himself, smacking the desktop high-five-style with both hands. "All right!"

He'd won—he'd beaten them at their own game. Revenge might be a solitary sport, but he'd managed to tell the world about the hypocrisy called Planetlife and the lie called Isaac Arrow. And with this transaction, he'd hit Waters and his friends where it hurt, too: right in the pocket. For Marty, being four hundred fifty million dollars richer was just a bonus.

As he paused in the doorway of the VR lab, taking a final look at Del Waters, Marty heard Che's gentle voice whispering in his head: "Good triumphs over evil in the sacred ball game."

"Yeah," he said softly. "And for the hero, death is the final play."

Del Waters saw the walls of the VR chamber melt away, replaced by a dark hole encircled with bamboo, a space no bigger than a coffin. He could barely move. A nightmare of remembrances came flooding back, becoming his only reality.

And suddenly, the putrid stench of decaying human flesh—there was no other smell like it—pressed over Waters's terrified face like a dead man's hand, hanging in his throat, threatening to choke him, to suffocate him. He wretched and vomited a dark pool of blood. It was then that Waters heard the wriggling sound. The sound of a million worms and ants and grubs and rats, slithering things, chewing their way toward him, eating their way through the other men's rotting carcasses.

At the feel of the insect legs and antennae, tapping and threading over his moist flesh, searching for a soft spot, for some point of entry, Del Waters let out a long, low scream.

On his way out, through Isaac Arrow's immense marble lobby, Marty returned the guard's disinterested wave and then stopped beneath the painting of Isaac Aronstein. "Got a piece of advice for you, Isaac, old man," he said, looking up with a smile. "In case you haven't heard, it's not nice to fool Mother Nature."

Epilogue

Reiki was in overalls and sneakers. She sat cross-legged, at the foot of Marty's chair, on the wide porch of the dilapidated farmhouse, a house she'd taken to calling "a work in progress." Her gaze was directed past the meadow of yellow daffodils spreading out before them, to the budding woodland beyond.

"So," she began softly, her solemn brown eyes turning up to him. "I guess we've been avoiding talking about the hearing, huh? Maybe we've been distracted. . . ."

"Honeymoons have a nasty habit of doing that." Marty chuckled, reaching over to ruffle her tawny hair with his hand.

She smiled and then gave out a sigh. "How are the attorneys saying you should plead? I mean, jeez, the hearing's tomorrow." She waited for his reply, twiddling nervously with the gold band around her finger.

Marty grinned. "They think I'm screwed. The case is so high profile, they think the FCC's going to make an example out of me. They think I should plead guilty to violating about seventy different laws and regulations."

"So how *are* you going to plead?"

Marty leaned back in the wicker chair and rocked back and forth. "Not guilty, of course," he replied with a smile.

And that's how he felt, too: not fucking guilty. Hell, what kind of justice was it that put the good guy behind bars?

Whatever happened to Perry Mason and the long arm of the law?

The FCC might get the red ass about somebody jamming the network's satellite system and inserting their own version of *America's Funniest Home Videos*, but hell, it all boiled down to just thirty seconds in the Super Bowl. Just thirty seconds of nothing, after all.

Postscript

Isaac Arrow president Frank Torello and vice president of marketing Carson Page were arrested at Planetlife on Super Bowl Sunday and charged with narcotics trafficking. They were found guilty and sentenced to twenty-five years in a federal penitentiary.

On Tuesday morning, January 27, Suzy Cameron, Doneeta Jackson, Crissie Sinclair, and Pike Stevens opened their mailboxes and each discovered a cashier's check in the amount of one million dollars.

Suzy Cameron moved to Florida, where she bought herself a condo on the beach. Doneeta Jackson put the money in a trust fund for her children's college education. Crissie Sinclair opened the Ford Sinclair Children's Home on Chicago's westside. Pike Stevens took a windjammer cruise around the world and bought a set of *Sea Hunt* videos.

During the week following the Super Bowl, Wynn Bergman Advertising was awarded the $1.6 billion Hexall/NHP account.

The dismembered body of Arch Templeton was found floating in Lake Michigan. An Iranian terrorist group claimed responsibility for the murder.

A group of Maya Indians in western Belize was featured on the cover of *Time* after receiving an anonymous donation of fifty million dollars for the establishment of the Balam Che Rainforest Preserve.

Roger Kemper was granted limited immunity in the "Fallen Soldier Slayings" and given a ten-year sentence with the condition that he testify before Senate and Congressional Committees investigating alleged CIA involvement in illegal activities. As a result of Kemper's testimony, six of the Central Intelligence Agency's top-ranked officials were sentenced to fifteen years in the federal penitentiary in Marion, Illinois.

Videotapes confiscated from Tony Inglesia's home by the FBI led to three hundred indictments against fifty underworld kingpins and twelve politicians.

Del Waters was placed under psychiatric observation at Bethesda Naval Hospital in Bethesda, Maryland. Waters was found unable to stand trial by reason of insanity and was subsequently transferred to the Detroit Institute for the Criminally Insane.

About the Authors

SAM GIANCANA is the godson and namesake of Sam "Momo" Giancana, the notorious Chicago mafia boss. Sam and BETTINA GIANCANA met in the field of advertising, where Sam was an executive and Bettina a sales rep. They are now a happily married couple who reside in Florida. 30 SECONDS is a first novel for both of them. Sam Giancana is coauthor of the bestseller *Double Cross*.